HE CALLED ME SON

Barbara Arnold lives with her husband in Christchurch, New Zealand, where as well as writing novels, she teaches creative writing. She has two sons and nine grandchildren.

He Called Me Son is her debut novel and the first in the trilogy *The Blountmere Street Series*, followed by *The Best in Blountmere Street*. The third novel in the trilogy is expected to be available early 2012.

HE CALLED ME SON

By

Barbara Arnold

Published by B. Arnold

This book is based on some true events. However, it has been fictionalised and all persons appearing in this work are fictitious. Any resemblance to real people, living or dead, is entirely coincidental.

ISBN 978-0-473-18641-8

To Roger
With my love for your belief in me

Acknowledgements

With profound thanks to all those who have had input into this novel. Writing can be a lonely craft and I am appreciative of your fellowship and encouragement.

To my "Editor In Chief", Caitlin, for helping me download, upload and often offload!

To Simon Garner for his cover design.

To Sid1, Flickr.com for the cover image.

To Margaret, for her web design, and for being so patient with this queen of computer dummies.

To Janet, for designing promotional material.

Special thanks to Barbara, Bryan, Freda and Stuart, without whose input I would probably never have even begun this novel.

My deep gratitude to editors: Judith, Gary, Aidan and Lisa.

To all those in my writing classes over the years and my many friends and writing colleagues for spurring me on to finish this novel and, of course, to edit, edit, edit …

To my sons, Simon and Nick for their unwavering support.....

With special love and thanks to Gwen for her sometimes thrice-daily calls. Go well, my friend!

AUTHOR'S NOTE

From the late 19th Century, Britain operated migration schemes which sent more than 100,000 children to Australia, New Zealand, Canada and other Commonwealth countries. These children did not travel with mothers or fathers but alone in groups. Taken from poverty and disadvantage, it was believed that they would have a better life working in the clean expanses of the British Empire where they were a source of much-needed labour.

During the final period in which the British migration policy operated from 1947 to 1967, it is estimated 549 children, mainly between the ages of three and fourteen, were sent from the United Kingdom to New Zealand.

Excerpts from House of Commons Health Third Report and Liverpool National Museum – Child Migration Exhibition.

PART ONE

Chapter One

London 1949

I heard the sound of crockery as it hit the wall and The Old Man's drunken bully-boy demands for food. There would be more dents in our cardboard-thin walls, and the grey roses on the wallpaper would be drooping even further on their stems. Worse, Mum's face would be bruised and bleeding.

I pulled the threadbare blanket over my head. In summer, it scratched and made my arms and legs itch. In winter, I had to double it to keep warm. I held my breath and curled myself into a ball. I could hear my sister Angela doing the same, pushing her head down further, so that if the Old Man came in, he wouldn't be able to grab hold of her hair and drag her out of bed.

I could hear a woman's voice. The Old Man had brought another of his floosies home from the pub and was ordering Mum to feed her. The bedroom door opened with a telltale squeak and the light came on. I peeped through a hole in my blanket. Instead of the Old Man, a woman entered, bringing with her the smell of cheap perfume and gin. She crossed to me and pulled back my blanket. Her finger-nails, painted a gaudy red, penetrated its loose weave, tearing another hole. Her face looked as if it had been coloured with crayons, crimson circling her mouth, deep blue, violent around the eyes, bumpy lines along the eyebrows.

''eaven preserve us, what 'ave we 'ere? A couple of kiddy-winkies. I thought it was the lav. It might as well be; there ain't much more in 'ere.' The woman bent closer to me and I pushed myself higher up the bed.

'So Ted's got a couple of sprogs. They always 'ave.'

The woman wore high heeled shoes. They tip-tapped on the floorboards as she crossed to Angela and whisked the blanket off. 'Not so bad looking either. What's yer names?'

Angela stayed sulky and silent. The woman looked to me for an answer. I clamped my lips together.

''ave yer got tongues in yer heads, or 'as the cat got 'em?'

'Clear off!' Angela eyeballed her.

'So you *can* talk.' The woman traced a finger down Angela's cheek. Angela shuddered and shoved her away.

From the kitchen I heard the ring of metal on metal and Mum's muffled pleas. It made me tremble inside, and I felt ashamed I couldn't face up to the Old Man and rescue her.

'Poor little perishers.' The woman took a shilling from her purse and offered it to Angela, but Angela smacked it from her hand. It hit the floor with a clink and rolled under the bed.

The woman shrugged and turned away.

I heard our Old Man yell, 'Come on, Bunty, there ain't no grub 'ere. Let's get out of this 'ole. The stench's getting up me nostrils.'

The woman put her finger to her lips as she tottered from our room. 'It's all right. 'e won't know I've been in 'ere. Poor little perishers,' she repeated, closing the door quietly behind her. ''Ere I am, Ted, just been to the lav. Fry you up an egg and a bit of bread at my place, all right loveykins.'

I heard our Old Man lurching his way towards the stairs, stumbling, half falling down them. His final shot of, 'I can promise yer one fing, I ain't never comin' back to this dump again,' were welcome words.

As soon as the front door banged shut, I flung myself out of bed and on to the floor. I ran my hands over the fluff-covered floorboards under the bed until I felt cold metal, and I scooped the shilling into my hand, tightening my fingers around it.

'She gave it to me. It's mine. Give it to me,' Angela whined, already out of bed and standing over me. She grabbed a handful of my hair, pulled me to my feet, and tried to loosen my grip on the treasure.

'It's mine now,' I said, elbowing her away.

'Let's go half each. Please, please.'

I held on tight and ignored her. Suddenly I remembered Mum in the kitchen. She was probably trying to tidy herself up. A going-red-inside feeling burnt me up. I had thought of the bob before I had thought of her.

I clutched it all night, and for the next two days, I held that bob tight, changing it from one hand to the other when it became sweaty. I didn't put it down when I went to the lav, trying to cling to my willie with one hand and the coin with the other. Once I got my hands muddled. The shilling clinked into the pan, and I had to roll up my sleeve and fish it out. Having that bob made me feel rich.

The following Monday at school I sat at my desk fingering the coin. It was sticky and stank of pee, but I didn't care.

After we'd recited the Lord's Prayer, our teacher Mrs Colby began calling the class register, sort of singing our names in alphabetical order. Fascinated, I stared at her face. I reckoned she had as many hairs sprouting from her chins as there were kids in the class. Some of the hairs curled upwards towards her nose, while one particularly coarse one like an electric wire wound its way past her throat in the direction of her chest.

She began *The List.* 'Those paying for school dinners come forward.'

Alice Aborne - one shilling. Tick. Alice stepped up to Miss Colby's desk and handed her a bob.

Victor Acton – one shilling. Tick.

Tony Addington - one shilling. Tick.

Usually there were thirty five names, thirty five shillings, thirty five thick black ticks for kids who could afford to pay for their school dinners. But today there were thirty six. I was off the poor list, at last. I handed my shilling over. *My* shilling. I didn't care if the dinners smelt and tasted like cold sick. I'd paid for them with my own shilling. I gave the coin a final pat before passing it to Mrs Colby. If I could, I would have thanked it out loud. I scrambled back to my desk next to Dobsie.

'You off the *Poor List*?' he whispered.

'The Old Man's cleared off, and Mum's got herself a job. We've got money now.'

I sang it in my head when I was in class, in the playground, on my way along Blountmere Street to the

Gang's Camp on the bombsite, opposite our flat. *We've got money now.*

That afternoon at the camp, as usual Dobsie took charge of our game of cowboys and Indians. 'I'm Hoppalong Cassidy. You can be Roy Rogers, Tony, and you can be Gene Autry, Herbie.'

'What about me?' Dennis asked.

'You can be Gabby Hayes.'

'But he's old. He can't blinkin' walk, let alone ride a horse.'

'D'you want to play or don't you?'

Dennis nodded grudgingly.

Dobsie began to move stones. 'Come and help me with these. We'll pile 'em up so we can hide behind 'em and shoot at each other.'

'What about Indians? We've got to have some Indians.'

Dobsie considered for a moment. 'Dennis can be an Indian as well as Gabby Hayes.'

But Dennis had already gone off the idea. I had a suspicion he had been waiting for the chance to show off something he thought was pretty special. He pressed his lips together in a smug half smile and fiddled with something in his inside pocket. Then he brought out a crumpled copy of *The Eagle* which he spread on a moss-covered breezeblock. 'Pinched it from Old Boy Barkers' shop,' he said, flicking over a couple of pages. 'I nicked some liquorice while I was at it.'

'How'd you do that? If Old Boy Barker isn't watching you every flippin' minute you're in his shop, Ma Barker is.'

'Quick as a wink; sleight of hand.' Dennis held his palms flat to show they were empty, then twisting them together in a mysterious move, he put them behind his back and brought them to the front again. This time a stone sat in the middle of his hand.

'Anyone with a bit of savvy can do that.' Dobsie sniffed.

'So why don't *you* nick something then?' Herbie asked.

Dobsie drew in the dust with a stick. 'Done it 'undreds of times. Tony's turn to nick them tomorrow. Fags and a couple of comics. Easy.'

'I'll nick 'em. It don't make no difference to me.' I said, but all at once the bubbles that had been fizzing in my stomach all day flattened and disappeared, leaving me feeling like a glass of day-old Tizer. Even reading *The Eagle* wasn't enough to keep me at the camp and the song in my head had gone.

Making some excuse about Mum not being well, I shinned the wall behind the camp. With my hands in my pockets, I shuffled across the road to our flat. Yanking at the string around my neck, I pulled the key from under my jersey and opened the door, I bounded up the stairs two at a time, and barged into our kitchen. Mum and Angela were dishing Spam and potatoes onto our three remaining china plates. Mum had her vague far-away look. She looked sick. Her face was the colour of cheese and there were lines like pencil marks around her eyes. It made me feel scared.

'Where d'you think you've been?' Angela demanded.

I pretended not to hear her and snatched at the plate with the most food. I took the plate to the table, plonked myself on a chair and began forking spud into my mouth. I saved the Spam until last. Spam was a treat. I swallowed it with gulping noises, in a hurry to get to Lori Lorimore next door to listen to *Dick Barton, Special Agent* on her wireless set.

'I said, where've you been?' Angela looked to Mum for support, but Mum kept her gaze directed on the door. I wondered if she might fly through it and far away.

'Mind your own business.' Mouth full, I spat bits of food onto the newspaper that covered the table. It had been there for days and greasy stains smudged the ink.

'Why should I? 'Cos I'm a girl I have to do everything round here. I can't go out with *my* mates after school.'

There was no way I was doing the washing up and that was flat, so I ignored Angela's carry on and concentrated on scraping every last bit from my plate. It made Angela as mad as hell when I didn't answer. I repeated the word *hell* to myself. Men who said *hell* could nick fags and comics without blinking.

'Well! What've you got to say for yourself?'

Nothing. So that's what I said - nothing.

'If you won't open your stupid mouth, I'll make you.' Angela lunged across the table at me, grabbing the front of my shirt. 'I'll get you, you lazy little rat. I'm older than you, and I'll get you.'

'Be quiet, the pair of you and eat your tea.' Mum rested her elbows on the table and held her head like she had a headache. She hadn't touched her dinner and I wondered if she'd let me eat it. She was always going on about not wasting food.

'It's not fair. He doesn't do anything. Tell him it's his turn to do the washing up.'

'It's not. I'm going into Lori's to listen to *Dick Barton*. She said I could.'

'For once, you'll have to stay home, won't you?' Angela struck her fork on the table. It made a tear in the newspaper.

'Now don't start getting upset again. We can wash up. It won't take us long.'

The way Mum was talking to Angela, she might as well have been toadying to the Old Man when he came back boozed. I hated it. It was fear rolled up in smarmy words.

She pushed her plate with the untouched food towards me, limped outside to the scullery and filled the kettle. A rush of water juddered through the pipes. She brought three enamel mugs into the kitchen, and spooned condensed milk into them, putting a soothing spoonful into her own mouth.

'But it's not fair.'

'*But it's not fair*,' I mimicked.

'Will you two stop.' Mum raised her voice, which was unusual for her. 'It's almost a quarter to seven, Tony. You'd better finish eating quickly and be getting next door.'

'You always take his side. You never let me away with the things he does.'

Mum didn't answer. She hated quarrels. I wouldn't mind betting she'd already taken off to the secret place in her head that was quiet and peaceful: somewhere our Old Man never existed, and where she didn't have to struggle to buy a tin of Spam.

When I got to her flat next door, Lori was already warming her wireless set. Like our kitchen, hers smelt of paraffin, but apart from two rickety chairs, the table and a sideboard propped up with books, our kitchen was bare. In Lori's, there were photographs everywhere. They hung in rows on her walls, and covered the top of her sideboard; even round the skirting boards. And anywhere there was the smallest space she had tucked a cup, a bowl or some ornament. The thing that frightened me, though, was an alabaster dog that kept watch over the fireplace with its mouth wide open displaying jagged teeth. Its eyes were yellow and I didn't like to turn my back on it for fear it would forget where it belonged and attack me.

'Sit down, Tony, the programme's about to begin.' Lori indicated a bulging armchair and handed me a plate with two chocolate biscuits on it. I stuffed the biscuits whole into my mouth, in case that dog got hold of them.

'Dick Barton, Special Agent.' Da de da, da de, da. As soon as I heard the announcement and the opening music, I fidgeted to the edge of the chair, and for the next quarter of an hour *Dick Barton* made me forget about nicking a few fags and a couple of comics.

When the programme finished, Lori turned off the crackling wireless set. 'I'll make us a quick cup of tea, shall I?'

Lori was a funny old biddy (that's what Herbie called old women: biddies), with grey-blonde frizzled hair, and scarves she wore winter and summer trailing to the ground.

But she was all right, really. If it hadn't been for Lori, we might have starved. She probably gave Mum the Spam we had for tea.

'Tea's a funny thing. We see it as the solution to all our problems.' Lori turned on the tap and filled the kettle, calling over the sound of moaning pipes. 'I know people say it was those Americans and of course, dear Mister Churchill who got us through the War. I believe it was the good old British cuppa that kept our spirits up and gave the nation the willpower to keep going.'

I got up, moved from my place in front of the wireless to the sideboard, and began picking up photographs: sepia ones of stern looking men and women, and solemn boys in sailor suits posing next to girls in long dresses with starched pinafores. Men with watches draped across their waistcoats stood to attention beside women in huge hats decorated with feathers. Why was it women in old photos always sat, while men stood? Perhaps it was supposed to show that men were stronger, although some of the women looked as if they could have gone a few rounds in a boxing ring and come out winning; they were a bit like Angela.

I peered at a photo of a scrawny man standing beside an enormous woman.   Then I moved from the sideboard to look at the photographs on the wall. Although I had been in and out of Lori's flat since I was a baby, I liked to look at these photos every time I came. We didn't have any photos in our flat, and I pretended Lori's family was mine, too.

'How's your mum, tonight?' Lori asked. 'Being on her feet all day in that shop, especially with those legs of hers, is too much for her. I hope you and your sister appreciate what she's doing.'

In the few days since she'd started work, Mum had begun bandaging her legs. All that stuff wrapped around them reminded me of the Egyptian mummies I learnt about at school.

I moved around the room touching things. Next to Lori's well-used Bible was her India box. It was my favourite thing in the room. A great-aunt had given it to her. This aunt had been married to a Colonel or some high up bloke in the British Army, and she had lived in India. I didn't know where India was, and Lori had showed it to me on a map. She said that India was hot and the box was made of sandalwood, which I thought must be a lot different from the tree at the top of Blountmere Street. When you opened the box it smelt like the spice on top of penny buns.

'If you ever want a gadget, I'm the one to ask,' Lori often said. 'I've got everything in my India box. I could live on a desert island and not want for anything, if I had it with me.'

When we were little, Lori had let Angela and me play with some of the things inside it - a spinning top and a doll in a bit of material called a sari. Once Angela stuffed the doll down her knickers and took it home, but Mum found it and gave it back to Lori. Angela cried all night.

On top of the India box was Lori's handbag: the old grey one she always carried. Sometimes, she even tucked it under her arm when she was hanging out her washing. The straps had worn out hundreds of years ago, and she often said she must get a new bag, but she never did. Inside it, I could see a whole lot of rubbishy stuff like Lori's powder puff she patted her nose with when she got flummoxed and one or two sweet papers. In the middle of it all, I saw her old green purse and it was bulging, really bulging. There was probably more money in it than Angela and I would see in ten years. Enough for a half crown not to be noticed. Then I could pay Old Boy Barker outright for the fags and comics. It was the answer to my problem. Lori had so much she wouldn't miss it, and I wouldn't risk Old Boy Barker catching me nicking. I fumbled for the purse, undid the clasp, grabbed a half crown, and stuffed it into my pocket.

Lori came into the kitchen with two cups of tea and told me to sit down, but I couldn't keep still. A fiery feeling burnt my throat. 'I think I'd better pop back to Mum,' I said, getting up and leaving the tea untasted.

'That's very thoughtful of you, Tony,' Lori called after me as I tore out her front door and down her path on my way back to our flat.

'Give my love to your Mum,' I heard as I opened our door, but I didn't answer. I had to get away. I didn't want to think about what I'd done.

The next day on the way to school, I told the Gang I had left my exercise book at home and I would catch them up. When I could see them well down the road, I put on a confident smile and skipped into Old Boy Barker's. I chose the comics and took them to the counter. Old Boy Barker stared at me, his red bladder of a nose practically throbbing when I asked for twenty Players.

'And you say these cigarettes are for your Gran?'

'My Gran smokes like … um …*hell.*' I choked over the word. 'My Gran smokes a lot.'

'What about the comics?'

'They're a special treat.'

'I didn't know you had a Gran.'

I thought quickly. 'Dad's mum. Step mum. She lives in ... India, but she's on holiday at the moment. She's got a box full of knick-knacks and that.'

I passed the half crown over the counter and Old Boy Barker gave me the Players. Then he rolled The Dandy and The Beano and put a rubber band around them, before handing them to me. He still looked suspicious and I made my smile bigger. It was a pity I wouldn't be able to have the penny drink of Tizer I had been looking forward to, but although I tried, I couldn't control the trembling in my belly or keep the fire from my throat.

Smoking! All that sucking and blowing. It was a waste of money.

Except for Herbie, we all threw up, lumpy sick, bright with carrots from our school dinner.

Afterwards, I made straight for our flat. Along the Dibbles' side of the front path, red flowers smothered their rose bushes, and their doorstep left ours looking grey. Their front door was half open. In the brightness of their hall, I could see Paula Dibble's two-wheeler propped against a wall. I kicked one of the rose bushes and it shed red petals on the path, like drops of blood. There was no way I would ever get a bike. Even when I got my hands on a measly half crown, I sicked it up.

As I turned my key, Lori opened her front door. Her scarf trailed the path as she bent to put an empty milk bottle on her step. She straightened, and looked directly at me.

'You look a little peaky,' she said. 'Cigarettes don't do much good to a nine year old stomach.'

Chapter Two

Most summer Saturday afternoons, I sat on the back doorstep with Paula Dibble from the flat downstairs reading comics. I was glad her old man's bushes hid us. If the Gang or Angela found out, they would call me a sissy. Angela said Paula was the stuck-up daughter of a stuck-up mother, paraded around in fancy outfits.

'She's a jellyfish, a spoilt, prissy jellyfish who's got everything but a backbone,' Angela said whenever Paula's name was so much as mentioned. 'What if she's always had every single thing she's wanted. Who cares? And Lily *Dribble* can carry on all she likes about *her wonderful Les*; he's still a bully.'

When we told each other secrets, Paula called it confiding. I liked confiding to Paula. I didn't throw stones at her like the Gang did, or chant, "*Dribble, dribble, all she does is dribble.*" But I wouldn't be caught walking to school with her. There was nothing wrong with her. It wasn't as if she was dirty. She smelt of soap, nice and flowery, not like that horrible coal tar stuff Mum bought when she had the money. Inside, I felt guilty as if a thousand worms squirmed.

'I had a nightmare last night,' I told Paula one thundery Saturday afternoon when the sky was so low it almost touched us. 'It's the same every time, about a giant stomping along Blountmere Street looking for me. He swooped on both our flats. He shook them and roared my name. I hid under the table, but he found me and squeezed me tighter and tighter, until I couldn't breathe.' I put my fingers over my eyes to get rid of the picture. 'Did you hear me scream?'

'Not really. Anyway, I expect you hear Dad shouting. He does sometimes - you know - shout. He doesn't mean to … He … It can be a bit frightening. In between, well, mainly he doesn't talk to Mum and me.'

'I never hear a dickey bird.' I lied. 'Sometimes me and Ang used to hide under the bed after our Old Man had a skinful in case he bashed us. A lot of the time he did, see … and Mum. He cut her eye once. She had to wear a patch over it.' I cast a half glance at Paula. 'He used to bring these fancy women home and force Mum to feed them. One of them came into our room once. She gave me a bob.'

With the lengthening days, the Gang spent even longer at our camp. We even went back there after we had all listened to *Dick Barton*. We each squatted on our own stone and talked, starting with *Dick* and his latest adventure, then on to all sorts of other things, while the shadows made the ruins look as if they had stripes painted on them.

'Any of you joinin' the Cubs up the Wesleyan Church, then?' Dobsie asked, poking a finger through a hole in the pullover he was always boasting his Gran had knitted him. I reckoned she had bad eyesight because you could see where she'd dropped some of the stitches. Both Dobsie's socks were pulled right up, without even a crinkle. Dobsie was fussy like that, but when he stretched his legs in front of him I could see he had a hole in the sole of his shoe.

'Kenny Withard said the Cubs have a camp at the seaside every year at Bognor? And it don't cost?'

'Bognor! And it don't cost?'

'Not a penny. Kenny says you have to be there a while before they take you. They have a Christmas party with presents as well. And you have adventures and get badges for having them. You wear a uniform and everyfink.'

'You thinkin' of going?' Herbie asked.

'I'll see,' Dobsie replied, as secretive as he always was.

'What about you, Tony?'

'I might.' A chance of going to the seaside without paying. You bet I'd be joining. I'd never been to the seaside. I wasn't sure about the uniform, though. Mum wouldn't be able to pay for that. With her having to take a week off work because of her legs, at the rate things were going I'd be back on the *Poor List* before you could say *Bognor.*

Two weeks later, Mum lost her job.

'The company were very good to me,' Mum told Lori when she popped in with some tea and sugar that she said she'd come across at the back of her cupboard. 'But I couldn't stand all day. Finally they asked me to leave.' Mum leant back in her chair, and even from my usual place in the corner, crouched next to the side board, I could see her face was that yellowish colour again.

Lori fiddled with the strap on her handbag. 'I know you don't want to hear this, Dolly, but you can't sit there pretending things will be all right. Unless you do something, we both know they won't.'

Mum's eyes were closed. I was pretty sure she'd mind-travelled to her secret place.

'How do you propose looking after yourself and the children without a job?' Lori bent closer to Mum, and lowered her voice. I suppose she thought I wouldn't be able to hear her. 'Why don't you let me make some enquiries to see if we can find Ted's whereabouts? The least he should be doing is making regular payments towards bringing up the children.'

That got Mum's attention, catapulting her from her land of make-believe. 'I don't want his help, and I won't have his name mentioned here.'

'If that's how you want it, Dolly.'

Mum stretched her legs in front of her, the bandages around them thicker than ever. She looked as if the last thing she wanted was to be dragged back into our kitchen from wherever she was trying to escape.

'You can sew, can't you? Why not take in sewing? And before you say you don't have a sewing machine, you can borrow mine.'

'Do you think I'm good enough? People can be very fussy.' Mum said, although her voice had perked up.

I held my breath, willing her to say yes. Mum had to take in sewing. She just had to, or I'd have to go back on the *Poor List*.

'Of course you're good enough. You made a couple of dresses for Olive Kingsley, didn't you, and they turned out all right.' Lori wound and rewound her handbag strap. 'The way I see it, sewing's the answer. Between times you'd be able to put your legs up.' She sent a quick glance in my direction. 'Tony and Angela could ask to put advertisements for your sewing services in the High Street shops. And, of course, they could ask Mr Barker to put one in his window.'

I shuddered. The last thing I wanted to do was to toady to grumpy shopkeepers. It was begging. As for asking Old Boy Barker to put an advertisement in *his* window, I'd been avoiding him since I'd bought the fags and comics. When the Gang popped into his shop for a bit of liquorice or a penny drink, I made an excuse to stay outside. I'd make Angela ask all the shopkeepers. She'd be better at it than me.

'That's settled.' Lori stopped fiddling with her bag strap, and the way she smiled lit up her face. 'Now you need something to bring in a little extra until the orders start coming.'

Mum sighed and closed her eyes again.

'A lodger! That's it, a lodger.'

'We don't have room,' Mum said, coming back fast.

'Of course you do.' Lori was as unstoppable as the rag and bone man's horse, when it got loose and galloped down Blountmere Street. 'You've got your front room. Needs must, Dolly. Needs must.'

'I really don't ...'

'But, of course. I should have thought of it before! I have a good friend, a retired naval officer who's looking for digs in this area. I'll get in touch with him straight away.'

For a moment I thought Lori was going to dance a jig.

'But ...'

Lori was already galloping through the door like that horse again, complimenting Mum on "a jolly good suggestion".

'There are times when Miss Lorimore gets carried away,' Mum sighed after Lori had gone.

When it came to taking in a lodger, Mum was right. The last thing we needed was some old geezer staggering round the place and bashing us up.

I could tell Fred Stannard had been in the Navy. Perhaps it was the way he held his shoulders and looked directly at me, but I somehow knew he had been one of our boys who had fought Jerry, and won The War. We watched films at Saturday Picture Club about it. I especially liked the ones about destroyers and mine sweepers. Those sailors were so brave. I always felt proud of them. Our Old Man had wheedled his way out of fighting. According to him there was something wrong with his feet.

'This will do me extremely well, Mrs Addington.' Fred Stannard was wearing a blue shirt. His skin was brownish and his hair a sandy colour. He looked around the room, and I felt ashamed we couldn't have given a brave sailor like Mr Stannard something better than old furniture Lori didn't want.

'Five shillings and sixpence seems a fair rent,' he said.

Mum smiled, though I could tell she was still uneasy about taking in a lodger.

'My friend Miss Lorimore tells me it will suit if I move in tomorrow.' Appearing not to notice Angela and me peeping round the door, Fred Stannard continued. 'Miss Lorimore also tells me you have two delightful children, whom I should very much like to meet.'

Mum gave us one of her looks and pushed us into the room. 'This is Angela.'

'How do you do, Angela? It's a pleasure to meet you.'
Fred Stannard shook Angela's hand.

She scowled and wiped her hand on her skirt.

'And Tony.'

'It's a pleasure to meet you, Tony.' Mr Stannard
pumped my hand until it tingled.

'Trust Lori to have a stuck-up friend like him.' Angela
sneered as soon as we got out of the room. 'All la de da and
posh. It's going to be horrible having him living with us.'

After Fred had settled in, he often invited me to play a game of
Spin The Globe, where he spun his globe and I pointed to a
place on it. If he'd sailed there, he told me about it and some
of his other voyages, as well.

Fancy having sailed round the world not once, but
dozens of times.

I began making excuses to the Gang about having to
help Mum, but I couldn't get to Fred quick enough. He had
put model ships in the alcoves either side of the fireplace, and
there was a half-finished model on the table by the window. I
liked the gluey smell.

'Take a pew,' Fred said, smiling. I perched on the
edge of a chair. It was old and the springs creaked.

'How's school been today?' Fred asked, offering me a
liquorice allsort.

'Fine.' I took the sweet and held it while I spun the
globe. I didn't want to talk about school. I only wanted to
spin and hear more of Fred's adventures. It was better than
listening to *Dick Barton*. When it stopped turning, I closed my
eyes and pointed.

'Well, well, well, South America,' Fred smiled. 'Brazil to be precise.'

'Have you been there?' I chewed on my sweet.

'I surely have. Of course, I haven't seen all of it. It's a very big place.'

'What's it like, then?'

'The beaches are some of the best in the world, with fine white sand and the sea is the colour of a blue summer sky.'

'As good as Bognor?'

'Just as good as Bognor,' Fred smiled. 'There are many churches. It's very hot, and the churches are cool inside and good places to go to get out of the heat.' Fred crossed to the window and looked out. I wondered if he was seeing Brazil instead of our bombsite.

'Vast areas are jungle where there are monkeys and a lot of other wild animals. There are still tribes of people who haven't ever seen a white person.'

Fred came back to the globe and rubbed his finger over the patch that was South America. 'Brazilian people speak Portuguese, because it was Portugal who discovered it.'

'What do they eat?'

'Mainly beans.'

'Baked beans?' What a place to live!

'I'm afraid not. They're a different kind entirely – not to my liking at all. Give me a good plate of Irish stew any day. But the people are happy-go-lucky and dance a lot. They call their national dance the samba.' Fred laughed. 'Not a dance for bones that are getting old like mine.'

I rested my chin in my hands and tried to imagine such a faraway place. When I grew up, I was going to travel like that. Maybe I'd join the Navy.

'Why don't Miss Lorimore and I take you to the library tomorrow? You can get some books on South America, and Angela might like to choose a couple of books too,' Fred continued.

'Thanks, thanks very much.' Having Fred live with us wasn't at all horrible.

October came and it was too cold to sit on Paula's back step. We took to reading in her kitchen, where it was warm and Mrs Dibble often gave us queen cakes or date slices. I was reading a Biggles book I'd got from the library when I'd last gone with Fred. Since Fred came to live with us, I'd gone up two reading grades at school and earned some progress stars.

'Fred's got a wireless set and he's put it in our kitchen. He said, what's the point of having it in his room, when we can all enjoy it.' I told Paula. 'Now Mum listens to *Housewives' Choice* while she does her sewing, and Lori pops in to listen to it, even though she's got a wireless of her own. I think she comes in all the time because Fred's a friend of hers. It's funny the way she acts when he's around.'

'What do you mean?'

'When she calls him *Fred*, she says it as if she's *Betty Grable*. Fred acts a bit strange in front of her too. The other day he called her by her first name and said she was looking as lovely as when she was eighteen. He had this silly grin on his face.'

'What's Miss Lorimore's first name?' It can't possibly be Lori. That's only her nickname.'

'I think it's Amelia.'

'Girls in books have that sort of name. They're the ones that go to posh boarding schools. They don't come from Blountmere Streeet.'

'The other day while I was getting my shoes from the cupboard in the passage I overheard Fred and Lori talking.'

'What did they say?' Paula asked.

'Lori said something about it not being proper they were alone in Fred's room, and what would Dolly think. Fred said that if he hadn't been a fool all those years ago, they wouldn't have to worry about what anyone thought now.'

'What did Lori say to that?' Paula leaned forward and rested her elbows on the table.

'Lori said she had waited for a long time.' I scratched my head. 'What had Lori waited for, do you think?'

'Perhaps it was a wireless.'

'Maybe. Anyway, Fred went on about regretting whatever it was.'

'Why did Fred regret Lori had to wait for a wireless?'

'Dunno, but he sounded like he had water in his voice box. Then he said, "I've asked her to let me go, but she refuses." Things went quiet after that and I didn't want them to catch me snooping, so I collected my shoes and crept back down the passage.'

'Grown ups have the strangest conversations.'

'How are things going, having Fred around?' Lori asked Mum one afternoon. Although she had always been in and out of our place, now Fred had come, Lori practically lived with us. As usual, I was in my corner reading. My present book was about Australia. I'd chosen it the last time I went to the library.

'Everything's going very well.' Mum actually sounded enthusiastic. 'Now I'm beginning to get busy with sewing, he's such a help, and I can't tell you how good it is to have him take over the housekeeping.

Our Old Man never lifted a finger to help with the dishes or cleaning. He said it was women's work. Going shopping would have sent him barmy.

November rolled in with fog, and our bombsite looked like it was covered in a curtain. The fog burnt my throat and made my eyes scratch.

Mum was speechless when Fred lugged in a bucket of coal and put it on the hearth.

'Wherever did that come from?' Mum asked looking up from her sewing.

'I budgeted a little from the housekeeping to have a couple of hundred weight delivered and persuaded Les Dibble downstairs to let me keep it in the shed in his back garden,' Fred explained. He knelt in front of the fireplace, screwed paper into balls and criss-crossed wood over them before heaping on the coal. He struck a match and held it to the paper. Before long our flat was cosy and warm for the first time I could remember.

'What a difference it makes,' Mum smiled. Her face had lost some of its sadness.

Fred straightened. 'Now, young Tony, how about popping down those stairs and fetching some more coal?' Fred handed me the coal scuttle. I could tell it was a way of getting me out of the room while he spoke to Mum.

I bounded down the stairs, opened and shut the door with a bang, then I crept back again. I wedged myself behind the door peeping through the crack.

'I wanted to give you this, Mrs Addington. It's the money I've saved on the shopping. I thought you might like to buy the children their Christmas presents with it,' Fred said.

Mum's voice was shaky. 'I've never had the opportunity to save anything before. It's like an inheritance, Mr Stannard.' I heard Mum blow her nose.

'Tony was telling me how much he'd like a Meccano set the other day. I think you'll find there's enough to buy him one, and it would still leave plenty for Angela's present.'

A Meccano set! I concentrated on keeping my feet on the floor in case I jumped up and down.

'I've always said I'd like to get Angela a musical box, one with a ballerina on top like the one I once had. Do you think this will run to one?' Mum asked, her voice still sounding quivery.

'I'm more than sure it will, and I think I know where you'll find just what you're looking for. Jousins the jewellers in the Old Town have one in their window. I'll come with you to get it if you like.'

'I'd be most grateful, Mr Stannard.'

'Not at all, Mrs Addington'

I thought Christmas would never come. Keeping my secret from everyone was like trying to keep a door locked when the key wanted to jump from my pocket and straight into the keyhole.

'I don't care what stupid Paula *Dribble* gets, it won't be as good as this,' Angela said on Christmas morning. The ballerina twirled on top of her musical box to the tinkling of *The Sugar Plum Fairy*, while Angela pretended to be a ballerina. I sprawled on the floor in front of the fire and screwed together pieces of Meccano to make a tank. The smell of chicken and Christmas pudding wafted from the scullery. There was a Christmas tree in the corner of the kitchen and Angela danced towards it. 'Our lights are real, not stupid little candles like the Dibbles have on their Christmas tree,' she sneered.

'It doesn't do to make comparisons,' Fred smiled at Angela and she smiled back. She hardly ever smiled and I couldn't believe how different it made her look. I must have been going soft or perhaps it was the Christmas tree lights, but she looked a bit like the angel Fred had tied to the top of the tree.

'We'll be able to listen to the King's speech after dinner. You can always rely on His Majesty to deliver a good few words, even if he does have a bit of a stammer.' Lori called from the scullery. Old Man Dibble downstairs was abusing his wife and she had to raise her voice to make herself heard over the row. 'Let's turn the wireless on, so that it warms up,' she said.

Chapter Three

Soon after Christmas, the weather turned nasty. North winds froze our blood. I had chilblains on my fingers and toes. Fred gave Mum an old jersey. She unravelled it and knitted Angela and me a pair of gloves and a scarf each, the first we'd ever owned. Sometimes when the wind rattled the window panes, and ice painted the insides of the glass with a thick crust, Angela and I wore our gloves and scarves around the house.

'Look at that icicle.' I pointed to a length of ice, hanging like a dagger outside the window.

'It's not as big as the one outside my classroom. It must be at least two feet long.'

'Why d'you always have to go one better,' I began.

Mum interrupted our argument. She looked nervous. 'I've been thinking. It's … well … I want to have you both christened.'

'You can't mean it.' It was one of the soppiest things I'd ever heard Mum say.

Mum's interest in God had begun a few months earlier when the vicar of St. Nicholas' Church came knocking on our door. I think he was trying to persuade people to join his congregation. After talking to him, Mum dusted off her old Bible and went to church. Sometimes Fred and Lori went with her. They came back singing hymns and with a pint of winkles which Fred bought from the stall outside *The Perseverance*.

'Your father didn't have any time for religion, but it doesn't seem right somehow that you haven't been sprinkled with holy water and blessed,' Mum continued.

'Babies get christened, not kids of our age. We'd look daft. Anyway, the vicar wouldn't be able to pick us up,' Angela said, and scowled.

'He wouldn't have to pick you up. It would be more of a grown-up service.' Mum sounded as if she had rehearsed what she wanted to say.

'You mean we wouldn't have to wear christening robes?'

She smiled at Angela. 'Of course you wouldn't. You'd wear your ordinary clothes. I might even be able to make you a new dress.'

I knew she was bribing Angela, like Herbie's Mum bribed him when she offered him a tanner if he went and got her a packet of fags.

'I've spoken to the Reverend Roberts. He says you should be christened, and he'll be happy to do it.'

'We won't get struck dead if we're not done, will we?'

'Of course not. It's just that the Reverend Roberts says every child should be dedicated to God.'

'I don't care what stupid Reverend Roberts says, I'm not getting christened; dress or no new dress.' Angela folded her arms.

Mum wasn't to be put off. 'Part of being christened is that you'll need godparents.'

'Godparents!'

'Two people who, if anything should happen to me, promise to support and look after you. Of course it's more of a tradition these days.'

'If it's only a silly tradition, why bother?'

'The Reverend Roberts says we must.'

I wondered if the Reverend Roberts would have so much to say if someone wanted to christen him when he was ten. He wasn't the one who'd look a chump. What would the Gang say if they found out?

'I'm sure it won't be bad. Reverend Roberts will only make a small cross with water on your forehead. And if it makes you feel better, we'll ask if it could be done in a private service with only your godparents there.'

'And who are going to be our godparents?'

'It's usually people from your family, but Aunt Jess and Uncle Albert live in Northumberland, so we can't ask them.'

I puffed out a relieved breath. Uncle Albert picked his nose and Aunt Jess had a squint that made it seem as if she was looking at you even when she wasn't.

Mum squared her shoulders. 'Actually, Miss Lorimore and Mr Stannard have said they'd do it'

'Fred and Lori!' Angela uncrossed her arms and the sulkiness drained from her face. 'And you say I can have a new dress?'

'Yes.'

'Can I choose the material and the pattern?'

'Maybe not the material, but the pattern. Miss Lorimore's also suggested a special tea afterwards to celebrate.'

Angela stroked the sides of her face the way Fred did when he was considering something. 'I suppose that makes a bit of a difference. And you say no-one else will be there?'

'No-one needs to know.'

'In that case, I suppose it'll be all right.'

'Yeah, I suppose we might as well go along with it.' I said, giving my opinion even though no one had asked for it.

'I'll ask the Reverend Roberts to book us in, shall I?'

'Might as well.'

As soon as she finished, I fled along the passage to Fred's room. 'Mum says you're going to be our godfather,' I blurted as soon as he opened the door.

Fred nodded. 'I like to think I'll do a good job. I'm afraid I didn't do so well with my own children. I was away too much to have any influence on them.'

'I didn't know you had kids.'

'Two - a boy and a girl. They both live abroad. Shirley's in Canada with her husband and two daughters, and Ronald's in New Zealand. He part-owns a business there.' Fred reached inside his jacket and pulled out his wallet. He took out two photographs and showed them to me. One was of a young woman, the other of a tall man wearing glasses and dressed in a checked shirt and jeans like a cowboy. Fred studied them as if he was trying to set every detail in his head. When he had replaced the photos in his wallet, he crossed to the window and stared out at yet another snow flurry. I edged closer to him and brushed my hand against his. If his children didn't appreciate him, I did.

Fred stroked my shoulders, but it felt as if he was stroking my heart. 'Sometimes we're given a second chance, what do you think?' Fred asked me.

On the afternoon of our christening in St. Nicholas', our breath swirled in front of us like white candyfloss. Lori had exchanged her scarf for a fur stole, and Fred could have been an Admiral in his navy blue blazer and freshly pressed slacks, a crisp white handkerchief peeping from his top pocket. The five of us stood around a strange looking basin which was half-filled with water. I hoped the water wasn't too cold. At least it hadn't frozen over like the ponds up The Common.

Lori and Fred had given each of us a Bible. There was a coloured picture on the inside cover that showed Jesus, surrounded by children. Underneath the picture, it said: "Suffer Little Children To Come Unto Me". I clutched my Bible to my chest, while Lori clung to Fred's arm, Angela fidgeted and Mum gave her the sort of smile that said it wouldn't be long now. Reverend Roberts put on his spectacles and read from the black book in front of him. After reading, he looked upwards and called out to God. 'Our Father, bless these, Thy children.' His voice bounced off the pillars and echoed from a hundred stone creases around the church. My concentration wandered, and in my mind I tried to create a picture of God. Each time, I imagined Him differently. Old and bearded, like a cleaner version of Gabby Hayes in the films at Saturday Picture Club. Next I imagined Him to look like the picture of Jesus I had in the front of my Bible. I even saw him as a version of Old Dibble downstairs, silent and angry.

Something wet touched my forehead, making me pay attention as Reverend Roberts drew a cold cross on my forehead

'May the God of Heaven watch over you,' he said in a sing song voice. I wished he hadn't said those words. I didn't want God spying on everything I did.

Next, Reverend Roberts turned to Fred and Lori and asked them to promise to carry out their duties responsibly. I looked at Fred, who was standing upright like the trunk of the sycamore tree in Blountmere Street. I knew he wouldn't let me down or run off with some fancy woman. Reverend Roberts called God "Father", but God wasn't like my Old Man. God was like Fred.

Chapter Four

'Checkmate!' Fred pointed to the chess piece resting on the board.

I pushed my fingers through my hair. 'I'm never going to pick this chess lark up.'

'Of course you are. Anything worth doing takes time.' Fred's voice was sort of sad. 'We've both got plenty of that. Now let's start again.'

He moved the pieces back to where they had been, and I stared at the chess board, concentrating hard. Hesitating, I slid my pawn in front of Fred's queen.

'Good lad. Excellent tactics.'

As if the longer days couldn't bear to hold off, it was becoming lighter in the late afternoons. Across the street, the bombsite was covered with green lace, as new growth crept over it. Fred got up and stood by the window gazing out.

'Come and have a look at this. Would you believe there's a couple of ducks on the water in that large bomb crater. There must be a reason they've decided to take their chances here, instead of somewhere like the ponds on The Common. Let's hope any eggs they lay are well hidden. They wouldn't stand much of a chance with some of the young tykes around here.' Fred beckoned for me to have a look, and I went to stand beside him at the window, pressing my nose against the windowpane. The glass felt cold. My breath made misty circles and I used one of my cuffs to wipe them off.

I stood staring at the ducks. They seemed out of place there. I wondered if Angela had seen them. She was dotty about animals. I swore she would have preferred a world without any humans to muck things up.

Angela and I had owned a kitten once, when I was about three, I think. We had called it Berry or Barry; I couldn't remember which. Somewhere in the back of my head was a faded image of its lifeless body covered in blood, with an eye dangling onto its nose. And I vaguely recalled Mum as she stood over it. She was crying and the Old Man was shouting at her to stop her snivelling.

'I think we had a kitten once.' I told Fred.

'I do recall Amel … Miss Lorimore mentioning something about it.'

'Mum won't let us have another one. Angela wants some white mice, but Mum doesn't like them.'

'Not everyone does.'

'Can we finish this game tomorrow?' I'd lost interest in chess. I felt fidgety and wanted to get outside.

'The ducks call, do they?' Fred guessed. 'Be off with you, then. Why don't you ask Miss Lorimore if she has some bread to spare?' Fred called after me as I skidded down the passage.

I practically danced on Lori's doorstep, I was so eager to get to the ducks. 'Fred suggested I ask you for some bread,' I said, as soon as she answered my knock. I could hardly keep from turning my back on her to look at the ducks. 'There's ducks on the bombsite and I want to feed them.'

'Yes, I've just noticed them. What a surprise. I'm sure I could spare a little of the cottage twist I bought yesterday. Come on into the kitchen and I'll cut you a piece.'

Lori laughed what I always thought of was a frizzy laugh, like her hair. 'I can see these ducks aren't going to go hungry.'

Instead of popping across the road there and then, I jumped Lori's path to our place. I opened the door and shouted to Angela. I must have been going soft in the head or something to actually tell Angela.

When it was filled with water, the crater looked like a real pond and a bit out of place on the bombsite. But the ducks seemed to like it, because when we got there they were sitting on some stones sunning themselves. That soon changed when we threw some of Lori's bread on the water. Then they quacked and paddled towards us as if they hadn't eaten before.

'D'you like that, ducky ducks,' Angela spoke to them in a voice she only used for animals. 'You're lovely,' she crooned.

After we'd used all the bread, Angela settled herself on the ground, continuing to talk to them. They kept swimming up and down past her, as if they could understand what she was saying to them.

After ten minutes I'd had enough. 'Are you coming home? I asked, but Angela waved her arm in the air as if she was glad to be getting rid of me. 'No, I'm staying here to look after them.'

'Go across to the bombsite and tell your sister her tea's ready, and don't take no for an answer. I know she wants to protect the ducks, but she's not eating her tea over there. Anyway it's getting dark and even ducks have to sleep.' It was plain

Mum didn't understand how we felt about them, I thought, as I nipped across to the bombsite to fetch Angela.

'I know they have to sleep. I'm not stupid,' Angela huffed when I passed on what Mum had said.

'I want to stay for a while to make sure they're safe.' The tough look on Angela's face changed to something soft like the inside of one of Old Boy Barker's bulls eyes.

'Honest, Tone, I can't let anything happen to them, not after what happened to …' She broke off abruptly.

'What?'

'Nothing. It doesn't matter.'

'Keep it to yourself, then. See if I care. Anyway, Fred said he'd pop over later tonight to check on them. I expect he'll bring Lori with him.' I tugged on her sleeve. 'You've got to come now. Mum's getting mad.'

Angela shrugged me off. 'I'm not frightened of Mum.'

Just the same, she collapsed the camping stool she'd been using. It was Les Dibble's, and Paula had smuggled it out of their flat for us. Angela folded the blanket she had taken from her bed, and hid it with the chair behind a pile of rubble. Before she left, she called to the ducks, telling them to hide while she was away, and then she belted off home.

I followed, thinking she was daft calling out to ducks. 'Don't you want your blanket?' I called after her.

'I'm coming back later. I'm not going to leave those ducks alone all night. I don't care what Mum or the King of England says. I'm coming back to check on them after tea.'

Mum had our meal on the table. We didn't even stop to wash our hands before we attacked the food.

'Your manners are getting worse, the two of you,' Mum complained, as we bolted our tea down so fast Angela got the hiccups and I let out a loud burp.

'You haven't given yourselves time to digest your food,' she continued, but we were already making for the door and bounding down the stairs. With Mum's legs the way they were, I knew by the time she'd hobbled to the bottom, we'd already be on the bombsite.

'Who said *you* could come? I don't need you or anyone else.' Angela was still hiccupping.

'The ducks are ours, remember.'

For a while neither of us spoke, as we concentrated on getting across the ruins in the dark.

It was cold, not ordinary cold, but the sort of misty cold that gave you the willies. There was no moon, only the light that seeped between cracks in the curtains that hung in the windows of the prefabs which surrounded the bombsite. The broken walls that sprang up in front of us looked like a monster's teeth.

'D'you reckon there are ghosts here from people who were killed in The War?' I asked.

'Not scared are you?'

'Course not. What about you?'

'It'd take more than a few stupid ghosts to put the wind up me.' Just the same, Angela hung on to my jersey.

I heard a rustling sound, followed by the noise of stones crunching together. I stopped and looked around to see a slit of light moving towards us.

Angela heard and saw it too. 'What's that?' She asked, screwing a handful of my jersey into a ball.

I made a grab for her hand. We moved closer to each other as the sound of a voice floated towards us.

'Blimey, it *is* a ghost! Clear off. Leave us alone,' she shouted, but her voice shook.

I felt the edge of a broken-down wall beside us, and pushed Angela behind it, then practically fell on top of her. 'Keep your head down and the ghosts might not be able to find us.'

From behind the wall we heard footsteps getting closer and I tightened my grip on Angela's hand.

'Don't touch the ducks,' she cried out. 'Please, please don't touch them. They haven't done you any harm. Don't kick'em with your boots 'til their eyes drop out.'

'It's all right, wherever you are. It's us, Mrs Dibble and Paula!'

'I told you there weren't any such things as ghosts, didn't I.' Angela hissed. 'You're nothing but a cry baby.' She shook off my hand.

'But it wasn't me who … and who was it who ...'

Angela ignored me. 'We're here, over here.'

'We've almost broken our necks trying to find you two,' Mrs Dibble stumbled over to us. She held on to Paula to keep steady as she bent to rub her ankle. 'Paula knew you stayed over here. She said you were guarding those blessed ducks, and she thought we should give you a bit of company. She wanted to come on her own, but I wasn't having any daughter of mine wandering round a bombsite alone at night. She could have broken her neck or fallen in that crater and drowned.'

'We're not guarding *the ducks*. Fred said they were safe enough at night. It's *their eggs* we're protecting. We don't want them getting nicked.'

'Mr Dibble and I think it's too early for ducklings.'

Angela's sniff was enough to tell Mrs Dibble what she thought of that.

The Dibbles stayed for a while. I liked their company. Having an adult with us made me feel less afraid of ghosts.

When we had to leave, it took a bit of persuading to get Angela to come home.

'You have to be prepared for those ducks to fly away whenever the instinct takes them, or in fact if the water in the crater dries up.' Fred told us the next morning as he spread a thin layer of marmalade on his toast, and Angela stirred another spoonful of condensed milk into her cup of tea.

Mum tapped Angela's hand to indicate that it was to be the last spoonful and said, 'That's exactly right. And you certainly can't take time off school to stay with them, Angela.'

'What if someone tries to hurt them or takes them to … to eat? Mavis Dodds said her brother has a duck's egg for breakfast every morning.'

'I'm sure nothing will happen.' Fred tried to assure Angela.

'You're not taking a day off school and that's flat,' Mum said.

The sound of a knock at the door interrupted what looked as if it was going to be one of Angela's outbursts.

I jumped down the stairs three at a time – my record – I was aiming for four, but I hadn't quite made it yet. The last time I tried, I ended up in a pile at the bottom and Mum was certain I'd broken my ankle.

Paula Dibble was at the door hovering from one foot to the other. As usual, the pleats in her skirt stood to attention, and her blouse was snowy against the greyness outside.

'The ducks are swimming on the crater now. Have you seen them?'

'Course we have.' Angela was close behind me down the stairs. She looked as if she was about to bite Paula.

Paula stepped backwards, saying, 'I'd better go, I've got to finish packing my satchel ready for school.'

'Thanks for last night,' I said. 'Angela's upset because Mum won't let her take the day off school to look after her precious ducks,' I explained.

'Blabbermouth!'

'I'm sure the ducks will be ...'

'I'll stay at the bombsite for the day and look after them,' I said, beaming at the suddenness of my idea.

'And how d'you propose doing that, clever clogs?'

'I'll bunk school. Mum didn't say *I* couldn't have the day off.'

'But won't people see you?' Paula seemed unsure.

'I know just the right place to hide.'

'Well, I s'ppose you could.' Angela looked like she was considering it. 'You'll need a note for Mrs Colby, though.'

Paula took us by surprise when she offered to help. 'That's easy, I'll write one. They might suspect something if it came from you, but I'm good at forging other people's handwriting.'

'You!'

'Why not?'

'Because you're always such a ...'

'When Mum's not looking I'll put a couple of pieces of writing paper and an envelope in my satchel. I can write the letter in the alley next to Jack Moody's yard, then you can give it to Mrs Colby. I've already packed my fountain pen. I'll say Tony's been up all night vomiting. You'll have to tell me how your mother signs her name.'

'That sounds all right.' The word vomitting impressed me. I would have said spewing or chucking it up.

'You'd better hurry up if you're going to write the note and go to the ducks. Mornings are the most dangerous.' Angela still wasn't completely out of her bad mood, but, then, when was she ever!

'Nobody's going to find out. Who's going to suspect me? It's quite fun, really.' Paula smiled at me and I smiled back. It was smashing sharing a secret, even though Angela had to be in on it. It was probably the first time in her whole life that Paula Dibble planned to lie.

The mist that had made the bombsite appear so eerie the night before had melted away and the place didn't seem half so spooky. I settled myself in a dug-out behind an ancient fireplace. It was the best hiding place I knew. I used it a lot when we played 'Can't Be Found' with the Gang. From there I could see everything that was going on all around, without anyone seeing me.

I wrapped Angela's blanket around me which was still damp from the night air and smelt of cats' pee. Paula had managed to sneak two queen cakes from her mother's tin. I stuffed them into my mouth whole, wishing she'd brought me more.

Further along Blountmere Street I could see Vic Newnham delivering coal. His face was as black as Paula's cat, Betsy. A couple of women from further down the street passed by, wheeling their prams. I heard one threaten to give her toddler a "good hiding". Mrs Dibble was on her way to clean the bakers. She raced along as if a cheetah was chasing her, with Ma Barker having to gallop by her side to pass the time of day.

Just as my legs were going numb and I was considering climbing out of my spy hole, Fred and Lori sauntered by, arm in arm. They stopped to look at the ducks. I lowered myself deeper into my hiding place as the skuffing of stones told me they were getting closer.

'Goodness, I don't know how these kids play over here without injuring themselves,' Lori seemed to be struggling to get her breath.

'I'm sure you did it once,' Fred laughed. 'At least we can tell Angela we've been to see her precious ducks. Have you got the bread?'

There was a rustling of paper, then a short silence, followed by a plop, a splash, a quacking and swift movement of the water as the ducks paddled towards the bread.

'She's obsessed about them,' Lori continued.

'From what you've told me, it seems to have something to do with that kitten they had.'

'It's amazing how small children remember things. Mind you, who could forget it? I know I've never been able to. It was awful. As usual, Ted Addington was the worse for drink and … he kicked it down the stairs, then trampled on it. I helped Dolly clear up the mess and Mr Dibble next door buried it in his garden. We told him a car had run it over.'

They strolled away, with Fred saying, 'That poor girl. She's probably sitting at school worrying about her ducks now.' Their voices trailed into the distance and I wriggled further up and saw them rounding the bend into The High Street.

I wondered where exactly our kitten had been buried. Then, trying to get rid of the pictures in my head, I tugged the copy of *The Girl* Paula had left me from my pocket.

The ducks were still swimming around the sides of the crater. I supposed they were hoping there would be more people to throw them bread. I guessed it must be dinner-time. Suddenly I realised I had missed a school dinner. What a waste! I imagined the gang tucking into shepherds pie, which was what we usually had on a Wednesday. I wished I hadn't eaten the queen cakes in one go. I was tempted to leave my hideout and sneak back home. Only thoughts of what Angela would do to me if she found out kept me huddled there, cold, stiff and hungry.

The first thing Angela said when she got back from school was, 'Those ducks been all right?' She was breathless from running straight from school, and her hair was hanging in strands over her eyes. Two of the buttons on her blouse had come undone.

'Course they have.'

'What they been doing?'

'What d'you think they've been doing? What ducks always do – swimming, stupid.'

'All right, keep your hair on.'

'What about the letter? Did you give it to Mrs Colby?'

'Course I did.'

'What did she say?'

'She said to tell you, she hopes you get better soon, and some claptrap about Mum being a sensible woman making you stay at home'

'And what about Paula?'

'She acted all innocent, a right Goody Two Shoes.' Angela stretched her arm down to help me out of the hole. 'You can go now I'm here.'

She was ordering me away as if I'd enjoyed myself all day.

'I'll go when I'm good and ready.'

'What's the matter with you, grumble guts? I thought you might want to go home to Fred or meet your chums, now I'm here to look after Bert and Bertha.'

'Bert and Bertha? Who are they?'

'The ducks, of course. You can't spend all this time with them without giving them a name.'

'But you don't know if they're a boy and a girl and, anyway, who's the boy and who's the girl?'

'That's the boy,' she said pointing a finger blue-black with ink at the duck closest to us.

'But how can you tell? I can't see any difference.'

'Of course *you* can't, but *I* can,' Angela was her usual snotty self.

'Well, I think they're daft names,' I sneered, needing to have the final word.

Three days later, the ducks had gone. Angela scoured every inch of the bombsite but she didn't find Bert and Bertha. I could tell by the red circles around her eyes she'd been crying. I was glad she hadn't done it openly in front of everyone. That would have been too embarrassing for words.

'I did tell you, didn't I, that one day they might take flight.' Fred said in a soft voice. 'In all probability they've returned to the ponds on The Common.'

'But didn't they know they were safe with us?'

'They obviously didn't know where they were well off.' Fred smiled, backing out of the kitchen and into the scullery. 'But perhaps these young fellows will recognise their good luck.' He walked back into the kitchen carrying a cage.

'They might make up for losing the ducks.' He placed the cage on the table. 'Go on, open it.'

Angela undid the catch on the door. She reached into the cage and took out one of two hamsters.

'They're lovely, really beautiful.' Angela passed the first hamster out to me, before coaxing the second one into her hand and stroking it with her still inky finger.

'Now you have a pet each,' Fred said, looking from Angela to me, and back to Angela. 'They're a present from Miss Lorimore and me, with your mother's blessing, of course.

I peered into the cage. 'They've even got a wheel to run on.'

'And they're really ours?' Angela queried.

'They're your pets.'

I nuzzled the little creature against my face. 'I'm going to call mine Brian.' It seemed as good a name for a hamster as any. Brian Bamfrey at school was the best one in the class at leaping over the vaulting horse. Anyway, we'd had another pet once whose name had begun with a B.

'That's a stupid ...' Angela began, then, ' Benjy. Mine's going to be Benjy.'

'Do you think you'll be able to tell them apart?' Fred asked.

'Mine's got a patch on his ear,' I interrupted before Angela could say she would know Benjy anywhere, without saying why.

We stroked and stroked them until at last we put the hamsters back in their cage, to their wheel running and to a much safer world than Berry had known.

Chapter Five

'Morning, sonny. Does a Frederick George Stannard live here?'

I stared at the policeman on our doorstep. What would a copper want with Fred?

'Well, does he?'

'Yeah, I'll fetch him.'

'Good lad, and while you're getting him, what about letting me stand inside. There's nothing like a copper on the doorstep to set tongues wagging.' The policeman glanced behind him at the group of kids already gathered on the pavement outside.

'What's the problem, Constable?' Fred asked, entering the hall, at the same time unrolling his shirt-sleeves.

'Frederick George Stannard?'

'That's right.'

I looked at Fred, but his face didn't look any different – not guilty or frightened. He looked just the same as he did every morning after he'd shaved.

'Is there anywhere we can talk privately, sir?'

Without answering, Fred led the policeman to his room, and I zoomed to the kitchen as if I was on a spaceship mission over on the bombsite with the Gang.

'A copper's here for Fred. He's in his room now.' I told Mum and Angela, even before I had fully opened the door.

'What's he want him for?' Angela asked, swallowing a mouthful of toast. She looked like a goldfish gulping air.

'How should I know? I told you, he's in his room now. D'you think Fred's committed a crime? I mean, he wouldn't have stolen anything, would he? Not Fred.'

'He's probably murdered someone,' Angela answered, as if it was nothing.

'Don't be silly, Angela,' Mum said.

'The way Tony carries on, you'd think Fred was Jack The Ripper.' Angela spoke through the piece of toast in her mouth.

'That's enough, Angela,' Mum reprimanded. 'I expect we'll know what it's about soon enough.'

'You don't think he'll be taken to prison, do you?' I didn't know how Angela could go on eating as if nothing was happening.

'I told you. We'll know when Mr Stannard is ready to tell us.'

As if hearing what Mum had said, Fred opened the door and walked into the kitchen. His face had white patches where the light brown usually was. His shoulders seemed to have drooped. 'I suppose Tony's already told you that it was the police knocking at the door.' Fred's voice had lost its up and downness. 'I hope it won't cause you any embarrassment,' he said to Mum.

What people in Blountmere Street thought had never been important enough to bother Mum. I suppose she thought what was another policeman on the doorstep after all the rigmarole there used to be with the police and the Old Man when he was boozed.

'Unfortunately, he came with the news that Eileen, my wife, has been killed in a bus accident.' Fred stared at the floor and I wanted to put my arm around him, although inside

I was relieved he hadn't been arrested. I felt that if I were to let go of the chair I was holding on to, I might float to the ceiling.

Mum took a breath, I think to say how sorry she was, but Fred held up his hand and said, 'As you know, my wife and I were estranged. But this has come as a bit of a shock.' He pulled a chair away from the kitchen table and sank on to it.

Suddenly my appetite came back and I pinched a piece of Angela's toast while she wasn't looking.

Straight after telling us, Fred popped next door to let Lori know about his wife's accident. While we were putting our coats on in the passage, Angela said, 'I wonder if that bus squashed Fred's wife flat like the hedgehog we saw in The High Street, but with a lot more blood.'

'How should I know?'

Angela's talk of blood and people being squashed, straight after breakfast was disgusting.

'I wonder if Fred'll marry Lori now?' She continued.

'Dunno.' I couldn't imagine Fred wanting to marry again when he had us.

'What was Old Flat Feet doing at your place?' One of the crowd of kids asked as soon as we opened our front door. 'Your Old Man in trouble again?'

'No, their Old Lady's done him in,' another boy shouted.

'It's none of your business.' Angela shot a warning look at me. She needn't have bothered. Having a secret made me feel important.

Now that the warmer weather had come, the Gang began visiting our camp in the evenings after school. Although we met practically every day, we hadn't noticed the changes in each other until we got back to the camp. Herbie was the only one who didn't seem to have grown, as if his bones had refused to get any longer and couldn't take the weight of any extra flesh on them. The stones Dennis and I perched on last year now needed us to draw our legs right up to our chins to squat on. Dobsie had grown so tall, he needed another stone, a bigger, flatter one that took him a whole evening to find and lug back to the camp.

Both Dennis and Dobsie now smoked as if they'd been doing it since they were babies, bringing crumpled packets of Woodbines with them. Dennis's stealing had become a hobby. Dobsie's parents had been paid out from the thrift club and had bought him a train set. He boasted the train was just like a real one.

Our camp was now bordered on every side by prefabs, each one enclosed by a square fenced-in garden. Having people living all around us took away some of the mystery of our stone circle, although our camp was still hidden behind the jagged wall. It made The Common a more attractive place to act out our adventures, especially on a Saturday afternoon after a morning at Saturday Picture Club.

The Common might not belong solely to us, but going "Up The Common" was highly rated by the Gang when it came to having adventures.

"Up the Common" was the most grass and trees we had ever seen. "Up The Common" the ponds were like oceans. "Up The Common" was the best playground in the whole universe. "Up The Common" was a smashing place to be on a spring day when the wind was blustery and the sun shone through silver clouds.

'Race you,' Herbie shouted to the three of us, as he began running towards the horse chestnut trees, heavy with pink and white candles. The other three of us were quick to follow him, at the same time curving and swerving in a game of "*It*".

'Where we going now - over the Spinney?' Herbie asked, as we leaned against tree trunks getting back our breath. The Spinney was the most thickly grown part of The Common. Although it covered a fairly small area and the trees themselves weren't as tall as the ones we were resting against, The Spinney was the ideal place for playing *Tarzan*.

I beat my hands on my chest, shouting, 'Me Tarzan,' and Dennis, swinging on a branch, yelled back 'Me Jane'.

'Swing upside down, Den, like Tarzan does. It's easy.' Dobsie shouted.

'If it's so easy, you do it.'

'I would if I wanted to, but I don't want to.'

'If you two are going to argue, let's play something else,' Herbie suggested. 'What about pirates?'

Using hollows in the trees as ships, and twigs as swords and daggers we sailed around the world a dozen times, bringing back treasure which we fought over. We killed each other and simply came back to life, ready to set sail again for faraway places. It was Saturday afternoon at its best.

'What about riding the lizzies?' Dennis suggested when we were beginning to tire of shouting, "Ho, ho, ho and a bottle of rum", and "Aha, me hearties".

"Up the Common" the playground didn't have one lizzie, but two, and riding the lizzies the way we did wasn't for cowards. The last time we had ridden them we'd frightened a group of stupid girls into screaming. The playground attendant called us nothing but a bunch of hooligans, and banned us from the playground. 'I'll have you for trespassing if you so much as set a toe past the gate.' He had poked his finger into each of our chests.

'You know we're not allowed,' I replied.

'It's all right, the attendant's not here. I've just had a look. Gone home to his missus, I reckon,' Dennis said. 'So we can ride the lizzies in a bit of peace and quiet.'

I grinned. There was nothing peaceful or quiet about the way the Gang rode the lizzies.

We jostled each other through the gate, Dobsie spitting his usual glob of saliva into the sandpit as he walked past.

'Oi, you filthy little whatsit, you stop that,' an angry mother shouted, picking up her toddler.

Both lizzies were in use, gliding backwards and forwards. They were going so slow, the half a dozen or so riders on each hardly needed to hold on to the iron handles.

With sneering looks, the Gang watched the girls at either end of each lizzie driving them, each girl clutching two vertical bars, while they worked the rollers with their feet. They swung the lizzies backwards and forwards, at the same time lifting the lizzies higher. They weren't riding them like the Gang rode them. When we rode them they went so high, it was like flying and my stomach turned over and almost came out of my mouth.

'Call that riding the lizzie,' Dobsie shouted. 'You're a lot of lily livers. Now scarper.' He picked up a stone and shied it. 'Anyone of you got the guts to ride with us?' He yelled, but already the lizzie was slowing and losing height. The children riding it were preparing to flee.

'Hop up then,' Dobsie ordered when the previous riders were already on the other side of the playground. 'Tell you what, let's race each other like they do in the Boat Race. Den and Herb, you're both Cambridge, so you can go on either end of that one.' He pointed to the first lizzie. 'And 'cos Tone and me are Oxford, we'll take this one. You'd better watch out. We're going to give you the hiding of your lives.'

We began cranking up the lizzies, at the same time taunting each other.

Dobsie shouted, 'We'll beat you, just like we beat you in the Boat Race.'

'Beat us! You couldn't knock the skin off a rice pudding. Oxford are a bunch of nancy boys,' Dennis yelled back as we worked the rollers and the lizzies swung higher.

'Oxford's stronger than Cambridge.'

'Cambridge is cleverer than Oxford.'

'We're winning. You're sinking,' I shrieked as we worked the rollers and the lizzies swung like sky boats. 'Swing high! Swing low!' I chanted inside my head. 'Swing high! Swing low!'

Gradually the lizzie rose. Dobsie and I were definitely higher than Dennis and Herbie. Up and up we went, and I had to arch my back and grip the vertical bars really tight.

As the ground disappeared, swinging the lizzie needed the sort of strength Popeye got from eating spinach.

When I drove forward, my body and arms were stretched as if they were made of elastic. The lizzie made strange screeching noises. Dobsie and I still kept our feet on the rollers, though. Now the whole frame began to shudder, and the metal burnt my hands. My arms ached and gasping sounds came from my throat, until I couldn't keep my foot on the roller any longer. I clung to the bars, concentrating really hard on not letting my fists come undone. But Dobsie was taller than me and his foot still reached the roller. He kept pushing, and my bones began twisting in their sockets. My spine was stretched as if I was being tortured. 'Take your foot off,' I yelled to him. 'Don't push.' But my words didn't reach him.

Suddenly, at the other end of the lizzie, Dobsie's body jerked and his right hand lost its grip on one of the vertical bars. It swung like a monkey's, trying to get its hold back. It aimed and missed, aimed and missed, near but not near enough. Dobsie's other hand began to slide down the sidebar until it slid free and Dobsie sort of fluttered from the lizzie like a flag in the breeze.

I could never remember how I slowed the lizzie, or how I came to be standing over Dobsie's body. His trousers were ripped, and his legs looked like snapped twigs.

The ambulance came and the men lifted the body out of its blood and placed it on a stretcher. Then they covered it with a red blanket. I remember thinking they used red because it soaked up blood without it showing. They spoke to each other in whispers, a few words at a time, as they lifted the stretcher into the ambulance. Before they closed the door, I heard one of them say the word, "dead" and then I saw them pull the blanket over the face.

The playground attendant came from out of nowhere. 'I knew one of 'em would end up killing himself. I told 'em.'

He pointed his finger at the policeman, who somehow just seemed to be there. 'I banned 'em, I did. I told 'em they wasn't to come here. If they did they'd be trespassing, I told 'em. Silly little devils.' He pushed his cap back on his head.

'Is this true?' The policeman licked the end of a pencil and wrote in a blue notebook. The woman with the toddler clinging to her legs was cradling Herbie. 'D'you have to question them now?' She asked, but the policeman continued writing.

Dennis was already beside the sandpit and running. He fled through the gate and along the outside of the playground. He had messed himself. It stuck to his legs like treacle and he left brown footprints on the path as he ran.

'Oi, come 'ere,' the policeman bellowed, but the brown footprints continued until they ran on to the grass, and Dennis became a distant figure.

Whenever I thought about that afternoon, what was most vivid in my memory were Dobsie's snapped bones sticking through his flesh, and the brown slime sliding down Dennis' legs.

In the days that followed, I couldn't link that twisted body with the know-it-all Dobsie who sat on the stones at the camp reading comics and smoking. That disgusting shape, oozing blood haunted me with pictures I couldn't chase from my head. That, that 'thing' wasn't – couldn't possibly be - my mate who walked backwards and forwards with me to school every day. Nobody could change like that in less than a couple of drags on a fag.

The policeman returned and said, with regard to the deceased, Alan Dobson, although theoretically there was some argument as to whether it had been a case of trespassing, under the circumstances, and this time, the authorities would not be prosecuting. As if there would be another time, another body, another red blanket. I listened as if from a long way off, puzzled by "theoretically" and "authorities" and "prosecuting".

Mum smiled gratefully and said thank you. The policeman replied that I had best try to get it out of my mind. But I knew the memories would never leave. They were glued there forever.

Dobsie's father called and said I had nothing to feel guilty about. His face was lined with sadness and his eyes were swollen. He placed a hand on my shoulder, but I stared ahead. I didn't feel guilty. I didn't feel anything. I wondered what would happen to Dobsie's train set.

Mum said we must pray for Dobsie and his parents, and that I should go to the funeral because one day I would be pleased I had. I didn't think I would feel pleased ever again. Everything would always be filled with nothingness. I wished Fred was at home. He shouldn't have gone away to his wife's funeral. She had deserved to die for not loving Fred, but Dobsie, not Dobsie. Dobsie had earned a place on this earth for being young, and my pal. The people in my life became confused. Perhaps I would never set eyes on Fred again, but I would see Dobsie walking to school tomorrow.

I refused to go to school. Instead I spent my time watching Brian's wheel-walking, or sitting on Fred's bed and reading the pile of comics Lori got from a jumble sale.

Sometimes I wandered round Fred's room looking at Fred's models, stroking them as if they were a body.

Mum tried to encourage me back to school. 'It'll take your mind off things. I'm sure you'll find everyone very kind,' she said.

I didn't know what I wanted, but it wasn't for people to be very kind. I didn't want people to be anything. I didn't want people at all. I couldn't bear to stand there in the hall while Old Williamson announced Dobsie's death, lowering his voice, like Fred did when he had talked about his wife being killed. I couldn't bear everyone's sympathy mixed with their blood-thirsty questions. I never wanted to see anyone from school ever again or to set foot in Blountmere Street. Life was cruel and it waited like an axeman the other side of our front door.

One afternoon from Fred's window, I saw Dennis. He was wearing his pullover back to front. He kept his gaze directed at the pavement and didn't look in the direction of our flat. In the same way, I kept my eyes from Dennis' legs in case I saw the brown slime still there, oozing like the blood had from the body.

Dennis wasn't at the funeral. I didn't blame him. There wasn't any point. I wouldn't have gone if Mum hadn't made me. It was a mark of respect, she said. Herbie and his father sat on the other side of the aisle. Herbie and I wore black armbands that looked like soot rings on our jackets. People smiled their funeral smiles, but neither of us took any notice of the other.

Mum took hold of my hand. I wish it had been Fred, and I kept my eyes fixed on the stained glass window at the front of the church. I studied a red disciple's robe and a blue angel's wing. I didn't want to have to smile a funeral smile back to other funeral smiles. I didn't want to see the white coffin with the body inside with the snapped legs.

The Reverend Roberts called the body "Our dear departed child" and declared, 'God hath given and God hath taken away'. Still I stared at the disciple's robe and the angel's wing, even when they sang *The Lord's My Shepherd.* Even when Dobsie's mother called out, "Alan!" "Alan!" as if it wasn't Dobsie's funeral but someone else's.

For the first time I allowed my eyes to rest on the coffin with its red flowers spelling SON. It was sissy. Dobsie would have wanted a train, a plane, a spaceship, with no stupid flowers on top.

Then they carried the white box to the back of the church and out into the spring softness. It should have been taken to the bombsite camp to our circle of stones hidden behind a half-destroyed wall. Instead they slid it into a hearse and drove it slowly away.

Chapter Six

The Gang didn't seem like the Gang without Dobsie, and we hadn't been to the camp much since he - well, since he - I couldn't say the word "died", and "passed away" was what old people did – since he left. That was it, since he left the camp and Blountmere Road School; since he left the earth and went somewhere else, like Jet in Journey Into Space.

Now that Fred was back I preferred spending time with him in his room, helping him work on his latest model sailing vessel.

'This is one Vasco da Gama might have sailed to Brazil in during the reign of Henry The Eighth, but don't you want to go out with your chums?' Fred asked.

'Nope.' How could I tell him I was afraid that if I left him for too long, he might have an accident, too. As it was, whenever he went out, I felt pulled tight inside, and I couldn't settle to anything. I usually ended up sitting on the stairs waiting, praying he would walk through our front door in one piece.

'The last time we went to the camp, Herbie cracked stupid jokes and laughed all the time,' I told Fred.

'Laughing, and making light of it, is probably his way of dealing with things,' Fred replied, running his finger along the piece of wood I had just glued, pressing it into position.

'I s'ppose.' I couldn't imagine anyone wanting to laugh to forget something like Dobsie's accident.

I didn't want to think about Dobsie any more because the words, *It was all my fault,* circled around my head.

Changing the subject, I said, 'Mrs Colby's been telling us about that King Henry bloke, the one who had lots of wives. He had some of their heads chopped off, didn't he?'

'Unfortunately, he did.' Fred wiped his hands on a cloth to remove the glue. 'Actually, with the school holidays coming up, it might be a nice outing for us to go to Hampton Court, where Henry used to live some of the time. The four of us could go together – you and me, Angela and Amelia … Miss Lorimore. Hampton Court isn't difficult to get to from here,' Fred said. 'We can catch a bus from the High Street that goes all the way. I don't suppose your mother would want to come. It would probably be too much for her legs.'

Making a day of it to Hampton Court with Fred! It was the first time I had felt anything other than dagger stabs of fear and guilt since Dobsie had left.

On the day we went to Hampton Court, Lori was wearing a scarf I hadn't seen before. It seemed even longer and had flowers scattered over it, like one of Old Dibbles' flower beds.

'It gives things a floral, summery look,' she said when Fred commented on how "fetching" she looked. "Fetching" must be a good thing to look because Lori blushed and smiled.

We waved to Mum who stood on the doorstep. Some of the Blountmere Street kids stared at us as we rounded the bombsite, but we ignored them as we walked past the prefabs and on towards the High Street.

'I bet they've never been to Hampton Court,' Angela said, sticking her nose in the air.

It seemed we had no sooner got to the bus stop than the bus arrived and Lori said, 'Well, I never. Many's the time I've taken this bus, but I've never had such a short wait.'

'It must be a sign that today's going to be a good one,' Fred smiled. 'I suppose you youngsters want to go upstairs,' but Angela was already halfway up.

The top deck was smoky, emphasising the blueness of the sky and the greenness of The Common outside. All at once, I realised we were going to have to pass the playground. I hadn't been there since Dobsie's accident, and I squeezed my eyes shut. Fred was sitting behind me seeming to sense my dread. He put his hand on my shoulder. I don't know if his touch gave me courage, but I opened my eyes just as we passed the playground. The lizzies had been replaced by two piddly rocking horses.

'Look out for Bert and Bertha,' Fred said, keeping his hand on my shoulder, as we passed the pond that had an island in the middle. I could see ducks launching themselves into the water and others waddling about on the grass.

'All right, lad?'

'Here, have a lemon drop,' Lori offered.

'We've never been as far as this in our whole lives,' Angela said, as she peered at her image reflected in the window, and primped her hair.

The further we went, the more spaced out the houses became, with grass verges and lots of trees.

When we got off the bus I stood looking at some of the houses that were covered with leaves. Lori said the green stuff was ivy. I thought it was pretty funny because the ivy only left gaps for the windows and doors, which looked like eyes and noses peering through the leaves.

'Some of those houses are very old. It's probably only the creeper that's keeping them from falling down,' Fred said.

I didn't know how old our place was, but it was probably held together by soot, and the only leaves were those in Old Dibbles' garden.

'Let's walk across Bushey Park, which will lead us to Hampton Court Palace,' Fred suggested, and we set off.

To me, Bushey Park was like a jungle, with a tangle of dead leaves and twigs that crunched beneath our feet. The trees grew so close, I couldn't see the sky, and I wouldn't have been surprised to see monkeys swinging through the branches. 'This must be just like South America,' I said to Fred.

He laughed and said, 'Not quite.' Then he winked at Lori, who, as usual was hanging on to his arm.

Just as Angela started complaining about how far she had to walk and that she couldn't manage another step, we came to an open area.

'This seems an ideal place for our picnic, Fred,' Lori's smile was wide enough to show a good few of her teeth and Fred rubbed his hand against her arm. I hoped they weren't going to be lovey-dovey all day. Angela raised her eyebrows in a way that said she felt the same.

Fred had brought a bag with him that was almost as big as a suitcase. He put it down, opened it and pulled out an old blanket which he spread on the ground. Lori had packed sandwiches and a flask of tea, and I thought she was going to make her usual comments about the good old British cuppa and dear Mr Churchill and The War. Instead, she rummaged in the bag, her head practically disappearing into it, and with a sort of whoop, she pulled out a bottle of Tizer.

'Much better than tea, don't you think?' She said.

Fred had bought a shillings worth of cakes from the baker's on our way to the bus stop and he offered me the bag. I shut my eyes and dipped my hand in. I wanted the doughnut, and I knew Angela wanted the shell cake. As it happened, I got the shell cake and she the doughnut.

'Swap them,' Fred advised.

I thought how straightforward things were with Fred. There was no arguing or trying to get the biggest or the best, nor was there any using it to lord it over the other person. Fred was fair and not a bit selfish.

We finished our picnic, with Fred and Lori having one last cup of tea. Then we made our way across a green and into some of the Palace gardens that made Old Dibble's bit of dirt nothing to show off about, although he always did. The roses, which were the only flowers Angela and I knew the name of, were a silky sheet of colour, and when I breathed in their scent, my nostrils seemed to capture it. Their smell stayed with me for the rest of the day, sweet and in some way comforting.

I'd had enough of gardens by the time we'd trudged round one that had a lot of small bushes cut into shapes and criss-crossed by gravel paths. Fred said this type of garden had been very fashionable a few hundred years ago. Lori replied it was too orderly for her liking. 'Give me a bit of clutter,' she said, making me think of her kitchen.

In a teasing way, Fred said, 'I wonder how I knew this wouldn't be your type of garden, Amelia,' and winked at her.

Angela lifted her eyebrows again. She could get them so high they almost touched her hair. 'I think gardens like this are boring,' she said.

'Perhaps the maze will be more to your liking,' Fred suggested, hoisting the picnic bag higher up his shoulder.

'It's not another lot of bushes, is it?'

'Actually, it is, but they're taller, and they're planted in such a way that once you enter, it's difficult to find your way out. It's a game, a sort of puzzle.'

'We'll get out, though, won't we?'

'Eventually,' Fred told her. 'I haven't heard of anyone being imprisoned in the maze for a lifetime.' He grinned at Lori and her face turned the colour of one of the pink roses we had just seen. As much as I liked being out with Fred, this courting lark was a bit much.

To begin with, the maze seemed simple enough, but after we had been going round and round for what seemed hours, and Lori was complaining of her bunions and Angela beginning to panic, it stopped being fun. Perhaps we would be the first never to come out. We were all being punished because of me and Dobsie. *It was all my fault.*

'We need to think about where we've come from and retrace our steps.' Fred sounded as confident as he always did, and led us round endless bends, each one looking the same as the one before. Eventually, we found ourselves on the outside again.

'I told you there was nothing to worry about.' He patted Angela's arm, but she said 'I wasn't worried. It'd take a lot more than that to put the wind up me.'

I looked up at Fred. How could a maze be difficult for a man who had sailed round the world hundreds of times!

Sitting on a bench overlooking the River Thames, we finished the last of the cakes, this time iced buns, before going into The Palace. It was the biggest building I had ever seen, not high like the ones I made with my Meccano set, but stretched wide as if the bricks were on elastic.

Walking round the huge entrance hall reminded me of Mum's church, echoey and cold. The walls were covered with paintings and tapestries of men on horses wearing silver and red armour, and women sitting in gardens under rose arches sewing or just talking to each other. I wondered if any of them had been Old Henry's wives. If they were, they might not be as carefree as they looked. Perhaps they were discussing how they could avoid having their heads chopped off.

'This is much more to my liking,' Lori said studying all the paintings, and I thought Fred was going to say he wondered how he knew that, too, but he didn't, although the corners of his mouth turned up.

I reckoned our kitchen would have fitted into the Palace kitchen a hundred times. It had huge pots and pans hanging from beams and a fireplace you could walk into.

'I couldn't imagine how much coal this fireplace would have taken,' Lori exclaimed. 'If my grate was this big, Vic Newnham would be making a delivery every day of the week and weekends as well.'

'Fancy eating your Spam in a room like this,' Fred laughed, as we walked through what he said was the Great Banqueting Hall. Again, it was massive with a carved stone ceiling and oblong windows.

'Can you imagine Old Henry at the top table drinking from a golden goblet as they brought in a roasted pig with an apple in its mouth and all the trimmings. Do you know people actually came to watch him eat,' Fred told us.

'Did they get the leftovers?' I asked.

'I shouldn't have thought so,' Fred replied.

'They should've saved their time. Who would want to see some old bloke scoffing grub, and not get offered anything, even if it was only a biscuit.' Angela was scathing.

Upstairs, one room led into another, all looking out on to the gardens or the river - wide and winding its way on forever. How could one person need so many rooms, even if he was a king?

We continued walking along a gallery that all at once seemed chill. Like every room in the Palace, paintings of strangely dressed men and women looking serious and important, stared down at us. Some had a faraway, mysterious look and the ones of Old Henry scared me. Our Old Man had been bad enough, but he hadn't chopped anyone's head off.

'This place is supposed to be haunted by one of Henry's wives. She walks along here at midnight screaming.' Angela whispered, trying to be dramatic and frighten me.

'How can she scream if she's had her head cut off?'

'Don't ask me. I'm only telling you what the guide said. How am I supposed to know what ghosts do?'

'I don't know if I should have liked to live in these times. What about you, Fred?' Lori asked, before a fight could develop between Angela and me.

'I'm not certain. The Elizabethan period would have been an exciting one for a sailor. I think I should have liked to have sailed with Sir Francis Drake or Sir Walter Raleigh.'

'Well, I wouldn't have liked to live when Henry was alive,' Angela said, frowning at the portrait of a girl who was probably about her age. 'I'd hate having to wear one of those dresses and a stupid hat. I wouldn't have liked not having electricity. Candles are all right, but I reckon you'd soon get fed up with them.'

For once I had to agree with her. I couldn't imagine life without *Dick Barton* and cowboys and Indians. I liked living right here and now, where I had everything I wanted: a bob for school dinners every Monday, a tanner for Saturday Picture Club, a Meccano set, a Bible and Spam once a week. Best of all we'd swapped the Old Man for Fred.

On the bus back home, Angela sat next to Lori in case she sicked up, which meant Fred sat next to me. We talked about Hampton Court.

'I've got some history books about the Tudor and Elizabethan periods in my room at home. I'll show them to you if you like.'

'Thanks.' I was interested all right, especially now we'd been to a real palace. I doubted anyone in Blountmere Street had been there, but I wouldn't say anything to Dennis and Herbie about liking old buildings or anything like that. I'd still act like a dunce when Mrs Colby gave us a history lesson, although I'd already memorised Old Henry's dates, and the names of his six wives. I didn't want to be thought a sissy like Harry Billings, who wore glasses, and had his hair parted in the middle and smarmed down. Every lesson he asked questions and nodded and said "thank you so much" to

Mrs Colby when she answered him, and he never looked at the rude pictures that got passed around the class.

'Do you think Henry ever felt guilty for what he did?' I asked Fred.

'Henry deserved to feel guilty, but often we load guilt on ourselves that doesn't belong on our shoulders at all, especially after people have died.' He squeezed my arm, and I knew he was talking about me and Dobsie. *If I hadn't tried to go so high; If I'd slowed the lizzie sooner, he wouldn't have been killed. If I hadn't suggested we went up The Common in the first place he would still be alive.*

'It wasn't your fault, lad. Everyone has to take responsibility for their own actions,' Fred said. He took hold of my hand and pressed it hard.

The sky was striped pink when we passed The Common, and the playground looked lonely with shadowy arms stretched across it. This time, though, it was easier with Fred sitting beside me, holding my hand.

Chapter Seven

Lori didn't usually knock before she came into our kitchen. She had a key to our front door and usually barged straight in - that was after she'd popped her head round Fred's door "to pass the time of day". But today she tapped at our kitchen door, coughed a rippling little cough and waited, though the lavender water she was wearing had already wafted into the kitchen. She twisted her hands together, and Fred stood behind her, sort of grinning, but I could see red blotches on his neck and on his scalp where his hair didn't grow.

'Well, come in the two of you,' Mum said. 'Since when have you had to be invited?'

Lori coughed again, and she and Fred sidled to the table, where I was making a crane from my Meccano set and Angela was threading some beads she had got for her birthday on to a string. Although Mum indicated some chairs for them to sit on, they kept standing like the statues on Lori's sideboard.

'Is anything wrong?' Mum asked, and Angela looked at me, putting her finger to her temple, winding it round and round, mouthing 'They've gone nutty.'

'It's … well …' Fred began.

'We wanted to …' Lori stopped.

'Spit it out,' Mum said, while Angela continued her winding action.

'With Eileen, Fred's wife … um … ex wife having passed away practically a year ago.' Lori did a couple more coughs before looking to Fred for help.

'Perhaps we should have waited a little longer, but circumstances have precipitated things,' Fred continued.

I didn't know what "precipitated" meant. I couldn't even pronounce it. I would just have to try and make sense of the rest of what they were stuttering and stammering about.

'So to cut a long story short.'

'I wish he would,' Angela whispered.

'I've asked Amelia to become my wife and she's accepted.'

'That's wonderful news! I couldn't think of a better matched couple.' Mum was unusually quick to her feet. Just as unusual was the way she flung her arms around them both.

'So you don't think we'll be the centre of Blountmere Street gossip?' Lori asked.

'Probably, but since when did that matter?'

Lori stopped twisting her handbag strap and I realised she had been covering her left hand with her right one. 'Would you like to see my engagement ring?' she asked, holding out her hand.

'It's beautiful,' Mum said, gazing at the half-circle of emeralds as green as the grass in Bushey Park, before darting a look at her own hand which was bare of any rings at all.

'Congratulations. We're very happy for you both, aren't we?' Mum said, looking at Angela and me. We both stood up and mumbled, 'Yes'

'When's the wedding and where's it going to be? Will you have it here or in Portsmouth where your sister lives?'

'We've decided to have a quiet wedding at a Registry Office here in London, in a month's time.' Lori paused, 'I know bridesmaids aren't really necessary, but you would make such a pretty one, Angela. Would you like to perform the duty for me? Perhaps we could call you a bridal attendant. Of course, if you don't want to …' Before she had time to finish, Angela hurled herself at Lori, and of all the sick-making things, she kissed her. 'Thanks! Thanks millions.'

Turning to Fred, she hugged him like she did Benjy her hamster, causing Fred to have to clear his throat.

'What sort of dress will I have? Will it be long? And what colour?'

The way Angela was carrying on, anyone would have thought *she* was the one who was getting married.

'How about you choose it yourself? We can go shopping for the material and a pattern, and perhaps your mother will make it.' Lori stopped. 'I had actually meant to ask you first, Dolly, but we seem to have got a little ahead of ourselves.'

Mum, smiled a soft sort of smile. 'I'd be delighted to make Angela's dress, and a month would give me plenty of time. 'What about yours? She asked. 'I'll make that too if you like.'

'I thought I'd wear a suit.'

'I could cope with a suit,' Mum assured Lori in her usual quiet way. Mum's eyes hadn't looked that bright with glinty lights in them since our christening.

'Now, Tony, I think it's our turn.' Fred put his arm around my shoulder which always made me feel proud, especially if he did it when we were out.

'As you know, my son is in New Zealand, and I don't have any family member living close who I could ask to be my best man, so I was wondering if you would take on the role?'

In contrast to Angela's noisy and unusually lovey-dovey reaction, mine was the opposite. Gulping and swallowing, I looked from Fred to Lori, across to Angela and Mum and back to Fred.

'Do I take it, you'll agree?' Fred asked.

'Yeah, sure.'

Fred gripped my hand and shook it. 'While the ladies are sorting out their paraphernalia, we'll get ourselves fitted for a couple of suits. What do you think?'

But all I could manage was a strangled, 'Smashing.'

I couldn't wait to get downstairs to the Dibbles to tell Paula all the wedding plans. As soon as Fred and Lori had left our kitchen, holding hands and giving each other dopey looks, I bolted down our stairs, tugged open our door, crossed our doorstep to the Dibbles' one, and hammered on their front door.

'Guess what? Fred and Lori are getting married,' I told her as soon as Paula opened the door. 'Angela's going to be a bridesmaid and I'm going to be Fred's best man.' I waited for Paula's usual enthusiasm, but all she said was, 'That's nice.' Her voice was as flat as the hedgehog in the middle of the High Street.

'And the wedding's going to be ...'

'Look, I've got to go.' And before I could finish my sentence, she darted back inside and closed the door.

Paula wasn't the only one who showed no interest in Fred and Lori's wedding. Dennis and Herbie hadn't seemed to care that I was being Fred's best man and wearing a proper suit.

'My cousin had a suit and he looked a right chump. I wouldn't want one. I'll tell you that for nothing. I'd rather have a cowboy jacket with fringes down the sleeves like the ones Roy Rogers wears. Anyway, your suit'll only have short trousers. You're not old enough for longs.' Dennis finished by waving his arm about, as if he was dismissing the idea of a suit altogether. Herbie nodded in agreement, while I tried to force down a sensation as if a log had become jammed in my throat. I hadn't expected Herbie and Dennis to be interested in the wedding itself, but I had thought they would think I was lucky to be getting a proper suit. Instead, all they did was laugh at Herbie's silly jokes.

I would never have believed a wedding of all things would bring Angela and me closer. With Paula drooping round like Sunday's celery on Monday, and Dennis and Herbie continuing to make stupid comments, Angela and I began to talk to each other about things we would once have thought drippy.

A few days after Fred and Lori announced their engagement, as she promised, Lori took Angela to choose the material for her bridesmaid dress.

Afterwards Angela bounced into the kitchen as if she was on a pogo stick.

'What d'you think of this,' she asked me, untying the string from around a brown paper parcel, and carefully lifting a shimmering piece of material. 'See, it changes colour. Pick it up and move it round,' she invited me. 'It's called shot taffeta. We got it from Bon Marche, not that stall where Paula *Dribble* got the stuff for *her* ballet dress.'

I knew how much it meant to Angela, and I took hold of the fabric as if it might dissolve in my hands. I held it towards the window and then away from it. One way it became pale pink, delicate, fragile. When I held it a different way, it darkened and almost sulked, becoming altogether more dramatic. It was like Angela's personality, although I'd never before thought of her as having a fragile side.

'Gorgeous, isn't it?' She exclaimed, taking it from me, twirling this way and that.

'It's pretty,' I replied, noticing how the pale pink made her face look softer.

'We bought a pattern as well. Look it's got a frill round the neck and at the bottom and Lori's going to buy me a headdress of silver leaves and silver shoes to go with it. What d'you think about silver shoes?' Angela asked, willing my enthusiasm.

'They'd be nice.'

'And a silver basket with pink roses and that white stuff old *Dribble*'s got growing in his garden, but better than his.' Angela folded the material back into the paper as if she was wrapping a baby into its shawl.

'What colour suits are you and Fred having?'

'Fred wants navy, but Lori says he's to have a change, so we might choose grey ones.'

'Grey'll look smart and go a treat with my pink dress. We'll match really well.' Angela paused. 'I was wondering if Dad might turn up to see me in my bridesmaid's outfit.'

'What would he do that for? He couldn't give two hoots about us. Anyway, how would he know about the wedding?'

'I was only wondering.' Angela busied herself putting the material into a cupboard.

'Good riddance to him. We've got Fred now.'

Mr Bendle, the tailor, lifted bales of cloth off shelves from which cobwebs hung like the Dibbles' lace curtains. Unwinding the material, he invited Fred to feel the quality.

Taking his time over each roll, Fred rubbed the cloth between his thumb and forefinger, before dividing the material into two groups. 'I don't think these ones are quite suitable,' he said, pushing one lot further along the workbench, and I watched as the shiny blue material I'd been eyeing slid out of reach.

'We're thinking of grey. This one looks good. What do you think?' Fred pushed some material towards me, and I took the cloth between my thumb and finger and rubbed it as Fred had done. 'It's good.'

Next, Mr Bendle ran his tape measure along my arms and across my back and chest.

'Now about the trousers for the young man?' He asked.

'Long ones,' Fred smoothed the flat of his hand across the material.

A quick scowl like one of Angela's when she wasn't happy about something, passed across the tailor's face, before he let the tape measure drop the length of my leg. 'Isn't he ... the young man ... a little young for long trousers?'

'Long,' Fred repeated, winking over the tailor's bent form. I winked back. A grey suit with longs! A grey suit with long trousers!

'And I'm having a grey suit with long trousers, the same as Fred,' I told Paula the next morning, as she stooped to put a milk bottle outside. I would have stood with a loud hailer at the top of Blountmere Street and announced it to everyone if I could have. As it was, Paula would have to do. I was banking on a better reaction from her than I'd got from Dennis, who had said he hoped I didn't look as ridiculous as his cousin had. But Paula was the same as she had been for the last couple of weeks, as if she hadn't heard a thing I said.

'Angela's dress is really pretty as well. It's going to be a swell wedding.' I liked the word "swell" because they said it a lot in the films at Saturday picture club. 'Afterwards, we're going up West to Lyons Corner House. You and your Mum could come to the Registry Office, if you wanted to.'

'I don't know,' Paula seemed as if she didn't want to go. Then looking back over her shoulder into her passage, presumably to make sure her mother wasn't around, she whispered, 'You're not to say anything to anyone, but Mum well, she's ill.' The back of her hand was wet where she'd rubbed it across her eyes. 'You've got to promise me you won't tell anyone.'

'Course I promise.' I couldn't think of one reason why I would want to tell anyone Mrs Dibble was ill. Lots of people had things wrong with them – Mum, for a start. She had bad legs, but we hardly mentioned it, and there was no way I'd cry about it, nor would Angela.

'I've got to go. I don't like leaving Mum on her own for too long, and I want to write to Damielle.'

'Who's Damielle?'

'A girl I made friends with on holiday. You'd really like her.'

I wouldn't like anyone with such a daft name. I bet Paula hadn't been so snotty with her as she was being with me. She would have toadied to her, like she did to the girls at school. There were times when I almost agreed with Angela that Paula Dibble had liquorice for guts.

I made my way to the bombsite, shinning a broken-down wall and kicking stones into anything that would clatter or bang. It was a bombsite and it didn't deserve any peace and quiet.

When I got back to our flat, Mum had just finished fitting Lori for her wedding suit. At the sight of me, Lori hurriedly fastened her blouse and smoothed her hair a little flatter, while Mum took one pin after another and pushed them into the jacket she was making.

'We're going to look like dukes and duchesses,' Lori laughed. 'It's exciting, isn't it?'

'It's a pity nobody else thinks so. You'd think your friends would try to be interested, instead of being so wrapped up in themselves.'

'That's the way it often is, I'm afraid. You'll be back at school next week. Perhaps you could write an essay about it?' Lori suggested

I was doubtful about that. Essays weren't something I liked writing, even if I did have a grey suit with long trousers to write about.

'In the meantime, how about doing a little gardening for me? I've been so busy, what with everything that's going on, my garden's been quite neglected.'

Even though I had difficulty telling the difference between weeds and flowers, Lori usually gave me sixpence when I'd finished. A tanner was good payment for one flowerbed under her kitchen window.

'Come with me and I'll give you a trowel. And while you're gardening, I can put some washing out. It must be the first time we've seen the sun in a week.'

When I got to Lori's garden, Mrs Dibble was already at her clothesline next door.

'How are you?' Lori asked, scooping a handful of pegs from a tattered bag with *EGS* embroidered on the front.

'Our holiday set us all up a treat.' Mrs Dibble spoke through a mouthful of pegs. 'How are your wedding plans going? I suppose you're getting things ready at your place for the two of you.'

Lori was noticeably slower than Mrs Dibble and had only pegged two things to her line, by comparison with the load that was flapping in the Dibbles' garden.

'I've been thinking about it but I don't seem to have had much time lately, what with one thing and another.' Lori pegged up a pair of pink knickers that, when the wind blew and filled them, looked like a cow's udders. 'It's difficult imagining the two of us living in my flat. I've been on my own there such a long time.'

Why hadn't I thought about it before! I had been so taken up with the wedding and getting the suit, it hadn't occurred to me that Fred would be moving out of our place and into Lori's. I didn't think Angela had thought about it either. Mum and Fred must have discussed it. At Lori's he might only be next door, but he wouldn't be there in his room to pop into and have a chat with whenever I felt like it. All at once a suit with long trousers seemed an unfair exchange.

'Will Dolly take in another lodger?' Mrs Dibble pushed the prongs of her clothes prop into the clothesline and her washing became a row of coloured flags.

I crawled a foot or so further along to make it look as if I was doing something.

'I think she'll have to. I know a very nice woman in business in the City who's looking for lodgings in this area.' Lori replied.

Mrs Dibble dropped her voice and exaggerated her pronunciation, at the same time casting a glance my way. 'Those kids'll miss Fred living with them, especially young Tony. I know you'll both be next door, but I suppose things will change a bit.'

'Nothing stays the same,' Lori was speaking so softly I had difficulty hearing what she was saying. I looked across at her and she turned and met my gaze, before looking at the ground and quickly swivelling back to her washing basket. Lori, the most honest person I knew, couldn't face me.

With only the two of us, The Majestic seemed a good place to spend Fred's stag night celebration. Fred had invited old Dibble, but he said he was too busy, although that morning I heard his razor blade voice rising from their flat shouting there was no way he was going to any stag night with bleedin' Captain Cook, and that was flat.

'The film was smashing. I like Gregory Peck,' I said, after we'd watched the film and were strolling along the High Street. 'I've never been to the pictures at night before. It was better than Saturday Picture Club.'

'What about stopping at Issy's for fish and chips?' Fred suggested. 'It would be a good way to finish a stag night, don't you think?'

We sauntered past David Greggs, the Bata Shoe Shop and Nivens, the shop where toffs bought their kids fancy clothes. Crossing the road, we looked in Wakeleys the sports shop window, before continuing on along the side of the bombsite towards Issy's.

Inside, Issy's smelt of fish and dripping and security. If the world caught fire, you would be safe in Issy's.

'What will you have, young man?' Fred asked.

'Rock salmon and chips, please.'

'Rock salmon. There's nothing like it, is there?'

'With plenty of salt and vinegar.'

'Wrapped in newspaper, of course.'

'It's the best food in the whole world, I reckon,' I said, saliva building up at the corners of my mouth.

'No-one can fry fish like Issy. In all my travels I've never tasted anything as good.' Fred gave our order to a rotund man with a glinting head. He beamed at us across the marble-topped counter. Then, without warning, Fred's smile seemed to flicker away. 'I'll always remember Issy's,' he said.

'Issy's will always be here, so you won't have to remember it.'

'Yes, of course.' But a sadness had settled on Fred not even Issy's rock salmon could lift.

Chapter Eight

The scent of roses filled the taxi, pink ones, tumbling from Angela's basket and peeping from Lori's small bouquet. Angela fidgeted, smoothing her dress, and Mum straightened the silver leaves around Angela's head. Angela didn't look like Angela at all. I would never have told a living soul, but she looked prettier than any girl I'd ever seen, including the ones who spoke with funny American accents on the films at Saturday Picture Club.

'I feel very grand.' Lori told us. And she looked it. She was wearing a suit in a colour she called wisteria or something like that. When Mum was making Lori's outfit, I had thought it looked like the colour of the stuff in old Dibbles' garden that their cat Betsy rubbed itself against. But now Lori was wearing it, it didn't look too bad. You could see Fred thought Lori looked wonderful, because he kept telling her so and squeezing her hand. Lori wore a purple hat perched on her frizzy curls. It looked like a bird's nest and reminded me of a picture at school of Elizabeth the First. Fred, using one of his favourite words, said it was "fetching".

I thought we looked "fetching" too in the grey double-breasted suits Mr Bendle, the tailor, had made for us. We wore pink carnations in our buttonholes, the same colour as Angela's roses.

'It's like being Princess Margaret.' Angela waved a lace-gloved hand to a group gathered on the pavement outside our flat.

'I think one or two people are a bit put out I've seen my bride before the ceremony. Folk are very superstitious like that,' Fred said.

'I'm certainly not worried about it,' Lori replied. 'It's much more sensible that we all go together. Anyway, I think it's wonderful to actually go to my wedding with my husband to be.' She bent forward and kissed Fred's cheek, while something in my stomach squelched.

As the taxi drew away, Herbie and Dennis walked past, appearing not to be interested, although I saw them giving us a sideways sneak. I had not so much as set a foot on the running board of a car, let alone ridden in one, and never, ever, in a taxi. I wasn't going to let anything spoil that, so I pretended not to notice them. I turned my Brylcreemed head to scan the group for Paula. She wasn't anywhere to be seen. I'd been sure she would at least have watched from her doorstep. Fingering the crease on my trouser leg, I glanced at the Dibbles' front window. There didn't appear to be anyone watching from behind the fancy net curtains. I turned away and smiled at Fred. I wasn't going to pull clouds over today's sunshine.

'Have you got the ring, son?' Fred asked. I took the white box with 'James Walker, Jewellers' written on it from my jacket pocket and showed it to Fred, He patted me on the shoulder.

"Son!" Fred had called me "son"! I fingered the creases in my trousers once again and looked from one face to another. Even though Fred wouldn't actually be living in our flat anymore, he would only be next door, living with Lori. Things wouldn't change too much. This was my family. I belonged with them. They belonged to me. Glue stuck us together. You couldn't slip a thread between any of us.

When we arrived at the Registry Office, Paula and her mother were waiting on the pavement outside like an official welcoming party. I suppose I should have known they wouldn't forget about the wedding completely. But Mrs Dibble and even Paula, who was always dressed in something posh, didn't look a fig compared to us.

'You look beautiful, Angela.' Paula bent to smell the roses in Angela's basket. 'And I love your silver shoes.'

'We got them in Pratts at Streatham.' Angela pointed her silver toes at Paula in a boasting sort of way which, for once, I could understand.

Creeping next to me, Paula whispered. 'You look really smart … like a man.' She hesitated. 'I'm sorry I haven't been interested in the wedding,'

'That's okay,' I mumbled. It wasn't okay really. I thought she was my friend, yet she hadn't wanted to share the best time of my life.

'Come on, it's time to go in.' Mrs Dibble took hold of Paula's arm, but Paula shook herself free, grumbling, 'All right, I know. You don't have to tell me what to do every minute of the day.'

Mrs Dibble made a clicking sound at Paula to let her know she was being rude, but Paula just glared back.

The ten minute ceremony didn't seem worth all our dressing up. A poe-faced man said something about marriage being honourable, causing Angela to nudge me and whisper, 'Did he say marriage was horrible?' Mum, in turn, nudged

Angela and put her finger to her lips. I was too busy keeping the creases in my trousers sharp, and thinking about leaving the Registry Office in yet another taxi, to listen to what else the bloke said. Then before I knew it, Fred had asked me for the ring, and I was fumbling for the box.

When I pulled it from my pocket, lifted the lid and gave the ring to Fred, I had the same feeling I'd had when I put the bob Dad's fancy woman had given us, into the dinner money tin.

After that, Fred, Lori, Mum and Mrs Dibble walked to a table at the side of the room to sign their names in a big leather book.

That was that, Fred and Lori were married.

Outside, it was much more like a wedding, with a photographer who took pictures of us. He told us to think of something that tickled our fancies and to flash our pearlies. Paula and Mrs Dibble showered us all with confetti. Paula even stuffed some into my pockets, and poked it down the collar of my new shirt. Angela joined them, gathering it up from the pavement and throwing as much back over herself as she did over the rest of us.

When the photographer had finished and the confetti thrown, Mrs Dibble said it was time for them to go, or they would miss the bus. Anyway, our taxi was about to arrive. For a short time we stood in an awkward group on the pavement, before Fred pumped the Dibbles' hands, thanking them for coming and Lori kissed them both. For one moment I thought Mrs Dibble was going to kiss me, and I held myself stiff and sucked in my cheeks. Instead she kissed Angela, who didn't seem to mind at all.

Just as we had in Blountmere Street, we climbed into the taxi as if we were film stars. This time Angela waved at everyone we passed, and most shocking of all, she even blew some of them kisses, so that I was relieved when we arrived at Lyons Corner House for the wedding reception.

In the murky afternoon light it seemed like a shining palace. Violin music floated through the revolving doors when we entered. The sound was like our own national anthem being played.

With my new shoes still squeaking, and picking confetti from my suit jacket, my feet sank into thick blue carpet as we followed a waiter into a huge room. I had never seen so many tables. They were covered with white tablecloths, and looked like a sky full of clouds, the blue of the carpet slanting through like an April day. Along with the music, I heard the clink of glasses, the scraping of cutlery on china and a buzz of voices like bees in a warm and friendly beehive.

Still following the waiter, we walked between the cloud-tables, Angela's long dress swishing, its colour altering from delicate and gentle to dark and threatening as the light changed. I was sure the diners around us were watching us, smiling at the beautiful girl in her long ever-changing frock, and at the boy, his curls refusing to be completely flattened, wearing his grey suit with long trousers.

At last we reached our table and the waiter actually pulled our chairs out for us. We sat, and he handed us each a black and gold menu. When he asked Fred if there was anything we'd like, Fred ordered a glass of orange each. The waiter actually bowed before turning to leave, which made Angela giggle.

We all ordered chicken with stuffing, because that seemed the most special thing to eat at a wedding. When they came, the roast potatoes were just as I liked them – crunchy on the outside and soft in the middle. Even though it wasn't the season for them, we actually had brussels sprouts. In a funny kind of way the dining room smells mixed with the scent of roses, giving the place a homey scent.

For afters, there was trifle with real cream on top, and it wasn't even Christmas.

'It's such a lovely day,' Lori kept saying, each time stroking Fred's hand, and once Fred said, 'At last, Amelia,' and he looked at Lori in a way I knew none of us was meant to see.

All Mum kept saying was, 'My, my,' although I wasn't sure what she was "my-mying" about.

'When d'you think the pictures we had taken'll be ready?' Angela asked, sucking red jelly into her mouth and making a disgusting noise.

'In a week or two.' Lori smiled, seeming to understand Angela's impatience. 'When they're developed we'll have a couple framed and you can put them on the sideboard in your kitchen. They'll remind you of us.'

'We won't need any reminding. We'll remember today forever and ever. Anyway, you'll always be there, so we won't need anything to remember you by.'

Lori put her napkin up to her face in a fit of coughing. 'Something caught in my throat,' she croaked but when she took the napkin away, it looked as if she was about to cry.

Angela said all brides cried at their weddings, but I thought Lori was too old to get so soppy.

'Now it's time for the official part,' Fred rubbed Lori's shoulder. Then he tapped a spoon lightly on the table. 'I'm aware, of course, that normally the bridegroom rises to make his speech, but since we're surrounded by other people, if you don't mind I'll stay seated.'

The reason we all laughed, I think, was because the word, "bridegroom", didn't seem to suit Fred. He was middle aged and not at all like the young blokes you imagined bridegrooms to be. We agreed it was all right for him to stay seated.

'I'm not sure if we've got it in the right order,' he began. 'But first, I'd like to thank you all for coming.' Fred swept his arm around the table as if he was making a speech to a whole shipload of sailors.

'Angela, you're the prettiest bridal attendant it's been my pleasure to set eyes on.'

Angela cuddled into Mum, as if she was actually shy.

'And, Tony, you have been an exemplary best man, although your duties aren't over yet because you have to read out the cards.'

'As long as I don't have to make a speech.'

'Not if you don't want to. You need only propose a toast,' Fred said, to my relief. 'As for you Mrs Add ... Dolly, your dressmaking talents have helped to make Amelia the most beautiful bride in the world. So I'd like you to charge your glasses and drink a toast to "my wife".'

I lifted my glass, glad to cover up the burning in my cheeks.

'Right, Tony, now it's your turn.' Fred nodded at Lori. She opened up her new handbag, which already looked as cluttered as the old one and pulled out a number of cards which she handed to Fred. He slid a knife along each envelope flap, took the card from it and handed it to me.

'There's one here from …' I squinted at the writing, 'from …'

'Betty and Bob.' Lori, leant across me and whispered.

'Betty and Bob,' I repeated, wishing I could understand the writing without Lori's help.

'Betty's been a good friend since we were in school together, although I haven't seen her for years,' Lori explained.

We went through all the cards like this, with Lori reading who it was from, saying something about them and finishing with, "I haven't seen them in years". In the end I didn't bother reading the cards myself, and handed them straight to her. It made me feel a bit of a dope, sitting there passing the cards from Fred to Lori. Then Fred handed me a telegram that I needed no help to read.

'It's from Joyce and Len in Canada,' I read. 'And it says, "To Dad and Amelia. Love and Congratulations. Wish we could be with you."

Fred ran a hand over his eyes, while Lori patted his arm and I hurried on. 'That's it. Now I'd like to propose a toast to …'

'Wait a minute! I'm sorry I'd forgotten this. You dropped it, Mr Stan … Fred, as you were walking down the path. I guessed it was a wedding card and popped it in my bag. At least, I think it's a card.' Mum passed an envelope to me. I could tell from the stamp, it was from New Zealand where Fred's son, Ronald, lived. He had written to his father several times lately, twice in one week not so long ago. Fred had soaked off the stamps, and given them to me to swap at school. I slit open the envelope myself. The writing was neat and I didn't need any help from Lori. I read out the message of congratulations and best wishes. I was about to put it on the pile with all the others, when I noticed a line of small writing at the bottom of the card. 'Hold on a mo, it's got something else written here. It says, "We're counting the days until you and Amelia emmigrate to New Zealand in November".'

Chapter Nine

I hardly heard the music or noticed the blue carpet and white-clothed tables as we made our way from the restaurant. A few hours ago I had practically skipped in there, now my feet felt so heavy I could hardly lift them.

Outside, the lights seemed to have dimmed, and the atmosphere in the taxi was so thick I could have cut it like Fred and Lori had just cut the wedding cake.

Lori sobbed and whispered, 'I'm sorry,' every few minutes.

Angela clung to Mum, her voice getting higher and higher. 'Don't let them go. Please don't let them go.'

I pushed myself into a corner and considered opening the door and running for it. It didn't matter where I ran to, just as long as I could escape from the truth. Fred and Lori wouldn't really leave us. Something would stop them. They wouldn't go through with it.

Fred bent forward and held his head in his hands, pushing his hair backwards and forwards and I knew what was in the telegram was as real and binding as what was written in that book in the Registry Office to say they were married.

Even as we drove along the dark London streets, a different life was waiting for them far, far away from us. There was nothing I could do to change it. They'd made fools of us. Fred had made us think our lives were safe since he moved in, but they were built on sand after all. Fred was clearing off, just like the Old Man, abandoning us. And Fred and Lori weren't popping round the corner, or going to be a bus or train ride away. They were disappearing to the other side of the world.

My chest was so tight it felt like a boulder was crushing me.

What would I do? How would I live without Fred? He had been everything I had ever wanted in a father. Hadn't he called me his son?

The next morning Fred stood in our kitchen with Lori beside him, her eyes looking like puffy slits.

'We never wanted you to find out this way. We can see now that we should have told you before the wedding, but we didn't want to spoil things. You were so excited. We didn't want to take that away from you'

'These things happen. You should probably have told us before the wedding, but hindsight's a wonderful thing. No time is ever the right time when it comes to giving people difficult news.'

I couldn't understand how Mum could take it so lightly. She was going to lose Lori who had kept us afloat when otherwise we would have gone under, and here she was saying, "These things happen". She was weak and without a backbone. She should fight. Fight for herself, fight for *us*. She should be trying to keep our lives on concrete. Even Angela, sitting at the table stuffing toast into her mouth, appeared to have got over it.

'As you can imagine, this wasn't an easy decision to make.' Fred avoided looking at me. If he had cast his gaze in my direction, he would have seen how much I hated him.

'But my son in New Zealand desperately needs me to help him with his business.'

Lori continued. 'And Fred has never really taken to retirement so …'

'Your son can rot in hell. You're no better than the Old Man. Clear off. See if I care. I don't need you or your bloody things,' I grabbed my Meccano set from on top of the sideboard and hurled the box against the wall. The pieces fell out and scattered across the floor. One of them hit Lori's foot, leaving blood on her ankle.

'Tony,' Mum exclaimed.

'Leave him,' Fred said.

I raced out the kitchen and flung myself down the stairs, banging our front door so hard I heard something crash to the floor in the Dibbles' place.

Outside, I ran and ran around the bombsite yelling, punching the air, swearing, cursing Fred with every word I could find. In my head I planned how I would run a knife through him and leave him in his own blood to die.

On and on, round and round, until my breath caught in my throat and my sides ached. I climbed into my dug-out and looked at the place where we'd found the ducks. We hadn't left those ducks to fend for themselves like Fred and Lori were leaving us. They'd promised in front of God to be there for us. They'd lied. Tears fell on to my knees and slid down my legs. I couldn't stop them. How could Fred say his son in New Zealand needed him more?

I heard the rattle of stones and looked up through a blur of tears. Paula was lowering herself into the hole beside me. We sat there squashed together not speaking until my tears became a trickle, streaking my cheeks.

'The pair of 'em are hypocrites. We were all going to be a family … the five of us … forever.'

'Fred and Lori?'

'They're going to New Zealand to live with his *precious* son. Why? Why? We're more his kids than that stupid Ronald. I hate him. I hate the two of them. I hate all of them.'

Paula picked up a handful of stones and let them run through her fingers. Then she put her arms around me and we wept together.

In spite of all my prayers beseeching God to stop them from going, Fred and Lori left for New Zealand on a late October day, when the sun painted a golden outline round the kids playing conkers on their way to school.

Outside our flat, we stood in a huddle together, dreading having to finally say goodbye. Lori was clinging to Mum as if she couldn't bear to let her go. 'We've left you some money and some stuff in the larder to help you out.' Lori was half speaking, half crying. 'And we'll write every week.'

'We wish you every success in your new life,' Mum said in a stiff voice.

I didn't wish them every success. I hoped they hated it; and that they were let down by Fred's son as Fred had let us down.

Next Lori hugged Angela, saying, 'You've always been my special girl. Do well in your life.' Lori stroked Angela's back. It heaved up and down as she cried.

She moved towards me, but I wouldn't let her hug me, and I stepped back, looking down at the pavement.

Fred shook hands with Mum and stroked Angela's arm, before offering me his hand. I declined it and Fred rubbed my shoulder instead. I shrugged him off. But as the taxi arrived, Fred pulled me to him, holding me so that I couldn't get away. 'Take care, son. Look after your mother and sister.' His voice faltered. 'I did my best,' he said.

I didn't answer him. He hadn't done his best for me - for us. He'd failed us and he'd caused Lori to do the same.

As the taxi made its way along Blountmere Street with Fred and Lori inside waving at us from inside, more a sad moving of their hands than a wave, it looked to me like a black bird carrying them away from us forever.

The weather turned to a damp chill, which brought fog and ultimately smog.

'Mum, Tony won't turn on the wireless and he's sitting right on top of it,' Angela screwed up a piece of paper. She threw it across the room, and it hit me in the eye.

'Oi, pack it in. Just for that you can do it yourself.'

Mum sighed. The ulcers on her legs were worse. I could see her pain in the lines on her face and the circles under her eyes. 'Don't be awkward, Tony. Just switch it on for your sister.'

I didn't answer, but I knew it was an effort for Mum to have to sort out our squabbling.

'Fred left the wireless for all of us, not only you, Mr High and Mighty,' Angela shouted.

'So what! I'm still not turning it on.'

'Mum!' Angela whined, but our bickering had driven Mum to the safe mind-place that she had again begun visiting since Fred and Lori left. Instead of feeling worried or sorry for her, she irritated me.

Shaking Mum's shoulders, Angela demanded, 'Why don't you say something? Don't you care! You've got sewing to do, but you're not doing it. That Mrs Clemence will be round here soon for her skirt, then what'll happen if it isn't made?'

'Don't go on, there's a good girl.'

'Can't you see, the food and stuff Fred and Lori left isn't going to last forever, nor is the fifty quid they gave us.'

'Why don't you stop shouting your mouth off.' I hated the way Angela was taking charge. I didn't want to hear things were getting tight again. It reminded me of the *"Poor List"*. 'We've got old Selska's rent, so I don't know what you're going on about?'

'It's not going to feed and clothe us if Mum doesn't do her sewing, pea brain.'

I made a grab for her hair. 'Don't call me pea brain!'

'Vat is going on?' Miss Selska, our new lodger, her hot water bottle under her arm, and carrying a Bakelite mug, entered our kitchen. She brought with her the smell of camphorated oil. The front room, once the home of Fred's models and his magic globe, was now a different place altogether. We were never invited into it, like we used to be when it had been Fred's. On the odd occasion when Miss Selska left her door open, all we could see were rows of medicine bottles and jars of pills.

'Vhy is it you children alvays fight? You do not know how lucky you are.' She shot the words at us like machine gun fire. 'Vhen I vas a child though ve have no food and any day may be our last, ve never fight. Never! Ve know how lucky ve are to be alive.'

'Here we go again,' Angela whispered, our bickering forgotten for the time being.

Giving Mum an accusing stare, Miss Selska carried on. 'Our mother did not permit us to fight and argue. She taught us to walue vhat ve had.'

I glanced at the wireless set, wondering whether I dared turn it on and drown her voice out.

'Vhy are not you children in bed, I ask?'

'Cos we're not,' I answered, but Miss Selska ignored me.

'As you can see, I am ready to retire to my bed now. Early nights are one of the secrets of good health. You children do not get enough sleep that is vhy you fight.'

I moved closer to the wireless. How could the old bag say she was healthy. She was as thin as a piece of string, and everything about her was khaki: her hair, her skin, even her eyes.

'And vhile I am on the subject of health, I do not think the children are ad-e-quate-ly dressed Mrs Ad-ding-ton. Angela should not be vearing such thin clothes.' Miss Selska moved her gaze from Mum to Angela. 'She should vear voollen things and …. how do you say …. a liberty vest.'

'I wouldn't be seen dead in one, so why don't you …'

'Angela!' Mum interrupted quickly, and then to Miss Selska, she said, 'We're just about to listen to the wireless, would you like to join us?'

'It is wery kind of you, but I cannot accept your offer. I have to go to vork in the morning. As you know, I have a wery important job in the City of London.'

'How can we forget, when she tells us every day,' I whispered to Angela.

'I vill fill my hot vater bottle and make myself some cocoa. Then I vill take my beauty sleep.'

'She'll need to sleep for hundreds of years, then' Angela sniggered as Miss Selska walked into the scullery.

'You shouldn't be so rude,' Mum told Angela mildly.

'Why not, I hate her guts, the horrible old dragon.'

'So do I.' I loathed her face and hair and her smarmy smile, her voice with its stupid accent and her parroting on about health. Most of all I hated her for taking Fred's place.

Since Fred and Lori had left, I preferred to stay at the Dibbles' place, where a fire flickered in their fireplace. It smelt of Mrs Dibbles' baking, and I could get away from bossy Angela. Even though Mrs Dibble treated me like an orphan, and Old Dibble never spoke except to grunt when he wanted something, it was better than having Angela telling me what to do all the time.

On a particularly dismal afternoon after school, when I called at the Dibbles, Paula was sitting at the kitchen table writing. She dipped the nib of her fountain pen into blue-black ink and lifted the lever at the side to fill it.

'Are you doing your homework?' I asked. Since Fred had gone, I didn't do mine, even though Mrs Colby gave me lines every time I missed it.

'I'm writing a letter to Fred and Lori. I thought you might like to write one as well. Then we could send them in the same envelope.'

I shrugged. I wouldn't have come down if I'd known all we were going to do was write stupid letters to stupid Fred and Lori.

'Don't you want to write one?' Paula asked.

'Nope.' I had brought my Biggles book with me to read. I was beginning to get fed up with it, but since Fred had gone, the library had become the boring place it had been before he came. I didn't go there anymore.

'I thought you might like to drop them a couple of lines to thank them for the postcards they sent you.'

They had been sent from South Africa, some other fancy place in Brazil and the latest one was from New Zealand. It had a picture of sheep on it with snowy mountains in the background. I liked my postcards better than the *Boys Own Annual* Fred and Lori had bought me for my birthday. My postcards were a way I could follow them. I carried them with me everywhere in my jacket pocket. When I thought no one was looking I rubbed them, especially the one from New Zealand.

'Couldn't you write a little bit? I've got another pen here and you can use my fountain pen. It makes your writing look much better. And I know Fred and Lori would love it if you were to write to them.'

'No thanks, I've bought my book to read.'

'You'd like using my fountain pen.'

I'd only used a fountain pen once when I'd pinched Mavis Dodd's pen when she wasn't looking. I liked the way it sort of glided over the paper, the way Bert and Bertha had on the crater pond.

'I've got a dictionary to help us with our spelling.'

I knew she didn't mean "*us*" but "*you*". I wasn't much cop at spelling. I wasn't much cop at knowing where the full stops and commas went either.

'Go on,' she held out her fountain pen to me, then placed a couple of pieces of paper in front of me. It was mauve and smelt of violets.

'It's pretty paper, don't you think?'

'Yeah, nice.' It was girls' stuff. I took hold of the pen as if it was as fragile as an egg. I sat there staring at the paper.

'Aren't you going to begin?' Paula started scratching at her writing paper.

'I don't know what to say.' It was the first letter I'd written in my life.

'Have you got their postcards with you?'

'No,' I lied. 'I've chucked 'em away. Anyway, how d'you find things to say?'

'I write whatever pops into my head. At the moment I'm telling them about how we're getting ready to sit the Eleven Plus examination.'

I shuddered. The last thing I wanted to write about was the Eleven Plus exam.

I supposed I could say something like I thought of them when I listened to the wireless and when I played with Brian. It didn't give too much away. I began, biting my lower lip, and tried to concentrate. I wished the words would bounce and tumble across the paper like they seemed to for Paula, then I could really be truthful. I would write to them about how our lives had changed since they'd gone. About Mum's legs and the pain she was in, and the way she lived in her head most of the time. I'd tell them how she hadn't once mentioned them since they left. Instead, when we spoke about them, she stared in front of her as if she didn't know who they were.

I wanted to tell them that the the money they left was running out, and it wouldn't be long before I went back on "*The Poor List*". But I didn't have the words, only unspoken longings and paralysing fear.

'Do you want to blot it?' Paula asked. Her letter was two pages long in comparison with my four lines. She had finished hers, "Love Paula" with a row of crosses after her name. I continued biting my lip. There was no way I was going to send them my love or put any kisses in my letter. When Mum got letters, mostly bills they ended, "Yours faithfully".

'How d'you spell "faithfully"?' I asked.

'Here you two, have a cup of tea and a ginger nut. But you'd better eat your tea, young man, or I'll be in trouble and that goes for you, too, Paula.' Mrs Dibble said as she came into the kitchen carrying a tray.

Not everything had changed. The Dibbles were still the same: Paula, gentle and genuine, Mrs Dibble, bustling, always fighting time, Old Man Dibble, grumpy and silent. Even so, I knew I couldn't depend on them. One day Paula might smile her innocent smile and say they were moving. "San Fairy Ann, pal, we're off." I wouldn't let the safety of the Dibbles' place make me feel too good inside.

As soon as I opened our front door, the stink of ulcers punched me in the face. It was sweet and sickly but not nice sweet, rotting sweet, going bad sweet. The stench was like a blanket that threw itself over the pongs of paraffin and camphorated oil.

'It stinks in here,' I said, as soon as I opened the kitchen door.

I went straight to Brian's cage and took him out. 'What's for tea?' I demanded sitting in a corner with Brian on my lap, as far away as I could from Mum and her stinking legs.

'I've made us some jam sandwiches.' For once Angela didn't come back with a smart crack or boss me around. Her face was red and sweaty and I noticed her dress was dirty.

'Blinkin' jam sandwishes. I want Spam.'

'That's enough.' Mum replied. 'Your sister's doing her best and you're to come straight home from school every day to help her.' Mum talked in little gasps and I noticed her legs jerking, as if she couldn't keep them still. 'Now put Brian back and make me and your sister a nice cup of tea.'

I scowled and poked my tongue out at Angela, but instead of coming directly back at me, she looked as if she was going to cry. She turned away, and went to sit beside Mum and patted the sweat from her forehead with a piece of rag.

'I reckon you should go to the doctor. That's what Lori would have said.' Angela didn't seem to mind the pong. She moved closer to Mum and spoke really softly to her

'She didn't know everything. I'll be all right in a couple of days.' Mum took some deep breaths. As I put

Brian back in his cage, I noticed her clenching her lips together.

The next morning Mum wasn't up as she usually was to see us off to school.

'Mum's not well so I'm staying at home to look after her,' Angela said, being her usual bossy self. 'She wants to see you before you go to school so you'd better get into her bedroom.'

'All right, all right.'

I took my time eating my toast, putting off going into Mum's bedroom. Even the thought of it gave me a queasy feeling. When I eventually forced myself in there, Mum's face was the colour of a primrose, which was all right for a primrose, but not Mum's face. Her eyes had sunk into black hollows in her head. Drops of water were shining above her lip and Angela was dabbing her forehead with a piece of rag, like she had yesterday, while Mum blew out her breath in short spurts. I didn't know what to do or say, and I stood at the foot of her bed tapping the iron bedstead with my fingernails making ringing sounds.

'You'd better be off to school.' Mum said in a hiccuppy voice. 'Now come and give me a kiss.'

I edged round the bed and bent over her, but my lips hardly touched her skin, before I fled through the door.

Relieved to be out of the room, I left the house before Angela could give me any more orders.

Outside I took deep breaths of thick smokey air. At least it didn't smell of ulcers. Inside me, though, I felt more afraid than I'd ever felt.

I knew Mum had asked me to go straight home after school but I couldn't bear the thought of seeing her like she'd been that morning and I went to Herbie's place to borrow some comics. I stayed there reading them for half an hour. Although I told myself I wasn't frightened of Angela, I knew I'd be in for trouble when I got home, though I didn't expect Mum would say much. For some reason, that made me feel bad.

I ran from Herbie's flat, and took a shortcut, skirting a wall on the corner of Whitely Square. Someone had chalked, *"Betty Grable's got legs like a table"* on it. The smokey atmosphere made it difficult to breath, but I kept running, reciting in my head what I would say to Angela. I would get the first words in. I'd tell her she wasn't going to order me around like she did Mum. I'd go where I liked; when I liked.

As I came into Blountmere Street. I could make out Angela racing towards me. Inside, I quaked. I thought of hot-footing it back the way I had come, but instead I slowed my pace, put my hands in my pockets and began whistling. Angela kept hurtling towards me until I could hear her shouting my name. I slowed my steps even more.

'Tone, Tone,' she called and I knew something wasn't right. Angela only called me "Tone" when she was in a good mood, or wanted to borrow something, the same as when I called her "Ang".

As she got closer, even through the murk, I could see she was crying. Without meaning to I began running.

'Tone, they've put Mum in hospital, and they're taking us away.' She sobbed in a little voice, and her tear-smeared face touched me somewhere deep inside.

'Taking *us* away? Who's taking us away? No one's taking me.'

'They're putting us in a home 'til Mum gets better. They're coming for us soon.'

'They can't do that. We can look after ourselves.'

'They say we can't. They say we're too young and we've got to go into an orphanage. Old Selska can't have us 'cos she works all day.'

'What about the Dibbles? Can't they look after us?'

'They haven't got room. When the doctor said Mum had to go in hospital, Mrs Dibble said she thought she could have us, then when old *Dribble* came home for his dinner, she said they didn't have enough room. I hate him, I really hate him. If we knew where Dad was perhaps ...' Angela began really crying, and I turned away and tried to talk tough.

'Well, we don't know where he is and who cares? Anyway, he wouldn't want us.'

I wished Fred was here. He would have known what to do. Who were *they* and *them,* anyway, and who said *they* had the right to take us from our home, and order us about, without even asking *us* what *we* wanted? I clenched my hand into a fist and smashed it into my other palm. I hated *they* and *them.*

'Lock the door,' Angela said as soon as we reached our flat. We climbed the stairs into the kitchen and sat at the kitchen table not knowing what to do. After a while, I said, 'Look, Ang, I'm going to have to go out again.' I couldn't see any way round it. I had to go to Herbie' place.

'Don't you dare go away and leave me,' Angela gripped my arm so hard she made a red blotch on it.

'I've got to go to Herbie's. If I can get his old woman to let me stay there, Mrs Dibble and Paula might be able to persuade Old Man Dibble to change his mind and let you sleep in Paula's room with her.'

Angela took a shuddering sob and blew her nose on the piece of rag she had dabbed Mum's head with. It made me think of Mum and how ill she was, and of the ulcers' smell.

'I've got to do it, Ang. I won't be long. I promise. While I'm gone you can make us some grub.'

Grudgingly, Angela let go her grip on me. 'Be quick then. I'll make us some jam sandwiches.'

'That'll be smashing,' I said. This time I managed to jump four stairs at a time to the bottom.

When I opened our front door, I saw a man and woman walking up the path. Beneath the light of the street lamp outside our place, they looked like black ghosts.

'Tony Addington?' The man asked in a gravelly voice.

'What if I am?' I tried to close the door, but the man wedged his foot between the door and the door frame.

'We've come to take you and your sister to be looked after for a while.' Pushing me in front of them the couple began climbing our stairs.

'Blimey, there's a stench in here,' the woman said, holding her nose between her fingers.

'What d'you think you're doing?' Angela stood in front of them with her hands on her hips. I knew she was trying to look fierce and scary, although I could tell she wasn't far from crying. 'Clear off. We don't need to go into any home. We're all right as we are.'

'Our orders are to take you both to orphanages.'

'I told you, we can look after ourselves.'

But the pair ignored her. Opening the large shopping bag she carried, the woman brought out two brown paper bags which she shoved at Angela and me. 'Put your stuff in these. I'll come with you. Where d'you keep your things? You'll have to move a bit sharpish, your carriage awaits,' she said trying to be funny.

'I'm not going and I'm not packing anything.' Angela refused to move.

'In that case, I'll have to do it for you.' The woman began opening and shutting doors until she came to our room. 'This looks like your bedroom; it's got two beds in it, at any rate.' She moved to our rickety chest of drawers and emptied the few things we had in it into her bag. 'It'll be your hard luck if something gets missed,' she said.

'Right, down you go.' Approaching the top of the stairs, the woman pushed Angela and me in front of her.

'I'm not going,' Angela shouted, clinging to the stair rail, while the woman struggled to prise her fingers from it, and called the man to help her.

'Why can't you be sensible like your brother and come quietly?' The man asked, trying to undo her grip.

Angela sneered at me. I could tell she thought I was a coward.

Eventually the man loosened Angela's hand from the rail, and half dragged, half carried her down the stairs.

'You filthy pigs,' she screamed. 'Filthy rotten pigs.'

'I'm letting go of her to open the door, so you'd better hold on tight,' the man ordered the woman.

'I'm not going, I tell you.' Angela bent her head and bit the woman's arm.

'You little bitch,' the woman slapped her hard across Angela's face, causing blood to spurt from Angela's nose, and I had to stop myself from running to her.

Outside I walked obediently down the path towards a blue van waiting under the street light.

'Help! Please help us, someone!' Angela called shrilly into the empty street, causing the woman to clamp her hand over Angela's mouth.

'You just stay where you are while I help with your sister,' the man commanded me, and slipping his hands under Angela's armpits, he began dragging her backwards towards the van.

'Help me, Tone, please help me!' Angela pleaded.

'I can't, Ang, not yet,'

If I was going to escape, now was the time. If I tried knocking at the Dibbles' front door, the man would reach me before they answered. Going to Herbie's was still the best idea. I was sure I'd be able to outrun this man. He was old. At least thirty. Herbie's old man might be home from work. He'd come back with me and explain everything. I began haring along Blountmere Street.

'Oi, come here,' the man chased after me, calling to the woman, 'Tie the girl up if you have to, then lock the door.'

I sprinted in the same direction from which I had recently come. Crossing a rough patch of grass, I turned out of Blountmere Street, my breath swirling in front of me. Shinning the *Betty Grable* wall, I stumbled and righted myself. I could hear the man's footsteps a little way behind me. My lungs felt as if they were filled with sand but I kept sprinting. I rounded the side of the bombsite we didn't often play on and then into Whitely Square, past the tenement buildings where quite a few of the kids at school lived. It was tea time and there wasn't anyone in the street. In the misty darkness, the street lights appeared like hazy stars. I pushed myself on, until I could see the lighted windows of the block where Herbie lived, but the man was gaining on me.

'Come here, you little sod,' he panted. I fled across the road. I had to keep going. In the distance I could see the blurred outline of *The Perseverance* and hear the smoky voices of early customers heading in for a pint or two on their way home from work.

'Hey, help me,' I shouted, but my voice was weak from running and the black blanket of night wrapped my words in it and smothered them.

I pushed myself onwards until I was unable to carry on any longer, and I stopped and bent to get my breath back, uncertain what to do next. I knew I would never reach the pub without the man catching up with me. Just the same, there was still safety to be had with Herbie. He would let me in.   But I'd taken too long and the footsteps were coming closer. I darted into the entrance of Herbie's building, kicking a rusty corned beef tin out of the way, then scaling the stairs three at a time. Only one more flight and I would be outside Herbie's flat..

I swung myself up the final few stairs. When I reached Herbie's front door, I banged the door knocker over and over again, shouting, 'Open the door. Please, please open the door.'

'Gotcha, sonny.'   A hand encircled my leg, yanking me to the ground. 'Thought you could get away from me, did you? I ain't a footballer for nothing.'

I struggled to get free, but the man pressed his knee hard into my chest.

'You're not getting away this time.' Standing and hauling me to my feet, he rammed his knee into the small of my back, urging me forward into the darkness.

'Herbie!' I yelled. 'Herbie!' But the doors to the tenements stayed closed. My voice struck the walls and echoed back at me.

I saw Paula and Mrs Dibble standing outside as the man pushed me towards the van. I noticed a torn piece of Angela's dress caught in the van door.

Paula rushed towards us. 'Where are you taking them?' She took hold of my arm. 'Where are they taking you?'

'We're not at liberty to tell you that.' The man said, still panting.

'You can't take them like this. If you wait, perhaps we can work something out.' I could see Mrs Dibble was agitated.

'We've got our orders. Anyway, a home is the right place for these two hooligans.' The man indicated to the woman to open the van door and shoved me inside. 'Don't move a muscle, or it won't just be your head that's cut.'

'I'll write, I promise,' Paula called into the van. 'I'll find out where they're taking you and I'll write.'

Inside Angela was weeping loudly. It was a horrible sound.

'Shut up.' The woman shook her.

'Leave her alone. When we get to where you're taking us, we'll report you. Just wait.'

'We're really frightened, aren't we, Jim,' the woman laughed. 'Anyway, there won't be any "we". Brothers and sisters are separated. No, Sunshine, you two are going to different orphanages. That should cool you both down a bit.' The woman pulled her collar up and around her ears. 'Hurry up and get this thing started, Jim. The sooner we get rid of the pair of them the better.'

Chapter Ten

'Pass the glue,' Joe called, lifting the tangle of paper chains further over on to the work bench. I swore his hair was more orange than the marigolds in old Dibble's garden, and his face was polka dotted with freckles the same colour as his hair. I handed him the paste pot and brush. We had made the paste from flour that cook had grudgingly measured out. She had grumbled that if we weren't careful, there wouldn't be enough for the dumplings to go with the stew we were having that night. If the dumplings tasted like the stew smelt, wafting into the orphanage recreation room in overpowering waves, the flour was best used to glue together paper chains.

'We must have miles of them here, enough for Balham High Street.' Joe picked up another armful and dumped them on the floor. 'There's enough for the whole of the blinkin' orphanage, and Matron's allowing us to hang 'em in our rooms, as well.'

I shrugged. Who cared? I didn't give a tinkers about paper chains or the Christmas tree Monica the housemaid said was coming today. She had already begun to moan about the needles it would drop.

'These decorations'll finish off our room nicely. We'll drape them round our beds, because they're next to each other, then loop them up and hang them over Micky's and Tom's beds. It's a marvel only having four of us in that great big room. At our dump at home, there was six of us in an attic the size of a pea. Packed in like cockroaches we were, and there were plenty of *them* about, too. And fancy having carpet in your bedroom! I still can't get over it.' The polka dots on Joe's face seemed to expand and join each other in orange splodges.

'So what! We had carpet everywhere in our place at home. Angela and I had a bedroom each, with our own bedroom suites,' I lied. I couldn't understand how Joe actually seemed to like this place. 'Don't you care you're not allowed to write to anyone, even your old lady, and that they don't let you get letters either?' I asked. 'Monica told me, they don't even tell your family where you are. Not that it bothers me,' I added. It didn't do to show your feelings to anyone, not even your friend.

'My old lady can't read, nor can any of the family, not much at any rate. They don't want me. I'm one less mouth to feed. They've probably already forgotten about me.' Joe finished pasting the last green circle, linking it to an orange one. 'Anyway, we're best pals, ain't we? We both came here on the same day. We sleep next to each other and I know The Common a bit. In my book, that makes us closer than family.'

'Yeah.' I liked Joe. We stuck up for each other, and he'd once been "Up The Common," but he didn't take the place of Mum and Angela, even Paula. And the rooms might be warm and the mattresses springy, not like the ones Ang and I slept on, but this place would never be like our flat in Blountmere Street, especially when Fred had lived with us.

All I wanted was to hear from Mum, so she could tell me how she was, and how Ang was doing in her orphanage. I remembered Paula writing Christmas cards, sitting at the Dibbles' kitchen table, drawing holly leaves in the corners and stars on the envelopes. If only she'd send me one. She said she would write to me when we were taken away. But how could she when she didn't know where I was?

On Christmas Day, Father Christmas arrived early at the orphanage recreation room with two sacks.

'It's bleedin' daft having Father Christmas. Anyone would think we were babies. Anyway, it's the gardener,' Joe whispered. 'He's still got mud on his boots.'

Matron had fixed a piece of mistletoe in her wiry grey hair and Father Gardener Christmas kissed her full on the lips. Then he plonked himself onto a chair covered with a piece of frayed red satin. 'I hopes you've all been good child-ren,' he said in his strange country accent.

Matron said she was sure we had. Holding the register, she began calling out our names. It reminded me of Mrs Colby and the school dinner lists. Because my surname began with an A, I was one of the first to walk forward to Father Christmas' throne. 'How old be you sonny?' Father Christmas asked. His front teeth were rotten and his neck was ridged with dirt.

'Eleven,' I answered. He gave me the willies, dressed in a tatty robe that smelt of last year's Christmas dinner, and wearing a beard that looked as if mice had nested in it. He delved into his sack and brought out a box. He shoved it at me, before waving me away with a grimy hand.

I walked back to my place next to Joe. 'What you got?' Joe asked, helping me tear the paper from the box. Even when I was tearing paper from a present, I was noticeably slower than him. As the strips came off, it became obvious it was a puzzle. The picture on the front was of a large lady sitting outside a cottage, knitting. The corners of the box were crushed and there was a white label at the top which read "To an Orphan. Two pieces missing."

'I had a Meccano set once and a suit with long trousers,'I said to Joe, sucking the tears back down my throat. I wished I could put my foot on the box and flatten it and the woman knitting.

'I swear you ain't smiled once all day, and it's Christmas,' Joe walked across to me after we'd eaten our Christmas dinner, as I sat at one of the work tables in the recreation room picking up puzzle pieces and putting them down again. 'And what d'you reckon about the turkey and Christmas pud. It wasn't bad, was it?'

'I s'ppose.'

'Is it 'cos you're worried about your old lady?'

'Course I'm not. Why would I be bothered about Doll?' Recently I had begun calling Mum, "Doll." It sounded tough to call your mother by her first name. 'Do you think I'm soft, or something?'

'Well, if you wanted to get in touch with her, I've thought of a way you could do it,' Joe continued, ignoring what I'd just said.

'How?' I tried to sound as if I wasn't interested.

'You could write the address of this place on a bit of paper. Send it to one of your friends and ask them to get it to your old woman.'

'And how am I supposed to post it?'

'Ask Monica to do it. You know she's got a soft spot for you, always calling you her curly haired angel and all that carry on. I'm pretty sure she wouldn't snitch to Matron.'

'I'll think about it, not that I care one way or the other.'

'You'll get me hung, drawn and quartered, you will,' Monica said when I handed her the envelope addressed to Paula. If I sent it to Dennis or Herbie, it would probably end up in a puddle. Anyway, I didn't know their exact addresses.

'But you'll do it?' I asked, wiping my hand across my face so that she couldn't see my eagerness. 'I haven't got a stamp.'

'Buying a stamp won't break the bank, but you're to keep it to yourself. I can't afford to lose my job. I've got a sick mother at home to keep. I would have handed in my notice years ago if it wasn't for her. I'm too kind hearted for this sort of place and always being at the beck and call of that dried up prune of a matron.' She ruffled my hair, which was something she did a lot when she came into our room. It embarrassed me when she did it in front of the others.

'You understand you won't get a reply, or if you do, it won't be given to you.'

'Yeah, I know. It's just that I want Mum to know where I am, in case they haven't told her, then when she's better she'll know where to come to get me out.' I liked saying Mum instead of my Old Woman or Doll, and Monica said, 'Your Mum's a lucky lady. I'd have loved a boy like you. A bit late now, though.' She took a handkerchief from her sleeve and blew her nose. Tucking the handkerchief back, she patted the pocket of her apron where my letter, or more accurately a scrap of a paper bag in an old envelope, was hidden. 'Let's hope it does the trick, eh?'

'If you stand at that window any more, you'll become a blinkin' statue and stay there forever,' Joe vowed as I gazed at the gravel drive below. I'd done it every single day of January, willing Mum to limp along the path on her way to collect me. Instead, the gardener trundled his wheelbarrow along it, still gathering dead leaves, delivery vans drove to and fro, orphans walked in crocodiles on their exercise walks, the vicar cycled twice a week to see matron, but Mum's shabby navy blue coat and hat never appeared in the distance.

Clumps of what Joe said were snowdrops peeped through the grass and around the trees. Midway through February, it snowed and smothered the snowdrops. I knew then that Mum wouldn't come, not for a while. She would wait until spring came fully. I would see her walking down the gravel path edged with daffodils, or on a warm summer's day, dabbing her forehead with a handkerchief. Although I tried to silence it, a voice inside me kept whispering that she might not come at all. After all, like Joe, I'd only be another mouth to feed. If she had to choose between who should go home with her, it would be Angela. At least Ang did things around the place, made herself useful, and it wouldn't be long before she could get a job. That's when I stopped staring out the window. I wouldn't even let my eyes wander to it, no matter how much I wanted to look.

I hated Saturday afternoons. I hated every single minute at the orphanage and at school, but I hated Saturday afternoons the most, because we had to make a model for Sunday School the next day. Although I'd made models with Fred, now I could never get mine right, and I was slow, much slower than Joe. I seemed to be slow at everything these days. Perhaps it was because I didn't sleep or eat much.

'What's that supposed to be?' Joe asked, pushing his hair back to reveal even more marmalade splodges.

'The whale that swallowed Jonah, what d'you think it is, Scotch mist?'

'It looks like a bit of cardboard you've painted grey.'

'And what's wrong with that?'

'I'll give you a hand. I've finished mine. I'll just pop over to the workbench and get what we need.' Joe darted across the room. He was getting quicker while I was becoming slower.

Without meaning to, I glanced up and out the window. Ribbons of cloud tied up the sunshine, making the landscape look as empty as I felt. Remembering my promise to myself not to look, I directed my gaze back to the table, but something red flickered at the edge of my vision. Immediately I looked up. A girl in red was walking slowly past the window. Her coat was open, and her short brown hair blew around her face. Just as quickly as I had seen her, she disappeared. I remained staring in front of me. It was probably only seconds, but it seemed minutes before she returned, peering in the window, shading her eyes with her hand. I put my hand up to wave, then dropped it. This girl wasn't real. I was dreaming, like I sometimes did when I eventually fell asleep. Then a gust of wind blew her coat open, and I saw her pleated skirt.

'Paula,' I mouthed, already running from the recreation room.

'I thought you were never going to see me,' she said, when I got outside and she guided me away from the window and towards a doorway, where Mrs Dibble and a man were huddled.

'What're you doing here? We're not allowed visitors. Is everything's all right? There's nothing wrong with … ?'

'Everything's fine. Paula and her mum wanted to make sure you were all right,' the man explained as we squeezed bedside them. 'They told your mother they'd come if they could.'

I stared at the ground willing myself not to cry.

'By the way, my name's Bill Masters, a friend of the Dibbles. I've got some transport and when Paula said she wanted to see you, I offered to bring them down.' The man extended his hand. 'How d'you do? I've heard a lot about you. All good, of course.'

'My word, Tony, you've grown.' Mrs Dibble was wearing a pale blue coat I hadn't seen her in before. It made her look a lot younger, and her face was reddish. Suddenly she embraced me and I raised my arms a little, then dropped them to my side, uncertain what to do.

'Who would have thought we would all be meeting together in a beautiful country place like this?' Mrs Dibble smiled.

I knew she was trying to be cheerful, while all the time she was taking in my frayed jersey and trousers that sagged below my knees.

'Paula's been on about you ever since you went, so we thought we'd bring you a few bits and pieces.'

'We'll have to hatch a way for Tony to smuggle them in,' The man stopped Mrs Dibble from unloading everything there and then.

'Are you likely to be missed?' he asked. Funny I hadn't heard Paula mention him before.

'I reckon they won't notice I've gone for a while. We've got to make a model and I was just starting mine.'

'It sounds a very nice place letting you do interesting things like that.' I knew Mrs Dibble was trying to be encouraging, but I didn't answer her.

'What if Mrs Dibble and I go for a walk while you two have a chat? It's a little cramped here. We'll be back in ten minutes. Come on Lil.' Bill Masters said.

'As long as they're not found.' Mrs Dibble looked concerned.

'They'll be all right. We've got to make sure we're not seen either, so we'd better creep back the way we came.'

'Honestly, Bill, this cloak and dagger stuff's not for me,' Mrs Dibble complained, but the man, his arm around her shoulders, was already leading her away. I wondered what Old Dibble would have said to that.

It was draughty and I kept looking towards the door, in case someone came through it and caught us.

'What's it like here?' Paula asked.

'It's all right.' Now that someone I really wanted to see was here, I couldn't think of a single thing to say. Perhaps matron was right. We were better off without visitors.

'Have you made many friends?'

'Not many.'

A bird settled on the gravel and began rummaging through it.

'There's this boy called Joe. He's in my room. We get on all right.'

'Your mum sends her love and says to tell you she really misses you. She's getting a lot better. It can't be long before she's home, then you'll be able to come back.'

I stared at Paula, trying to work out whether she was telling the truth or only saying what she thought I wanted to hear.

'Your Mum's heard from Angela. She's settled down where she is, and she says she's made a lot of friends.'

'Good.'

It hadn't been like this between Paula and me when we read comics on Saturday afternoons. Then we hadn't had to struggle to find things to say to each other.

'We've brought you a letter from your Mum, and Fred and Lori have written to you from New Zealand. Even Miss Selska's sent you something about how to look after your health. We've brought them with us to give to you.' Paula tried to penetrate the wall between us that seemed to be six feet wide.

'You're not missing anything in Blountmere Street. It's just the same. Nobody's been able to go over the bombsite because it's been too cold and wet. The only news is that Kenny Bryant and Marjorie Hicks got married last week. She looked lovely in this brocade dress with those pointy sleeves brides' dresses have, and she had ever such a long veil. The bridesmaids were in red, which is very unusual, don't you think?'

Another bird joined the one already on the gravel, and began to peck amongst the stones, making soft scrabbling noises.

'I would have written, but we didn't know where you were until we got your letter,' Paula explained.

'They don't let us have letters, anyway. They say it will unsettle us.'

'Do you have lessons here?'

'We all go to school in the village.'

'Is it better than Blountmere Street School?'

'Nope.' I looked down at my feet.

'Did you sit the Eleven Plus exam?'

'Yeah.'

'How did you do?'

'All right.'

Paula hesitated. I knew she was trying to think of something more to ask, while I couldn't bring to mind anything I wanted to say.

'With all this ground, I bet you play lots of outside games.' She pressed on.

'Not in winter.'

'I suppose not, but there must be some good things about being here.'

'There's nothing good about being here.' Even though I was talking to Paula Dibble from Blountmere Street which was something I would have given anything for, I wanted to run away.

I picked up a stone from the path and began gouging the brickwork with it.

Mrs Dibble and the man came into view. They were laughing. Even from a distance, I could see Mrs Dibble's face was still flushed and she looked a lot different from the woman who scurried along Blountmere Street as if she was responsible for looking after the whole earth.

'Bill's a friend of Mum's from before she was married. He's really nice,' Paula said, and I watched with panic as they came closer.

Without meaning to, I clutched hold of her. 'Take me home with you. I hate it here. It's horrible. Your mum could have me. It wouldn't be for long.' I shook Paula's arm.

'I don't think we'd be allowed to.'

'What aren't you allowed to do?' Mrs Dibble asked in a fluttery voice, as she and the man drew nearer.

'Tony wants to come back home with us.'

Mrs Dibble shot the man an "I knew this would happen" look before replying. 'I'm sorry, Tony, but it wouldn't be allowed. Anyway, you won't be here much longer. Your mother's well on the road to recovery. She'll be sending for you soon. Make the most of it, eh? After all, it does seem a very nice place.'

I turned away, my shoulders slumping forward, my head low on my chest.

'Now, come on, cheer up!' Mrs Dibble urged. 'Let's see how much of this stuff you can take in with you.'

'I won't be able to take any of it.' I swiveled back to face her. 'If they found out, I'd be in for it.'

The man took the bag from Mrs Dibble. He began sorting through its contents.

'Take the letters. Have you got a drawer of your own that's private?'

'I've got a drawer, but it isn't private.'

'Well, put them under your mattress, and here are some sweets. Stick them in your pocket.'

'They're Old Boy Barker's special mix,' Paula added.

I allowed Mrs Dibble to tuck the bag into my pocket.

'We'll give your Mum your love, and tell her you're being well looked after. Have you any messages for anyone?'

'Nope.'

'Then, we'd better go before you're missed.'

After allowing Mrs Dibble to kiss me on the cheek, but without saying goodbye or looking at them, I walked to the door. My footsteps dragged with the weight of my abandonment.

'Wait! Wait!' Paula began running after me. 'It'll be all right. Honestly. I'm sorry you can't come back with us. I wish you could, but your mum will come and get you. It won't be long. If she had to, your mother would fight to have you with her, I know she would. She might be quiet, but she's strong inside. You've got to believe that, Tony.'

'Yeah, I know, but you don't understand what it's like here, and I miss everybody at home, especially Ang. It's funny really, 'cos I always thought I'd like the country. We're not far from the sea either, but it doesn't feel right.' My top lip quivered.

'I didn't mean to upset you. I only wanted to see you and let you know we're thinking of you.'

'I'm glad you came. I'm sorry I got the pip. I wasn't expecting you, that's all. Thanks for bringing all that stuff.'

'I'm sorry you can't take much of it. We'll give it to you when you get home. It'll be like Christmas.' She paused. 'I've got to go.' Then, as if on an impulse, she said, 'Why don't we make a promise to think of each other every afternoon at four? That way you can stay in touch with Blountmere Street. Perhaps it won't be so hard to be here for a little longer then. We'll have to concentrate hard so that what we're thinking reaches each other. And no-one will know, only you and me.' She kissed me on the cheek. 'I love you, Tony,' she said. This time I didn't squirm.

Chapter Eleven

As soon as the Dibbles had gone, I dashed back up to my room. I hoped for a glimpse of them leaving the orphanage, but they had been swallowed into the bare landscape. I took the letters from my inside pocket: one from Mum, another from Miss Selska and a third from Fred and Lori. I tore the top from the last envelope, and snatched at several sheets of thin paper like posh lav paper. They were covered with Fred's precise writing and paragraphs in Lori's scribble. I scrutinised the pages as if I could magic Fred and Lori right there into my room. Although they didn't exactly say so, I could tell they weren't happy. They didn't belong thousands of miles away. Their home was in Blountmere Street with me and Angela and Mum.

'What're you doing?' Joe barged into the room, as he always did, swinging round the door. With one leap he landed in the middle of his bed. 'You know we're not s'pposed to be here at this time on a Saturday afternoon. What happened? One minute you were at the table, the next you'd scarpered. I told everyone you'd gone to the lav.'

'The people who live downstairs to us in Blountmere Street turned up. We had to hide because matron wouldn't let them in, the old bag. They brought me some letters and stuff, so I came up here to read them.'

'You're lucky.'

'I s'ppose.'

'We'd better get downstairs quick, before they notice we've gone, or we'll miss our crumpets tomorrow. Sunday night and crumpets is the best night of the week. Saturday afternoons aren't bad either.'

As far as I was concerned, nothing about this place was good.

'What did your mates say about your old lady?' Joe asked.

'They said Doll's getting better. She'll be sending for me soon.'

'There you are then; I reckon you've got nothing to moan about.'

'I'll hide these letters under here.' I began lifting the corner of my mattress.

'Three's a lot to have under there. Why don't you put one under my mattress. That way it'll be safer,' Joe suggested. It was typical of Joe to think of something like that.

'Good idea,' I handed Joe Miss Selska's letter. I didn't want to sleep that far away from the other two.

'The Dibbles brought me some sweets – Old Boy Barker's special mix. I'll hide them in my socks then we can have them tonight. It'll be easier with only a couple of us.' I looked across at the two empty beds that, until a few of days ago, had been occupied by Mickey and Tom. The beds looked as if they were wearing uniforms of grey blankets hemmed with red stitching. 'We're sure to get another couple in here soon, so we'd better eat them quick. You'll love 'em' For the first time that afternoon I smiled - properly, not that silly raising of my lips I'd done for the Dibbles.

The next afternoon at four o'clock, the time Paula and I had arranged to send mind messages to each other, I screwed up my face in concentration to receive her message. Now it had actually come to it, I found it impossible to chase away all the thoughts that dodged and darted around my head like naughty puppies. No sooner did I catch one, than another and another took its place.

'You in pain or something?' Joe asked, looking at me funny.

'I need some peace and quiet, that's all.'

'Please yourself.'

Paula made swapping our thoughts sound easy, like receiving letters in your head. I was sure she was sending hers right now. If Paula said she would, she would. I gritted my teeth and grunted, but nothing came. Joe gave me another of his funny looks.

It had been a crackpot idea, but if I couldn't catch hold of Paula's thoughts, I might as well let my own wander where they would. Paula might be better at picking them up.

I closed my eyes and pictured the model I had been working on, or at least Joe had been working on for me, when Paula had come yesterday. It had been judged by the local vicar as the best in the Sunday School.

Inwardly I cringed as I recalled over-hearing the vicar telling one of the women from the village that they usually chose an orphan to win, because they felt sorry for 'the poor souls'. It was like being on the *Poor List* again. Forgetting Paula might be picking up what was in my head, the shame I'd felt blazed into anger. They were nothing but a bunch of do-gooders. I loathed their smug faces. When I got home, I'd show them, and all the others like them.

'I've just heard they're sending another four kids to that there halfway home Micky and Tom got sent to.' Joe loved tittle-tattle, good or bad, and I wondered if it was because his ears came to a point at the top that he got to hear so much. He kept scraping at his potato. Spud bashing was our special duty every morning before school. If we didn't fill the cauldron, we had to clean the lavs.

'Alfie Barchard says it's 'cos they're getting ready to go on this adventure to another country.'

'Why would they want Mickey and Tom and the others to have an adventure? They hate us having adventures. Anyway, why do they have to have them in some other country? Can't they have them here? It's crackers.'

'Alfie Barchard says it's hot where they have their adventures.' Joe threw a spud into the cauldron. Water splashed the bench and trickled on to the floor. 'I wouldn't mind an adventure in a hot place mesself, except I'd frizzle up with these.' He pointed to the freckles covering his arms that made them look a completely different colour to mine. 'That's the trouble having ginger hair. I wouldn't mind if my old man or woman had it. I'm the only one in the whole blinkin' family who's a carrot top. I reckon I must have been the milkman's.'

'Did he have ginger hair?'

'I don't know, do I? It was a joke. Where've you been all your life!'

'Learning how to punch people like you.' I grabbed hold of Joe's jersey and hauled him towards me.

'Let go, for pity's sake, I was only joking.'

'Yeah, well. Let it be a warning to you, or anyone who takes the mickey out of me.' I let go of his jersey.

That night I had another of the nightmares I had been having of late. A cannibal was chasing me across a desert. The heat pressed down on me like a rock. It caused my head to bang inside and my lungs to long for a cool English day. The soles of my feet were criss-crossed with bloody tramlines. My feet sank into the sand, making them difficult to lift.

As the chase went on, a paralysis began creeping into my legs. I struggled to keep going, pushing one foot in front of the other as the savage with a spear hared after me. Numbness was taking hold of me as my attacker drew nearer.

The heat didn't seem to affect him at all. Gradually my whole body lost feeling, and I fell onto the sand.

With a whoop of victory, the cannibal dragged me towards a fire with a cauldron, hanging over it like the one we used for the spuds. I could feel the heat like blisters on my skin, and hear fire roaring in my ears. My lungs wouldn't blow up and I was having difficulty breathing. Sweat trickled into my eyes and down my face until I could taste its saltiness. Effortlessly, as if I was made of cotton wool, the cannibal lifted me up and into the cauldron, where Mickey's and Tom's faces leered up at me. I fought to suck in the next breath. Then, while I was being lowered into the pot, my lungs filled with air as if a pair of bellows had been pushed into them.

'It's all right, Tone. It's all right. You were having one of those nightmares again,' Joe was sitting on the edge of my bed holding my shoulders while I sucked in air, trying to breathe properly.

'It was horrible, horrible. He was cooking Mickey and Tom. I was next.'

'What's going on in here?' Matron opened the door and waved torchlight around the room.

'He's had a nightmare, Miss. He'll be all right in a minute. He needs a drink of water, and it'd help if we could have the light on for a bit.'

'You most certainly can't have either.' Matron's whispering was louder than if she spoke normally. 'The rules are no lights after half past eight. He's not a baby. He doesn't need a drink at night. We can't make exceptions for him. Before we know it, everyone will be pretending to have nightmares, then where will we be!' She closed the door with a click. We heard her footsteps disappearing along the landing.

'He was going to eat me, Joe.' My voice still trembled.

'Who was?'

'A cannibal. He was going to put me in the spud pot.'

'You gave me a turn screaming like that.'

'Promise you won't tell anyone.'

'What' d'you take me for? Mates don't grass on each other.' By now, Joe was sitting cross-legged at the foot of my bed.

'I wish I could have the light on. I don't want to go back to sleep in case he gets me this time.'

'I won't let him. I'll cover myself up with a blanket and sleep at the end of your bed. At home I was used to kipping in half inch of space.' He pulled back the blanket and crawled under it. Knowing he was there at the foot of my bed made me feel safe and eventually I fell back to sleep.

When I awoke, Joe was hunched like a hibernating animal at the bottom of my bed. I wiggled my feet and gradually the hillock flattened and Joe's face emerged. 'Best night's kip I've had for a blinking century,' he grinned.

A white skin of frost covering the countryside was beginning to melt as we walked to school.

'You don't think horrible things really do happen when they send them to have these adventures, like being eaten by cannibals, do you?'

'Course they don't. Cannibals come from Africa, and Africa's too far to send them to have adventures. Stop worrying.' Against the frost-blue sky, Joe's hair was an orange crown around his head. 'Come here and I'll show you something.'

'What is it?'

'A bird's nest. I found it yesterday. There's no eggs in it, so it might be old, or a bird might be going to lay some soon. I'm going to try and get a book on birds, then perhaps I can find out what sort of nest it is.' Joe stooped to pick a snowdrop from a clump emerging from behind a tree trunk. 'I never saw a flower growing 'til I came here. I saw them in shops, but not actually coming up out the ground. And the only birds I ever saw were sparrows and pigeons. It's real lovely in the country.'

I found the bombsite far more beautiful. Each season it changed, even at different times of the day. Eerily it rose from the fog on a winter's morning like a ghost city. Evening shadows stretched long fingers across it, leading it into the secret night. Dandelions thrived in yellow clouds, afterwards their petals dropping, leaving their fairy-down to be blown away in countless games of "Telling the Time". Flowers that had once been part of someone's garden refused to give up and kept up the same colourful display year after year. And when the sun shone on the sycamore tree by the bakers, it actually glimmered, while in the autumn it dropped its seeds like tiny brown helicopters.

'Dirty orphans! Dirty orphans!' A group of village children began careering towards us, yelling, 'You've got fleas and stink!'

'I'll kill you. I'll kill all of you.' Instant anger flared inside me, but Joe was already dragging me through an opening in the hedge and pushing me down behind it.

'What d'you think you're doing? There must be a dozen of 'em. They'll murder us.'

'Nobody's calling me a dirty orphan.' I struggled to free myself from Joe's grip, but his hands were like a vice. He was surprisingly strong for someone with such a small frame.

Reluctantly, I ducked low as the chanting grew louder and the cows in the field munched on, oblivious to the din.

'Come on out, you dirty orphans.' The group of boys was close now. 'Leave it until we get to school. We'll get 'em then,' one of the boys boasted and, satisfied to wait, the group passed by.

'Sticks and stones can break your bones, but words can't harm you,' Joe actually laughed.

'Wait 'til we get to school, then we'll see whose bones are going to be broken.' I clenched and unclenched my fists.

'Don't be so daft. We couldn't take that lot on, even if we were Tarzan. There's other ways round things. Leave it to old Joe.' He touched his nose with his forefinger.

'We've got a horrible disease,' Joe cautioned the group that confronted us later that morning in the playground. 'If you get too near us, your tongue'll go black and your eyes pop out of their sockets. The next thing you know, your balls will have dropped off and you'll be sicking up every last part of your guts. If you don't believe me, go to the orphanage. There are eyes and balls and guts all over the floor. It's the most horrible sight you've set your eyes on.' Joe pulled a grotesque face and the boys' eyes widened. Looking from one to the other, they waited for the first one to make a move.

'If you don't clear off, we'll spit on you, then you'll die in agony. If you snitch about what's happening at the orphanage, your fingers and toes'll snap off like twigs!

Without waiting to consult with each other, the group fled.

'I told you to leave it to me.' Joe rubbed his hands together as if he had sent each of them packing with a punch on the nose.

'Now no-one'll talk to us. Not that I care,' I added.

'Neither do I, so there you are. We've got each other. Anyway, *you* won't be here much longer. Your Mum'll be collecting you before you can say "balls"'.

In my experience, although you pretended words didn't hurt you, they punctured your insides, and the pain never went away, not really. Yet words, when they were kind, warmed you like an oven in your belly. It was because of words, written ones, I couldn't wait to get back to the orphanage every day after school and take my letters from under the mattresses. I knew every letter by heart.

Fred was busy helping his son with his business, although he didn't say exactly what it was. Something to do with tractors, I thought. Lori helped Fred's son's wife with their new baby, but she didn't mention going shopping, or to the library, or having afternoon tea with friends like she did in Blountmere Street. Instead, she asked strange questions like the price of lamb, was I enjoying the winter and how many times we'd had Spam lately.

Mum's letter wasn't very long and consisted mainly of news that Angela was in an orphanage in the country, like mine, and that she seemed happy with her new friends. Quite a few times, she told me to be a good boy and seven times – I know because I counted them every day – she told me she loved and missed me, and that it wouldn't be long before we'd all be back home together in Blountmere Street.

I even read Miss Selska's letter every day, although it was full of advice on using camphorated oil and eating my vegetables.

My letters filled my mind all day at school, even when Miss Magdalen told the class, looking directly at me and Joe, that there were some children who would never amount to anything.

Every afternoon I tried to get in touch with Paula. It brought a sort of relief being able to pour out the day's happenings, even if I did feel as if I was talking to myself. Even though I concentrated really hard and wriggled around and squirmed, I couldn't pick up anything from her. But my letters – well – they were real, not airy-fairy. My letters told me that people were thinking about me. Mum wasn't going to let me rot in this place. Soon she was going to come and take me home to be with her and Ang.

'What're you doing?' Joe lurched into the room in his usual door-swinging fashion.

'Nothing much, just reading my letters.' I stuffed them into their envelopes and back under the mattresses.

'It's a wonder you haven't read the words off the pages,' Joe said, at the same time seeming to be having difficulty getting something out of his pocket. 'Here, I got this for you, seeing as how they won't let us have the light on at night.' At last he loosened a small torch from his trouser pocket.

'How did you get hold of it?'

'Ask no questions, and you'll hear no lies.'

'You nicked it!'

'As if I'd do a thing like that? I knew Joe was pretending to look shocked.

'Where am I going to keep it? If I put it underneath my pillow they'll find it, and I can't put it under the mattress.'

'I've already got the place. They don't call me Einstein for nothing.' Joe walked across to the window. 'I was having a decko yesterday and behind the curtain, I found a hole. I think that torch will fit it nicely.'

I had never thought to probe behind the curtains. They were covered with tired yellow flowers and dull brown leaves that extended well beyond the window on either side.

'I reckon they must have been going to put a socket in or something. Anyway, it's big enough to squeeze your letters into it as well.'

I pushed the batteries into the torch, tested it to see that it worked, then wedged it into the cubby hole. Brick dust floated to the floor. Joe knelt and rubbed it into the carpet with the sleeve of his jersey.

'I'll put my letters in later.' How could I tell Joe the hole in the wall was too far away to be from my letters?

'Hurry up will you, or we'll be put away in that halfway house they're sending 'em to. I've heard Charlie Butcher and Bruce Levene are off there tomorrow.'

It reminded me of my nightmare and I looked towards the curtain for reassurance.

'Thanks, Joe.'

'What for?'

'The torch and that.'

'Now don't go getting soft,' he said.

Miss Magdalen entered the classroom looking even more sombre than usual. She stood in front of her table, paused, then cleared her throat. 'This is a very sad day for us all.' She paused again, as if not knowing how to bring us the news. 'We have just heard that our dear King George the Sixth has tragically passed away.' She hesitated, then in a loud voice announced, 'God Save The Queen.'

Matron declared the next day one of mourning "for our dear departed Majesty", which meant total silence at breakfast and when we returned from school. A black-framed banner appeared in the hall from which a picture of the late King looked down on us, as if it had been placed there in case we dared utter a sound. The whole orphanage was ordered to attend church to pray for our new Queen.

'Church is bad enough on Sundays, let alone in the week,' Joe lisped out of the side of his mouth, even though we were still alone in our room. Matron could hear and see things that normal people couldn't.

That afternoon I thought I heard Paula speaking to me. It was a vague impression. She was talking about the King. I could visualize the sadness in her face, the expression in her eyes. Or was it because I knew that was what she would have been talking about? Just the same, in my head I responded, telling her about the banner, going to church in the week, even about matron wearing a black ribbon tied around her head with a bow in the front.

'You're a dirty, disgusting boy!' Matron was making one of her surprise morning inspections. She didn't make them often. We never knew when she would appear in our room at seven in the morning, and order us to take the sheets and blankets from our beds. Matron's face was close to Joe's. 'What boy of your age wets the bed! Get here.' She grasped the top of Joe's pyjamas and yanked him towards her. I watched as she ordered him to take the wet sheet off his bed. I knew what was coming, what always happened when a bed wetter was discovered.

'You know what to do, Joseph.'

'But Miss, it's horrible.'

'It is entirely of your own making. Now put the sheet over your head! Right over!' With the sheet covering Joe like a shroud, matron propelled him through the door and on to the landing, calling, 'Come here children. Witness a dirty bed-wetter.' Joe stumbled up the corridor, the wet patch sticking to his face, outlining the shape of his nose, his lips pressed together so that they looked like one. At the doors of their rooms, the other boys called out, 'Wet the bed! Wet the bed!' as they were expected to.

Although we never mentioned it, I knew Joe often peed himself at night, but he had always managed to get the bed made in time, and it remained a secret. When Monica came to change the sheets, she took no notice of the urine stench and stains, she just stuffed the sheets into a large laundry bag. Now Joe had been caught, and there was nothing I could do, only refuse to go to the door and join in.

'Get out here immediately, Tony Addington,' Matron ordered.

'No I won't. I'm not going to watch my mate have the mickey taken out of him. It isn't his fault: he can't help it.'

'Are you daring to answer me back?' Matron marched towards me, caught hold of my ear and dragged me behind her. 'You'll stand there until I tell you to move! Come here and help me take the mattress off this dirty boy's bed,' she called to Monica, who, well used to the rigmarole, was sweeping the stairs, appearing not to take any notice.

With a lot of puffing from matron, she and Monica hauled Joe's mattress clear of the bed. As they did so, Miss Selska's letter fell on to a blanket.

'Joseph Fisher, get here immediately!' Matron had forgotten the bed-wetting incident in the light of a greater crime. Joe fumbled with the sheet and, forgetting matron's warning not to move, I fled to help him free himself

'What is this?' Matron poked the envelope into Joe's face.

'It's a letter, Miss.'

'I can see it's a letter.' She began taking the pages from the envelope and reading them. 'This appears to be yours.' She rounded on me. 'It is yours, isn't it?'

I remained silent.

'How did you get it?'

I clamped my lips together.

'If you won't tell me, there is only one thing to be done.' Deliberately she tore the letter into strips, then the strips into pieces and stuffed them into her pocket.

'I will be calling for both of you in my office later.' She began to leave, then stopped. 'Monica, before you go, perhaps you'll help me with the other two mattresses and Tony's as well. Boys like this can't be trusted.'

My mattress was the last to be taken from the bed. All the time Matron and Monica were turning the other two, I wondered how I could retrieve the letters under mine. I knew I had pushed them well into the middle. Perhaps we could divert matron's attention. I looked at Joe for help, but he was still recovering from being laughed at by the other boys. He shrugged his shoulders in a hopeless sort of way.

When matron and Monica took my mattress from my bed, matron immediately snatched the envelopes.

'Please don't tear them up,' I pleaded. 'I'll do anything, anything, just don't get rid of my letters. You can keep them in your office. I swear on God's honour, I'll never read them again.' I turned to Monica, 'Please don't let her do it.' As if she hadn't heard me, however, and without opening the envelopes, matron simply tore Mum's and Fred and Lori's letters into the same strips and pieces as she had Miss Selska's. She shoved them into her pocket. Then she swept out of our room, saying, 'I'll be calling for you both in my office.'

'I'm sorry, so sorry,' Monica was weeping as she placed her arm round my shoulder. 'She's an old cow to do that.'

I shrugged her hand off me. My letters had been taken. Nothing was left, except a square that had fluttered from Matron's bunched hand and concealed itself in the bedclothes strewn across the floor. On it were the words, "Love Mum".

After Monica had gone, I skirted the mound of covers to the window, where I pulled back the curtain and inserted the square of paper next to my torch. No one would ever take it from me, no one, ever. I would kill them if they tried.

'They're sending me to that half-way house,' Joe said later that day after he had been summoned to matron's office. There was still a lingering smell of urine about him. 'They're sending me somewhere abroad. They said I was a-good-for-nothing and lucky to have the chance of a fresh start.' He cuffed tears across his face. All at once I knew how much I would miss him.

'I wish you were coming with me.' He suddenly seemed very small and frightened, but my sadness for Joe was mingled with relief that I wouldn't be in this horrible place much longer. Anyway, Joe was going to have an adventure. I was sure he would enjoy that.

It was a couple of weeks before matron ordered me to her office. Every day I had been expecting to have to confront her and explain the letters, but when I passed her she ignored me.

One afternoon after school, when the wind was blowing so hard every window in the place rattled and everyone seemed restless, Monica came running to our room, puffing, 'Matron wants to see you in her office. She's got some high-up bloke with her, too.' She began brushing me down with her hand, then trying to flatten my hair. 'You'd better make yourself presentable. Rub a flannel over your face. It's black. If you ask me, it's something important.'

Monica insisted on taking me to Matron's office, even though I knew the way perfectly well. She babbled on and on as we walked down the stairs and along the narrow corridor, but I wasn't listening. At last Mum was better and the man had come to take me back to her.

'Come on in,' matron invited me into her office. Her desk was swept clear of everything except a vase of daffodils. She wasn't scowling as I expected her to be, and my hopes rose.

'This is Mr Grasley,' matron indicated the man standing by the window. He walked towards me and put out his hand. His fingers were bony like a skeleton's.

'I'm afraid we've got some rather bad news.' Matron screwed her face into a funny shape. It couldn't be anything bad. Mum was better. I was going home. The man coughed, swallowed and coughed again. 'Anthony Malcolm Addington?' He enquired, and without waiting for a reply, continued, 'I have to inform you that your mother has passed away and you are being conscripted on to the Government's Child Migration Scheme with your destination, New Zealand.'

There was no explanation or words of sympathy.

I wondered how Mum died and what would happen to Angela. Did the Old Man know or even care, but I was dismissed before I could even form the questions.

PART TWO

Chapter Twelve

New Zealand 1953

The wind was whipping the sea into a frenzy when we docked at Wellington. It caused the ship to be tossed about as if it was made of balsa wood, like the ones the kids sailed on the pond Up The Common.

Joe and I were part of a string of orphan boys who clutched on to the rope of the gang plank, as we tottered from the ship and on to the quayside. We clasped our empty cases, and studied our strange surroundings, while the wind slapped at our bare legs and penetrated our jackets.

'I thought you said it never gets cold here.' Despite the chill, Joe stuffed the cap we were ordered to wear on disembarkation into his pocket. 'It makes me look like Little Lord Fauntleroy,' he complained.

I hardly heard him as I scanned the waterfront, then up to the bush-clad hills, dotted with wooden bungalows painted different colours like lumps of marshmallow. Even though it was cloudy, the light was bright and I shielded my eyes with my hand. Perhaps Fred and Lori lived in one of the marshmallows and were hurrying down one of the steep streets to meet us.

When I had been in England, a woman from the transit orphanage, wearing gold rimmed spectacles hung round her neck on a chain, had written down Fred and Lori's names.   She had thanked me and smiled.   Smiling was something people who worked in orphanages never did.   I returned her smile, seeing myself racing down the gangplank into Fred and Lori's arms.   On board, it made the cramped conditions and seasickness bearable.   At night it helped me not to cry.

'I thought you said your precious friends would be waiting for you.'   Micky Bricks jeered, waving his arm around at the emptiness.

'They'll be here,' I replied.

Some men in shirts, their sleeves rolled up and wearing caps like the one Old Dibble wore, herded us across the wharf into a long wooden building.   We were still not used to being on firm ground, and we staggered and tripped. Inside, people were bunched around the edges of a long room.   They stared at us I heard someone say, "You'd think they'd be different coming from the Homeland."

My gaze travelled from person to person as I searched the knots of people for Fred and Lori.

'Can yer see 'em?'   Joe enquired as we were manhandled into a row.

'Give us a mo.'   I found a chair, stood on it and continued looking round the room.

'Get down immediately,' ordered a man in red plaid shorts and long socks.

'Well?' Joe asked.

'They're a bit late, that's all.'

When we were in position, an official-looking man with hair parted down the middle, told us we would have opportunities in New Zealand we'd never dreamt of.

Outside the wind howled. Inside it was damp and drab. He droned on. One of the boys wet himself. It made a hissing sound on the floor.

The man used strange words like, 'New Zealand pride", while the people nodded, and I stood there not knowing what was going on.

At last the man finished and another man stepped forward. He was from what sounded like "The Agency". He spoke with the same strange accent, and said things like gidday and nemes instead of names. He said that some of the children would be placed temporarily in orphanages, until they found all of us foster homes, although some of the boys had foster parents waiting to take them immediately. At least, I think that's what he said.

All the time the speeches were going on, my eyes never stopped sweeping the room for Fred and Lori.

The next thing I heard, the Man from the Agency was saying we were very lucky and privileged children. Our lives would be so much better than the ones we'd left behind. We'd actually eat lamb and drink plenty of milk. Then he pulled a piece of paper from his briefcase and began reading names from it.

'Perhaps your Fred and Lori can't get here, and they'll put us in a home while we wait. We mustn't let them split us up.' Joe moved closer. He clung to the hem of my jacket, while kids started walking towards uplifted hands. It left Joe and me exposed and conspicuous. Someone slipped in the urine and cursed.

'Mr Eleod Downston?' We were led to a man who had two distinct lines across his face: his eyebrows thick and joining like a black hedge and his lips thin and straight that stretched from one weather-beaten cheek to the other.

'This is Anthony Addington and Joseph Fisher,' the man said.

Joe's grip tightened on my jacket, pulling it off my shoulders. 'Is that the name of your Fred and Lori?' He whispered.

I shrugged myself free of his grip and brushed my sleeve across my eyes, spreading the moisture towards my temples. I didn't answer. They'd given me to someone else. Fred and Lori didn't want me.

'I asked for girls,' Eleod Downston complained. 'The missus needs 'em to help her around the place.'

'I'm afraid there aren't any girls on this shipment.' The Man from the Agency might as well have been talking about sacks of sugar or flour. 'I'll definitely put you down for a couple. Any preferences?'

'Young.'

'Young?'

'The Missus likes 'em young, so she can train 'em.'

'Quite, quite, and may I say how generous it is of you and Mrs Downston to offer a home to these deprived children.'

The Man glided away, avoiding the urine.

Eleod Downston hawked phlegm into a piece of rag. He looked us up and down and measured the circumference of our upper arms with his circled fingers. 'A couple of scrawny bastards they've given me,' he sneered.

'I'm Joe and this 'ere's Tony.' Joe began. His voice sounded funny.

'When I want to know your names, I'll ask for 'em. Until then, keep your mouths shut.' Downston grabbed hold of my chin and forced my face up. My teeth locked together.

'Get your eyes up, boy,' he ordered. 'Never could stand whingers. Well, pick up your stuff. What d'yer want – a housemaid to do it for yer? We breed 'em tough here, so you can forget yer fancy mummy's boys' ways.' He strode towards the door. We followed, while The Man from the Agency called after him, 'Hooray, Mr Downston. We'll be at your place to go over the paperwork and check everything's all right. Give us time. You're a fair ways out in the wap-waps.'

'And don't forget the girls. Young 'uns.'

'Good as gold.'

We exchanged one ship for another, this time sailing from the North Island to the South Island.

'What a carry on, but pretty, though,' Joe said as we sailed through a channel, flanked on either side by inlets and islands smothered with vegetation. I ignored him. I imagined natives like the one in my nightmare darting from the forest all around. I stood outside on the deck and clutched on to a pole, trying to put another layer of concrete over my heart. I pretended not to care about natives, or Fred and Lori not wanting me, or this godforsaken place, or Eleod Downston below deck drinking.

The harbour we sailed into was quiet, with a street of shops and a few houses, the same as the ones in Wellington. Beyond were more and yet more hills.

On a strip of grass by the waterfront, a group of kids played games that didn't look much different from the ones we'd played in Blountmere Street.

We left the ship and Eleod Downston lurched along the jetty. Although he was slower than Joe and me, he shouted, 'Get a move on! You're not in bloody London now.' Heaving for breath, he caught up with us and, for no reason, slapped the side of my face with the flat of his hand. He said something, but I couldn't hear beyond the ringing in my ear. I held my hand to it to ease the stinging.

A truck was parked on the quayside.

'Well, jump in,' Downston slurred. He seemed to expect us to know the truck was his. We struggled into the back and immediately slid on animal dung. The stench was so strong it hurt my nostrils, then hit the back of my throat. It made me want to gag.

'Blimey, what a pong,' Joe said, holding his nose between two fingers.

Although we couldn't see through to the cab of the truck, we heard Downston slam the door, turn on the engine and grind the gears.

'Where d'you reckon we're going?' Joe asked as Downston revved the motor and began throwing the truck round endless corners. It caused us and our cases to slither from side to side and become coated with animal doings.

The only light came from two small windows at the back of the truck and I slid to the end, wiped a patch in one of the windows with my sleeve and squinted out.

'I can't see much out there,' I said.

'I hope it's not far. I'm so hungry, my guts are rumbling.' Joe's voice vibrated, as the truck shook and swayed along gravel tracks and the engine made a graunching noise as we began to climb.

I continued to wipe condensation from the window and looked out at the landscape. Outside, there was nothing but a mat of trees. I wondered how long it would be before we were out of this forest and we would see a house or someone walking along. But the trees stretched on and on. Joe crawled further up the truck and huddled next to me, as our stomachs became emptier.

'You frightened?' Joe asked.

'Course I'm not.' I hoped he couldn't hear the fear in my voice.

Snippets of light began to appear and the sky became wider. Down below, a river wound its way through a haphazard band of shingle, and mountains rose behind it like monsters with pointed heads. I shivered at the emptiness – nothing but trees; not tall like the ones in Bushey Park, but smaller, a bit like the ones in the spinney Up The Common. It was as if the mountains refused to allow them to compete. The river in its shingle case appeared and disappeared, playing a game of hide and seek, but the mountains stayed there all the time, keeping guard.

'It's like *Journey Into Space*,' Joe yelled, as the road curled round and round, up and down, through the undergrowth, finding and losing the river, all the time watched over by the pointed-headed monsters.

Unexpectedly, the sea appeared and we travelled alongside it for a few miles. We watched the waves break on the rocks. It left them ringed with foam like soap suds.

Then we turned inland and away from it. Still there were no houses or people.

After we'd travelled for what seemed hours and the daylight had become purple before it finally disappeared, Downston took a sudden turn, causing the truck's tyres to spin, and the truck to tip as if it was going to topple over.

'Blimey, he's trying to kill us.' Joe fell across my legs. We slithered in circles, and clutched each other for support.

No sooner had the truck righted itself, than it lurched in and out what felt like a series of potholes. My stomach rose and fell.

Eventually, the truck skidded to a squealing halt. We heard the door open and Downston jump from the cab. He flung open the back doors on to blackness. 'Don't just sit there. Shift yourselves.' He commanded, leaving us to scramble from the truck.

'I said, move your backsides,' Downston struck us both a blow across the back of our heads.

Our cases, like us, were caked with dung, as we stumbled after Downston towards the outline of a broken-down wooden building.

Downston opened the door, and punched us through the opening. Inside, two men were playing cards by the light of a kerosene lamp. Sacking was nailed at the windows, and the place smelt of food, sweat and farting.

'A couple of hands for you. Useless by the looks of 'em. You'll 'ave to thrash 'em to get anything out of 'em. But, then, a couple of nice little boys might suit the two of you.' Downston's eyes glazed over and his mouth slackened.

'Beggar me, Boss ...' The older of the two men began, but Downston was already striding through the door. The hinges groaned. It was a frightening sound.

'Beggar me,' the man repeated. Tufts of hair sprouted in clumps from midway across his head and down his neck. He was wearing a tattered singlet from which more straggly hair protruded. 'What's the Boss thinking of? What do we know about kids?'

'Perhaps we should start by telling them our names and finding out theirs?' The younger of the two men got up from the table. He walked towards us. He had an Irish accent and was taller than the older man. 'This here's Murray, and he's the shepherd at Downstons Farm. I'm Fergus, a rouseabout, a bit like yourselves.'

'Tony and Joe,' I mumbled. I wondered what a rouseabout was.

'Well, me boys, it seems you're going to be sharing the men's quarters with us. You'll have to use the bed we keep for the swagmen. Stinks a bit, but then the two of you don't smell too sweet,' Fergus said. 'Old Candlewax, the last swagman to use it wasn't too clean in his habits, but you can sleep one at each end until we can knock together a couple of bunks, and get some more sacking to cover them. To be sure, it seems you're going to be here a whiles.'

Chapter Thirteen

A bellbird called into the morning hush of the men's quarters, as I turned on my wafer-thin mattress and wiped the window beside me. Outside, the first light of day was splintering the sky and smudging the mountains purple. Even now, the New Zealand landscape seemed alien, with its folds of hills rolling towards the mountains. In winter, they were crowned with snow. In summer, they faded to a hazy mauve. In the distance the river snaked through a steep gorge which was edged by tangled bush. From there, it forged its way onwards into nothingness.

I prodded Joe awake. 'Come on. You know what Downston's like if we're late up.' I kept poking Joe until he stirred, and his head appeared from beneath his sacking bedcovers.

'All right, all right, I ain't dead.' In spite of being warned by Downston that he'd beat his Pommie accent out of him, Joe remained defiant. 'I've spoke like this all me life and I ain't talking different for him nor nobody.'

Like Joe, I wanted to cling to every bit of my Englishness. It would be all too easy in this place on the edge of the earth to forget where I came from. At Fergus's suggestion, Joe and I wrote our birthdays and the year we were both born on the margin of a piece of newspaper. We tore off the strip we had written on, and hid it in our cases, for fear we might miss a year in this land of topsy-turvy seasons.

I pulled on my shorts, and made my way outside to the pump, leaving Joe to huff and puff his way out of bed. I filled a tin bowl, and dunked my face into it. I shook off the water, then plucked a frayed piece of cloth from its usual place on a nearby bush. I rubbed it over my top half, which was weathered the colour of the logs I had recently been splitting. Months of working on the land had hardened my body and although, as Joe said, I was still as thin as a whippet – the Missus' tucker saw to that – I had grown upwards like a tree starved of light. My shirt which had been given to me less than a month ago now finished above my midriff, while my shorts crept higher up my legs, and cut into my groin.

Murray and Fergus brought our clothes back from the Catholic Mission when they were in the township collecting supplies. They probably chose them after a skinful at *The Travellers*. What would two men like Murray and Fergus know about the clothes boys wore? They had once brought me back a girl's pink blouse, patterned with milkmaids! 'The nuns at the Mission said it would do just as well for a boy as a girl,' Murray tried to persuade me, but Downston had laughed himself silly, snorting, 'Can't tell if you're Arthur or Martha. A proper poofter you're turning out to be.'

The only thing I hated more than that blouse was not having underpants. Not wearing underpants was shameful. When things had been at their worst, Mum had seen to it we had underwear. "Well mended, but respectable," she'd said.

If clothes were a problem, shoes were equally so. The work boots sent by the Mission were either too big or too small. They caused blisters on my feet that burst and stung. At night they rubbed on the sacking covering me. They kept me awake, and made me wish I was more like Joe, who hadn't grown much since we'd arrived. His shoes were at least comfortable, even if they were almost in pieces.

I hung my wash rag back over the bush, and ran my fingers through my matted hair in an effort to subdue my curls. There was no mirror in the men's quarters. Once, as I waited outside the homestead to collect the nightly boil-up, I noticed the Missus had left the kitchen. I could see a mirror, and I slipped through the door and sidled along the wall. The mirror was spotted with fly dirt and chipped around the edges, but I was able to see myself well enough. My face had changed as if it had become more permanent. I ran my fingers over my nose, then along my lips, up my cheek and to my eyebrow. I doubted anyone in Blountmere Street would recognise me. The thought of appearing a stranger to them was unbearable. Although I'd had the opportunity a few times since, I'd never looked in that mirror again.

I pulled my shirt over my head, and struggled to button up my shorts. Beyond the men's quarters, Fergus was on his way across the paddock to milk the house cow. I waved and in answer Fergus called out his usual morning greeting, 'To be sure, today's a clean slate.'

I had no idea how an educated man like Fergus came to be working on a back country farm in New Zealand for someone like Eleod Downston. He belonged in a nice house in Ireland with a nice lady who kissed him goodbye every morning. He needed to be nearer a library, like the one Fred and Lori used to belong to. And he needed to have someone other than me listen to him when he recited poetry. But when Fergus and Murray went to the township for supplies, Fergus always arrived back paralytic. Downston banned liquor from the men's quarters, saying he'd got no time for a man who couldn't hold his drink. He could talk! Often in the far off distance of the homestead when I went to the long drop at night, I saw Downston himself staggering around the place, drunk. I finished my business as fast as I could, and raced back to my bed in the corner of the men's quarters, well away from him. He was even swifter with his fists than the Old Man had been when he was drunk.

Murray and Fergus said that Downston was partial to young girls and that he was in and out of the scullery maid's bed so often, he was wearing a hole in her mattress. They said that all the time there was a young girl about, Joe and me would be all right on that count, even if we were seldom free of a black eye or bruises from Downston's boot or rock-hard knuckles. Although Joe just shrugged and recited that stuff about "sticks and stones", it made me seethe with anger and swear that one day I'd get even with him.

I made my way across the scrub to the pigsty, where the squealing and grunting of pigs shattered the serenity of early morning. It was one of my easier jobs. It allowed my thoughts to transport me back to Blountmere Street; at least to a Blountmere Street that had once been, before Fred and Lori left, and Dobsie and Mum died. It was the one freedom I had; a secret to be savoured, a place nobody knew I went to, or could stop me visiting. It was exquisitely sweet and unbearably painful. Yet, every morning in my head, I visited my old home – my only home. To Mum smelling of coal tar soap, sitting in her chair staring at something or somewhere only she could see, as I was doing now. I imagined the Gang, as it had once been with Dobsie, squatting on our stones at the camp on the bombsite.

My thoughts roamed to Paula, who stepped out of her front door on her way to school, with her satchel hanging across her chest, while Mrs Dibble brushed a speck from her daughter's pleated skirt, and checked she had a clean hankie. Behind them, Old Dibble loaded ladders on to his motorcycle cart. Then into my mind came Lori, calling something about the weather from her front door and looking up at the window to wave to Fred, who, as usual, was immaculate as if he hadn't been to bed to get creased and crumpled like everyone else.

I wondered whether Angela was still in her orphanage or whether, like me, she had been put on a ship and sent somewhere. I wished with all my heart I had been nicer to her. I imagined myself catching in my hands every unkind word I'd ever said to her, and throwing them far, far away, so that they couldn't touch and hurt her anymore.

I remembered the softness of Paula's cheek when she had kissed me at the orphanage, and told me she loved me. What school would she be at now? It was probably one where she wore a posh straw hat and a fancy blazer. If I was back in Blountmere Street, I would be at Grigham Road Secondary Modern, a dump. It would still be better than getting no tuition at all other than what Fergus gave me at night by the light of the oil lamp, or outside on the ridge when it was light enough.

I carted buckets of swill backwards and forward, used to their heaviness and the rank odour, like the pig bins in Jack Moody's yard.

In the distance, Joe was dragging his mattress outside to air. It made the place stink like a piss house, Fergus and Murray complained. They threatened Joe he had better get it outside or he'd be sleeping under a tree where he could pee to his heart's content.

The "piss house" was a long drop, a few yards away from the men's quarters, and was enclosed by a wooden structure with gaps that the south-westerly whistled and sliced between, and through which you could see and be seen. Murray said that by rights we should put lime into the pit, but the Boss was too mean to buy it. When it was full, Joe and I had to cover it over, and dig another, while once a week we cut newspaper into precise squares, which Murray skewered onto a hook hanging on the back of the door. "Better than all that fancy stuff," he asserted, and scratched his backside as if he could already feel it. "So what if it does leave newsprint on yer arse. Who's goin' to look at yer arse?"

I finished filling the troughs and began hosing down the sty, before making my way back to the men's quarters.

Inside, Murray was standing over a potbellied stove stirring the morning mutton in the blackened pot Joe had just collected from the homestead. This morning the Missus must have been feeling generous, because she'd sent us over a bit of bread with it. Murray took four tin bowls from a shelf and placed them on the rough wooden table. After he'd brought the boil up to the table, he gave it another stir to dissolve the soft white paste that had already begun to form a fatty cap on the top. Then he returned to the stove, which stood in the corner like some fat and kind protector, took off the lid, and stuffed more wood inside. The flames shot up. Immediately, the hut was caressed with warmth.

'Worth its weight in gold, this stove.' Murray said the same thing at least five times a day.

'To be sure 'tis a blessing from the saints themselves,' Fergus replied, coming through the door. He stamped his feet. It disturbed the cobwebs and caused the calendars around the walls to flutter. The calendars dated back at least ten years.

Murray took another pot full of water and put it on top of the stove ready for a mug of tea that would be the colour of mahogany, or later to wash away the grime of the day.

'Tucker's up,' he said, as if it was some kind of banquet we were being invited to. 'Worse where there's none.'

I sat down carefully on my chair. It was creaky and I was sure one day it would refuse to hold my weight and I'd break a bone or something.

'To be sure, the Missus must have climbed the spire of St. Patrick's to throw in the mutton. There's so little of it. By all the saints, why doesn't she toss the whole thing away and start afresh,' Fergus complained.

Joe grimaced, and said it shouldn't be used as pig swill. But, like me, he devoured it. We were too hungry to be fussy.

Sometimes the Missus, her hair scraped back, her overall pulled flat over her chest, brought the boil-up over herself. Her ball-bearing eyes constantly darted round the hut, before she left without uttering a word although Murray always said, 'Hooray, Missus.' And afterwards, Fergus said.

'To be sure, tis because she wants a few minutes respite, poor soul.'

I didn't think she was a poor soul. I hated her expressionless face and her shuffling way of walking. Being married to Downston meant she was as evil as he was.

As usual, the following Sunday, a larger cauldron which took all day to heat gurgled on top of the stove ready for our baths.

It was the week Murray washed his hair and his work clothes in the bath water. He did it monthly, using a small piece of Ma Downston's soap. It gave little lather and smelt like the fat on top of the boil up. All four of us shared a few inches of water, and we bathed in order of seniority, Murray first.

'I swear this water puts more dirt on to you than it takes off. Can't you wash your clothes in the tub outside like the rest of us?' Fergus grumbled to Murray.

'There's no hot water outside. Anyways, there's nothing wrong with this bath water. It's full of good, clean dirt,' Murray replied.

'And what sort of answer is that?' Bath-times were the only occasions when Murray and Fergus argued.

When Murray had wrung out his clothes, he finished washing himself. Then Fergus stripped himself of his trousers and shirt, shuddered and lowered himself into the water, while I turned my gaze away from his shriveled willie, and Murray hacked at the hair growing in his armpits. He let tufts of it drop to the floor to join months of dirt. On the weeks he didn't wash his clothes he mended them, grasping the needle with work-thickened fingers.

'After I've done this, I'll have a go at your hair, Ginger. It looks as if it could do with a hack,' Murray observed.

'D'you 'ave to? Those scissors are as blunt as a butcher's chopping board. I end up looking a right sight. It's more a scalping than a hack.'

'Better that than the Boss plaster your hair with sheep shit, like he did the last time you let it grow too long.'

'I s'ppose so.'

'Good as gold. I'll do it after Fergus has finished his toe nails.

Because I was older than Joe, I was the next one in the bath. Even so, the water was lukewarm and smelt of sheep dung. I thought of Paula and her flowery smell, even Mum and her coal tar soap.

'Be sure, not to forget yer lugholes,' Fergus said as he snipped at his toenails. I took no notice. I didn't need anyone to tell me how to keep myself clean, which was more than you could say for Joe.

'I hate the scum on top when I'm the blinkin' last in the bath,' Joe moaned when it was his turn. 'I'm not that dirty. I don't need it.' He continued to make an assortment of excuses not to get into the water.

'Right, Ginger, that's it.' Murray laid down the scissors and walked towards Joe. He began dragging him towards the bath. 'If you won't get in yourself, you'll have to be helped.'

'Pack it in,' Joe shouted, but he was laughing as he yelled. It was the same every week. I had my suspicions that Joe's reluctance to bathe had little to do with the scummy water. It had more to do with the attention of being chased and caught by Murray, and the camaraderie they shared.

As I rubbed myself dry with another piece of rag and hurried to get my clothes on I wondered how Joe could have settled into this place in the far reaches of the earth so quickly.

When we all finished bathing, Joe and I carried the bath outside. We emptied the water over the piece of scrub surrounding our quarters.

'This bit of land's wasted, you know,' Joe said, bending to pick a piece of coarse grass. 'I could make it into a vegie patch if they'd let me.'

'If they let you do what?' Murray asked walking to the rope clothes line strung between two stunted trees and pegging his recently washed clothes on to it.

'Let me have this bit of land for a garden.'

'Beggar me, boy, but it'd be hard work digging this lot over.'

'I could do it and make things grow, I know I could. And we could put the vegies into the boil-up.'

'I don't know what the Boss would say.'

'We wouldn't have to say anything, would we?'

Murray squeezed the last of the bath water from a trouser leg. 'Well, Ginger, if you want to have a go, where's the harm in it? I'll buy you some seeds and get you a couple of books on gardening from the library when we go to the township.'

'Will you really? You're a real … a real pal.'   At that moment I knew Joe felt the same way about Murray as I had about Fred.

Murray revved the engine of the truck, while Fergus jumped in beside him on their way to the township. Exhaust smoke plumed into the crisp winter air. 'Watch over things while we're away. Anyroad, the Boss doesn't want you leaving this place. Says you'll be safer here.'

'Don't want us to squeal on him's more the truth,' Joe scowled.

'We'll see you both when we get back.'

When Murray and Fergus returned, they were too drunk to see anything. Joe and I lifted each of them from the truck, carried them into the hut, and dumped them on their bunks.

'How did Murray manage to drive in the state he's in? The truck must have made its own way back. It's a wonder the two of them didn't kill themselves,' Joe exclaimed.

I shrugged. We'd be lucky if we got the books and the shirts they were going to bring us back. We'd be saddled with tight shirts and no books until the next time they went to the township. Another promise broken. Fergus had given me his word he would bring some poetry books back. I loved reading poetry with Fergus. The Gang would never have spoken to me again if I'd ever shown an inkling for the stuff. I had sniggered with the rest of them, when Mrs Colby made us take *The Red Book of Verse* from our desks. I couldn't remember much of it, just odd lines like *Water, water everywhere, nor any drop to drink.* I hadn't known where it came from or who had written it.

Reading poetry with Fergus was different. He didn't recite poetry like Daphne Johns used to in a smug, singsong voice. Fergus spoke the words on a soft breath, tasting them, causing me to tingle and shiver, even when I didn't understand them.

I often recited verses while I was working, keeping rhythm with what I was doing. *By the shores of Gitche Gume.* Swish! *By the shining Big Sea Water.* Thwack! Some of the poetry was so tender, I hid it inside me to treasure silently.

Even though Fergus often let me down, the next time he and Murray went to the township, I pressed an envelope into his hand. I asked him to post it for me. 'It's to England. I'll pay you for the stamp as soon as I can,' I said. It was a rash promise, when Downston never paid us a cent.

'To be sure, there's no need to worry about the money, lad. To someone special is it?'

'Paula, the girl who lived downstairs to us in London,' I replied, not wanting to divulge any more.

'Right you are, young Tony.' He struggled to lift himself from the seat and stuff the envelope into his back pocket. 'Consider it done.'

Another summer had come without there seeming to be much of a gap between this and the last one. The heat that had hovered over the paddocks all day was beginning to dissipate. Outside our quarters, Joe's garden was flourishing, helped no doubt by the frequent handfuls of fertilizer he pilfered from Downston which he scooped into his hat and smuggled back. As he usually did on hot summer evenings, he cajoled us into helping him water his garden, threatening, 'If you want to eat the stuff, you've all got to do your bit.'

When we finished, we forsook the stove for the ridge outside, while the sun hid itself behind the mountains and the mantle of night draped itself across the sky.

Murray, mellowed by the softness of a dwindling day, recalled his childhood on the West Coast, saying, 'Beggar me, if they weren't golden days', and Fergus sang, *When Irish Eyes Are Smiling,* as if the "eyes" belonged to someone he once knew. It reminded me of Mrs Dibble singing the same song when she was peeling potatoes at her sink. It made me want to cry, and I tightened the muscles in my face so that no one could tell.

With the speed that days in the southern hemisphere lose their colour, darkness overcame the macrocarpa trees in what seemed no more than a dozen blinks. It turned the homestead to a ghostly outline, and transformed the road leading to and from the farm into a thin moon-illuminated ribbon. I once imagined Fred and Lori coming down that road to collect me. I had kindled such dreams of life in New Zealand. The pain of leaving England, and of Mum dying, had been blunted by my anticipation that I would live with Fred and Lori. But I had never heard from them.

I hugged my knees, and looked up at the stars. The more I concentrated on them, the closer they became, until I imagined they were near enough to throw a rope over.

'Blinkin' marvellous those stars. D'you know, I 'ardly knew there *were* stars when I lived in London.' Joe made circles with the thumb and forefinger of both hands. He peered through them as if they were a pair of binoculars.

I continued daydreaming. If I could connect the stars with the rope I could swing on it, from one to the other, on and on and on across the land and the sea until -

'When the baby Jesus was born, it must have been really hard for those shepherds knowing what star was the brightest if they all looked like this lot.'

- until I got to Blountmere Street. Then I could perch on a star and look down on them all, and watch - watch and listen. It would be better than visiting them in the pigsty every morning, far better. I might find out what had happened to Mum and Angela, because now I knew with a certainty I wasn't going to receive a reply to the letter I had written to Paula. Fergus said it took as long for a letter to get to England and one to come back, as it did to ride a bicycle to Baliclarny. But I could tell by the look on his face he was lying. I doubted my letter ever got any further than the *The Travellers*. It had probably been swept up with the sawdust on the floor and burnt.

Chapter Fourteen

Joe pushed his hat from his forehead to reveal patches of freckles, shiny with sweat. Although Joe and I both hated the job of grubbing thistles, at least we could do it together and suffer the after-pain of a thousand stings jointly.

Joe laid down his grubber. He clasped his hands around his bony knees. 'Something's up with the Boss and the Missus.' He blew his breath upwards to cool his face. 'Don't it sound odd, the Missus is going to start giving us lessons in her front parlour after all this time? Murray says they're sending their own kids to the Boss's brother's place on the West Coast to finish off their stuck up boarding school holidays, so we can do our lessons at the homestead. He says the Boss is sending him and Fergus to the township to get exercise books and things for us. Murray says …'

'Perhaps they think it's about time we had a bit of education.'

Joe gave me a scathing look. 'You've been listening to too much of that poetry Fergus reads. You're talking about Downston and the Missus as if they had hearts. She ain't said one word to us since we arrived here, neither would he if he didn't have to. All they want from us is free elbow grease, so don't go getting soft in the head.'

'I'm not going soft, and I'll soon shut the mouth of anyone who says I am.' I glared at Joe. There were times when he had too much to say.

When Fergus and Murray returned from their latest visit to the township, Murray began unpacking a box. After taking from it some seed packets and a couple of library books, he held up two pairs of short grey trousers, followed by two white shirts still in shiny packets and two black jerseys with a yellow stripe across the chest.

'They're for their snotty nose son, I suppose. I thought he'd consider himself too old for short trousers.' I pictured Paul Downston sitting astride Flinders, his horse, in his check shirt and stetson, riding round the farm like a stuck-up cowboy.

'The Boss said they were for you two to wear while you're doing your school work in the homestead.'

'Blimey! They're new ain't they?'

'Too right they're new, the whole rig out: shoes, socks, the lot. Got 'em from Old Witchery's place on sale or return. Old Witchery wasn't too happy about it.'

'Shoes and socks! The Boss must have had a brainstorm.'

'Any underpants?' I asked expectantly.

'What d'you want underpants for? They'd only be something else to wash. Anyways, as far as I can recall, they get up the crease in your bum. There's two exercise books and a couple of new fangled pens;' Murray continued.

I fanned the crisp, lined pages of one of the books. I would have preferred underpants.

'The pair of you are to report to the homestead at one every afternoon for the Missus to give you some lessons. Make sure you're not bloody late, 'cos if you are, I promise you there'll be hell to pay. And give yourselves a wash before you come. The Missus don't want you stinking out the place.' Downston concentrated on picking his nose, his finger well up his nostril.

Joe whispered, 'Blimey he pongs as if he never wipes his bum.'

'You're lucky to be given an education, so don't let it go to your heads.'

'I thought that was where it was meant to go,' I mumbled, and Downston said, 'Don't start getting mouthy with me, boy, or you and me'll fall out, and it won't be me getting the worst of it.'

Lori used to say that red was a warm and welcoming colour, but the Downstons' front parlour with its red flock wall paper, red sofa and chairs with red cushions, was neither warm nor welcoming.

'It doesn't feel as if anyone's ever been in here.' I shivered, and rubbed my arms. All at once I missed our flat in Blountmere Street.

'It's just like my Gran's place. She had this front room nobody was allowed in. 'eaven knows why she had chairs in there 'cos you weren't allowed to sit on 'em. Her place smelt of fly strip and polish, just like it does in here. It was all for show. When she wasn't around, up the pub or shopping, me and my brothers used to sneak in and bang away on her piano. Then we'd jump like chimps on her armchairs, pretending we were in a circus.' The thought prompted Joe to bound across the room and begin jumping on the sofa.

'Get off. If the Missus comes in she'll kill you.'

'Blinkin' thing's as hard as she is.'

'Get off quick.' I grabbed his arm, and yanked him to the floor. 'You know how quiet she is. We'd never hear her coming.'

Sure enough, Maggie Downston appeared to come from nowhere; warily, as if she could feel the disturbed sanctity of her parlour. She looked around for something to confirm her suspicions. Finally, her gaze rested on the two desks pushed against the wall. She indicated that we should sit on the chairs in front of them, and slid an exercise book in front of each of us. She produced a book entitled *English for Everyone*. It smelt musty and its pages were loose and brownish yellow. She turned to a chapter headed, 'Nouns and Pronouns'. 'Copy, swap,' she told me. Taking a piece of paper covered with grease patterns and a list of sums from her apron pocket, she gave it to Joe, saying, 'Add! Take away! Swap!' She pointed to the paper, to Joe and then to me.

I hadn't noticed how crooked her face was. Her skin was coarse, too. It wasn't smooth and unblemished like Mum's and Angela's. Lori said they had "English skin". "It's because we eat our greens. Not like those Australians. It's their pores," she told Angela and me.

For the next week, the Missus simply appeared in the front parlour. Without reading what we'd written, she planted a tick at the bottom of each page, saying, 'More! Quick! Quiet!'

Fortunately, the next day we were studying instead of playing noughts and crosses or drawing, as we often did when the Missus wasn't around.

When Downston barged through the parlour door, he created dust the Missus had endeavoured so mightily to keep from the place. He began by examining our exercise books before pulling back our ear lobes and peering inside our ears. 'Grow a bloody field of corn in 'em.' The flat of his hand made a dull thud as it connected with the side of Joe's face.

'As from today you'll be living at the homestead,' he announced. 'So have a bloody bath, keep your mouths shut, and only speak when you're spoken to. Understood?'

'But...'

'I said, *understood*?'

Joe nodded, but I wouldn't give Downston the satisfaction of my obedience. Instead I lifted an eyebrow in as slight a way as I could.

'On Wednesday there's someone coming from the Department of something or the other, so you'll be able to tell him you're having lessons. You're to say you're well fed, and lucky to be living here with the Missus and me.'

'But we've only ... '

'Remember what I said? Only speak when you're spoken to! When you're asked questions, you're to say, *yes* or *no*, nothing else. Leave me to do the talking.' Downston's eyebrow and lip lines threatened to merge. 'And if either of you pisses the bed I'll cut your dicks off.' He strode from the room, causing the cut glass bowl on the piano to wobble and a company of dust motes to gloat in the sunlight.

That evening, we ate our meal in the homestead dining room in silence, apart from the clink of metal and china and the smacking and gulping sounds Downston made swallowing his food without chewing. The dirt under his finger-nails made them look like beetles. As he forked his food into his mouth, some of it fell back down his chin and onto his shirt.

'When the Man comes, you're to tell him about this bit of silverside and the mustard sauce the Missus made to go with it.' He loaded more food on to his fork and crammed it into his mouth.

'Silverside! Sauce!' the Missus echoed, while Elsie the kitchen girl sidled through the door carrying two more dishes. Her lank hair fell across her face as she placed the dishes on the table. It was not before I saw the wheals on her forehead and cheeks and her half-closed eye. Downston watched her as she stepped away from the table. His eyes were glassy, and she half-curtsied to him before she backed and finally scampered away.

'And don't forget to mention the apple pie and custard,' Downston ordered.

'I thought we weren't supposed to talk unless we were talked to,' I mumbled.

'Watch your lip, boy.'

'If we can talk to this bloke, then we might as well tell him about the boil up we get every night and the …'

Downston rose, food falling from his shirt to the floor. 'I said, watch your lip.' He advanced a few steps towards me, but as he did so, the Missus got up from the table. Shuffling between us, she collected our plates, pointed to the kitchen and said to Joe and me, 'Wash! Dry! Now!

In the kitchen, the girl was standing on tiptoe scrubbing a saucepan. She looked as if she was about to disappear into it. Her sleeves were rolled up past her elbows revealing scrawny, bruised arms.

'There's a bowl on the shelf and some hot water on the stove,' she said without looking up. Her voice was high pitched, and she lisped. I reckoned she was no more than ten.

'You're going to be at the homestead for a while, aren't you? The Missus asked me to get Mr Paul's bedroom ready for you. It's a bit different from the men's quarters,' Elsie said.

'Have you been here long?' Joe asked

'Since I was seven. Gran died and I didn't have anyone else, so the Boss took me on to help the Missus.'

'Do you like it here?'

The girl swivelled back to the sink and recommenced her scrubbing 'I can't remember much else.' She paused and her voice softened. 'I like it when Miss Gaylene's back from her school holidays. It's not so lonely then. She helps me. She knows how to cook silverside just the way the Boss likes it. Very fussy about his silverside, he is. I'm in for a good thrashing if I don't get it right.'

'Why don't you come up to the men's quarters sometimes. It would give you some company and a bit of a rest.' I wondered how she managed to stand all day on legs that appeared no sturdier than a couple of pipe cleaners.

'The Boss wouldn't like it.'

'Why not?'

'He wouldn't. That's all.' She took a cloth and began drying the pot. 'You have to be careful of the Boss,' she said.

Paul Downston's bedroom had blue striped wallpaper, on which were pinned pictures of blokes with funny hair, wearing strange clothes and playing guitars. Beneath one of the posters were the words, *Rock'n Roll*, which I supposed must have something to do with music, although Joe said it sounded religious to him. It was probably something to do with The Salvation Army he said, though they didn't look much like blokes from the Sallies. I couldn't imagine Paul Downston wanting pictures of the Salvation Army on his bedroom wall.

The Missus entered the room without knocking. Immediately, she padded to a wardrobe. 'Clothes! Away!' She said, and pointing to a chest of drawers, 'Fold! Tidy!' She looked at the posters and made a clicking sound, before pulling the blue bed cover straight. She left as quietly and quickly as she had come.

I shuddered at being so close to the Downstons. 'I wish we were back in the men's quarters.' I blew on my new shoes in case a speck of dust had managed to settle on them, since I had last looked. 'This place is like an undertaker's. I don't give a tinkers if it does have an inside lav. The long drop gets more air.'

'If you don't mind your privates getting chilblains.' Joe bounced up and down on the bed. 'Make the most of it. It won't last.'

I climbed on to the bed and lay on my back staring at the ceiling. The room was twice the size of the one I shared with Angela in our flat in Blountmere Street. It had a yellow rug with blue circles on it, and a bedside lamp. They were things our bedroom never had.

The encroaching twilight transformed the apples on the tree outside into black orbs. Beyond the homestead, I could hear Murray whistling the dogs. Murray and Fergus would have lit the lamps. After Murray had fed the dogs and shut them up for the night, the two men would hang up their hats and settle in their chairs to read or doze in front of the stove. I felt as far from the men's quarters as I did from Blountmere Street.

Sometime in the night, I heard Eleod stagger along the hallway to the small room at the back of the house that I knew was Elsie's. I heard the door being opened, then closed again. There was a scuffle, and the rasping of bedsprings. Although they sounded muffled, I could hear Elsie's cries, followed by Eleod's grunts. Later, the door opened and closed again. I expelled a breath as I heard Eleod pass our bedroom. I lay awake for a long time wishing Elsie would stop weeping.

'My word, but it's a hot one for this time of the year.' The Man from the whatever-department, unwound himself from behind the wheel of his Austin. He mopped his forehead with a handkerchief before stuffing it back in his pocket and extending his hand to Downston.

'Harrington.' He introduced himself.

Downston stretched his neck and jutted out his chin, clearly uncomfortable in his yellow cravat. 'G'day. Eleod Downston.'

'Been meaning to get to you before this, but pressure of work, Mr Downston, pressure of work.'

The Man turned to Joe and me. 'And these must be your boys.'

'Yes, these are the ... our two ... lads.' Downston rammed a hand into the small of our backs and thrust us forward.

'Smart young men.' The Man took in the creases in the sleeves of our shirts, our polished shoes and smarmed hair that had been slicked down by Downston with axle grease.

'You must be proud of them.'

'Um, very proud.'

'You've certainly got a beautiful place here. A fair bit of land. Do you have any help?'

'That's why he has ...'Joe began.

'What the lad's trying to say is, we have a shepherd and a rouseabout who help run things round the place.'

'So you two boys don't have to do too much, eh?' The Man chuckled.

'Actually, we have to work ...'

'They have so much school work, they don't get any time to help.'

'You're very lucky boys. Not all our orphans are in such ideal situations, although we try to make sure everyone's happy,' the Man added.

In the parlour, our exercise books were displayed on our desks, our pens laid on top. The Missus, in a dress that rolled tightly over her stomach and hips, stood like a guardian beside them.

'So how's their tuition progressing?' the Man asked her.

'Going. Well,' the Missus pronounced.

At an attempt at mateyness, the Man ruffled my hair. 'Not all orphans get the chance to have this kind of education, and certainly not in such a luxurious classroom.'

The Man rubbed his hands together in order to try and rid them of the grease.

'We don't … ' I tried again.

'They … um … don't know how to thank us for what we're doing for them, but … um … charity begins at home.' Downston cleared his throat in an attempt at modesty. With a warning glance at me, he marshalled us out of the parlour.

'It certainly does make everything worthwhile when one observes children so well looked after, so privileged.' The Man followed the Missus to our bedroom for his inspection.

'Treat 'em just like our own.' Downston had a touch of pathos in his voice as he patted the bed.

'Own,' the Missus repeated.

'Laudable,' the Man exclaimed, glancing around the room. 'Like rock and roll, do you?' he asked Joe, eyeing the poster and looking as if he was about to ruffle Joe's hair, then thinking better of it.

'Never been much of a one for religion,' Joe replied.

The Man grinned at Downston. 'Got a sense of humour, these lads of yours.'

After walking the Man around the homestead garden, Downston led the way back into the house and into the dining room.

'I'm sure you won't say no to some afternoon refreshment,' Downston said in his most smarmy voice.

'Being on the road most of the time, afternoon tea's a rare treat for me. With a bit of a journey ahead of me I certainly won't say no,' the Man replied. 'Are the boys going to join us?'

'Always eat with us. We share our table and our home with them.' It looked as if Downston might cry at the thought of his own generosity.

'And your own children?' The Man took four triangular sandwiches from the bone china plate the Missus held in front of him. I had glimpsed Elsie making them earlier. She had fresh bruises on her face. Now she was nowhere to be seen. I wondered what the Boss had done with her.

'Our own kids are on the Coast with my brother, so we can concentrate on these two.'

'All good friends together, are you?' he asked me.

'We don't … '

'Real good mates,' Downston butted in.

'And you teach your own children at home too, Mrs Downston?'

'They're at boarding school,' Downston answered for her. 'They're happy enough there and … ' Downston took a noisy swig of tea, 'it gives us a chance to give these two a bit more attention.'

'They certainly seem to get that. Plenty of good food, eh?' The Man's gaze lingered on the ginger gems and pikelets on another of the plates that were usually kept in the glass cabinet in the parlour.

Joe stuffed a sandwich into his mouth whole and said, 'We only ever get boil-up.'

'He means if they had their way, that's what they'd like to have every night.'

'My kids are the same.' The Man put another three sandwiches on his plate. 'They'd eat fish and chips all the time, if we let them.' It sounded as if he'd said fush and chups.

'Tell Mr Harrington what you had for dinner last night.' Downston was determined the silverside wasn't going to be forgotten. He inclined his head towards me, his neck pushed forward, causing his veins to protrude.

'Meat and …'

'A nice bit of silverside and mustard sauce, it was. And what else? Tell Mr Harrington what you had after that.'

'Apple pie and custard,' I muttered.

'My, my, and yet you haven't got an ounce of fat on you.' The Man patted his own ample stomach. 'Just look at the two of you.'

'We can't look at ourselves 'cos we've never had a mirror.'

Downston pulled at his cravat. 'We don't encourage vanity. Humility's what we're aiming for.'

'Laudable,' the Man exclaimed again.

'More? Tea?' Maggie enquired.

'I don't mind if I do.'

'I'll fill up the teapot again.' Joe jumped to his feet and took the silver teapot in to the kitchen.

'No, I …' Maggie began

'Let him, Mrs Downston.' The Man beamed his approval. 'It's seldom one sees a young man, and certainly not one who's an orphan, so willing to help.'

'Aren't you two boys going to have another cup?' the Man asked when Joe returned.

'I'd like …' I ventured, suddenly thinking of Lori and what she'd said about the good old British cuppa.

'No thanks, me and Tony have had enough,' Joe cut across me.

'Good to know when you've had enough,' the Man spluttered, washing down his fourth ginger gem.

When the Man had finished his third pikelet, he belched and rose from the table and opened his brief case that had been resting next to his knee. He took some papers from it and flicked through them until he came to the one he wanted. He placed it on the table, fished in his inside jacket pocket and produced a fountain pen, unscrewed the top and placed some ticks on the form. 'Everything seems to be perfect. And the boys have had no illness?'

'Never - crook!' The Missus drained the last of the tea from her cup.

'I need you to sign here, then, Mr Downston.'

Downston placed his empty cup on the table and took the pen. His finger-nails had been cleaned for the occasion. They looked like brown insects rather than black ones.

'And remember, if you have any problems you can always contact me.'

'What if we have any?' I faced him square on.

'What problems could you possibly have, young man? You're as close to living in paradise as you're likely to be.'

'But that's not ...'

'You'd better get back to your lessons. Now!' Downston managed a weak smile. 'Don't like them to get behind.'

'I thought I told you only to speak when you were spoken to. You had far too much to say.' Eleod ground out the words as the Austin laboured up the hill and away from the farm. 'Get your stuff and clear off back to the men's quarters where you belong.' Downston raised his boot and aimed a punishing kick to my shin. 'And don't forget to bring your clothes and shoes back to the Missus.'

'That's the finish of our education, is it?'

'You'd better watch your mouth, boy, or I'll shut it for you. It'll get you into trouble one day. Let that be a warning.'

Inside, my anger churned.

Back in the men's quarters, Joe flung himself on his bunk. 'It's like being home,' he said.

At least Joe and I were comparatively safe here - as safe as we were likely to be. But I had learnt from experience that when you felt at your most secure it was the time when you were most at risk. When it came to it, you couldn't trust anyone. Look after number one was my motto. But when I thought of Elsie, I knew Joe and I should be grateful we were away from the homestead and with Murray and Fergus, even if they were funny old blokes.

'I reckon we won't have to worry about the Boss for a day or two.' Joe stretched on top of his bunk, his hands behind his head, elbows akimbo. 'I'd say the Missus won't feel too good, either.'

'Why?' I wouldn't care if Downston and The Missus dropped down dead there and then.

'Crook I'd say, the pair of 'em. And that high and mighty Harrington.'

'Crook?'

Joe crossed one leg over the other and smiled up at the rafters. 'You didn't think I offered to make the tea out the goodness of my heart, did you?' He began to laugh. It made his whole body shake and his bunk rocked. 'When I went into the kitchen to fill up the teapot, I took it outside and peed in it.' Joe could hardly draw enough breath to talk.

'You peed in the teapot?'

'Funny how tea and pee look the same, ain't it?'

Chapter Fifteen

Candlewax dumped his swag on the bed. It was kept in the corner of the men's quarters for the various swagmen who called at Downstons.

'You 'ad the boil-up yet?' he asked.

'Not yet,' Murray replied.

'Blimey, he stinks. How we supposed to eat with that pong?' Joe complained.

'You'll get used to it.' Murray took a pile of newspaper squares we had recently cut and handed them to Candlewax. 'Mind you use 'em,' he instructed.

The man's hair was long and greasy. 'You got a jacket?' He mumbled. It's cold out there at nights?'

'We might have something, but you mind what I've just told you.'

Without seeming to hear what Murray said, Candlewax untied his swag and took out a tin. He unscrewed the top and immediately the smell of the sludgy green ointment inside it filled the men's quarters. It made my eyes water and forced me to rush for the door.

'Good for cuts and the sort. Seen it heal a cockie down south who nigh on cut his hand off.' The swagman offered the tin to Murray. 'You can have it for a double helping of boil-up. Plenty of mutton in it, is there? The Missus give you chops and bread for breakfast?' Candlewax seemed unaffected by the smell, although his nose dripped on to the floor.

'Mornings I throw in a few potatoes the boy grows,' Murray said.

'Sounds like poison to me,' Candlewax spat on the floor.

'Outside for that sort of thing,' Murray grumbled.

'Getting fussy now you got a couple of pommies with yer.'

That night when Candlewax wasn't calling for someone called Gladys, he was farting, causing Fergus to complain into the darkness, 'For the love of all the saints, can't someone put a cork in one end of the wretched man, and a gag at the other?'

The next day, as soon as he had downed two bowls of boil-up, Candlewax was off, wearing a jacket Murray had somehow managed to lay hold of. He left a bed that Fergus and Murray threw into the undergrowth, and a stench that took days to fade.

I didn't envy Candlewax with the weather getting colder. He'd need the jacket. I guessed he wouldn't use the newspaper squares he'd taken with him for the purpose they were intended either, but to pad his coat against the freezing blasts.

I blew on my hands, and my footsteps crunched on the frozen ground as I walked to the pigsties. The snow that had coated the mountains flirted with the foothills, turning them into a succession of thinly clad white mounds. The distant sheep stood cold and lonely against a gun metal sky.

The sooner I fed the pigs and cleaned the pigsty, the sooner I could get back to our quarters and the potato porridge Murray had taken to making with the onset of colder mornings.

I heaved a bucket and tipped its contents into a trough. Today, it was too cold to take my time and dream my dreams of Blountmere Street. My jersey did little to combat the chill, and my short trousers left my knees exposed and purple. New Zealand wasn't the tropical place I'd boasted about to the other boys on the ship. At least this part of New Zealand wasn't.

Joe entered the hut, stamping his feet and clapping his hands to shock life back into them.

'Holy Mother of God, do you have to make that racket?' Fergus winced. Last night, he had returned from the township, drunk as usual. Murray had dumped him in a disheveled heap on his bed.

'Porridge?' Murray enquired. 'Nothing like potato porridge to warm the innards.'

Fergus lurched for the door.

'Hooray,' Murray called after him.

'Blimey, he stinks the place out when he's been on the grog, just like my old man. It stayed up your nose all day when he'd had a skinful.' Joe squeezed his nostrils between his thumb and forefinger.

Smells didn't stay with you for just a day. On the odd occasion, when I tried to conjure a picture of the Old Man, all that flickered behind my eyelids was a blurry cut-out figure. Yet, in my head somewhere, I still held the aroma of cheap perfume worn by the women the Old Man had brought to the house. The scent of Bunty - rotting violets - and with it came the memory of her painted face, bleached hair and the last time I heard the Old Man's voice.

'Spent his winnings at *The Travellers*,' Murray nodded towards the door Fergus had retreated through.

'Winnings? On the gee gees?' Joe had his spoon raised ready for when Murray placed his bowl in front of him.

'Too right.'

'You won?'

'Too right.'

'Did you win a lot? A fortune?'

'Enough.' Murray delved into his pocket. He pulled out a wad of notes. 'That reminds me, we put a bob each way for you young blokes on *Lucky Scoundrel*.' He began peeling from the bundle of notes.

'D'you mean you put a bet on for us, and we won, as well as you?' I asked. I hadn't ever won anything.

'Too right.'

'But we never gave you any money.' The last time I could remember holding money in my hand, was when Mum gave me sixpence for Saturday Picture Club out of what Fred and Lori left us.

'Our shout. We each put in a bit for the two of you.'

'And we've won thirty bob each?'

'That's right.'

'Blimey, we're blinkin' rich.'

'Steady on, Ginger.' Murray replaced the wad in his pocket, and began spooning porridge on top of the boil-up.

Joe stared at the money in his hand. 'One day I'll be stinkin' rich. And I'll tell you something; now I've got a bit, I won't ever be without cash again'

That evening, when Fergus' hangover had worn off, he suddenly asked me 'Have you thought any more about writing to those neighbours of yours?' He flipped over a dog-eared page of *Beautiful Ireland*, as the wind forced itself between the wooden slats of our quarters and rustled the calendars on the walls.

'Not really.'

'If you write a letter, I'll post it for you. The last one you wrote probably got lost on the ship. To be sure, that's what happened.' But Fergus's eyes never left his book. 'Anyhows, be that as it may, if you start a letter now, you'll have a couple of weeks to work on it.'

'I'll think about it.' What reason did I have to write? I wasn't likely to get back to England no matter how many wins we had on the horses. And, if Paula Dibble did decide to answer, I wasn't sure I wanted to hear how Mum died, and what had happened to Angela. I didn't want to know how things had changed in Blountmere Street. My dreams were all I had left.

'And those other friends, the ones who live in New Zealand. What about them? They might have a telephone number. If you give me their names and address, I'll try and find out. Now where's the harm in that?'

'No point. They didn't turn up to collect me off the ship, and that's that.' I resented Fergus' nosiness.

'Have you thought they might not know you're here?'

'The orphanage said they'd get in touch with them, and the orphanage always did what they said they would. They said they'd punish you if you wet the bed and they did. They said you were going to be sent to New Zealand, and you were.'

'Why don't you give me these people's names and address.' I could tell Fergus was trying to make up for losing my last letter but it was too late.

'They're called Fred and Lori.' I didn't want to say their names out loud. My voice was little more than a whisper.

'Fred and Lori who?'

'It doesn't matter.'

'Of course it matters.'

'Stannard.'

'Stannard?'

'That's what I said.' Why didn't Fergus stop asking questions. He wasn't always on at Joe to write to *his* folk.

'Where do they live?'

'Don't know.'

'The North or The South Island?

'Don't know.'

'So you didn't give the orphanage their address?'

'Didn't have one. The matron tore up their letter, and I couldn't remember their address in New Zealand.'

Fergus' face took on the sort of softness it did when he read poetry out loud.

'By all the saints, how could the orphanage contact them without an address?'

'New Zealand's not that big. There can't be many Stannards living here.'

Fergus sighed. 'You said they have a son in New Zealand. What's his name?'

'Ronald, but Fred said he didn't have the same surname as him, because he'd taken Fred's first wife's name.'

'It doesn't make things easy, to be sure, but let's have a go, anyway, shall we?'

'Do what you want.' I didn't care. Fergus could please himself. This time I wouldn't spend every waking opportunity with my eyes fixed on the distant road, expecting Fred and Lori to come round the bend and down the hill. It was a mug's game. I wasn't playing it any more.

Paul Downston galloped his horse, Flinders, in the paddock next to the pigsty. It was early for Downston's son to be out. During his school holidays, when he was back on the farm, he wasn't usually around until much later. If I could, I avoided him. He was as much a bully as his father. More so. Even Downston didn't treat the animals with the cruelty his son did. I could see the horse was tiring. Its breath created a white column in front of it, yet the boy kept applying his whip to the animal's rump, urging it to go faster. I walked back into the sty, my insides feeling as if they were being squeezed through the Missus' mangle. Just as I couldn't do anything to change my own life, I could do nothing to help Flinders. We were both captives.

Paul Downston tugged at the rein and turned Flinders towards the pigsty. My stomach experienced another turn in the mangle. As they approached, I noticed blood pumping from one of Flinder's flanks. I shivered. Like me, Flinders was at the mercy of a brute.

'Come here you, pommie bastard,' Paul Downston commanded me, as he reached the sty. He dismounted from Flinders, with another vicious crack of his whip to the mare's hind quarters. Flinders whinied. I hated hearing her pain.

'You slept in my bedroom while I was away, and ran it alive with fleas, you dirty orphan.' He accused. 'Now say, "Sorry, sir".'

I didn't answer, and went inside the pigsty. I took a piece of rag from a hook, returned and began dabbing at the wheals on Flinder's back.

'Don't try and be clever with me.' Paul Downston snatched the cloth. Flinders snorted in pain.

'When I say something to you, you're to answer, "Yes, sir".'

The only weapon I had against Paul Downston was silence. I wouldn't apologise or say "sir".

'Say, "Yes, sir"!' Paul Downston commanded. His lips, which were narrow like his old man's, straightened and merged into one. 'Now say, "Yes, sir"!'

Still I refused to answer, and Flinders whinnied as if she was on my side.

'Are you going to say it, or am I going to have to knock it out of you?'

Silence.

'Say it!' He had hold of my jersey.

Silence.

The punch, when it came, caught me on the side of my mouth, causing blood to spurt from my lip and two teeth to become loosened.

'Say, "Yes, sir"!' Paul Downston shook with rage, while he flexed and unflexed his fists.

At once my mouth swelled. I wouldn't be able to pronounce the words, even if I'd decided to.

I turned and began to walk towards the men's quarters. I readied myself for the next blow. This time, I wouldn't take it. This time, I'd turn and hit him so hard, he wouldn't get up. This time, I'd kill him.

'Call me, "sir"!' His voice was shaking. 'Call me, "sir"!'

But the blow I was expecting never came. Instead, I heard him mount Flinders and gallop away.

Back in the hut, Murray examined his pliers and wiped them on a piece of newspaper. 'Those two teeth are going to have to come out.' He practised at positioning the pliers. 'Open your mouth wide, boy, so I can get these inside it,' he instructed.

'He can't. His mouth's too swollen,' Joe answered for me.

'Open it as far as it'll go. Nothing to worry about. A couple of good yanks and they'll both be out.'

'Good job they're at the back, Tone. Nobody'll be able to see they're missing.' Joe tried to assure me, but every inch of me was quivering.

It took more than a couple of "good yanks" to extract the two incisors and Murray had built up a sweat before he dropped them both with a tinkle into a bowl.

'Holy Mother of God,' Fergus said, as he wiped perspiration from his own upper lip.

'I'll give him *"yes sir"*. I'll get him back for this, Tone. I promise you that. Paul Downston'll wish he'd never set eyes on us when I've finished with him. I'll bide my time, but I'll get him.' Joe held a blood-soaked cloth to my mouth. My whole head throbbed, and I barely heard him.

That night, I hardly slept, even when the shaking had subsided. It wasn't only because of the pain in my mouth, but because of my concern for Flinders. What if Paul Downston had killed her? She didn't deserve to die. She was a soft and trusting creature. She needed to be caressed and loved. I didn't know much about horses, but I knew she would have willingly done whatever Downston had wanted, without having to be whipped. The thought of being loved and caressed caused fresh longings to flare inside me.

The next morning with my face swollen the size of a full moon I visited Flinders in the stables before the first light appeared over the mountains. I knew Paul Downston wouldn't be about at that hour. Nevertheless, my actions were stealthy as I tiptoed into the stables, calling softly. To my relief, the mare made a snuffling sound, and scraped a hoof on the ground. 'It's all right, girl. It's only me,' I told her. With the orphanage torch, the one Joe had given me, I shone it along Flinders' back. Then, from my other pocket, I took the tin of ointment Candlewax had left. I scooped a liberal amount of the pungent grease into my hand. I rubbed it along the whip wounds, praying that it would heal as Candlewax said it would. Flinders whinnied and I said, 'Shush, girl, shush. We don't want anyone to hear, do we?' The horse nuzzled me. 'I'll be back,' I promised. When he's not around I'll come and put some more ointment on you, to make you better. You can rely on me.' Flinders rubbed her face against mine. Perhaps, like me, she felt a little less powerless.

'For the love of the Blessed Virgin, can't a man get any peace round here!' Fergus licked his pencil stub and frowned at the piece of writing paper in front of him.

'I was only saying I've got to cover my lemon tree, in case a late frost gets hold of it,' Joe said.

'Then, for all the saints' sakes, say it quieter.'

Joe poked out his tongue at Fergus' back and mumbled something about people getting the hump.

It had been the fourth night running that Fergus had laboured over what appeared to be a letter, before screwing it into a ball and tossing it into the fire.

'To be sure, you'd do well to be writing a letter yourself instead of watching me like a tawny owl.' He scowled at me.

'Fergus is finding it really difficult to write to whoever it is,' I observed to Joe as we draped a piece of sacking over his lemon tree.

'It doesn't mean he has to take it out on us. Anyway, I don't know why people find writing letters so difficult.'

'That's because you never write any.'

'I would if I wanted to.'

I tucked a corner of the sacking under a branch. There were people I wanted to write to; people like the Gang and the Dibbles. People who had left a chasm in my life much, much wider than the gap in my teeth that my tongue was forever probing. It was their reply, or lack of one, that worried me.

The next night, Fergus barely touched his dinner as he sat hunched on his bed, staring at a blank sheet of paper. He scrawled on it before he crossed out what he had written, cursed and began again.

Joe looked across at Fergus and raised his eyebrows, before saying, 'I think I'll have a couple of bob each way on *Den's Dance.*' He folded *The Betting News.*

Studying form had become Joe's preferred evening reading.

'What about you, Tone?'

'If you think it's going to win, why don't you put more money on it?' I asked.

'I told you, I'm never going to be without a bit of cash again. A couple of bob will do.'

'I suppose you want me to put it on for you?' Murray scraped Fergus's half-eaten dinner into a tin for the dogs.

'Yeah … please.' Joe gave Murray his most persuasive grin.

'And for me, too.'

'Beggar me, if the pair of you aren't worse than me and my brothers when we were your age,' Murray replied.

'Are you not going to be writing a letter, then?' Fergus asked me, as if from a long way off.

'Another time,' I replied.

Murray said Paul Downston had gone to the Boss's brother on the Coast. I didn't care where he'd gone, as long as he was away from the farm and I could visit the stables more freely. Downston himself had no interest in horses. I took the sugar lumps Murray and Fergus had pinched from *The Travellers.* The mare licked my hand clean, then she nuzzled my neck. I examined Flinders' back, where the whip had cut into her. Thanks to Candlewax's ointment, it was pretty well healed. I wished I could say the same about my mouth. From time to time my gum still ached, especially at night when the pain woke me.

I took a brush and began grooming her in long, loving strokes along her back until her coat was glossy. All the time, I crooned, 'Lovely girl. Good girl, Flinders.' When I finished, I fondled the animal's head and Flinders brought it up and nuzzled her nose against me, from my chin up to my forehead and back down. In the process, she spread the sudden tears of longing for Mum and Angela that had begun to flow.

'Keep touching me, Flinders,' I sobbed. 'Keep touching me'

'Well, come on. Tell us how we did.' Joe was at Murray's heels as the dogs usually were on Murray's return from the township.

'How we did with what, Ginger?'

'You know what?'

'My word, I don't.'

'The gee gees!'

'The gee gees?'

'*Den's Dance*!'

'Now let me see.' Murray turned away and put his hand into the inside of his jacket. 'He won, too right he did. Twenty to one.' He held up a handful of pound notes.

'I told you he would, didn't I? I told you studying form was what you had to do. We're going to be millionaires, Tone. Blinkin' millionaires.'

'What good will that do you, to be sure?' Fergus entered the hut, disheveled and stinking of booze. He reeled across the floor, and took the lid off the stove. Then he poked the letter he had finally written the night before into the flames. 'You had the right idea, Tony. By all the saints and the Virgin herself, letters are best kept in the head.'

He slumped on his bed with his hat pushed over his face, leaving only his mouth clear, and muttered, 'Not in the phone book those folks of yours, Fred and whoever ... not there.' His mouth slackened and he let out a sob before entering oblivion.

Chapter Sixteen

The air resounded with bleats, whistles and barks, as the dogs herded sheep into the woolshed.

Behind the shed, gorse flowers turned the hills gold while the mountains, almost free of snow, retreated to a hazy far off place. Summer was upon us, and the sun had leached moisture from the ground, leaving the grass struggling and a yellowish brown.

I licked perspiration from my lips, as I dragged another fleece to the wool table. My skin was slippery with lanolin, and my mission shirt had split under the arms. Yet no matter how fast I worked, I couldn't keep up with the two shearers.

'Shift yourself, boy. No slacking,' Downston yelled across the yard.

By the side of the holding pen, Paul Downston observed the activity, sitting astride Flinders, while Joe goaded the shorn sheep back into a paddock. His face had become one orange freckle, and his hair stuck to it in dagger shapes.

It was midday - feed time - when the shearers stretched and retreated to the rear of the shed, where they ducked their heads under the tap and drank deeply. It was uncanny how they knew the time. Fergus and Murray were the same, even Joe was getting the knack. The only reason I was interested in knowing the time was so that I could compare it to the time in England. As if by so doing, I could halt its relentless onwards march.

Recently, however, I'd had difficulty remembering details of my life in Blountmere Street, and some of my mind pictures had become fuzzy. It was like looking through windows that needed cleaning. I worried that some of my memories may have slipped into a place beyond recall without my realizing it.

Having quenched their thirst, the shearers sat propped against the woolshed. Their muscular bodies glistened. For the most part, they were uncommunicative. They were content to do their job, eat their fill and at the end of a day's work, drink well beyond their fill.

Usually, the Missus or Elsie brought bread, cold mutton and tomatoes, together with jugs of homemade lemonade for the shearers' lunchtime feed. Today, though, I recognised the Downston girl coming towards us, carrying the tucker basket.

'Looks as if the Missus has sent the girl with the kai. We're the lucky ones,' one of the shearers, with more hair on his body than his head, drawled. He barely raised his eyes, yet appeared to see everything. With the same lack of effort, his mate studied the girl as she progressed towards us, a gold and orange figure.

Feigning disinterest, the shearers watched through half-closed eyes as she set out the food. Her hair curled around her face and when she pushed it away from her eyes, it revealed Lori's *English* skin. It wasn't blotchy and lumpy like her mother's. But, then, nothing about her was like her mother. They might as well have belonged to two different species.

'G'day. Wanna hand?' slurred one of the shearers, who was negligently propped on one elbow.

'I need to bring some more things from the house. I couldn't carry it all at once, but Tony will help me.'

I reddened. I wasn't aware she knew my name.

'I'm Gaylene,' the girl smiled easily as we began crossing the paddock back to the homestead. A tingling sensation reached the roots of my hair and made me want to itch my scalp.

'You didn't mind me asking you to help, did you?' she enquired.

'No ... course not.' I tried to keep my voice low for fear it would squeak, as it sometimes did lately.

'Mum said the shearers aren't to be trusted and to ask you.'

I couldn't imagine the Missus trusting me. Trust wasn't a word Downston would have used when it came to me or Joe. He'd threatened us to keep well away from his kids. I looked around to check Downston's whereabouts. I didn't see him and guessed that he was in the homestead kitchen wolfing back his tucker. I hoped so.

'You're from England, aren't you?' Gaylene half skipped beside me. Although I gazed straight ahead, I was conscious of the orange and yellow skirt swishing beside me and, by comparison, the state of my shirt. How out of place this butterfly girl must be in the Downstons' front parlour, and not just because the colours clashed.

'You must miss your home and family.'

'A bit.' I quickened the pace so that she couldn't see the absurd tears that had sprung from nowhere.

'Have you got any brothers and sisters?' Gaylene skipped a little faster to keep up with me.

'A sister.' I hoped she wouldn't ask about Mum, although perhaps she already knew she was dead. I didn't know what I'd say if she mentioned The Old Man. 'My sister's name's Angela,' I said.

'Does she live in England?'

'She lives in London.'

'Do you hear from her?'

'Sometimes,' I lied. 'Look, we ought to hurry. The blokes'll go crook if they have to wait too long.'

At the homestead, I kept out of view behind the washing hanging on the line in the Missus' vege garden while Gaylene collected the rest of the stuff. The Missus' vegetables were yellow and stunted. I doubted the homestead garden would yield much that was edible, not like Joe's thriving plants in the garden at the back of our quarters.

On the way back to the woolshed, Gaylene seemed to understand my reluctance to talk about myself. She chatted about boarding school, her teachers, and friends.

I wanted to catch every word she spoke in my hands and let them out a little at a time so that they would last.

'Mum says you're to come to the homestead at lunchtime for the next few days to help me carry everything over to the woolshed. Will that be all right?'

It was more than all right.

After a day's shearing, the shearers settled for the evening in their quarters. One played a mouth organ, while the other sang. The sound drifted into our hut and Fergus said, 'To be sure, grog oils the vocal cords. You don't want to be joining them?' Fergus himself looked as if he would like to join them, for the beer, if not the singing.

'Not me. It stinks of sweat and farting in there,' Joe replied.

I recalled Mrs Dibble saying "fart" was a terrible word. She had only just managed to bring it to her lips, and then she had whispered it and blushed. She said you should say "windy" instead, and that it was all right for men to do "windies". Women shouldn't do them at all. It was funny I should remember that. At least it proved that I could bring some things I thought I'd forgotten to the front of my brain, even if others had evaporated.

'Anyway, it ain't right they're allowed booze,' Joe continued.

'They're shearers, and good shearers are worth the whole of the Emerald Isle. To be sure, it wouldn't do to go upsetting them. For the time being, though, it's safer not to go too near them when they're like this.'

'What d'you mean?'

'He means they've a liking for young boys, my word they have.' Murray joined the conversation

'The dirty … '

'Settle down, Ginger. You're safe enough here.'

Fergus arched his back. 'By the saints, a day hauling sheep around plays havoc with the nether regions.' He massaged his back and down to his legs. 'Tell me, Tony, was that young Miss Downston with you walking across the paddock to the homestead?'

'Blimey I must be going blind. I never saw you and that Gay Whatsername together.' Joe's interest seemed to make his freckles protrude.

'She couldn't get all the stuff to the woolshed in one go, so she asked me to help her.'

'What's she like?'

'All right.'

'What's she say?'

'Nothing much.'

'Honestly, Tone, why d'you play your cards so close to your chest?'

'We didn't say much, that's all. Anyway, what about you and Paul Downston? Why have you been toadying up to him lately?'

'No reason.'

'See, you're doing the same. There must be a reason.'

'The Paul Downstons of this world have their uses, that's all.'

The day was another of burnished sunshine as Gaylene and I walked through the paddock on our way to the woolshed with the lunchtime tucker. Suddenly, Gaylene stopped. 'I made some scones for Mum this morning,' she said. 'I've brought one each for us. We'll have to eat them before we get there, or the men will want to know where theirs are.' We crept behind a flax bush and Gaylene delved into her basket and brought out a tin. It reminded me of Candlewax's ointment tin, but when she took the lid off, it smelt of homemade baking. Gaylene offered me a scone. I took one and bit into it. Jam and cream squelched from the middle in a red and white frill.

'Cream!' I had only tasted cream once before – at Fred and Lori's wedding. It was special for trifles and knickerbocker glories. Mrs Dibble made scones, but only ever with jam in them.

'Your mother would go mad if she knew you'd brought me one of these.' I pulled the scone apart and licked the jam and cream from each side. I let it settle on my tongue, trying to keep it from melting. When the jam and cream were gone, I began nibbling round the edges of the scone.

'Actually, she suggested it.'

'You mean she told you to bring me a scone with cream?'

'She's not that bad. She just seems fierce because she can't smile or talk much. She had a stroke, you see, just after I was born. It affected her speech, but she likes you, honestly.' Gaylene ran her tongue along her lower lip to lick off the jam. I found her lip-licking almost irresistible. When she had finished, she brushed crumbs from her skirt.

'Mum finds looking after the house and all the cooking too much, especially at shearing time. When I'm on my school holidays I help her, even though she usually has a girl from the township. They don't always stay, but there's always more that need work, or ... ' she stopped abruptly. I was pretty sure she was going to say that there were always orphans from England, like me.

A few weeks ago, Elsie suddenly disappeared. Murray said she'd probably been packed off because she was in the family way. It wouldn't be the first time it had happened to one of the scullery maids, he said.

'Mum said you were very bright, and she wanted to keep on teaching you. But Dad wouldn't let her. You know what he's like. It's not easy for her, although he spoils me.'

I hoped that didn't mean he did the same things to her that he'd done to Elsie.

If Downston were to catch us together he'd kill me, but when Gaylene ran her tongue over her top lip again, what Downston thought didn't seem to matter.

'Do you mind not going to school? I mean, would you like to?' She asked.

'I've *been* to school.' I didn't want Gaylene to think I'd had no education at all. 'In London I went to Blountmere Street Junior School. Angela goes to Grigham.' I left out *Road* and *Secondary School,* because I wanted it to sound posh. Of course I had no idea what school Angela went to or if, like me, she didn't go to school at all. It was more likely she was at work now.

'So you were sent here instead. Do you like it?' she asked.

'It's all right.' I knew I should sound more positive, but Gaylene didn't appear to notice.

'Come on, we'd better get this over to the men, or we'll be in trouble.' The butterfly girl flitted from behind the flax.

The heat of the day lingered into the evening and Joe lent on his hoe, surveying a row of lettuces in his garden. Joe's garden was so established, it seemed as if it had always been there.

'You're still having a lot to do with Paul Downston,' I said. How Joe could be pals with Paul was beyond my understanding, especially after all he'd said when Paul had all

204

but knocked out my teeth. Anyway, Joe hated arrogant, stuck up people.

'Not really.' Joe began hoeing. 'At any rate he's coming round to my way of thinking.'

Every successive day, the ground became drier and harder and the mountains had practically disappeared into the distance. Wool bales filled the shed, piled to the roof. The shearers had said that another day should do it. The one with more hair on his body than his head, who for some reason was known as Curly, slurred that the Boss was sitting on a goldmine. He called me *Rousie*, and said wool was fetching a high price, and to make sure the Boss gave me a bonus.

'You think about it, Rousie. Clever bloke like you should be able to persuade the Boss,' he said, hardly moving his mouth.

But Gaylene Downston was all I could think about. Some days, Blountmere Street, like the mountains, seemed to have receded from view.

With only one day left to carry the men's tucker together, Gaylene and I lingered over our time walking across the paddock from the homestead.

'I often wonder what you do over there in your quarters,' Gaylene said, the wind blowing her skirt into a swirl of colour.

'Joe reads his seed packets and books about gardening.' I left out his recent obsession with *studying form*. 'Murray messes around cleaning up and reading the paper, and Fergus and I read anything Fergus brings back from the library. Mainly…' All at once, I wanted to measure the distance our friendship had come. 'Mainly, we read poetry. We like to read it aloud.' I waited for her response.

'Who's your favourite poet?' She didn't look surprised, or seem to think it was sissy.

'I don't know if I've got one particular favourite. I like some of the First World War poets, but then I like Browning and well … lots of others as well.' I hoped I didn't sound a show off. 'I don't know much about it. I just like reading it and listening to Fergus read it.'

'Will you read some to me?'

I didn't know if I'd get the opportunity, but I replied, 'If you want me to.'

I was still thinking about reading Gaylene Downston poetry as I passed the shearers' quarters on my way from the long drop that evening. At first, I didn't see Curley propped against the doorway. As I passed, he caught hold of my arm. 'Where you going, boy?' he asked. 'Pretty, with all that hair.' He ran his hand up my neck. At the same time, he pushed me through the door and into the shearer's quarters. I tried to pull away from him.

'I've got to go. I … '

'Not so fast.' Curly pulled me towards him. 'Much too pretty to go to waste. Get that bonus, did you?'

'Get off me.' I struggled to free myself, but he easily overpowered me. 'Get him off me,' I urged the other shearer who was in his usual propped position on his bunk. But his mouth curled into a lazy smile.

'Come to me, pretty boy,' Curley drawled. His breath was rank, the hair on his body was sticky with sweat and lanolin.

'Joe! Fergus! Murray! Help me,' I yelled.

'They won't hear yer.' Curley's breath came in short spurts.

'Get off me. Get your hands off me.'

But Curly had a strong grip .

'Help me,' I implored the other shearer, but he stayed where he was, still smiling.

Suddenly a hard slap caused the shearer's head to slump forward. He sagged to his knees, making a gurgling sound in his throat.

I hadn't realized Murray had entered the hut, or that he was so strong and at the same time agile.

'I'll kill you if you lay a hand on the boy again.' Murray dragged the shearer to a bunk and flung him on to it.

'You'd better watch yer mate!' Murray ordered the other shearer. 'And make sure you keep your own filthy hands off both the boys.' Murray's anger made his voice sound strange.

'You threatening me?' The other shearer sneered.

'I'm telling you, keep away from them or I swear I'll murder the two of you's. Come on, boy, let's get away from this place.' Murray practically carried me out and into the freshest air I'd ever breathed.

To my relief, the shearers packed up and left the next day.

Murray and Fergus were busy with the clean up, leaving Joe and me alone in our quarters.

Joe pulled his orphanage suitcase from under the bed. He struggled with the rusty catches, opened it, and pulled out the handkerchief he'd found on the quay at Wellington when we'd first arrived. It was marked with an H in one corner. He lifted the sacking from the window and checked to make sure Fergus and Murray weren't around. Then he unfolded the handkerchief and placed a five pound note into it. 'Keep your mouth shut about this,' he warned me.

'Where did you get it from?'

'Somebody.'

'Who?'

'It don't matter. Someone who got into a bit of trouble.'

'Come on, Joe, we never keep secrets from each other.' It wasn't true. I hadn't told him about Curley. Murray said it was best kept between the two of us. That was where I intended to keep it. The shame flamed inside me like a burnt-off paddock, leaving me feeling blackened and ugly.

'I told you he'd come in handy one day, didn't I?'

'Paul Downston? You got the money from Paul Downston. How?'

'I found out he'd got himself into a bit of trouble.'

'What sort of trouble?"

'If you really want to know, when we were staying at the homestead, I had a bit of a nosey. You've got to take your chances when you can. Anyhow, I came across a few things that pointed to the fact the Boss' boy had got himself into a bit of strife with a girl.' Joe winked.

'How come the Missus didn't find out when she cleaned his room?'

'He had the evidence hidden like the blinkin' Crown Jewels, but I had this feeling, like I do with the gee gees.'

'So that's why you've been … '

'Toadying to him? Too right. I wouldn't touch him with a barge pole otherwise.'

'So why did he give you the money?'

'Use your loaf.' Joe tapped his head with his forefinger. 'I told him I'd grass on him to his old man if he didn't give me a tenner.'

'Ten pounds!' The Gang might have threatened to squeal on a kid for some of Old Boy Barker's special mix, even a packet of fags, but ten pounds!

'Where did he get the money?'

'I don't care where he got it, though I reckon it came from the same place as the cash to pay the girl off: his uncle on the West Coast.'

Joe rummaged in his pocket and brought out another five pound note. 'Here's your half.' He handed it to me. 'Share and share alike. A fiver each.'

'But it's blackmail.'

'D'you want it, or don't you?'

I took the money and stuffed it in my pocket. When the time was right, I'd still ask the Boss for a bonus. I deserved it.

Chapter Seventeen

I felt round my chin for the hairs that had begun growing on it. I wondered whether I should ask Murray if I could borrow his razor. Joe said he couldn't see any bum fuzz and not to be so daft. 'Since you've become keen on that Gay Whatsername, you've done nothing but worry about your looks,' he said.

It wasn't only what I looked like that concerned me. Without warning, my voice could alternate from a growl to a squeak. Fergus said I was becoming a man, and laughed.

One blazing day followed another, and we all had our Sunday bath outside behind the bushes. Joe was, as usual, the last to have his. When he finished, he poured the remainder of the water onto his garden where the scum left a grey residue.

'Are you going to help me or stand there stroking your chin all night? What're you trying to do? Rub hairs on to it, or get rid of the ones you reckon you've already got?'

Due to Joe's philosophy to "waste not, want not", the garden wasn't only vibrant with colour but crammed with vegetable plants; healthy ones at that. Hardly a drop of liquid in our quarters went to waste. If I didn't watch over my cup of tea, even before I'd taken the first sip, Joe had the cup in his hand to throw over some plant or the other. I had to admit, Joe's veges improved the nightly boil-up. Ang and I used to make shuddery sounds and refuse to eat the vegetables Mum put on our plates.

'The veges'll be good for Christmas,' Joe scraped the ladle along the bottom of the bath, causing me to grit my teeth. 'It'll be here soon,' he continued. 'We'll have to get Murray to tell us what's in the shops. It'll be no good asking Fergus. He'll be knocking them back at the *The Travellers*.'

'Why d'you want to know?' I asked. We never took any notice of Christmas. There didn't seem much point when it was like any other day, except that in this upside down land, it was in the summer. 'There aren't many shops in the township, Fergus says.'

Joe swiped at a fly. 'Don't matter. They'll be *something,* and now we've got some dough, we can buy presents. I told you having a bit behind you would make a difference, didn't I?'

'But we're not allowed off the farm.'

'We'll have to ask Murray to get them for us.'

'That's daft. Murray and Fergus are the only people we'll be buying presents for, except something for each other.'

'Leave it to me, I'll think of something. Anyway, don't you want to buy that Gay Whatsername a present seeing as you fancy her?'

'We talk when we see each other, that's all.'

Joe sniffed.

'I haven't seen you talking to Paul Downston lately,' I said to direct the conversation away from Gaylene.

'Why should I? Our bit of business is finished. I don't want to talk to him, and he don't want to pass the time with me. I've got what I wanted out of him.' Joe chuckled. 'Until the next time. I haven't finished with him yet.'

Whenever I was working reasonably close to the homestead and her old man wasn't around, Gaylene still seemed to find a way to meet me. The others said it was because she had it bad for me. Murray told me never to trust a woman, while Fergus said true love was a precious thing. All I knew was that when Gaylene sat next to me, I was conscious of the feel of her skin, the sunshine smell of her clothes and her slender fingers making me think of swans' necks.

'I expect you saw the Queen all the time when you lived in London. What's she like? Is she as small as they say she is?' Gaylene asked, the next time we met, as we sat well hidden behind a clump of bushes.

'I've never seen her, so I don't know.'

Gaylene looked disappointed. 'But you must have been to Buckingham Palace.'

'No, I haven't.' Buckingham Palace was the last place the Gang had thought of visiting. The only time I had been to the West End had been for Fred and Lori's wedding. Dennis once went to Madam Tussauds. He told us all about the Chamber of Horrors. I had nightmares about it for weeks afterwards.

'The Queen came to New Zealand once,' Gaylene continued. 'Our whole school went. We waited on the side of the road for hours. We waved flags, but her car drove past so quickly, we couldn't see her. If I'd lived in London I'd definitely have gone to Buckingham Palace.'

I felt an urge to put my arm around her shoulders to say how sorry I was she hadn't been able to go. 'I've been on a London underground train,' I said, hoping it would make up for not having seen the Queen or Buckingham Palace.

'What's it like?'

'Crowded – well, it is in the mornings and at night when everyone's going or coming home from work.' I kept my hands between my knees, in case they strayed and stroked her arms. 'During The War, people slept on the platforms.'

'Really?'

'I think Mum might have taken Angela and me down there to sleep sometimes. It was like a long air raid shelter.'

'Was the poetry you read me about that War?'

'No. That was poetry from The First World War. Fergus said a whole generation of men enlisted to fight for their country. But thousands were injured and killed. He said that blokes like Joe and me lied about their age so that they could fight. They thought they were going to have an adventure and that it would soon be over. Instead it lasted four years.' I paused and gazed ahead. It wasn't unlike us orphan boys. We thought we were being sent to have an adventure. But we were banished from home forever. We were the ones who never returned.

'I've copied a war poem. D'you want to hear it?' I asked.

As an answer, Gaylene moved closer, and I felt a powerful need to protect her.

As bronze may be much beautified
By lying in the dark damp soil
So men who fade in dust of warfare fade
Fairer, and sorrow blooms their soul.
Like pearls which noble women wear
And, tarnishing, awhile confide
Unto the old salt sea to feed

Many return more lustrous than they were
But what of them buried profound
Buried where we can no more find
Who lie dark for ever under abysmal war?

Bees hummed in the manuka bushes, drowsily, without haste. Birds sang a midday song on scented air - an eternity away from the trenches, an eternity away from … I cuffed my eyes before the tears could spill.

The evening air held the day's heat as Murray, Fergus, Joe and I sat on the ridge outside our quarters. I looked at the distant river, a thin band at this time of year. My three allocated strawberries from Joe's garden, together with a sugar lump, remained untouched in my bowl.

'You're not still mooning about that Gay Whatshername?'

'And what's wrong with that, Joe me lad? Love's never to be taken for granted. To be sure, one day all you're left with are bitter-sweet memories,' Fergus answered.

'Well, *I* ain't going in for all that soppy love stuff.'

Murray reclined on the grass and pulled his hat over his face. 'Too right, boy, never trust a woman.'

At that moment, it wasn't Gaylene who was on my mind, although she had been mostly every minute I was awake and often when I was asleep. This evening, and throughout the day, however, she had only shared my thoughts.

That morning, before the light had broken and the birds had begun their dawn call, I experienced a stirring as if someone was trying to nudge me awake. I was sure it wasn't a dream. I could see Fergus' form rise and fall in slumber, hear Murray snoring and Joe's incoherent sleep talk. It had been a bizarre impression of someone wanting to reach me.

I sat up in bed, straining for more but there was nothing, only the desperation of a human spirit trying to touch my own.

'What d'you want?' I whispered into the stillness, but Joe muttered was it time to get up and the connection had been severed.

Throughout the day, I tried to re-establish the link. My thoughts became caught up with a thousand others, as they had when I tried to communicate with Paula at the orphanage. I wondered if it truly had been Paula. If so, I had let her down.

The next time Gaylene and I met was behind an old shed the rabbiters used. It was the ideal place to talk, she said, as she plucked at a blade of grass. She was wearing a yellow headband in an attempt to capture her curls, but a few wayward tendrils that looked like corkscrews had escaped.

Although it was two days ago, my strange early morning experience was still with me. My mind kept wandering back to it and I had no idea how Gaylene and I had got on to the subject of Downston and the Missus. They were the last people I wanted to talk about, but Gaylene said, 'Mum was going to be a teacher. All her family were teachers. Then she met Dad and gave up her training.' She hugged her knees. 'You should see their wedding photos. She was very beautiful.'

Trying to imagine the Missus as a beautiful bride was as difficult as liberating my thoughts to reach someone thousands of miles away. I found it impossible to understand why anyone would want to give up everything for a man like Downston, but, then, Mum had done the same thing for our Old Man.

'Mum's never really taken to farm life,' Gaylene continued. 'Things that farmers' wives are supposed to do don't interest her. She doesn't like making jam and bottling fruit or cooking, although she has to do it.'

I thought of the boil-up and nodded.

'I try to help as much as I can when I'm home from school,' Gaylene paused. 'You see, it was when I was born she had a stroke. She's never properly got over it. She's lost all her confidence. The men's quarters are about as far as she ever gets. I sometimes think if I hadn't been born Mum would still be all right and that it's my fault.'

'Of course it's wasn't your fault.' I stroked her hand. When I realized what I was doing, I became embarrassed, and placed it back in her lap. I was about to say she was silly to blame herself, but I often thought if it wasn't for me and Angela, the Old Man might have been different. Maybe it was only because of *me*. If it wasn't for *me,* Mum and the Old Man might have got on better.

'So Downston's away, is he?' Joe asked.

'On business.' Murray gave up trying to darn the hole in his sock and threw it on his bunk.

'And you've got to go into the township tomorrow?'

'That's the size of it,' Murray said, farting and scratching his bum.

'Right, Tone, we've got our chance. I told you I'd come up with something.'

'I don't know what you're talking about.'

'I'm talking about going into township to do our bit of Christmas shopping. With the Boss away, we'll be able to go with Murray and Fergus. We'll lie low in the truck so no-one can see us leave.'

'Steady on Ginger. There'll be hell to pay if the Boss finds out. His orders are that the two of you have to stay put here. And you both know as well I do, you don't go crossing Eleod Downston if you know what's good for you.'

'If he's not here, how's he going to know? You said yourself, now he's started going down south he never goes into the township these days.'

'Our work won't get done, for one thing.' I added. 'And what about the Missus. She might suspect something.' I suppose I could ask Gaylene to cover for us. I was sure she would, but it didn't seem fair to get her to deceive Downston and the Missus. They were her parents, after all.

'If it's work and the Missus you're worried about, I'll stay behind.' Fergus lowered his book. 'It's time you lads got off this place for a whiles.

'But what about *The Travellers*?' Joe asked.

'And to be sure, what about the *The Travellers*?'

'You know how you like your drop of sherbert.'

'Are you suggesting I can't last more than a couple of weeks without a drink?   Let me tell you, I'm capable of staying sober for a lot longer than two weeks. To be sure, you know nothing about me.' Fergus stalked outside.

The next day, Joe and I hid in the back of the truck, as it bumped up the hill and away from the farm on our way to the township. With the Boss away, the Missus and the kids were probably still tucked up in their beds, Murray had said. I wished that was where I was. I'd been awake most of the night, feeling like a rabbit about to leave the safety of its burrow for the first time. Murray and Austin were taking a mighty big risk for us. If Downston were ever to find out they would probably lose their jobs and only God himself knew what would happen to Joe and me.

When we arrived at the township, I shielded my eyes and looked across at a band of glimmering silver water beyond the township's main street. 'You never said it was by the sea,' I said.

'Nowhere in New Zealand's that far from the ocean.' Without locking the truck, Murray dropped the keys into a shopping bag. It was older than Mum's ancient string one that Fred used when he did the shopping. I'd almost forgotten it.

I returned my gaze to the sea that stretched to an empty horizon. It made me feel exposed and vulnerable. I longed to jump into the truck, and drive as quickly as we could back to the security of the men's quarters.

'Is this *it*?' Joe looked around him.

'Too right it is.'

'But there's nothing here.'

'What else d'you want?'

'Some shops for a start. It ain't exactly Balham High Street.'

'There's Old Witchery's place.' Murray sounded upset Joe didn't think the township compared with London. 'Old Witchery's been here years and his father before him. Farm supplies and the like, groceries, clothes, stuff from all over the world. Old Witchery sells the lot. You can even get a cup of tea and a steak and cheese pie in the back. Grannie Witchery makes 'em herself. When she's a mind to, she puts on lamingtons. No-one makes lamingtons like Grannie.

Murray pointed to a two storey building opposite Witchery's, with a board outside advertising, *"The best beer ever to hit the sides of the throat"*.

'There's *The Travellers' Hotel*. Townships crowded today,' Murray observed as two men entered the pub, and a woman with a small boy crossed the road. 'That place next to *The Traveller's* is the community hall. They have a monthly dance there with Rangi and the Flax Boys. Reckon half the folk hereabouts did their courting at one of those dances.'

'Where's the library?' I asked. The panic that had threatened to overcome me began to die down at the sight of a few buildings.

'Back of the Community Hall. My word, it's a credit to the place. That and the school.' Murray pointed to a hill on which perched a building much like the woolshed. 'All for education here. Got the Mission to thank for it. That's the Mission behind the school.'

It was unusual for Murray to say so much at once, and he gulped for air. His Adam's apple was like a grey and wrinkly golf ball 'We'll see what the Mission's got later.'

I shuddered. I'd never been sure about nuns. There had been a convent close to The Common. When I saw them, I always thought the nuns looked like black ghosts gliding along the road. Once, one of them smiled at me but I stuck my tongue out at her and ran away. No, I certainly didn't want any nun fitting me for clothes and trying to persuade me that things I knew looked ridiculous were exactly right for me.

'What about a bookie? Me and Tone want to put a couple of bob on *Wandering Minstrel*.'

'I'll do it for you at *The Travellers*. Don't want to put it on another gee gee, do you?'

'Nope. *Wandering Minstrel*'s the one.' Joe assured him.

'How can they call this a town when there's nothing here?' Joe grumbled as Murray retreated to the yard behind Witchery's to pick up some drench.

'Fergus did tell us not to expect much.'

'You can say that again. And since when's there been snow in the summer?' Joe indicated the mock snowstorm made from clumps of cotton wool stuck to Old Witchery's windows. In the centre angels blowing trumpets surrounded a picture of Father Christmas on his sleigh being pulled by eight petulant reindeers.

'Blinkin' snow when it's boiling hot. What next!'

Inside Witchery's store, unsteady arrangements of pots and pans, crockery and cutlery filled shelves from floor to ceiling. Boxes lined every aisle so that we had to walk with pigeon steps between the clutter. We held on to whatever we could to keep our balance.

Fly swats and strainers, feather dusters, dustpans and brushes hung like decorations from the few clear parts of the ceiling, while *Good Quality Manchester* was stacked in haphazard piles in every corner. Almost inaccessible counters overflowed with everything from hairnets to little liver pills. Christmas decorations, like the ones we'd made at the orphanage by linking pieces of coloured paper and gluing them together, clung to each other in sticky spirals.

'I reckon there's enough here to fill a dozen shops,' Joe remarked.

'You wouldn't think there'd be enough people to buy it.'

'We should be able to find a couple of things for Christmas. We'll just have to move the stuff and have a good gander. Old Witchery's still outside with Murray so we've got the place to ourselves for a bit.'

Joe lifted a box and stacked it on another. It gave him room to place both his feet together. He picked up a chamber pot, embellished with blue swans. 'We could buy this for Fergus. Save him having to pee round the back of the hut in the middle of the night.'

'I don't think he'd be happy with a po for Christmas.'

'Just a thought.'

I lifted the top from a box marked *Men Only*, and there they were! Underpants like large off-white sails! I looked at the labels marked *Dawkins Finest Menswear*. I searched until I found two smaller pairs. I pulled them from the box and held them against myself. They would do nicely; one pair on, the other in the wash. It was the sort of thing Mrs Dibble would have said. I folded them carefully and placed them on the counter.

'You want to be careful what you do with your money. Once it's gone, it's gone,' Joe warned.

We were considering a pair of socks for Murray which we found in a box marked *Feet* when Old Witchery entered. He practically hurdled over several rugs rolled up in front of the door at the rear of the shop.

'You don't think we should get Murray two pairs?' I asked Joe.

'He can only wear one pair at a time. We don't want to spend what we don't have to.'

'Skinflint.'

'There's nothing wrong in being careful.' Old Witchery walked on his toes between the boxes as if he was a ballet dancer.

'So you're the ones working out at Downstons. Heard a bit about you two. Here to do some Christmas shopping, Murray tells me.' Old Witchery rubbed his hands together. They were smaller than Gaylene's. 'Murray says Grannie and me have to keep our lips tight about the pair of you's being in the township, or your boss won't be too happy. Downston's a cruel bloke, always has been. There's a few here whose lives he's ruined. It'll be a pleasure to keep him in the dark. You can trust me and Grannie. When we've a mind to, we can keep our mouths as tight as a donkey's backside.'

He opened a pack of playing cards, took the cards out, fanned them and put them back. 'You can have these half price,' he offered. 'There's only a couple missing.'

Joe said we weren't interested.

'They say the two of you's from London. Got an uncle there by the name of Sid Grice. Know him? Big bloke with a glass eye.'

'Where's he live?'

'I told you, London. Need something to clear the wax out your ears? I got some oil somewhere.'

'London's a big place,' I stammered.

'You don't know him, then?'

'Well, no.'

'Why didn't you say so in the first place?'

Irritated, Old Witchery moved to another counter. His feet were small enough for him to walk easily along the rows as if early in life their growth had been stunted.

'What about a nice handkerchief to go with the socks. Had a shipment not more than ten years ago, quality Irish linen. Nothing to beat Irish linen. Like blowing your nose on a lily.'

We bought two, one each for Fergus and Murray. At the same time we declined a haircut from Old Witchery who, apparently, was also the township's barber.

'You'd better hide the presents quick,' Joe said as Murray entered through the back door.

He tripped over the rugs and grumbled, 'Beggar me, Cyril, isn't it time you moved these things?'

'You should be used to them by now. They've been there twenty years or more,' Old Witchery replied.

Joe and I chose a row each and continued inspecting boxes. I was about to walk further along, when I saw a black leather wallet lying between half a dozen rolls of toilet paper and some packets of jelly. Peeping from the wallet as if it was preparing to fly away, I noticed an orange butterfly. It didn't move and I put my hand out to touch its wing, when I realized it was a hair slide. I tucked the wallet and hair slide behind the toilet paper. When Joe was gone, I would come back and buy the wallet for him and the hair slide for Gaylene. It felt as if I'd found treasure.

'*Norwest arch out there,*' Old Witchery observed to Murray.

'*Too right there is.*'

'*That norwest's been blowing up all night.*'

'*Too right, it has.*'

'I think we should buy this for the Missus,' Joe called across to me, holding up a book entitled *Public Speaking For Everyone*.

'*It'll be a hot one today all right,*' Old Witchery forecast.

'*My word, yes.*'

'*Need to hang on to your wig in this wind.*'

Murray touched his hat. '*I reckon.*'

Elastic, buttons, zips, cotton in a box marked "*Ladies Personals*".

'*It'll turn souwest by six,*' Murray answered.

'*Nearer five.*'

'*Six is my guess.*'

'*Definitely five.*'

'There's a book on gardening here. Can you get across?' I called to Joe.

'I'm on my way.' Joe clambered across a counter. Old Witchery was too busy weather forecasting to notice.

'*You can see it blowin' in from here.*'

'*We'll get some rain by six.*' Murray was adamant.

'*Never seen a souwester that didn't bring a bit of dirty weather with it. Yes, here by five.*' Old Witchery crossed his arms and defied Murray to disagree with him.

'This looks donkey's years old, but I s'ppose gardening don't change. I'm not going to pay his price, though. He'll have to knock it down before I buy it,' Joe said, as he thumbed through a book with yellowing pages.

I continued to lift books from the box and placed them in small piles wherever I could find space. 'There doesn't seem much else here,' I said as I thumbed through a book entitled *Make Do and Mend To Help Win The War*.

'*I recall a couple of years back, a norwester took us up to a hundred. So hot, Grannie refused to make her pies.*'

'*I remember.*'

'*Then quick as a flash, in comes the souwest.*'

'*And before you know it we've got snow.*'

'*I was about to say that.*' Old Witchery glared at Murray.

'Wait a mo.' I picked up a book with a picture of a river. Behind it there was a large church. 'This one's called *Dublin, City of My Dreams*.'

'Ain't Dublin in Ireland?' Joe asked.

'I'm sure I remember Fergus saying he lived there once.'

'We'll get Old Witchery to give us a special deal seeing as we're buying a couple of books,' Joe said.

'*Forty-eight when that norwester blew the roof off the Community Hall, remember?*' Murray took the initiative.

'*Course I remember, but it was forty-nine.*'

'*Forty-eight. The year my brother went to Australia,*' Murray stated with some force.

'*Forty-nine. When I had that shipment of corned beef from Argentina. Sold the last tin not more than a month back.*'

When I'd finished shopping, I left Joe in Grannie Witchery's tea room tucking into one of her steak and cheese pies. I doubled back to the front of the shop and told Old Witchery I wanted to buy the wallet for Joe and the hair slide as a present for my sister. It would be perfect for Gaylene.

Murray, mellow after an afternoon at *The Travellers*, shouted to his mates inside. 'Don't forget, not a word to the Boss about the young blokes being here.' In answer came a chorus of 'Too right, we won't', and 'Mum's the word'.

'Not such a bad place, eh?' he asked me and Joe, as we waited outside.

'Grannie's pie was worth coming for, that's a fact,' Joe answered, forgetting his recent impatience at having to wait for Murray.

Murray searched the shopping bag for his keys and hesitated. 'Cuss it all, I've a feeling I've forgotten something.' He scratched his head under his hat, leaving his hat askew.

The Mission, nuns and clothes! Murray was about to remember. I braced myself.

'I've got it. It's come back to me now! Your winnings! I've got them right here.' Beer fumes wafted over us, as Murray handed us the money.

'Good old *Wandering Minstrel*. Joe kissed the notes as he usually did when we won.

'My word, no! *Tea Caddy*. There was never any doubt.'

'*Tea Caddy*? You put our money on *Tea Caddy*?'

'Too right I did, Ginger. If there's two things I'm not often wrong about, it's horses and the weather.'

Murray touched his hat to Old Witchery, who was standing outside his shop. He climbed into the truck. 'Jump in you two. Best be off. That souwester'll be here by six.'

Chapter Eighteen

When I asked him about the bonus, Eleod's weather-beaten face turned a menacing purple.

'Bonus! Bonus! You want a bloody bonus! *Because wool's fetching a good price this year*,' he mimicked.

'You'd still be in an orphanage if it wasn't for me. That's where the likes of you and your cocky mate belong. I give you three good meals a day, clothe you, put a roof over your heads and give you an education. You won't be getting a penny out of me.'

'But …'

'It's you who need to pay me!' He stabbed his finger into my chest. 'What have you got to pay me with, eh?'

'Nothing,' I mumbled.

He stabbed me in the chest again. 'Your pal's got something to pay me with.'

I felt the colour leave my face. Downston must have found out about the money Joe had screwed out of his son.

He continued, 'I should have thought of it before. The four of you living on the fat of the land over there, while the Missus and I struggle to feed ourselves.' Downston looked as if he truly believed his own words.

'You won't be eating extra tucker anymore. This afternoon I'll be over to those quarters of yours and watch you dig up every vege in the boy's garden and give 'em to the Missus and me. I'll teach you to complain.'

'But they're ours.'

'Nothing's yours, boy.' He caught me a blow around the head that blurred everything grey.

That afternoon, the sky was weighed down with cloud that sealed in the heat. Sweat poured from us in rivulets, as we thrust our spades into the soil and dug up the plants. Downston stood at the side and commanded. 'Put your backs into it, and don't think you can miss any.'

'By all the saints, Boss, is this really necessary? The boy's spent every spare minute he's had labouring over this garden,' Fergus intervened.

'His mate should have thought of that before he became lippy with me.'

I kept digging. If I'd kept my mouth shut, this wouldn't have happened. Joe's veges would still be there and Joe wouldn't have his hat pulled down over his eyes so we couldn't see his tears.

'They were for Christmas,' he muttered, and Murray kept saying, 'She'll be right, boy. She'll be right.'

When every plant had been lifted and taken to the homestead, Joe laid face-down on his bunk, his muddy shoes hanging from the end. 'I hope they choke on 'em'. Joe's voice shook, and my hatred towards Downston made it difficult for me to swallow.

'Now come on, Ginger, you can't let the Boss beat you.' It was unusual for Murray to give advice.

'What d'you suggest I should do? Go and pinch the veges back?'

'I don't rightly know, but you're a clever young beggar, you'll think of something.' Murray edged nearer to

Joe's bunk and patted him on the back. I could see it was an affectionate gesture. I knew that Murray was more upset for Joe than he was for the loss of the veges themselves. 'I reckon I can get hold of a few peas and potatoes from Old Witchery for Christmas. I don't know why we never thought of it before,' he said.

'To be sure, we all feel the same way, but Murray's right. You'll bounce back, and my reckoning is it'll be higher than before,' Fergus said.

Joe made a hopeless sort of noise and his body shuddered.

'Why'd the two of you stay here with Downston?' I asked Murray and Fergus.

'Too old to change now,' Murray said.

Fergus shrugged.

'Anyhow, we've got you two to think about,' Murray continued, and I realised he and Fergus would probably have gone long ago if it wasn't for Joe and me.

Usually, Christmas Day was no different from any other day; the routines remained unchanged. This year, true to his word, Murray managed to get some peas, beans and a few spuds from Old Witchery to go with the boil-up. For the first time, too, there were four thin slices of Christmas pudding on a plate next to the boil-up pan. I wondered if Gaylene had persuaded the Missus to give them to us.

'This Christmas pudding's not so bad. I reckon that new girl they've got helping the Missus made it.'

'I wish by St. Nicholas himself that she'd show the Missus how to do something different with the boil-up,' Fergus replied.

'Well, next year we'll be eating our own veges again, if my little plan comes off.' Joe's face wore its sly and secretive look. He had almost reverted to his old self.

'And, of course, you can't tell us what it is!' I said. Joe's secrets always irritated me.

'Not yet. Anyway, it's time for the presents.' All day Joe had been like an excited puppy expecting a bone. We'll give ours out first, Tone.'

'If you like.' I felt under my bunk and brought out three presents wrapped in newspaper. I took the first one. 'This is for you, Murray.'

Murray tore at the newspaper and pulled out the socks. 'My word,' he said, 'But you should have gone easy on the bum paper.'

'And this is for you,' I handed the book to Fergus. The paper had already come undone and I could see part of the picture of a church spire and the first word, *"Dublin"*.

'It's called, *"Dublin, City of My Dreams"*,' Joe told Fergus as if he couldn't read it for himself. 'Tony says Dublin's where you lived.'

'To be sure it was.' Fergus ran his hand across the cover. His face held a look of longing that verged on despair.

'And this is my present to you, Joe.' Joe practically snatched the packet from me and began ripping the paper. 'It's a wallet.' He held it up for the others to see. He put it to his nose and sniffed. 'Would you believe it's real leather, real leather,' he repeated.

I knew that when the others weren't around he'd transfer his mounting pile of pound notes to it. 'Real leather, what d'you think about that,' he said once more to Murray, and Murray, replied, 'Too right, it is, Ginger. One of Old Witchery's best if I'm not mistaken.'

Joe pulled back the sack covering his bunk, and brought out an unwrapped book. 'Merry Christmas, Tone. Old Witchery said he knew just where to put his finger on a book of poetry, and he did. Climbed across three counters and came straight to it, under a pile of trusses. On the cover it says it's love poems,' Joe explained as he handed the book to me. 'It sounds a lot of double Dutch to me, but I knew you'd like it.'

Fergus and Murray gave us a tooth brush each which, when we were on our own, Joe said weren't exactly the sort of presents that made you want to dance down Balham High Street. We'd got away without using a tooth brush all this time, why start now? It seemed a bit hypocritical, he said, when Murray and Fergus never cleaned *their* teeth.

'It's beautiful,' Gaylene caught the curls resting on her forehead into the slide I gave her. 'It matches my skirt,' she said as if it was coincidental. 'How did you manage to get it?'

'Murray got it for me when he went for the supplies. Um ... I told him I wanted something for my sister.'

Gaylene adjusted the slide so that it sat a little higher. 'I'm sorry I couldn't buy you anything, but I saved this from Christmas day.' She produced a Christmas cracker from the paper bag she had brought with her to our meeting place behind the rabbiters' hut.

When we had spent Christmas Day with Fred and Lori we'd had Christmas crackers, proper ones. Mine was red, I remembered. Inside had been a plastic chicken and a motto.

I offered one end of my cracker to Gaylene.

We've got to make a wish,' she said, closing her eyes. 'And we mustn't tell anyone what we've wished for or it won't come true.'

I had spent the whole of my life wishing. Dreams never came true. Nevertheless, I smiled and said, 'I won't tell anyone.'

We pulled and the cracker split open. An orange plastic ring rolled on to the ground. I picked it up and turned it over in my hand. 'Would you like it?' I held the ring out to Gaylene. 'It matches your hair slide.'

She took it and placed it on the middle finger of her right hand, stroking it as if it was a precious gem.

'Would you like me to read you some poetry the next time we meet? I've got a new poetry book.' My voice sounded strange even to me.

'Yes, please.'

'Right, tomorrow same time, if I can get here.' I rose abruptly and left. I knew I shouldn't have arranged to meet her or to read her poetry but how could I own a book like that without sharing it with her?

'Blinkin' heat. Never could abide hot weather,' Joe grumbled as we sat outside our quarters looking at what had been Joe's garden, but was now a tangle of dying plants and fresh weeds.

'D'you think you can get me some old tins and pots and pans when you go into the township? I'll give you the cash for 'em.' Joe asked Murray. As a concession to the heat, Murray had rolled his trousers up past his knees, revealing skinny hairless legs.

'I don't see why not, Ginger. What're you thinking of doing with 'em?'

'Hiding them.' Joe replied.

'My word, that's not what I was expecting you to say.'

'Hiding them full of earth and Downston's fertilizer and growing veges in 'em. I'll put them all over the show, in places he never goes to. 'It'll be a bit of a job when it comes to watering them but if we all get stuck in I think it'll work. I might even try a few flowers.'

'I said you'd find a way, didn't I? Clever bloke like you wouldn't be beaten by the likes of the Boss. I said that at the time, isn't that a fact. Count us in, Ginger,' Murray said looking into the hut at Fergus. But Fergus was rubbing his fingers over the picture of Dublin on the front of his book.

'And me, too,' I said, getting up and walking into the hut to sit next to Fergus on his bunk. I liked looking at the photos of Dublin. It reminded me of the times Fred and I spun the globe.

'We used to sit by the Liffey, Marion and I, on mild and smiling days with a breeze like petals,' Fergus said to no one in particular. 'Holy Mother of God it was beautiful. On the day we were married, we walked along the banks of the Liffey. She looked like the river goddess herself with her hair the colour of the bulrushes while all about us was blue and green. "You're not regretting it, Fergus?" She asked.

"Although 'tis a bit late now." She laughed and her laughter entered my soul.

'Never, and I never will. You're all I need, Marion.' And indeed she was. It didn't matter what the Church said about relinquishing my vows as a priest, even that I had broken my parents' hearts.

'I found a job on a farm that had a cottage going with it, a broken-down place but to Marion and me it was a palace. Not a jarring word did we speak in it. In the evenings I would read her poetry, while she knitted for the child we were expecting.'

Fergus got up. 'Tis like a furnace in this place,' he said and made his way out of the hut and across to the ridge.

I followed him. 'What happened?' I asked after a while. 'What happened to Marion?'

'She died. I told my sister to come and get the baby. I didn't look at the child, a girl, I believe, and I left.'

'Haven't you seen her, your daughter, I mean?'

'No. I don't even know her name. She's thirteen now. Whenever I see a young girl in the township, I look at her and wonder if my daughter is like that.'

'Is that who you were writing to?'

'I was foolish enough to think she might like to know who her daddy is, but why should she care?'

The next day when I arrived, Gaylene was propped against the back of the rabbiter's hut polishing her cracker ring on her skirt.

'Have you bought the poetry book?' she asked, looking at my empty hands.

'I couldn't bring the book itself in case someone saw me, but I've copied a poem.' I took a piece of crumpled paper from my pocket. 'I won't be able to stay or someone might come looking for me.' What I actually meant was her father might come looking for me.

Gaylene slid further down the wall, and settled herself beside me. I felt her breath on my neck.

'It's a love poem,' I said jerkily and she replied, 'Read it to me like you said Fergus reads poetry.' She closed her eyes, and I began.

She was a phantom of delight
When first she gleam'd upon my sight.
A lovely apparition sent
To be a moment's ornament:
Her eyes as stars of twilight fair,
Like twilight's, too, her dusky hair,
But all things else about her dawn,
A dancing shape, an image gay
To haunt, to startle and waylay.'

For a moment neither of us spoke. Gaylene still had her eyes shut. Finally she said, 'I didn't know poetry could be so beautiful. Who wrote it?'

'William Wordsworth.'

I studied the side of her face. Her skin was smooth and without any blemishes and I wondered if Fergus's Marion had been as lovely.

'If you want, we can read some poetry this evening. We can meet at the river by the flat rock. Do you know it?' She asked.

I nodded. Sometimes when I could get away without Downston or the others seeing me, I would go there to be alone with my memories. It was more peaceful than the pigsty and much more beautiful.

'About seven, before it gets dark,' Gaylene suggested.

'Your parents wouldn't like it.'

'I can slip out my bedroom window. They'll think I'm working on my school holiday project.'

'I don't want you to get into trouble.'

'It'll be all right. I'll be back and asleep by the time Mum pops her head round the door before she goes to bed.'

She stood and offered her hand to pull me up. 'Come on, we've got to go.'

The evening breeze brushed my body as I shook the water from my face, and begun rubbing under my arms with my washing rag.

'At this rate, you'll wash yourself away.' Joe looked at me, puzzled. 'Why do you want to wash after dinner as well as in the morning? It's not natural. Once a day's too much if you ask me.'

He hit his forehead dramatically with the heel of his hand. 'I've got it! You're going to meet that Gay Whatsername. I should've twigged.'

I wished Joe would leave me alone.

'Playing with fire, that's what you're doing. The Boss'll murder you if he finds out.'

'He's not going to.' Somewhere in my stomach fear mingled with excitement.

'Where are the two of you going?'

'To the river. Anyway, I don't know why you're making such a fuss.'

'I'm not making a fuss. I don't want to see you cut up in little pieces and fed to the pigs.'

'I told you that's not going to happen.' I felt round my chin.

'You're not going to shave are you? You've only got two whiskers.' Joe handed me my shirt. 'All this for a bit of hanky panky.'

'It's nothing like that. All we're going to do is read poetry. There's nothing wrong with that, is there?'

I didn't like Joe using those words about Gaylene. It demeaned her, though I wasn't sure what hanky panky was. I thought it was something in addition to sex, although I wasn't that certain about sex. When the Gang saw people kissing in a picture at Saturday Picture Club, we jeered and cat-called. We thought kissing was soppy. If it was soppy, why did I dream about kissing Gaylene?

'Nothing wrong with what, boy?' Murray asked, emerging from our quarters on his way to the long drop, already unbuttoning his fly.

'He's going to meet that Gay Whatsername tonight at the river?'

'Big mouth!'

Murray whistled through his teeth and said, 'My word.'

'I've told him the Boss'll kill him if he finds out.'

'Too right he will.'

'Aren't you going to tell him not to trust a woman?' Joe called after Murray.

'It's his own business.' Murray disappeared inside the dunny, shouting back, 'You can borrow my new socks, boy.'

Shadows engulfed the gorge, through which the river wound - a grey-blue thread, before it ran its course along a widening shingle bed. From there it forged its way on into a further canyon. A lonely birdsong soared upwards while insects in black clusters hovered in the pastel haze of evening.

Gaylene was already there when I arrived, low down by the river, sitting on a rock the shape of an ironing board.

'I thought you might not have been able to find me,' she smiled as I approached. Against the steep outcrop, she appeared smaller.

I clambered across the rock and sat beside her. 'Did you have any trouble getting here?'

'No. My bedroom's round the back of the house. At this time in the evening, Mum and Dad are always at the front so it was easy to slip away. What about you?'

'No.'

'It's lovely here in the evening.'

'Yes.' I sought for something to say but nothing came. We gazed at the river. All at once I became aware of the space between us filled with uncertainty and widened by a thousand unasked and unanswered questions.

'Are you going to read some poetry?' Gaylene asked at last. It was a relief she had spoken. This time I took my poetry book from my pocket. I opened it to a page I had marked with a bookmark made from the long-drop newspaper. 'I'll read another verse from the poem I read you yesterday by Wordsworth.' My voice cracked involuntarily and rose before falling. Embarrassed, I coughed as if to clear my throat. I struggled for an even pitch.

> *I saw her upon nearer view,*
> *A Spirit, yet a woman too!*
> *Her household motions light and free*
> *And steps of virgin liberty,*
> *A countenance in which did meet,*
> *Sweet records, promises as sweet,*
> *A creature not too bright or good*
> *For human nature's daily food,*
> *For transient sorrows, simple wiles,*
> *Praise, blame, love, kisses, tears and smiles*

Gaylene rested her head in her hands. 'I don't think my father has ever loved my mother like that. What about your parents?'

I blew my breath in front of me. 'The only thing my Old Man ever loved was the bottle. He left home when I was a kid. I suppose my mother must have loved him once.' I paused. 'Perhaps they both loved each other once.'

How could anything as beautiful as Wordsworth wrote about deteriorate into what Angela and I had witnessed? Yet love could overcome unimaginable obstacles, even survive death. I had only to listen to Fergus to know that.

Gaylene moved closer. 'Am I an apparition of delight?' she whispered.

As an answer, I took hold of her shoulders and stroked upwards to her face.

'You're beautiful.'
Her kiss was like dandelion down brushing my lips.

'You're moping around like a lovesick animal,' Joe observed the next day. He moved closer. 'What I want to know is, what the two of you got up to. Did you … you know?'
'I told you. We read poetry.'
'Pigs might fly.'
'Please yourself.' I began to walk away from Joe. I wanted to be alone to relive the previous evening, to feel Gaylene's lips touching mine, to recreate the tenderness.
'You going to meet her again tonight?' Joe shouted after me.
'What if I am?'
'You must be mad,' he called back.

This time I was the first to arrive, lying back on the rock, feeling its stored up heat from the day seep into me. Behind my closed eyes, a dozen Gaylenes danced in an orange swirl. When she arrived she was a manifestation of my daydream.
We took off our shoes and walked along the river's edge, jumping from stone to stone. We ran through the water, squealing at its chill. Then we pulled each other across deeper crevices and up steeper slopes until we found a clearing. There we laid on crackling leaves, entwined in each other's arms. I felt the smoothness of her skin and the roundness of her breasts as the canyon grew shadowy and the birds became silent.
The canyon was almost dark when we finally stumbled from it. Twilight had turned the grass grey as we

crept hand in hand towards the homestead. We kissed one final time behind the large flax bush.

'Blimey, where've you been?' Joe confronted me at the door.

Inside, Fergus was reading and Murray was tending the stove.

'We began to think you'd eloped, boy,' Murray laughed.

I coloured.

'Be taking no notice.' Fergus looked up from his book and took a sip of his cocoa. 'Would you be liking some?'

The everydayness of the act slowed my heart a little.

Then we heard it! The Bedford with the tailgate clanging as it tore along the rough track. It skidded on the gravel and pulled up outside with a great screeching of brakes. Fergus held his cup midair. Murray knelt unmoving in front of the stove. Joe and I clung to each other as the door was flung open. It swung back and hit the wall with a crash. Papers became dislodged from shelves and fluttered to the floor, together with the calendars. The cocoa slurped from Fergus' mug.

Downston flung himself into the hut. Everything about his face was aflame: eyes, skin, nose, mouth. 'I'm going to bloody murder you.' He advanced towards me.

Chapter Nineteen

We were all on our feet now.

'Steady on, Boss.' Murray approached Downston in an effort to calm him, but Downston lunged towards Joe and me. He caught hold of Joe before he realised he had the wrong one and hurled him across the room. Again, the hut quaked as if the ground beneath was in turmoil. Downston ignored Fergus's shouts of, 'Tis enough,' and seized my shirt. Leaving the collar hanging, he yanked me to the door and tossed me into the truck as if he was throwing a sheep there. 'Let's see what a night in the bush'll do for you!' He rounded the vehicle, jumped into the driver's seat and started the engine. The truck hurtled back along the track.

Dazed and shivering, I wedged myself into a corner and massaged the flesh above my elbow. My ripped collar flapped in the air rush.

We were on a wider track now and dust enveloped the truck. I bent over to protect myself from the piercing cold while, at the same time, trying to brace myself.

It was difficult to know how long we'd been driving when Downston screeched the truck to a halt and ordered me out. My eyes watered, my ears stung and my feet were numb as I levered myself from the vehicle and toppled on to the ground.

'Get up, damn you!' Downston booted me in the ribs. He produced a torch, grabbed the back of my neck and shoved me forward.

I stumbled over the uneven ground, catching my feet in the tangled undergrowth. At times, it seemed we were circling the same trees, as Downston half dragged me onwards into thick bush. Without warning, he stopped as if he didn't trust himself to go further.

'Dare to touch my girl! Dare to touch her! Stay here and don't move a bloody inch until I drive away or I swear I'll murder you.'

I remained statue-like until the flicker of torchlight disappeared and I could no longer hear the brittle sound of footsteps on tinder. I thought I heard the distant sound of an engine starting up. Only then did I slither down a tree trunk, relieved to be rid of Downston.

I rubbed my arm, probing it gently. It was lumpy and swollen. My legs were scratched and I felt my own blood warm on my fingers. All round me there seemed to be strange forest noises. I shivered as the dankness seeped into me and I wrapped my arms around myself for comfort.

I peered into the darkness trying to accustom my eyes to it. Slivers of moonlight penetrated the canopy above me. Shadows loomed, advancing phantom shapes. From somewhere within them came an eerie screech.

I couldn't stay here all night. I must get back to the road. I couldn't think beyond that. The road – any road – would be better than this place. I struggled to get up but my legs buckled. I sank back against the tree experiencing a rotating feeling in my head. I closed my eyes and waited for the dizziness to pass. 'Must find the road,' I whispered, afraid some hidden presence might hear me.

Weariness settled on me like a blanket. 'Must find the road.' I forced my eyes open. I would try to get up again in a moment. I extended my legs. Despite my efforts to keep awake, I fell into a sleep that wasn't a sleep at all, but more a lack of consciousness, full of dark images. Mum and Angela appeared and beckoned. Joe, Murray and Fergus tramped through the bush and on into oblivion. I was being driven deeper and deeper until I reached its vortex, from which I couldn't escape.

It was still dark when I came to myself. I was aware of the numbness in my hands and feet and the pain in my arm. Gradually, I recalled the events that had led to me being there. I swallowed down my fear and levered myself back up against the tree trunk. I wiggled my fingers to induce life back into them.

Like a theatre curtain being imperceptibly raised, the dimmest of lights silhouetted everything around me. Feeling began returning to my fingers and toes. I pulled off my shoes and socks and massaged my feet, before placing one foot over the other and burying them into a pile of dry leaves for warmth. I ripped off my loose collar, spat on it, and dabbed at the wound on my arm and at my scratched legs before discarding it. I folded my socks and placed them inside my shoes. Murray would have something to say if I didn't look after them.

A solitary bird's first call of the day encouraged me to my feet. I clutched the tree trunk for support. My legs trembled but held as I studied my surroundings through the pinpricks of light that infiltrated the forest.

With effort I raised one arm, then the other. After that, I slid my feet apart and then together, in a feeble attempt to ape the exercises we used to do in the playground in

Blountmere Street School. The sound of my shuffling on the forest floor seemed louder and more disturbing than jumping up and down on the tarmac of a London school playground. The forest was hallowed. Nothing other than its own sounds were meant to be heard.

A choir of birds joined the solo. Everywhere resounded to their song. Beyond them another chorus swelled and beyond them another. I marvelled at their ability to sing in this impenetrable jungle but, then, if they wanted, they could fly above the trees and escape. The thought disturbed me. I needed to find the road. But after the road, what? Where could I go? Downston wouldn't allow me back and I'd be lost anywhere away from the farm. I cast the thought away. I had to concentrate on finding my way out of this place to the road. When I got to the road, I'd decide what to do.

I brushed my feet clean before I replaced Murray's socks and put on my shoes. Then I set off in the direction in which I thought Downston had left. It shouldn't be difficult or he would never have brought me here for fear of getting lost himself.

The advent of morning transformed the bush from menace to safe tranquility, like the coming of daylight did to the bombsite. The Gang could have made a marvellous camp here. No one would have found us. No one would have found us! If I didn't find my way out, no one would find me! I pushed the thought away and trudged on.

I recalled Murray saying that shepherds were able to cover long distances because they walked to a steady rhythm:

consistent, not fast or slow as the mood and energy took them. One - breathe, two – breathe, three – breathe.

I began reciting poetry, measuring my steps to it. When I ran out of poems I knew, I started again.

Reciting poetry reminded me of Gaylene. I wondered what had happened to her. Had the Boss punished her, too? Perhaps he had taken her somewhere and left her like he had me. He might even have beaten her. I conjured a picture of the two of us together by the river and stroked my arm fleetingly, as if I was touching her. Was it only last night we had been together?

Resolutely, I pushed on brushing against black velvet tree trunks. A fungus caused the velvety parts, Gaylene had told me on our ascent up the side of the gorge. She said the trunks reminded her of long black gloves that ladies sometimes wore to balls. It was the sort of thing Paula would have said. I hadn't thought about Paula or Blountmere Street much recently. My friendship with Gaylene had driven them away. I allowed myself a wry inner smile. What would they say in Blountmere Street if they could see me now, deep in the bush.

The birdsong chorus continued. First, one bird took the lead, then another. Their song sounded as clear as church bells on frosty air.

Ahead, a patch of light widened to reveal a clump of cabbage trees. Joe said it was a stupid name for a tree that didn't grow cabbages. It was like calling a tree an apple tree when it didn't grow apples. That's what Joe said.

I couldn't be far from the road now.

Even with trees crammed one against another, forming a matted roof above me, I could feel it becoming hotter. I didn't know how long I had been walking, but it had taken much longer than Downston took last night.

I hadn't eaten since the Missus's boil-up the night before and hunger gnawed at me. My feet were becoming sore. Worse, my tongue felt pitted.

I found a sturdy tree root and squatted on it. Where was the road?

I wondered what the others were doing. I ached for the security of our quarters.

'Got to get going.' I hoisted myself to my feet. If there was a landmark, like the river, something to point me in the right direction, I could follow it, but discovering the river seemed an impossible dream.

I continued to claw my way through thick bush as the terrain rose steadily. Using both my hands to help me keep my balance, I scrambled upwards. Prickly young beeches, manuka bushes and bush lawyer raked me. My breathing came in painful sobs. My legs shook from exertion. I felt weaker than I could ever remember.

I was afraid that if I stopped, I might topple backwards. I pressed on, forcing my legs to move. I dared not look up for fear of losing my balance and I dreaded to let my gaze wander downwards. When I thought I was incapable of taking another step, the ground flattened into a ledge. It was wide enough to allow me to bend over and clutch my knees. My chest heaved and fell like bellows as my lungs sucked in air. The muscles in my legs twitched and complained. My fingers stung. My tongue cleaved to the roof of my mouth.

I didn't know how long it took for my breathing to become steady. Time had no meaning here.

At last, I straightened and looked around. Trees hemmed me in like prison walls. Murray once told us about someone, an American student Murray seemed to remember, who had gone into the bush for an afternoon stroll. They found his skeleton draped with the remains of his clothes two years later. That's what happened to fools who knew nothing about the bush, Murray had said.

Panic surged through me. Had the American called for help, or cried, or thought of his family, or prayed? Perhaps he lived in an American-type Blountmere Street and he kept a picture of it in front of him all the time he was trying to make his way out. He might not have been far from the road. If he'd kept going, he would have made it.

Wearily, I raised my hands above my head and attempted a stretch, before I slowly began a descent. I wedged myself against anything that felt solid to stop plummeting forward and used my diminishing strength to keep my balance. Down and down - slithering and clutching.

When the ground flattened, I hardly recognised that it had. The blisters on my feet throbbed and I sat on a flat stone and removed my shoes. Murray's socks were streaked with blood. Just the same, I folded them as carefully as before, tucked them inside my shoes and tied the laces together. I would be better off without them. It wasn't as if I always wore shoes on the farm.

Automatically, I stood up, hung my shoes over my shoulder and began walking again. I *must* keep going. If the American hadn't given up, he might be back in his American Blountmere Street, instead of ending up a pile of bones and clothes hidden in the New Zealand bush. It was a waste of his journey.

Although it was almost hidden by the overgrowth, the sun reached its flaring pinnacle, causing noonday lethargy. The bush rested.

Somewhere I thought I heard the sound of water, a far away hum. Gaylene said that farther along from where we'd sat on our ironing board rock, the river threaded its way for miles. 'The river! Lead me to the river where I can drink from it! Bathe my feet in! Splash in it! Dance in it! Be reborn by it!' I prayed to Mum's God.

Succumbing to the midday drowsiness all around me, I laid on a pile of leaves, heaping more for a pillow. *The river or the road.* I slept.

When I came to, the birdsong was gentler, not so exuberant, winding down, getting ready to set with the sun.

Bloody patches of leaves stuck to my feet and I tried to peel them off.

When I'd taken as many of them from my feet as I could, I once again started walking, listening beyond the birdsong for the mellow sound of the water I thought I'd heard before I fell asleep. But I couldn't attune my ears to it.

On and on I went in search of the water sounds.

There it was! Not water, but a clearing in the bush! I staggered headlong towards it. My spirits soared and I looked up to the sky and freedom. I couldn't be far now. I called out in excitement. 'I've found it! I'm here!' Even as the words left me, I realized it was the same plantation of cabbage trees I'd passed hours before.

Lying face down, I abandoned myself to sobs that parted the stillness. I was going to die here in this place. Not

250

in a bed like Mum probably had. Not even in the familiarity of the playground next to the lizzie, like Dobsie. Not screwed up with pain or with broken contorted limbs, just a heap of bones that had fallen asleep and never woken up, covered with my despised mission clothes. In the end, they would outlast me. I would go with no-one to pull a red blanket over my face, or say a prayer over me. I would go alone and with no one who really loved me. I would simply fade away into the forest, while the birds chorused unheeding above me.

I was crawling now. My shoes and socks lay discarded somewhere. Above me, the ragged edges of sky became tinged with twilight.

As if I had wept the last of the moisture left in me, my thirst superseded everything. My shredded feet and bloody arms were a mere blur of pain by comparison. Obsessive thoughts of water tormented me. Buckets! Lakes! Oceans! Cool and refreshing on my lips, trickling down my throat.

"I said you were crackers, didn't I. Bleedin' crackers! Crackers! Crackers!" Joe's red hair and freckles burnt under my eyelids. "Nobody'll look after you if you don't look after yourself. Crackers!" I cupped my hands to catch the globules that dropped from Joe's watering can, but they evaporated before they reached my fingers. I scratched at the ground for the last of the fallen moisture, but the earth was arid under my finger-nails.

I let my eyelids droop and relinquished myself to the bush. I had been abandoned for the last time.

The man was no more than a black outline in the early morning light as he bent over me. He seemed familiar and I raised my hand to touch his face.

'She'll be right, boy,' the man said.

I closed my eyes and waited. I had never imagined the touch of death to be whiskery and warm. Crackers!

Chapter Twenty

'I've never seen Murray and Fergus like that before,' Joe told me when we were both back in the quarters. 'You should have heard them, demanding to know what the Boss had done with you. The old sod blustered that he was giving you a couple of nights in the bush you wouldn't forget. It wouldn't do you any harm, he said. Just the same, he looked as if he had the wind-up, when Murray said the authorities would have him if anything happened to you. Fergus said it was a damn fool thing to do. The Blessed Virgin must be weeping over you, alone out there, he told the Boss.

'Like I said, it must have frightened Downston good and proper, 'cos even though he stormed around swearing he didn't know what all the fuss was about, he threw Murray the keys to the truck. He said he'd taken you to *Pikes Elbow*. If you'd got any sense you'd stay put there. He started going on about you interfering with his daughter. He ranted about you having to be taught a lesson, but Murray was already outside the hut, and running to the truck. I followed him. There was no way I was going to let him go without me,' Joe grinned.

'Even though Murray's a bushman, I thought we were going to get ourselves lost. But Murray knew what he was doing, all right. When we found the collar to your shirt, I knew we'd find you, if only you'd hang on, and not go conking out on us.' Joe gave a wobbly laugh.

Joe said when they got me back to the men's quarters, I slept for sixteen hours straight off. Even so, when I tried to get up my legs gave way. They looked like a pair of corkscrews and my feet were torn to shreds, Joe told me. I hardly felt the pain.

That evening the Missus brought the boil-up over herself. She'd mixed a bit of chicken with it.

Murray touched his hat and said 'Good on ya, Missus,' but she ignored him and walked across to my bunk. Without saying anything, she took a posh looking tin from the pocket of her overall. She unscrewed the lid, pushed me gently back, and began to rub honeysuckle-perfumed cream into my feet. Her hands were surprisingly soft and every now and then she put the tin to her nose and inhaled. I think it must have been expensive stuff. Just the same, it stung and caused me to suck in my breath. She touched my shoulder fleetingly and as silently as she had come, she left.

'My, but she's been a hot one today.' Downston appeared over the ridge as the four of us sat outside later that evening. He was carrying a chipped china jug and two glasses.

'I reckon she's still got a bit of summer left,' he said in an oily way.

'Too right, Boss,' Murray replied.

'Just having a stroll round the place to make sure everything's all right.' Downston explained casually. He acted as if he hadn't seen me.

'To be sure 'tis a good night for a saunter.' Fergus joined the conversation.

'Brought you a drop of something to wet the back of your throats, seeing as it's hot as a bloody furnace. Liquid gold, it is.'

'Good on ya, Boss.' Murray took hold of the jug and glasses, leaving Downston empty-handed and awkward. 'Too right she's a hot one,' he repeated and cleared his throat. 'Well, best be off then. There's still a bit to check on. Hooray.'

We watched as Downston stumbled over the ridge and retreated into the distance. Murray moved his hat back and scratched his head. 'The Boss is scared we're going to rap on him to the authorities, too right he is. That's what all this is about.'

'Why don't we snitch on him? Tony could be dead now if we hadn't found him.' Joe lowered his voice as if he was trying not to let me hear.

'No point, boy. It would only be our word against his,' Murray replied. 'And what would they do? My guess is they'd take the pair of you's away to a place where we couldn't keep an eye on you.'

'To be sure we've talked it over. But for everyone's sake it's best left. He won't do it again. Not with us around!'

'Too right, he won't.'

'*Nothing to worry about with us around,*' Joe mimicked, when Murray and Fergus had returned to the hut. 'Anything for a quiet life, those two.'

I kept my mouth shut. What was the point in making a fuss? Who was going to listen to what I had to say? No one ever had.

I hadn't seen Gaylene since being lost in the bush. Murray said they'd probably sent her to Downston's brother until it was time for her to return to school. Often, before I fell asleep I recalled the feel of her skin and the rise of her breasts, although I had difficulty picturing her face.

In the same way, a net had fallen over Blountmere Street that blurred details, obscured scenes and refused to lift even when with deep concentration I tried to raise it.

The torpor deepened. My thoughts and actions became sluggish and without purpose. Despair that I had neither the inclination, nor the energy to throw off settled on me. No reading of poetry by Fergus or cajoling by Murray could penetrate it. I was oblivious to Joe's endless chatter. Living or dying became indecipherable as choices.

As if each day some unknown finger pressed a button connected to my body, I went about my work and routines without thinking or caring what I was doing until the finger pressed again and released me to the relief of sleep.

Careless autumn sunshine gave place to the warning barbs of winter. Somewhere deep in a recess in my head, it reminded me of the bombsite. I think it was the only reason I noticed it.

'The sun's ripenened the tomatoes I've got hidden all over the place.' Joe caressed the ones he'd just picked. 'With winter coming, I want to use them all up, so Murray and me are going to make some chutney. Want to help?' Joe asked as we sat outside the men's quarters.

'Nope.'

Joe threw a tomato into the air and caught it. 'I'm real sorry about what the Boss did to you. And about your Mum dying and everything. But not everyone's done the dirty on you. I haven't, for one, nor have Murray and Fergus.

And we won't always have to stay here. Why d'you think we're saving our money?   One day we'll show Downston and the Missus a thing or two.'

'Blast Downston ! Blast him! Blast you all!' I grabbed the tomatoes Joe had been holding and hurled them like red grenades to the ground. Then I bent down, grabbed a handful of stones, and aimed them at the long drop. 'I hate everyone and everything about this place.' My words were interspersed with sobs, but I didn't care. 'You're a fool. We'll never get away. We'll die here. *You'll* die here next to your precious tomatoes.'

'Steady on boy. Can't a man have a wash in peace?' Murray emerged from the hut in his greying vest, tufts of hair sprouting from under his arms.

'Go to hell!' I fled across the paddock and headed for the bush. Before I got there, my chest was heaving and my breathing was becoming painful. My legs still weren't as strong as they had been. They buckled and I sank to the ground. Through my tears, I saw the far away river and beyond it the bush. That was where I belonged, away from everyone and everything; away from a poetry-reciting Irishmen and a lily-livered Kiwi; away from Joe and his tomatoes. I belonged with Mum and Dobsie. There was nothing for me here except a life of misery. There was no escape. I levered myself to my feet and slowly began walking to the river. I would take myself into the bush. This time they wouldn't find me. It was better to wither there now than to die an old man at Downstons.

I walked on and on, until I came to the ironing board rock Gaylene and I had sat on. Once I had crossed the river, I would be on the edge of the bush where I could take myself off into oblivion. I jumped on to the rock and stood contemplating the never-ending jungle in front of me. I trembled at its density and I urged myself to build up the courage to enter it again, to prepare myself for its loneliness. 'I'm coming to you, Mum,' I whispered, but my legs had become part of the rock. 'I want to be with you,' I called louder this time into the emptiness. 'Let me be with you. Please let me be with you.' But my legs stayed where they were.

I don't know how long I remained rooted to the rock. I called for Mum, and told Dobsie how sorry I was, as I pleaded with them to come and get me. But they didn't come, and I couldn't do it without them. I couldn't enter that place again. I couldn't let it take me. This time my legs moved and I walked away.

The rabbiters had been at Downston's for a couple of days now, and shots resounded all around.

'It's funny how you get used to the noise,' Joe observed, as he and Murray chopped onions ready for their chutney. 'But they're strange blokes, those rabbiters. Keep themselves to themselves and never say a word.'

'That's because the poor beggars are deaf. Too much gunshot in their ears,' Murray replied. 'Anyways, you just watch it. I've known more than one bloke who's been shot by the rabbiters unawares.'

Joe shuddered. 'We're best in here then. Sure you don't want to help with this chutney?' He called across to me, as I sprawled on my bunk. I didn't answer. I'd told him once. I wasn't going to waste my breath telling him again.

'Please yourself.'

A shot rang out and Murray said, 'Another bunny to add to their stash. Deaf or not, those guns earn 'em a good living. Never let 'em out of their sight. Even take 'em to the dunny.'

I rolled from my bunk and left the hut. With the rabbiters hard at it, now was the time to take a look in their huts. I knew what Murray had just said, but maybe by chance just this once, they'd left a spare gun lying around. I ran to the pigsty. I stayed there while gunshot echoed in the distance. Then I chased across a paddock to the rabbiters' huts.

I pushed open the door to the first one. It was dark and reeked of sweat and boil-up. I sidled through the door and waited for my eyes to adjust to the murkiness. The hut was only big enough for one bunk. It was covered with the usual sacking. A tin bowl, knife and fork and a mug were grouped together in one corner, while in another was an empty tin box with the lid open. There didn't seem to be much else there. I groped under the bed, but all I retrieved was a handful of leaves and a couple of dead mice.

I crept out of the hut into the next one. It was more or less the same, even to the dead mice under the bed. Outside I flattened myself against a hut, and sidestepped around the wooden boards, but there were no guns propped anywhere. Murray was right. The rabbiters were pretty careful with them.

When I returned, our quarters were thick with the smell of chutney, and the table was covered with jars full of the muddy red concoction.

'This'll spice up the boil up.' Murray wiped the outside of a jar on his trousers. 'It should last us at least a year, I reckon.'

A year! I wouldn't be eating the stuff for a year. I didn't intend staying around that long.

I left our quarters as quickly as I had entered them and ran towards the sound of the shots.

Across a paddock, I could see the rabbiters advancing. Their guns were at shoulder height and ready to fire. Their rabbiters' eyes were fixed on their target. They were unaware of my presence nearby as I slithered through the undergrowth on my stomach. Then I saw the two rabbits they had lined up, sitting stock still as if they could sense danger. They were so near, I could have touched them. I watched as the rabbiters took aim. Then as a bullet left a gun, I threw myself in front of the rabbits. The shot passed me with a high pitched whistle. I fell and the rabbiters ran towards me. I saw their lips moving, but the shot had deafened me. They patted me all over, then stood me to my feet and shook me a little. Their relief showed on their faces. I began to cry. The rabbiters had missed me. I was still alive.

It must have scared the rabbiters good and proper, and as soon as they'd made sure I was all right, they scarpered back to their huts. I don't think they told anyone what I'd done. At least no one said anything to me.

My confusion increased. I supposed I was relieved the rabbiters hadn't killed me, but my despondency remained and turned into a sense of futility. In my anger, I wanted to lash out at anything or anyone close to me. More than anything, I burned with hatred towards Downston.

'You!' Downston stomped into the hut, and advanced towards me. His one eyebrow had lowered. I turned on my bunk, experiencing an impulse to tread on his ugly face like I had Joe's tomatoes, to grind my heel into it, to leave it a bloody pulp.

'What d'you want?' I asked in the belligerent way I spoke to everyone.

'Stand up when I'm talking to you!' Downston ordered. Reluctantly, I rolled from my bunk and came to my feet.

'Did you rub chutney over the homestead windows and the Missus' washing?'

'What if I did? What're you going to do about it?' All at once, I realized I was a head taller than Downston and my shoulders were several inches wider.

'What're you going to do about it?' I repeated. 'Take me back into the bush? Report me to the authorities?'

A pulse ticked in the side of Downston's face. I moved nearer to him and grabbed his arms. Impulsively, I began to shake him, my fury at last let fully loose. Downston struggled to free himself but I tightened my grip and intensified the shaking. Downston's face was a crimson blur in front of me. I was unheeding of the choking noises he was making and of his pitiful protests. I shook him for the orphanage, for the authorities who had taken us away. I shook him for Mum and Angela. I shook him for Gaylene.

I pushed my knee into his groin and he yelped. Spurred on, I moved my hands to his throat. I felt his shrivelled skin like a lizard's and his Adam's apple moving up and down under my fingers. I circled his neck with my hands and twisted until he began to make deep spluttering noises. Saliva dripped from his mouth on to my hands.

'By the saints be done, lad.' Fergus' voice came from a distance. It vied with the roaring in my ears. I fought to free myself as Murray and Fergus took hold of me.

'I'm going to kill him. Let me kill him!' But they held me firm.

'You'd better leave, Boss. We'll calm him down. The boy's had a bad few months.' Murray puffed it out in disjointed sentences, using all his strength to keep me from escaping their grip.

'I'll have him out. Be warned. I'll get rid of him.' Downston held his throat and stumbled to the door. 'The boy's mad. He needs to be put away.' Downston's voice was weak and raspy.

Spent, I flopped on my bunk while Murray moved around hardly disturbing the air, picking the things up that had become dislodged. His hat had come off when he and Fergus had restrained me. He brushed it with his sleeve, pushed out the dents, and replaced it before disappearing outside. Joe mouthed and gestured he was going to one of his gardens. Fergus picked up a book and sat by his bed reading.

With my eyes closed, I lay on my bunk and waited for my taut muscles to relax enough to enable me to breathe properly and for my heart to resume a regular beat. When it did, I would take my suitcase and leave.

'Are you all right, lad?' Fergus asked after a bit.

'Why shouldn't I be?' The tension was giving way. Now, I felt as if I was wilting, like one of Joe's flowers after battling a day in the sun.

'The Boss'll have a headache for a day or two and some marks around his throat, not to mention a few other places.' Fergus allowed himself a half-smile.

'I wished I'd killed him.'

'Do you think you would have felt better if you had?'

Fergus wasn't going to practise his sermons on me. I wasn't a kid anymore. I'd do what I liked. I didn't answer. The silence stretched into minutes.

'Will you promise me something?' Fergus's voice was as tender as it was when he felt the pathos of a poem. 'Promise me you won't do anything hasty?'

No answer.

'Promise me, Tony.'

'Why should I?'

'Promise me!'

'All right, all right, I promise.' Relief and weariness swept over me. I would go, though. When I was ready, I would leave this place for good. I didn't need any of them.

Since I'd attacked Downston, a stilted air had fallen on our quarters. Even Joe seemed to consider what he was about to say before he said it. I sensed a collective exhaling of breath when I answered their questions civilly. I knew the atmosphere lightened when I left the men's quarters.

Fergus and Murray took to whispering to each other, moving guiltily apart when I approached. I didn't care, yet I was aware of the need to tread carefully, not with them, but with myself. I was frightened that anything: any out of place word or misinterpreted action could detonate another explosion inside myself. I had only meant to give Downston some lip. Instead, I'd ended up trying to kill him. What was packed inside me that a match of aggravation could ignite? I was glad Downston was away on business. Not that I was, or would ever again be, frightened of him. I feared myself more.

For once, Fergus wasn't drunk when he and Murray returned from the township the next time they went. Without saying anything, he placed a book of poetry on my bunk, but the whispering between the two of them continued.

The next day, after we'd eaten the boil-up, Fergus coughed awkwardly and Murray lifted his hat and replaced it again.

'We … er want to talk to you both.' Murray's voice wasn't his ordinary everyday one.

Joe pulled a chair up to the table. He turned it so that he could perch astride it, while I braced myself for more useless gabble.

'It's like this,' Murray began. He pushed his hat further back on his head and started again. 'It's like this.' He faltered. 'Beggar me.'

'It's not that we want rid of the two of you,' Fergus took over. 'But Murray and mesself are a deal worried about you, by the saints we are.'

I banged my elbows on the table, rested my head on my arms and gave an exaggerated sigh.

Fergus continued, 'The Boss has it in for you, especially you, young Tony. Who knows what he'll do next. He can throw you off the farm any time he wants and get another couple of lads to take your place.'

'All he has to do is tell the authorities the two of you buggered off and he doesn't know where you are,' Murray said. 'They'll believe him, my word they will.'

'So? I've told you, when I'm good and ready, I'll go.'

'To be sure we know that, but Murray and I are mindful the two of you's don't know the parts hereabouts, and if the Boss were to get rid of you … '

'Save your breath!' I made to go.

'I'd be obliged if you'd give us the courtesy of hearing us out, Tony.'

I flopped back into my chair, my legs extended, my eyes closed, feeling inwardly disciplined by Fergus's unusual severity.

'Our hunch is that it won't be long before the Boss gets you by the scruff of your necks and tosses you off the place. The two of you are growing up, and it can't be long before the authorities stop paying him.'

'He could be jacking up another couple of kids right now,' Murray added.

Joe replied, 'Flippin' cheek …', but Murray held up a hand. 'It seemed to us we'd better think ahead a bit and get in before the Boss. We've made a couple of enquiries, beggar me if we haven't. Jack and Peg Millard are looking for a couple of experienced blokes on their place aways north of the township.' Murray coughed, cuffed his nose with his sleeve and wiped his sleeve down the side of his trousers.

'To be sure the Millards are as gracious a couple as you're likely to find, even on the blessed Emerald Isle itself. They're more than happy to take the pair of you on, pay you a bit and give you board at the homestead. It's a lot more than you get now.'

'I don't need your help. I've told you I can find something of my own. It wasn't up to you to go to these people behind our backs.'

'Let's face it, Tony, you haven't been too approachable of late. We appreciate your independent spirit. 'Tis a good trait, but there comes a time when everyone needs to accept help when it's offered.'

'I don't need … '

'You mean we're going to have to go from here, and leave everything?' Joe opened and closed his hands, as if he was trying to gather everything to himself for safe keeping. 'Are you telling us that we've got to leave *you*!'

'It's all for the best, Ginger. She'll be right,' Murray replied. But Joe was already running through the door. It was the first time I had ever seen him cry properly, and I was glad he'd run away. It would be like watching Mum or Angela weeping.

'We'll think about it.' I slouched away, as if I was going for a Sunday afternoon stroll. It didn't do to let others know what you were thinking.

A breeze wafted along the valley like a woman's touch, ruffling my hair. I had taken my time walking to the woolshed. Instinctively, I knew that was where I'd find Joe.

'We've got to leave,' I said when I reached him. 'We don't have a choice.'

Joe was sprawled headlong, his face resting downwards on his arms and he didn't answer.

I continued, 'This place they want us to go to doesn't sound bad.' What I was saying was false and without hope. Our future stretched in front of us both like the distant bush, mile after monotonous mile of it.

Joe rolled on to his back, his eyes red-rimmed. 'You might not think much of the place, but it's the only home I've had, real home, that is. And Murray … he's been like a … anyhow, he wants rid of us now, so that's it.'

'I don't think he or Fergus want us to go.' I didn't know why I was defending them. The new Tony wasn't supposed to defend anyone other than himself.

Suddenly, Joe levered himself up. 'It's no good lying here wasting time. Let's get ready to sling our hooks. No one's going to say Joseph Fisher's soft.'

On the day we left, the truck was parked outside the men's quarters, ready for Fergus to drive to the township. 'Now creep along and keep your heads down,' he instructed Joe and me. 'I know the Boss is still away, but we don't want the Missus catching you.'

'Aren't you coming with us?' Joe asked Murray. Joe seemed to have shrunk and looked as if he needed Murray's support.

'Too much to do, boy.' Murray coughed a lot and pushed and pulled his hat about. 'Not to worry about your veges, Ginger, I'll look after them, too right I will. I know where they all are.' He chuckled but it was mirthless. 'Look after yourselves and take this.' He pushed his Christmas handkerchief into Joe's hand. 'You might need it where you're going.' He ruffled Joe's hair and aimed a fake punch at his chest. 'Look after yourself, boy,' he said, his voice gruff.

'Too right I will,' Joe replied, but I could see him swallowing back the tears.

'We'll meet at *The Travellers* and talk about the gee gees.'

'Yeah, course we will.'

The meagre contents of our orphanage suitcases rattled as Fergus lifted them onto the truck. Then we climbed into the back with them and laid flat. Fergus said when we were away from Downstons we could ride up front with him

My trousers were tight across the thighs, and I yanked at them in order to make myself more comfortable. At least, it was the last time I would have to wear mission clothes. Once I had things figured out, I wouldn't stay around for anyone to make a fool of me with their empty promises. Joe could do what he liked. Fergus jumped in the cab, started the engine and the truck began to chug away from the men's quarters and towards the road leading from the farm. 'No looking back, Joe,' I said.

Chapter Twenty-One

'To my way of thinking, everyone needs good food and a comfortable home,' Peg Millard said as she showed Joe and me around the homestead. She reminded me of a woman Friar Tuck in her brown skirt and jumper. Rolls of fat protruded from above and below a belt tied around what must have once been her waist. Peg believed a plump person should automatically be a happy one.

To me, she seemed as strange as the Missus in a different sort of way, with her booming laugh and wobbling flesh.

'I'll soon put some meat on those skinny frames of yours. I don't know what I do wrong with my Jack, though,' she sighed. 'I never can get an extra ounce on him, no matter how big the feeds. Mind you, if he weighed twenty stone he couldn't be more content. Get on and do what you can with what you've got. That's Jack's way - the Kiwi way.'

Peg stood between Joe and me. She put an arm round both our shoulders and guided us along the passage. 'This is the lounge room, where we sit in the evenings.'

Everything about the room was faded: curtains that might have started out the colour of corn were now off-white; cream walls that I reckoned had once been yellow, carpet and armchairs – brown, turning beige.

'I don't believe in keeping a room for best. Open the curtains up, let the sun in and use it.'

I wondered what the Missus, in her darkened red lounge, would have thought of that and of the half-finished puzzle covering the occasional table. Books spilled from a cupboard, records were scattered across the floor and there was an empty beer bottle by the side of what looked to be Jack Millard's armchair.

'It was like this in the men's quarters,' Joe replied as if to remind Peg hers wasn't the only place that was cosy.

'I'm sure it was.' Peg's eyes were a peculiar brown-green, like a bird's. 'You'll miss it for a while, but you'll be right,' she said.

Joe snorted his doubts, and Peg directed us back along the hall. 'These are your rooms. You've got one each.' She pointed to two doors next to each other. They were open. Sunshine painted slants in the hallway.

'We don't want … ' Joe began.

'That's good, thanks.' I hadn't dared hope for a room of my own.

'They're much the same, and there's a rug next to each of your beds, so the lino doesn't strike cold when you get up in the mornings.'

'We had sort of rugs in the men's quarters. Well, they were sacks, but what's the difference. Fergus and Murray put 'em there.'

'Well, I'll leave you to unpack,' Peg said, as if she wasn't aware of Joe's defensiveness or of the obvious lightness of our suitcases. 'When you've finished, come along to the kitchen. I'll make you a nice ham sandwich with plenty of mustard. By the way,' she called back, 'There's pyjamas under your pillows. They should do you for the time being.'

I closed the door of my room. It had a key. I turned it in the lock. At last I had somewhere of my own.

I circled the room – my room - touching the walls, stroking the furniture, fingering the bed cover that Mum would have called a counterpane. I wondered if the Queen had a rug by *her* bed so that the floor didn't strike cold when *she* got up.

A white towel was folded over a chair beneath the window. I took it and pressed it to my face. I would never use it in case it lost its fluffiness. I wanted to keep everything in the room the same as this first time I walked in.

Outside, Joe rattled my door handle and called, 'Let me in for pity's sake.'

'Won't be long.'

'Be hoity toity, then. See if I care,' Joe grumbled from the other side of the door.

As I passed the dressing table, a stranger stared back at me from the mirror. I made a puckered face at it. I posed sideways, left then right. Moving closer to the mirror I peered first at my chin, then my teeth. I pulled my lip back and looked at the empty gum socket where Paul Downston had practically knocked my teeth out and Murray had finished the job with his pliers. I put my thumb into each nostril and examined inside. Then I squashed my nose flat, rubbing the crevices either side.

When I had finished examining myself, I placed my case on the desk in the corner of the room. I opened it and removed my clean pair of underpants, the piece of rag I'd tied my winnings in, my tooth brush, and the poetry book Joe had bought me. Inside it, I had hidden my 'Love Mum' piece of paper and the scrap with my age and birthday written on it. I placed everything in one of the dressing table drawers – my drawers. Then I took the pyjamas from under the pillow on my bed. I held them up, and folded them again. They smelt of fresh air and lemons. I wouldn't wear them. They might get creased.

I never thought I'd miss my daily work in the pigsty, but I did. It was perhaps the only thing I did miss, apart from Flinders, the dogs and, strangely, the far off river. I didn't miss Murray and Fergus like Joe seemed to, mooning about the place, talking about them all the time, saying how much they'd done for us. He said if it wasn't for the responsibility they'd felt towards us, they would have upped and left years ago. Actually, I thought the only reason they stayed was because they didn't have the gumption to do anything else.

Although Jack Millard seemed to think we were hard workers, the work was easier than at Downstons. It came without the constant cuffs around the ears, punches and kicks up the backside. And Millard didn't goad us and call us nancy boys, lazy good-for-nothings, or pommie bastards. When he asked you to do something, he actually said, "please" and, when you'd done it, he replied, "Thanks". Joe said it was slimey and you didn't know where you were with someone like that. Perhaps he was right. But it reminded me of Fred, who had been the master of manners. I still missed him and Lori. I wished I knew where they were, although I would never have admitted it to anyone. I was tough Tony Addington, and tough Tony Addington didn't wake up crying at night for his neighbours.

We had been at Millards' a week and had just finished Peg's dinner of home made fish and chips, followed by her special chocolate pudding when Jack fiddled in his coat pocket and produced two small, brown envelopes. He offered one each to Joe and me across the table, saying, 'There you go.'

'You giving us our marching orders?' Joe asked defiantly, pushing his empty pudding bowl away from him.

'Why should I want to do that? I'm paying you. What else would I be doing? These wee brown beauties are your wages. You've been here a week, haven't you? A fair day's pay for a fair day's work, isn't that what they say?' He laughed just like Peg, but without the quivering flesh.

'Downston never said that.'

'Be that as it may, we're not like that here.' Jack got up from the table and crossed to a calendar hanging on the back of the kitchen door. 'Now about your day off.'

'We get a day off?'

'I expect you to work hard, but not seven days a week.'

'At Downstons ...'

'I reckon you'll be wanting to go into the township to get rid of that pay packet. Until you can both drive you can go in on Wednesdays with Tai. I reckon I can handle the work around here on my own for a few hours. As soon as you can drive, you can take the truck in yourselves. Just don't go asking me. It's bad enough when my good lady wants me to take her there for a day out. Not that I begrudge her an outing. My good lady deserves that and more.' He smiled across at Peg in a sickening sort of way.

A lot of the men in Blountmere Street called their wives "their old woman". Mainly it seemed like a joke, but sometimes it sounded hurtful and cruel. Jack made Peg sound like royalty and he was only half Peg's size!

'Sounds all right,' I said. It didn't do to show too much enthusiasm or gratitude. I had to keep remembering I didn't need anyone.

'So when can we start?' Joe asked.

'To spend your money?' Jack walked back to the table. He put his hand on Joe's shoulder, but Joe shrugged it away.

'You won't catch me spending my dosh. I meant when can we learn to drive?'

'How about tomorrow afternoon? It shouldn't be that difficult for the pair of you. Driven a tractor, haven't you?'

'The Boss didn't allow it.'

Jack acted as if he hadn't heard what Joe had just said and continued, 'You can go turn and turn about. Tai's a patient sort of bloke. He'll show you the ropes.'

The next afternoon, I sat on the hillock above the homestead. The sea was a deep band of cobalt on the horizon. Below me in the home paddock Joe was having his driving lesson. The truck hopped and the engine whined, then it stalled.

All around, the land rolled green and gentle. It was as untroubled as the Millards themselves appeared to be. I took my wage packet and pulled out the notes. Two pounds. Added to it, there was everything I could eat and my own room, warm and without the vicious draughts of the men's quarters. It would do for the time being.

Joe restarted the engine. It bounded forward in a further series of hops, then with a sound of skidding tyres, leapt forward and careered into the paddock fence. Tai jumped out and stood wordlessly over the pile of wood, rubbing his forehead.

'Blinkin heck,' Joe's voice floated upwards. 'I'm never going to get the 'ang of this.'

Our trips to the township with Tai were short and uneventful. There was little to do and it was seven weeks before our trip coincided with a visit by Fergus and Murray.

'Beggar me, if the two old codgers aren't in *The Travellers*,' Joe said, when he saw Downston's truck parked outside the hotel. 'It'll be good to see them again.' He sprinted to the hotel and pushed the door open so hard, I thought he might break one of the glass panels.

Spying Fergus and Murray sitting in a corner, he ran towards them, laughing. He was more animated than I'd seen him since he'd left Downston's. When he got to them, he pushed Murray's hat forward, and aimed the same sort of fake punch Murray had at him when we had left. He stretched across and rubbed Fergus' shoulder. 'How ya goin', mate? Missed the pair of us, have yer?'

'To be sure we have,' Fergus replied, but Murray, a glass in his hand, simply sat there grinning at Joe.

'So come on and be telling us about life at the Millards,' Fergus prompted, as we pulled out a couple of chairs and sat down.

'Well, they've got an inside lav,' I began.

'I'm not keen on it, personally. The long drop was healthier.' Joe continued.

Murray took a lingering swig of bitter and wiped his mouth on the back of his sleeve. He sighed with contentment. 'My word, the pair of you've filled out. Peg Millard feeding you well, is she?'

'S'ppose. Personally, I preferred the boil-up.' Joe had squeezed in next to Murray.

'How can you say that? Peg's food's a million times better than the horrible stuff the Missus dished up.' I pictured the lumps of meat coated in congealed fat.

'I can say it, 'cos that's what I think. All right?'

'For something you don't like, you eat plenty of it.'

'I didn't say I didn't like Peg's food, I just said …'

'I've brought you these, Ginger,' Murray interrupted, and placed a sack on the table. 'We hoped we might see the two of you's here. We thought you could take them to Peg Millard to see what she could do with them.'

'Lemons! They're my lemons!' And the Boss didn't nick any of them?'

'No. He seemed to have forgotten about them.'

'Blimey, who would have thought Joe Fisher would end up growing lemons?'

Murray rested his arm on Joe's shoulder. This time Joe didn't shrug or pull away like he had when Jack Millard had done it.

'You've got green thumbs, boy, beggar me but you have.'

Through the haze, Murray caught the eye of a woman straddling young and middle age, and raised the dregs of his glass to her. She was still reasonably pretty. I couldn't understand why she would want to work in a place that reeked of beer and cigarette smoke among men, who if they were sober when they arrived, didn't stay that way for long. This was the sort of place the Old Man had swapped us for -

Mum, Ang and me. He couldn't have thought we were worth much.

'So old Downston's got no new orphan kids, then?' Joe asked.

'No, he must have decided he'd be best not drawing attention to himself for a bit,' Murray replied. Joe let out a relieved breath. I knew it was because he didn't want anyone else to share Murray's attention.

'What's he say when you told him we'd upped and gone?'

'Very little.' Fergus' face was already becoming flushed. Two more foaming jugs sat in front of him waiting to be downed. 'To be sure, we reminded him of a thing or two … We told him if it wasn't for us … Well, as I said, he didn't do too much arguing.'

'It's true. If it wasn't for the pair of you, I don't know where we would have been, d'you, Tone?'

I drew a shape on the table with my finger. What was I supposed to do - kiss their backsides?

'And who's doing the jobs we did?' Joe asked.

'We are, and the sooner we get off the place, the better,' Murray grumbled. 'Not a pig or a chook bloke, me. If one lot's not rolling in the mud, the others are pecking at it. Give me my sheep and dogs any day. It's a sheep cockie I am, and a sheep cockie I'll stay.'

'Now you know what it was like for us,' I said. The three of them irritated me like gravel under my skin. Abruptly, I stood and said to Fergus, 'I'm off to Old Man Witchery's. After that, I'll be in the library if you want to come.'

'Once I've finished these jugs I'll be there in a leprechaun's leap.'

I rose from the table without even saying goodbye to Murray. The door slammed behind me.

I crossed the road to Witchery's. This time, I knew exactly where to look for the trousers I wanted to buy, while Old Man Witchery pigeon-toed his way down the aisles, telling me the latest gossip from the township: Harriet Allsop, her with the glass eye, had up and married a commercial traveller from the North Island, which Witchery swore made both her eyes sparkle. Alan Garitty had chopped the top of his finger off while he was tailing. Grannie had sewed it back on again, her being a seamstress as well as a bloody good cook who could give Peg Millard a run for her money. The weather was in for a warm-up, Old Witchery would bet all Grannie's lamingtons on it. On he went, while I said yes and no in what I thought were the right places.

At Downston's, all I'd wanted was to get out of my mission clothes, but now I was getting paid, I was loathe to spend any of my wages. If I saved everything I could, in a year I might have as much as a hundred quid. I'd be able to do a lot with that. Joe was right. Having some cash behind you gave you freedom.

But Peg had already made me buy new shoes, and more underwear. A few weeks ago, she'd pestered me into getting a couple of new shirts. Now it was trousers. She threatened she wouldn't feed me if I didn't get them, although I couldn't see Peg not feeding anyone.

'I don't know how *those people* could let you go around like ragamuffins. Disgraceful!' she'd said, making loud disapproving sounds.

After rummaging through only two boxes, I found the trousers I was looking for. I measured them against me and was surprised at their length. I'd thought they'd be too long. At least I was growing upwards, Peg said, although I was sure she'd be more satisfied if, at the same time, it had been outwards. I declined Old Witchery's offer to try them on in Grannie Witchery's kitchen. 'You don't have anything Grannie hasn't seen plenty of afore,' Old Witchery chuckled. I counted the money into his hand and fled before he could cross the counter and manhandle me towards Grannie.

Outside the shop, I slowed my pace and made my way to the Community Hall, where the library was crammed into a room at the back. After thumbing through a few books, I placed them back on the shelves. It didn't seem as if Fergus would be coming. I wasn't surprised. By now he would be well on his way to becoming legless, and Joe and Murray would in all likelihood be talking about the gee gees. Joe still *studied form* at night, while Peg shook her head. 'Fifteen and already gambling. You're on a downward spiral,' she forecast, but she laughed just the same.

I liked the evenings when we all sat together. It soothed away some of my pain.

I left the library and began walking towards the sound of the sea. I could already taste the salt on my lips. Even though it was winter, the sun was warm on my face. In a couple of hours, the air would cool again. Back at the homestead, Peg would be making soup for our evening meal, thick and meaty; roasting a leg of mutton perhaps; baking an apple pie.

The thought reminded me I hadn't eaten the lunch Peg had made for me. The package was still in the inside pocket of my jacket. I perched myself on a churchyard wall, pulled out the package and unwrapped the paper. The sandwiches were fat with cheese and Peg's homemade chutney. In a smaller packet were two ginger gems, oozing cream. Mrs Dibble might have known about ginger gems and pavlovas, but I'm sure Mum wouldn't have had any idea. Who cared if she couldn't cook like Peg Millard! She had never had Peg Millard's money for one thing, nor a husband to call her *his good lady*. She had been the best mother she could be. I squared my shoulders and blinked to refocus the fading picture of her in my mind.

I manoeuvred myself on the wall and turned to look behind me at the church. It was made of wood with an arch-shaped entrance. Surrounding it was a small graveyard. The ground around the gravestones was still white with frost.

I slid from the wall and for no reason wandered into the church. I remembered Mum's church as being like a cathedral. It was made of stone and had a pointed roof covered with all sorts of carvings, which I could still picture clearly. Perhaps it was because I had spent so long staring up at them every Sunday, while the Reverend Roberts droned the sermon. I supposed Mum's funeral had taken place there. How many pews had been filled? Not many. Not one whole row. There would have been the Dibbles – Mrs Dibble and Paula, at any rate - and a couple of neighbours. I imagined Ang standing there alone and defiant. The Old Man wouldn't have turned up. He probably didn't know even now that Mum was dead. The Reverend Roberts would have given another one of his sermons, and they would have sung *Onward Christian Soldiers*, Mum's favourite.

I ambled round, reading various memorials. On a side wall was a brass plaque with the names of the blokes from the township who had died in the First World War. It was a long list for a small township. Next to it was a headstone that read, *To Elija Pullston and his dear wife, Eliza – gone to their eternal rest.*

On the opposite wall, an embroidered banner spelt out *Mother's Union.* To the right of the altar, a board announced *Hymns.* I climbed up into the wooden pulpit, not as high as the one in Mum's church - only three steps - and turned a few pages of the large black Bible resting on it. What had happened to the Bible Fred and Lori had given me when I was christened? I turned to the altar with a wooden cross in the middle. Even with the light falling on it from the window behind, I thought it looked sort of sad and alone.

I descended the pulpit steps and sat for a while just looking at the cross. Then I felt under the pew with my feet for one of the cushion things they had at Mum's church. There was one there and I pushed it out. It was embroidered with flowers. I expected *The Mothers* had made it. I'd seen Mum kneel to pray, although Ang and I had stayed glued to our pew.

Despite the church's simplicity, the window behind the altar was of stained glass in vivid colours, showing men with beards and wearing long robes. Some seemed to be flying, while others had their arms outstretched. They all had bright yellow circles above their heads. The window reminded me of the pieces of coloured glass Paula used to collect from the bombsite. She kept them in a wooden box and called them her jewels.

In the middle of the window, a man stood with his arms outstretched and underneath were written the words, *Jesus said, I will never leave you nor forsake you.* Even though my memories of Blountmere Street were becoming a bit muddy, I could still see the look on Mum's face when she talked about Jesus. She'd said He wouldn't leave you nor forsake you. But He had, hadn't He? Where was Jesus when they'd taken Ang and me away? Where had He been when they'd sent me to New Zealand? Why had He taken Mum when we needed her the most?

I lowered my gaze to the cross on the altar and tried to recall the hymns we used to sing about it. I remembered the Reverend Roberts saying Jesus had died on the cross because he loved everyone individually. Mum had said the same but Ang had argued it was a load of codswallop. She would have said, if God loved us, he had a pretty funny way of showing it. But somewhere in the valleys of my mind, I heard him saying the cross brought hope as well. A bit of hope and some help thrown in for luck wouldn't come amiss. Only God, if there was one, could know about the hole in the middle of me. Not just a space, a whopping bombsite crater I'd given up on ever filling. And what could Jesus do about that? Could He do the same for me as He had for Mum? I supposed I could give God a chance. If it didn't work, I hadn't lost anything. After all, if God didn't exist, He wouldn't know I'd prayed. If He did exist, and had decided I wasn't one of the people at the top of His list, what had changed? I hesitated, clasped my hands together and squeezed my eyes shut. I tried to recall all the wrong things I'd ever done so that I could say I was sorry. Would God really care? I started on *Our Father*, but got stuck halfway through. Then, opening my eyes, I looked up at the man in the window. 'All right, I'll give you one last chance,' I called up to him.

Chapter Twenty-Two

As soon as I could drive, Jack asked me whether I'd mind driving Peg to church every now and then. I noticed he didn't mention Joe taking his turn with the driving. Perhaps it was because he treasured Peg's life too much.

'Can't say I'm much of a church-goer myself,' Jack confessed, 'but my good lady seems to get something from it. Tai used to go with her, but Uncle Rewi, being his real uncle, used to pick on him a bit too often in his sermons. Poor young Tai, shy bloke that he is, didn't handle it too well. Mind you he has to go every so often, or Uncle Rewi comes out here and preaches his whole sermon all over again in case Tai gets backslidden. Anyways, Old Witchery tells me you pop into the church from time to time when you're in the township.'

I couldn't very well say no to Jack. He was what Mum would have called "the salt of the earth", and who could refuse Peg anything when she cooked the way she did? I'd done a deal or two with the Almighty, as well, when I crept in and out of the church, hoping not to be noticed. I should have known not much got past Old Witchery. Although my visits somehow seemed to steady me inside, it still didn't mean I wanted to attend a proper church service any more than I had when Mum asked me to go with her.

'Yeah, that should be all right,' I tried not to sound too enthusiastic in case it encouraged Jack to ask me to take Peg every week. Christmas, Easter and the odd time in between would be quite enough.

"*And the mountains and the hills will break forth in singing,*"
Uncle Rewi read from the big black Bible resting on the
pulpit. "*And the trees of the field will clap their hands.*" His
voice grew louder, building to a crescendo until he burst into
song: "*Praise my soul the King of heaven.*" He climbed
down the three steps from the pulpit, his rich voice making
the tiny church shake.

"*Glorious in his faithfulness.*" The final note swelled
and went on and on.

Peg dabbed at her eyes and whispered, 'Beautiful'.

Peg had told me that nobody was sure how Uncle
Rewi came to preach at the church every Sunday. She didn't
think he was ordained. All she knew was that when it
became too much for the circuit preacher, Uncle Rewi
stepped in and he'd been there ever since.

'Everyday the Good Lord plunges his hand into His
bag of good things and flings them from the portals of heaven
to the earth for us to enjoy. Good eh!' Uncle Rewi begun his
sermon, strutting round the church, addressing members of
the congregation individually, asking them, "Good eh?"

Just when his sermon seemed as if it would last for a
week, maybe even a month, he burst into what Peg whispered
was a Maori song called a waiata. Someone Peg called
Auntie Aroha harmonized from the front pew.

'Amen! Amen! Amen!'

On the way from the homested, Peg had also told me
that Uncle Rewi had been known to preach another full-
blown sermon after his amens, which didn't exactly make me
feel excited about going. She didn't say that his closing
prayer would last round about five minutes. Perhaps she

thought I'd turn the truck round and drive straight back to the homestead if she did.

At last, Uncle Rewi and Auntie Aroha sung their final waiata. It was over.

'Inspiring,' Peg breathed. To my own surprise, I agreed with her.

Outside the church, Peg drew her fur stole around her. The fox's head rested on her breasts as she made her exchanges with various members of the congregation.

'G'day. How're ya going? Marvellous sermon.'

'Too right, mate.'

'G'day. Keeping well?'

'A box of birds! Bloody good sermon, eh?'

'G'day. She's a good one today and no mistake.'

'One straight out the box.'

'You work for the Millards, don't you?'

I found myself facing a woman who could have been anywhere between thirty and fifty. She stretched her hand towards me, instantly reminding me of Fred's handshakes, and especially of the time he first rented our front room in Blountmere Street.

'Barbara Jervlin. Teacher at the school here, for my sins,' she added. Her smile couldn't disguise the firmness of her jaw or the directness of her gaze.

'I'm Tony Addington from … ' My voice petered away. I wasn't certain where I was from.

'Peg tells me you're an avid reader.'

'I like books, yes.'

'She says you read a lot of poetry.'

'I used to read it with Fergus at Downston's.'

Miss Jervlin probably recognised Fergus as one of the men she saw when she went into the township. One of the ones who lurched from *The Travellers* and stumbled along the main street, sometimes collapsing in the gutter when the six o'clock swill was over.

'Good, you've found each other.' Peg pushed her way between us, her fox grinning. 'I've been telling Barbara here what a bookworm you are.'

I shifted uncomfortably.

'I told her that through no fault of your own.' She glared at a far off place, presumably in the direction of the Downstons'. 'You've not had any proper education since you came to New Zealand. Missed a lot, and you, such an intelligent young bloke. Disgraceful.' Her fox seemed to snarl. 'And education's so important. My kids wouldn't be where they are today without having had a good education. Part owner of a company, one of them, and doing well for himself.'

It must have been at least the sixth time she'd told me.

'You must wonder what all this is about.' Barbara Jervlin directed the conversation back to me. 'I'm quite prepared for you to come to the school, say, three afternoons a week at about four o'clock, for a couple of hours for you to catch up on your schooling.'

'Jack and me have talked about it, and it's all right with us. You can leave a bit early, maybe make up the time by doing some extra when you can. You can take the truck.' Peg looked anxious for my reaction.

'But what about … I mean how much will it cost?'

'It's all taken care of. You just do well with your studies. Can't have a brain like yours going to waste. You do want to do it, don't you? Me and Jack got the impression you did.'

I was sure I hadn't mentioned anything about my lack of schooling to the Millards, although it had been at the forefront of my thoughts recently. The Gang, who had never had a good word to say about school, would just about be finished their school years. Mine had ended a long time ago. If I was to meet them now, they would know all manner of things that I didn't. I would be backward and behind them and every other kid of my age or even younger in Blountmere Street.

'Is it all right with you?' Miss Jervlin prodded, obviously not used to being kept waiting by her pupils. 'It seems to me that one of those good things Uncle Rewi just talked about has landed directly at your feet,' Barbara Jervlin said.

I gave the teacher a quick sideways glance. Would lessons from her be a good thing, straight from the portals of heaven? I wasn't convinced.

'That's settled, then.' The fox appeared to open its mouth in a saber-toothed shout of triumph, as Peg wrestled it back into position.

If it wasn't for Peg sending Joe to look for me in case I'd forgotten I was due to begin my lessons that evening, I wouldn't have gone.

Steaming water was in the basin in my bedroom when I got back to the homestead. Peg handed me my towel, grumbling at me to use it to dry myself on, instead of that "silly bit of rag". 'It'll come up just as fluffy next time I wash it,' she assured me. A clean shirt was laid out on my bed. I knew she was hovering outside my door in case I needed anything else.

'I've packed you something to eat on the way there. Your dinner will be waiting for you when you get back, so don't worry,' she said, as I jumped in the cab of the truck.

Missing dinner was the least of my worries. Walking into the small playground in the opposite direction to some incredibly small children who stared at me and giggled - that was a worry. Looking into the classroom with its little desks, benches and multiplication charts - that was a worry. Miss Jervlin, a pile of ink-blotched exercise books in front of her, scolding a boy no more than seven - that was yet another worry.

When Miss Jervlin had finished dealing with the boy, she bade me a curt good evening and indicated a desk directly in front of her own table. Attached to the desk was a bench that I practically had to double myself to sit behind.

'I'm sorry, the furniture's a little small for you, but I'm sure you'll manage.' She handed me a timetable. 'You'll have as much homework as you actually do here at school. Unfortunately, you've got a good few years to make up. Either you grasp the opportunity that's being handed you, or you do without any formal secondary education. The decision is yours.' She managed a brittle smile, but I knew that between her and Peg I didn't have a choice.

'What's twelve twelves?' Joe sat on the wall surrounding the homestead garden, a trowel in one hand, a book of tables in the other. I had loathed school work in Blountmere Street, but to my amazement, now I enjoyed it – all of it, even mathematics and science. These days no one had to force me to do my homework. What would Ang and the Gang have said about that!

'A hundred and forty-four.' I regretted making paper darts to throw at the Gang or polishing conkers ready for a playground match at Blountmere Street School, instead of learning my tables .

'Thank gawd for that. Now we don't have to go over the blinkin' things anymore. Mind you, I've learnt most of them mesself now.'

'But don't you want to make up for all the other things you missed at school? Miss Jervlin said you could come with me if you wanted.'

'Why would I want to do that? I can count and read gardening books, study the gee gees and sign my name. You don't need nothing else to make money. As long as I can count my winnings, why should I spend all that time cooped up in a classroom? Good on ya, Tone, but it's not for me. I reckon I'll get on very nicely in life without it.'

Peg was probably right: Joe would survive by his wits.

'Give me one good reason why you can't go to the dance in the community hall,' Peg confronted me and Joe as we prepared to leave the homestead for a day's work.

'Cos we can't dance, for starters.' Joe adopted a defensive pose, standing sideways to Peg with his arms folded.

'That doesn't matter. Nor, I bet, can three quarters of the other people who'll be there.' Peg was at her most persuasive. She turned to me. 'You'll be coming, won't you, Tony?'

'No fear, not me.'

'I don't know what's the matter with you two. You get the chance to meet some young people your own age, have a bit of fun, even dance with some girls and the two of you are like a couple of wet fleeces.'

'We're happy as we are, aren't we, Tone?'

'And I'm extra busy with my school work at the moment.'

'That's precisely why you need to go. Don't forget what they say about all work and no play.' Peg began walking away, calling over her shoulder, 'Did I tell you I'm in charge of the buffet supper, so there'll be a good few of my special pavs there.

'I suppose we could go,' Joe said, loud enough for Peg to hear.

'Good. Saturday at seven. I've already got your tickets.'

That night, it happened again and it pushed the dance a long way from my thoughts. Like before, it wasn't a voice, not an audible one at any rate, and I wasn't asleep. Along the hall, I could hear Peg's's rhythmic snoring, while outside everything was still. It was like it had been at the Downstons when I'd been woken up with the same persistent tapping somewhere inside me. I levered myself into a sitting position, accustoming my eyes to the darkness. The feeling intensified, but there were no pictures or words to help me. It was more of an imprint on my spirit. I got out of bed and stood at the window looking down on what I was already beginning to think of as Joe's garden. Jack would say I was suffering from a touch of indigestion; too much of Peg's ginger pudding. But indigestion didn't make you feel as if someone was shaking you at your deepest point. Bad acid didn't contribute to the impression someone was pleading for your attention.

'What is it?' I whispered, but I knew even as I spoke that my words were hanging static there in my room. I continued to stare from the window as the first line of light appeared on the horizon.

The week before the community hall dance, Peg cooked herself into a frenzy. If she hadn't been able to listen to *Aunt Daisy* on the radio while she was doing it, she didn't know what she would have done, she said.

On the actual night, I couldn't imagine where everyone had come from; dozens of people jiggling and jostling each other on the dance floor. The dancing wasn't the kind they did in England, where men and women stood close together with their arms around each other, and which the Gang swore they'd never do. At this dance, men were flinging women all over the place, even throwing them over their shoulders and turning them upside down. All of it was done to a deafening drum beat and twanging guitars.

'This is sissy compared to *The Travellers*.' Joe wedged himself into a corner.

'What d'you mean?' I couldn't see what was sissy about this sort of dancing.

'There's no beer,' Joe complained.

'Are you going to ask someone to dance?' I shot a glance at a row of girls sitting with their hands clasped in their laps. Their skirts were well above their knees, and their hair was piled high on top and stretched wide at the sides

'Not on your nellie! Real men don't dance.'

I looked around at the crowded dance floor. 'They do here.'

'I'm going outside. This racket's driving me up the wall. Can't stand the crowd either,' Joe grumbled.

I knew how he felt. We hadn't seen so many people all together since the day we arrived in Wellington. Our isolation had changed us and we hadn't realised it.

'What're you two doing skulking in the corner?' Peg advanced towards us, licking her fingers free of cream. 'You should be out there on that floor enjoying yourselves.'

'We're all right as we are, thanks.'

'Of course you're not.' Peg wiped her hands on her apron. 'Come with me.' She yanked us from our chairs, put her palms into the small of our backs and before either of us could object further, she was shoving us to the edge of the dance floor.

'Ann! Merrin!' She called to two girls still sitting, waiting and hopeful. 'Come and teach these boys how to rock and roll.'

'I'm off,' Joe tried to free himself from Peg's grip, but a girl a head taller than him was already leading him on to the dance floor. 'I'm Ann,' I heard her say, as Merrin took my hand and pulled me towards the crowd of dancers.

293

'Haven't you really done this before?' Merrin made it sound as if I must have lived on a far off planet, or that I had been imprisoned somewhere. She was partly right.

'It's easy. All you have to do is flick me left or right, and that's the way I'll go.'

It wasn't so simple. To begin with, I was sure she'd swung left when I'd flicked her right, or right when I'd flicked her left. We bumped into people, almost fell over, but once or twice Merrin managed the perfect twirl, laughing, breathless, her skirt billowing.

It's shot taffeta ... It's for my bridesmaid's dress. See it changes colour ... gorgeous isn't it ... .and Lori's going to buy me this headdress of silver leaves and silver shoes to go with it.

Angela pirouetted in front of me as she had in our kitchen at Blountmere Street. I stopped for a moment and swallowed, struggling with the overpowering sadness that had suddenly fallen on me.

'Are you all right? Do you want to stop?' Merrin asked.

'No, no, I'm all right.' I said, but I knew then what I had to do.

The brave yet cowardly rollers mesmerized me as they attacked the sand then retreated. Above me shags circled, while seals reclined fatly content on flinty outcrops.

At last I found a smooth rock to lean against and, balancing a book on my knees to rest on, I began to write once again to Paula.

This time, my letter was longer. My life since leaving England at least needed some explanation. Once I began, it kept coming. It was like sitting on her back doorstep on Saturday afternoons. I told her about my first letter to her and how Fergus had lost it; about Joe and our time at Downstons. I confided to her my mind visits to Blountmere Street each morning. I told her about Fergus and the way we used to read poetry together in the evenings in the men's quarters; about my lessons at the township school. I asked her where she went to school and if she had been attempting to reach me in my head, as we'd once said we would. I'd often tried, I wrote, but it never worked.

Up and up it surged. And still it kept gushing like oil from a deep well. Where was Angela now? Did Paula still keep in touch with her? Was Ang all right? Was she working? Would she send Angela's address and ... and a photo? Would they all send photos? I would let them have one of me as soon as I could get it taken. And Lori and Fred? Did they still keep in touch? How were they? Had they said anything about why they weren't there to meet me?

The waves grew more courageous, pummeling the rocks. The seals, seeking revival, plopped into the white capped frenzy.

For the first time since beginning the letter, I hesitated. Mum – how had she died? Had she been in hospital? She hadn't been on her own, had she? Did Paula happen to know if Mum had said anything – left any message for me before she passed on?

And then it was over. The well was dry. I addressed the
envelope, sealed it, and walked back along the beach.
Purged. Very light.

Chapter Twenty-Three

'A cracker of a bird, this one.' Jack's sleeves were rolled above his elbows, and sweat glistened on his arms as he carved the Christmas turkey.

Outside, a snowy-clothed table was fast becoming covered with bowls as Peg set yet another dish on the table, this one steaming with freshly picked peas, fragrant with mint.

'I hope we're going to have enough.' Peg surveyed the table dubiously.

'For pity's sake, Mum, you could give everyone in New Zealand a feed with the amount you've got here.' Susan Millard shifted the baby at her breast. 'We're going to be very well-fed indeed, aren't we my possum?' She spoke into the soft down on the baby's head.

'Never knew a Christmas when Mum didn't cook for the nation.' Neville Millard was a male version of his mother.

Peg looked down on the baby. 'Your first Christmas, wee fella. Another addition to our family. It's a pity Roger, Jenny and the kids couldn't come, but that business of his keeps him busy, especially with his partner being away with his family and parents this Christmas.'

There was a general shuffling of chairs, while Peg ordered everyone to dig in.

Afterwards, we drank toasts to The Queen, Peg and her Christmas dinner, the new baby, to the success of the farm, absent family and friends, even to me and the exams I'd sat a few weeks earlier.

Then, drowsily full, we sprawled in deckchairs. A warm breeze blew across the homestead garden and ruffled the red pohutakawa flowers on the tree outside the backdoor of the homestead.

All around, eyes were closing. Jack emitted a whistling sound and Peg began to snore.

'Do you still see Ann Epsley?' I asked Joe, as if I'd plucked the question from the breeze.

'Sometimes.'

'Did you buy her a Christmas present?'

'Course not.'

'But you like her, don't you?'

'She's all right.'

'She's keen on you. I can tell.'

'Don't talk wet.' Joe closed his eyes as a sign the conversation was at a close, but I wouldn't let the subject go.

'So why do you keep seeing her?'

'Her old man owns a business.'

'And?'

'He's well off!'

'So?'

'Flippin' heck, d'you want a picture painted? You need to keep in with anyone who might be able to pull a few strings for you - someone you might be able to tap up for a bob or two.'

'So you're keeping things going with Ann because of her father?'

'Something of the sort.'

'That's terrible.'

'What's so terrible about it? If you had any sense, you'd do the same.' He lowered his voice. 'Take the Millards. You'd only have to tell them you needed a bit of cash to send to yer family in England, and they'd cough up, no questions asked. Why don't you? It'd be a start for yer. Get you set on your way to being well off.'

'But that would be using people who trust you. It would be betraying them.'

'Please yourself, but if you ask me, you've been listening to too many of that Rewi-bloke's semons.'

Peg roused herself from her chair. "I'd better start getting tea ready. The others'll be here soon.'

'Tea! You can't be serious! We've already eaten enough grub for a year.' Even Joe's appetite appeared to have been satisfied.

'It won't do any good telling my good lady that,' Jack spoke sleepily from the depths of his deck chair. 'Though it's amazing how you can always force down another fruit mince pie or brandy snap.'

Peg seemed to have invited most of the township for tea.

'Have you given any more thought to what you want to do with your life, Tony?' Barbara Jervlin bit into one of Peg's shortbread specials. I had difficulty directing my thoughts to my education after having eaten so much. Anyway, my life was still a question I couldn't find an answer for.

'Surely you've given it some consideration,' Miss Jervlin enquired. 'After all, the results of your exams should be here soon. I'd be surprised if you didn't pass. What are you going to do then? Call a halt to your schooling? I, for one, would be very disappointed if you did. If you're going to continue, what do you want to be?'

'I wouldn't mind being … a teacher.' It was just something to say. I had no idea what I wanted to be. I didn't know if I cared. If I could find someone I'd known in my old life in England, it might have been different. I wasn't sure how or why. I only knew instinctively that it would.

In that case, you'll definitely need to return to school.' Barbara Jervlin's features softened. 'I think you'd make an excellent teacher, Tony.'

The next time we went to the township, Joe spent longer in *The Travellers* than he usually did and hiccupped as I helped him back into the truck. 'Oops a daisy!' He was overcome by a fit of giggling. He hit his head on the dashboard, then fell backwards into the front seat.

'You're drunk!'

'Just a tinsy, winsy bit. Shellibratin' my good fortune.'

'Where are Fergus and Murray?'

'Gone. Flown away like little birds. Fly, fly, fly!'

'So, why did you stay at *The Travellers* on your own?'

Characteristically, Joe tapped the side of his nose. 'Had bushiness to do, my son, important bushiness.'

'You've been money lending, haven't you?'

'And other important thinsh.'

'I can't believe you wasted your money on booze. You've always said it's a mug's game.'

'Just thish once, 'cos I'm goin' to be very rish, very rish.'

Back at the homestead, Jack and I hauled Joe out of the truck, as we used to drag Fergus from the Bedford after his trips to the township.

'Silly young fool, but I suppose we've all done it. Part of growing up,' Jack said.

Peg wrinkled her nose, but Joe only murmured a soft whimper as she began stripping his clothes from him outside the back door. 'I won't have him reeking the place out,' she grumbled.

For the next few days, Joe was unusually quiet. When he wasn't working, he was skulking in his bedroom. To Peg's chagrin, he skipped breakfast twice. It was the worst nutritional sin a person could commit, according to Peg. 'Sheepish', she said. He was acting very "sheepish".

It was several days before I got a chance to speak to Joe. In all the time we'd been together, I'd never known him to withdraw but Joe had changed since we'd left Downston's. A year or so ago, he'd never have said what he had about using the Millards. I didn't know if Joe had detected it, but I knew that somehow our relationship had become fractured. I didn't share Joe's desire to be wealthy. I probably never would. My dreams were rooted in my past, while his rested very much in the future. The crack was bound to widen. There was nothing else for it to do.

'You don't have to feel bad about getting drunk,' I said, sidling closer for fear he might walk away.

'Why should I feel bad about it?' He leant on a fence, gazing at the homestead paddock.

'You've been a bit quiet lately. I thought …'

'It's not got nothing to do with getting drunk.' Joe brushed his sleeve across his face and to my dismay I realised he'd been crying.

'What's the matter? Have *I* done anything to give you the pip?'

'I ain't got the pip with you. Never have and never will.' He made a sobbing sound. 'If you must know, I'm leaving the Millards.'

'Why?'

'Ann's old man's opening up a farm machinery place. He's offered me a job.'

'And you're going to take it?'

'I'd be a mug not to. Could be the manager in a year, own it myself in a couple.'

'What's the matter then?'

'It's us, that's what's the matter. We've always been together, you and me. I can't hardly remember a time when we haven't. It's bad enough having separate rooms, but at least we're next door to each other. I managed to get through not having Murray around 'cos you were here. Now, I … '

'You'll be right.' I didn't know if either of us would be "right". I didn't feel anything. I had no idea how it would be for us. I patted Joe's shoulder in an awkward way and Joe sniffed up the mucous that had been frothing from his nostrils, but I couldn't forget what he'd said about using the Millards.

On the morning Joe left, Peg hugged him several times and cried, all the time reciting a list of what he should do to keep himself healthy. Jack shook his hand. He said he'd been a damn good worker, and wished him luck. It reminded me of the day Fred and Lori left Blountmere Street.

We stopped a few miles from the township, and ate the slices of bacon and egg pie Peg had packed for us. Joe took his time over it, wanting to defer his departure, I suspected. I ate mine a lot quicker. For me, the sooner we got it over, the better.

'We'll be able to meet in the township once a week,' I said, although I didn't want to spend too much of my day off in *The Travellers*.

'Too right, we will.'

'Have a drink at *The Travellers*, take a bit of a stroll along the beach.'

'Yeah.'

'It won't be much different from now.'

'Hardly any difference at all.'

'We just won't be living at the same place.'

Ann smiled coyly when we arrived at the Epsley's place, while her mother sat knitting on the white picketed verandah.

'I haven't got much, only my … only the one case.' Joe placed his orphanage suitcase between his feet. These days, it probably held a lot more money than it had when he'd left Downstons.

'That's it, then. Keep your pecker up.' He slapped me on the back and picked up his case.

'Come on, Joseph,' Ann threaded her arm through Joe's and led him away. 'Mummy's got afternoon tea ready. She's using her best bone china tea set.'

On the day I heard I had passed all my examination subjects, and eight months and two days after I'd posted my letter to Paula, the letter was returned, marked, "Gone Away".

It was impossible to imagine the flat downstairs in Blountmere Street without the Dibbles. I wouldn't try. I needed to keep my memories intact.

There was still something I could do. I could make more of an effort to find Fred and Lori. When I'd saved enough, I'd buy a car and travel round a bit. I couldn't imagine them living in the country, even somewhere like the township. Lori wouldn't have liked it at all. She needed people around her. No, they probably lived in one of the cities. There weren't too many of them in New Zealand. And it would be good for me to see more of the place. After all, this was where I was going to have to live the rest of my life. The pain under my heart was as acute as the day I had arrived here.

As for my examination results – I had passed. It would please the Millards.

'Jack and I are keen you do your Sixth Form Certificate, and then get your Bursary. You've obviously got it in you to get to university.' Peg clasped me to her, crushing my face against her bosom. She didn't mention anything of the other letter I'd received that morning.

'You do still want to carry on with your studies, don't you?'

'Yes … Yes. Of course.'

'That's it then. I'm sure Jack will give you as much time off as you need.'

'She'll be right,' I assured her, a pool of guilt eddying somewhere under my rib-cage. I was using the Millards, not in the way Joe had suggested, but, nevertheless, I was using their generosity simply because I had nothing better to do. I was excluding them from my own inner theatre, where the characters constantly played out the past against a backdrop they were no longer a part of. Just as long as the curtain didn't drop. Keeping the curtain lifted was where my best energies had to be expended, not in the classroom.

Fergus stood outside the community hall and wiped the perspiration from his top lip. 'Holy Mother of God, but I'm pleased to see you, Tony, me lad.' He wiped away the moisture with a grey handkerchief held in a shaking hand.

'Are you all right?'

'I'll be better when I get into the library, out of sight of *The Travellers*. The temptation is almost too much for a man to bear.'

We walked through the community hall where Fergus gulped in the stale beer fumes of the last dance. I pushed open the library door. Consciously, we lowered our voices as we entered.

'I'm needing some distraction, I'm thinking. It's funny how I manage to keep off the grog back at the hut, even when the shearers are there throwing it back to all hours. As soon as *The Travellers* comes into view, well now, that's different.'

'So you're not going to the hotel today?'

'I've got the Missus with me doing a bit of shopping, so I'm a-needing to keep sober, added to which, I'm wanting to save the pounds, shillings and pence.'

'What're you saving for?'

'I'm thinking of taking myself back to Dublin.'

'But you've never wanted to return.' We moved into a row away from the librarian.

'That was when I thought Eryn wouldn't want to see me.'

'Who's Eryn?'

'Eryn's my daughter.' From his inside pocket, Fergus took a photograph prematurely crumpled around the edges. 'Here she is. Isn't she a beauty? As fair as her mother.'

'How did she know where to find you?' I studied the photograph of a smiling girl who was probably about eighteen.

'Because, by St Patrick himself, one morning I woke up and realized time was too short for all my shenanigans, and I wrote the letter I'd been too afraid to write for years. No more agonizing over the words. I let what was in me come out. Then before I could change my mind, I posted it and waited. Holy Mother of God, I can't tell you how long every day was until I heard.'

I didn't have to be told what it was like to wait for a letter.

'Then one day, there it was: a letter from my daughter saying her name was Eryn, and that she was so happy to have heard from me. Imagine that, now will you! So happy to have heard from the father who didn't stay around long enough to give her a name!' Fergus ran the back of his hand across his eyes. 'She sent me this photograph and told me all about herself. She's training to be a nurse. To be sure, it would take a blind man not to see the compassion in those eyes.' He took Eryn's photograph from me and gazed at it.

'When are you going back?'

'As soon as I can.' Fergus replaced the photograph in his pocket. At the same time Noeline Stott, the librarian, appeared at the end of the row with a warning finger pressed against her lips.

'No compassion there, lad, none whatsoever,' Fergus whispered. 'Let's sit outside the church awhiles. We haven't had much chance to exercise our jaws together since you and Joe left Downston's. And we can't do it here with that dragon, Noeline, breathing down our necks.'

A plaque on the seat in front of the church read, "*In memory of those who fell in the First And Second World Wars*". So many young men from the township and surrounding farms had gone to war and never returned. The air smelt of roses, Grandma Witchery's steak pies and loss.

'Tell me. How're you getting on without that young leprechaun, Joe? I hear he's moved in with the family who own the farm machinery place. Works for them by all accounts. To be sure, you must miss him. I've always thought of the two of you as brothers.'

I nodded, agreeing how much I missed Joe, though I didn't miss him in the way I missed Mum and Angela. Not in the way I missed Paula and the Dibbles and the Gang and Fred and Lori. Not in the way I missed Blountmere Street. There wasn't room on my stage to miss Joe like that. But I harbour a sadness born of everything we'd been through together.

'We still see each other once a week,' I said.

'Not the same, is it, lad?'

'Not really. After finding out what we're up to neither of us can think of anything more to say. It's as if he's a different person now he works at Epsleys.'

Joe had even begun speaking differently, prefixing every word he possibly could with an 'h'. I presumed he did it to make himself sound upper class. 'We get interrupted by customers a lot. And when he comes into the township he usually brings Ann with him.'

'Or maybe Ann, if that's the young lady I saw him with last week, brings him, judging by the way she holds on to his arm. That's the way of a man and a woman. You're powerless to stop it.' Fergus sighed. 'I suspect the reason Murray doesn't come into the township much lately is because he fair misses Joe not showing up at *The Travellers*. Fergus turned to look fully at me. 'Indeed, the light faded for Murray when Joe left. Not that the pair of you shouldn't have gone. It was for the best. But you and Joe brought us a lot of pleasure.' Fergus's voice caught. 'I often question if we should have done more for the pair of you. Whether we should have called in the authorities and been stronger with the Boss, but we did what we thought to be right at the time. We looked after you as well as two old rouseabouts could. We did our best to keep you safe.'

The sound of gulls and ocean mingled, while I remembered the shearer with more hair on his body than his head.

Fergus picked up on my thoughts. 'Men's desires can be dark and young boys can seem sweet pickings. We couldn't keep you from a few nights in the bush, nor the back lashings of the Boss, but, the Holy Mother herself be praised, we did keep you out of the clutches of a few depraved souls.'

Above us, the squawking gulls severed the stillness. I thought of the children who had been on the ship bringing us to New Zealand. I wondered how many of them had been the victims of "depraved souls".

'To be sure, now we're getting maudlin.' Fergus felt in his pockets for his handkerchief. 'Let's go for a stroll. Nothing like a saunter for banishing the miseries.'

We walked towards the sea sounds, away from the smell of roses and pies. We talked of Fergus's dreams for himself and his daughter.

With less enthusiasm, as far as I was concerned, we discussed my education and my almost non-existent plans for the future.

'You'd make a good teacher, young Tony. Give it time,' Fergus assured me. 'Speaking of time, I think I'd better be getting back. Thank you for keeping me away from the wiles of the hotel.' Fergus grinned, causing the corners of his mouth to lift and his face to look ten years younger. 'I'll have just enough time to revisit the library for a book or two before picking the Missus up outside Witchery's. It's a rare day indeed when the Missus comes into town, so I'd best not be late.'

The Missus was already waiting outside Witchery's. Her eyes were like those of the gulls circling above. They darted over the window display, just as they had taken in everything in the men's quarters when she had occasionally brought the daily boil-up. She was dressed in grey, and looked as drab as a mid-winter tree.

'I'll come back into the library with you.' I had no desire to see the Missus, or that the Missus should see me.

We'd walked half-way through the community hall when we heard a woman's voice, strident and fierce.

'The caterwauling seems to be coming from Witchery's. By the saints, it sounds as if there's murder happening.'

Outside Witchery's, to my astonishment, Peg was confronting the Missus. Peg's breasts in their Sunday best twin-set were rising and lowering. Her sleeves were rolled to her elbows. 'You're disgraceful! DISGRACEFUL!' She advanced on the Missus, who edged backwards.

'Peg must have persuaded Jack to bring her into town after I left. She likes to get dressed up sometimes.' I whispered to Fergus.

'You need locking up. You and that good-for-nothing husband of yours,' Peg screamed. Her hat had slipped forward and she pushed it back. It looked like a dish on top of her head. 'You starved those two boys. Starved them!' Peg was close enough to dig a finger into the Missus' chest. 'Not just of food, no. You starved them of education, care - everything. Two orphans, and what did you do?' Her finger kept jabbing. The Missus attempted to turn away, but Peg took hold of her shoulders and swung her back towards her. 'What've you got to say for yourself?' she demanded.

'Tried .... tried.' The Missus held her bag in front of her to protect herself from Peg's jabs.

'Rubbish! Sheep dung! All you tried to do was make money out of them. You took advantage of two vulnerable children.' Peg's chest lifted precariously.

'Go … way. Go …way.' The Missus' voice had risen to a shriek.

'I best go break it up. Though 'tis a pity the Boss isn't here to get a walloping, too,' Fergus said.

'So Peg sticks up for us and gives the Missus a shiner. I can't get over it,' Joe exclaimed the next time we met at *The Travellers*. The tension between us had immediately dissipated with the news. 'Tell me what 'appened.' He seemed to have forgotten his recent efforts to talk posh.

'I've already told you half a dozen times.'

'Just once more. What happened after Peg walloped her?'

'The Missus fell and hit her head on the wall.'

'And?'

'As she slid down, her coat and dress got caught up somehow and I got this view of her suspenders and brown knickers. Anyway, at the same time as Fergus ran across the road, Jack came sprinting from *The Travellers* and dragged Peg away.'

'What did he say?'

'Nothing much, except that Peg was the last person he'd expect to get herself into a fight. At the same time, he laughed a bit, as if he was sort of proud of her. He called her his "good lady" a lot.'

'What d'you think Eleod'll do?'

'Jack doesn't think he'll do anything. Too scared the Millards will report him.'

'And will they?'

'Peg wants to, but Jack says, where's the point? The Downstons will lie themselves out of it. Anyway, it's over now.'

'It's not the issue, though.'

'That's what Peg says, but Jack doesn't want to get involved. He thinks it'll take too much out of Peg. It already has.'

Joe edged closer in his old conspiratorial way. 'The Boss's got a woman in Christchurch, so I hear. She's years younger than him. That's where he goes when he says he's on business. Dirty old sod.'

A week later, Peg still looked strained as she climbed into the truck, ready for Jack to drive her to the bus. It had taken all Jack's persuasion and my assurance we'd eat every crumb of her baking, before Peg agreed to spend a week with her son. She hadn't seen him or their daughter-in-law and grand-children for a while. It would be good for her, Jack said. She'd be able to help out, too, what with Jenny's hands full with the four kids, and Roger's partner away with his elderly parents again. The poor old couple had never settled. They were still homesick for the Old Country, Jack said. I knew how they felt.

Chapter Twenty-Four

The evening sun sketched shapes that flitted like phantom birds on the wall of the school room. Had I been coming here for four years?

Miss Jervlin voiced my thoughts. 'One day had to be the last time you sat at that desk.' Her hair may have grown greyer, the skin round her neck a little folded, but Miss Jervlin was as taciturn as when I had first met her that Sunday morning outside the church.

Four years of scrubbing off the grime of the farm and driving over potholed roads to the old wooden school. Four years doing what all the kids in Blountmere Street had done years earlier. Four years of discovery.

'And now in a few weeks you'll be off to university. You've done well.' Miss Jervlin smiled at me in what was, for her, the ultimate display of pride.

'I couldn't have done it without you.'

'Nonsense! Anyone with some tenacity could have got this far.'

Tenacious wasn't a word I would have used of myself. There had been so many times when Peg had to chase me from the house. But for Peg, I knew I would have given up long before sitting my bursary.

Mum never seemed to place much importance on education. If I'd won a place to a university when I lived in Blountmere Street, I would have been ostracized and called "toffee nosed", and "stuck up". But, then, in Blountmere Street, I would have been as far away from a university education as I was from the moon. I couldn't think of one person I'd ever known who had gone to university. Anyway, I was the last one they would have imagined going there.

Mum once said something about it standing a young man in good stead if he got an apprenticeship and learnt a trade. I thought it was Mum who said it, or was it Mrs Dibble? Anyway, I had no idea what "good stead" meant, and I couldn't see myself becoming a plumber or a bricklayer, even then.

It was Peg, too, who had encouraged me to buy a car and to take time off from studying, urging me to go to the township more. 'Everyone needs some fun from time to time.' She sighed one of her deep, heartfelt sighs. 'And why you haven't taken up with that Merrin Bensdyke is beyond me. The girl's a looker, and she seems keen enough. You make a lovely couple when you dance together at the community hall dances.' Peg looked into the distance as if she was seeing herself and Jack at that age.

I wasn't sure why I hadn't "taken up" with Merrin Bensdyke. She was all the things Peg said she was, yet when we drove somewhere or sat on the beach aiming pebbles at the ocean, it was as if her presence *created* a space in me, rather than fill it.

Joe said that "hit was hindeed a honour to 'ave a friend with henough brains to do all this 'igh-faluting stuff hat one of them there universities". He smiled expansively, although he was unable to resist looking up at the sign that read, "Epsley and Fisher, Agricultural Machinery" and underneath in smaller gold letters: *"Proprietors Bruce Epsley and Joseph*

Fisher." 'Not bad, eh? Part-howning a business hat my hage.'

As well as being referred to by the Epsleys and their friends as Joseph, and his now entrenched "h" habit, Joe's face had widened, and his freckles had expanded and contorted into shapes like an orange jigsaw puzzle. Due to Ann Epsley and her mother's influence, he had taken to wearing a black velvet waistcoat embroidered with a pink floral design. It was the closest Joe got to flowers these days.

Joe and Ann's engagement was announced at one of the community hall dances only a few weeks before Bruce Epsley took Joe into partnership. The exact date of the wedding hadn't yet been fixed, but Ann said she and her Joseph would be married early next year. Already, her "glory box" was full and their wedding would be a grand affair, quite the biggest the township had ever seen. The only time she'd mentioned my impending study at university was to say what a pity it was I wouldn't be able to attend their nuptials.

Joe, however, had confided to me that he was in no hurry to get married. "Plenty of time for hall that malarkey. All the time hin the bleedin' world," he said.

I doubted Ann Epsley and her family saw it that way.

On the day before I left the Millards to study at the University of Canterbury, Fergus gave me his copy of First World War poetry and returned to Dublin. It was yet another change at Downstons' since the Missus had died a year earlier after suffering a stroke. Peg had been fraught with worry that her attack on Maggie Downston had contributed to her death. She had even consulted old Doctor Marthwaite, who said that he would hardly have thought a slap two years earlier would have resulted in a stroke. It was much more likely to have been due to the Missus' high blood pressure. Nevertheless, I knew Peg had come to regret her attack. She had gone for the wrong one, she said. It should have been Eleod Downston, especially after he'd brought a girl no more than a youngster to live on the farm less than two months after his wife's death. It was shameful. SHAMEFUL!

I heard from Murray that Gaylene rarely went back to the farm these days, and who could blame her. She had got herself engaged to a banker in Auckland. I wondered if he ever read her poetry.

Apparently, Paul Downston got himself into a spot of trouble and ended up in gaol. 'Not that I'm surprised, my word I'm not,' Murray said. 'Nasty bit of work. Kicked that horse of his into such a bloody mess, the poor animal had to be put down.'

Murray, too, was considering leaving Downston's to work with his brother over on the Coast. As soon as he got things straightened out, he was off, too right he was. He had been bought so many farewell jugs by his fellow drinkers at *The Travellers*, they began to think his talk of leaving was a catch on Murray's part to get free grog. Crafty old bugger.

I closed the lid of my orphanage suitcase, smoothed my bedcover and tweaked the curtains straight.

In the yard, Peg wedged herself into the front seat of my Morris Minor.

'I don't know if I should be going, Jack. It seemed a good idea to get a lift with Tony to see our Roger and Jenny and the kids, and to make sure Tony gets settled into his lodgings, but now I'm not so certain.' Peg looked as if she might be about to cry.

'Of course it's the right idea. I'd come myself if it wasn't for the farm.' Jack bent and kissed Peg. She clung to his arm. 'It gets more difficult to leave you the older we get.' She looked into his face.

All I had managed to say to Merrin was a stilted goodbye, without even the promise of a letter.

'I've put a couple of cans of petrol in the boot. It's a long way.' Jack disentangled himself from Peg and walked round to the driver's door, beginning to extend his hand before abandoning his reserve and embracing me. 'Take care, boy. We know you'll give it your best.' He laughed a half-laugh to cover his awkwardness. 'Be careful of those Christchurch girls. I hear they eat blokes like you for breakfast.'

'Come on, Jack, let the bloke get in the car. It's not as if you won't see him again. He'll be back in the holidays. He's part of the family.'

How different it was from when Joe and I had left Downston's. Then, we had sneaked away, dispirited, willing ourselves not to look back. We hadn't wanted to be reminded of our years of incarceration.

Peg and I drove first to Epsley and Fisher's and waited while Joe, looking very Bavarian in his floral waistcoat, stood by a tractor. He patted it as if it was a dog, while he explained its features to an entranced farmer.

'Hanother 'appy cocky,' Joe rubbed his hands together as the farmer left. 'Just spent a packet and given

Hepsley and Fisher a tidy profit hinto the bargain. Come hinto my hoffice, I've got somethink for you.'

I left Peg sitting in the Morrie and followed Joe into his office.

He took a key from his waistcoat pocket and unlocked the drawer of a desk in the corner. He took out a package and extended it to me. 'Cop 'old of this, and don't go hopening it now.'

'How will I know what it is if I can't open it?'

'Cos it's a bit of dough to 'elp you out with your university heducation. It should see you through for a while. I've been keeping it 'ere for you. Don't altogether trust them there banks.'

'But …'

''aven't I hallways said what I 'ad was 'alf yours? I'm doing hall right 'ere, what with a few private deals. So 'ere's your share. Just between the two of us, now. You can tell Peg it's a pair of socks.'

'Look, Joe, I can't … '

'Don't go getting all sentimental. Just take it and do what-hever it is you do at university, you blinkin' brainbox. Who would've guessed it when we was in the orphanage. A right dunce you were back then.'

I looked at the splodged freckles, framed by spiky marmalade hair. 'I'm sorry if we haven't been, well, if we haven't been so … I suppose … close lately.'

Joe made a dismissive gesture. 'Now didn't I say you weren't to go getting sentimental on me. That's 'ow it is with brothers. Can't hallways be in each other's back pocket.' He cuffed me round the head. 'Don't go getting too big for your boots, that's hall.'

'That was nice of Joe to buy you some socks,' Peg remarked, as we drove from Epsley & Fisher's. 'Being the skinflint you are, he knows you probably won't buy any for yourself. Do you want me to open the parcel for you?'

'No thanks. I'll open it later.'

The road rose and fell, snaking between thick bush and the ocean.

'I always love this journey with the sea at your elbow.' Peg wound down her window and breathed deeply. 'We must be surrounded by some of the most beautiful scenery in the world. Though, I suppose if a place is someone's home, wherever it is must seem lovely to them.'

Even a bombsite. Especially a bombsite, awash with dandelions and fresh spring growth shining with dew.

'That older couple, you know, the parents of our Roger's business partner. They've never been able to settle properly in New Zealand. Jenny says sometimes she catches them sitting in the garden holding hands, looking into space as if they're seeing something no-one else can.'

We drove on a little longer, then parked and watched seals sunning themselves on shiny outcrops before they flopped back, satiated, into the water.

From sea to sea.

I'd sung the hymn a lifetime ago at Mum's church. Then, the words had struck the stone pillars and bounced back.

From sea to sea to sea to sea.

There had been a time when my only idea of what the sea looked like was in the book on Devon that Paula had got

from the library. I never did get to Bognor with the Cubs.
Perhaps Dennis and Herbie went. They might even have
thought of me now and then while they were there. Fred and
Lori promised to take Ang and me to the seaside, but they
never got round to it before they emigrated.
	Another seal plopped into the water.
	From sea to sea.
	I had to find Fred and Lori.

Peg said Christchurch was like an English city, but I didn't
think it was. Not that I'd seen much of England, except for
the bits closest to Blountmere Street. Most Christchurch
streets were unwaveringly straight and bordered by wooden
bungalows. And I was perfectly sure it wasn't the same 'Up
West' when we had gone to Lyons Corner House with Fred
and Lori. I could still remember it clearly. I didn't think
Devon had wide roads, either. In Paula's library book, the
streets had looked narrow, some of them no more than a strip.
If anything, it was the gardens that were reminiscent of
England, or at least of the Dibble's, with their precision-
planted regiments of red, white and blue.
	Yipsley Street, which was where I was going to
board, was identical to all the streets around it, but Peg
approved. 'Nice and quiet. Everyone keeps their gardens
well which is always a good sign.' Peg squinted at the
numbers on the post boxes. 'Number twenty-three's here.'
She opened her window and leant out. 'Yes, this is it, the one
painted yellow.' She appraised it as if she was thinking of
buying it. 'It looks tidy enough and the windows seem clean.

Nicely painted, though I would have preferred cream myself. Should be a good indication of what's inside.'

'We'll find out soon enough.' I couldn't understand the need for such speculation when we were just about to see inside the house. Anyway, Miss Jervlin had said that the place belonged to her cousin's friend, and she could vouch for it.

'Best to be prepared, and make a bit of an assessment,' Peg counselled.

Like many of its neighbours, number twenty-three had a fretwork butterfly hung at an angle next to the front door.

'Nice, very nice,' Peg observed.

The door-knocker was highly polished. The door was opened by a woman so straight and fleshless, she reminded me of a pencil. Peg immediately sniffed her disapproval. In Peg's opinion, anyone that thin didn't have a mere flaw in their make-up, but a deep sinful chasm.

'You must be Tony. I'm Mrs Munn.' The woman extended a bony hand. 'Come on in.' She lead us along a wood-panelled hall into the front room. It smelt of lavender polish. While it wasn't as cozily haphazard as the Millard's lounge room, it wasn't the mausoleum the Downston's had been. Above the red-brick fireplace was a painting of pink roses, their petals dropping into a silver bowl. Under it, but with no apparent relevance to the picture, were the words, *As for me and my house we will serve the Lord.*

'Good words, some of Uncle Rewi's favourites.' Peg nodded towards the painting, appearing to be getting over the shock of Mrs Munn's shapelessness. 'I'm Peg Millard, by the way.'

'I gathered you were. How d'you do?'

Mrs Munn escorted us through into another wood panelled room, with a red velvet seat built into a lead-lighted bay window. Above a fireplace, identical to the one in the front room, hung a picture of The Last Supper, under which the words announced: *The Lord is the unseen guest at every meal, the silent listener to every conversation*'.

'This is the dining room. We eat all our meals here,' Mrs Munn informed us.

'Very nice,' Peg surveyed the place. She was always impressed by people who ate in their dining rooms, on the assumption that if they went to the trouble of eating in a special room, then surely they would have cooked plenty of good wholesome food to go with it, as it were.

'Would you like a cup of tea?' Mrs Munn asked.

'We'd love one.' Peg edged her way to the door. 'The kitchen's through here, is it? We'll come and wait while you make it.' This was the crucial part of Peg's assessment. I followed, hoping Peg's son would soon arrive to pick her up and take her the rest of the way to his place. Personally, the only room I was interested in was the one that was going to be my bedroom. All I wanted was for this to be a base, not only for my university studies, but for my search for Fred and Lori. Christchurch was just the sort of place they would live. I had to find them.

In the kitchen, we sat at a table covered with red oilcloth in the middle of a scrupulously tidy kitchen. I wasn't sure if Peg would view it as commendable. She certainly appeared to be impressed by the row of preserves on the bench under the window. Not as many as she herself would have made, but preserves nonetheless. Mrs Munn busied herself with cups and saucers before opening a larder to reveal a tower of tins. 'You like cakes, Tony?' she asked.

'I love them.' I knew I dare not answer otherwise, with Peg sitting opposite me.

'I always fill my tins every Tuesday. Monday's washing day, Tuesday's baking.' Mrs Munn began extracting various dainties and placing them onto a cake plate with a chrome handle, much the same as the one Peg had.

'I wash on a Monday as well. Same routine. Monday's washing, Tuesday's baking. It's the only way to do things, in my opinion.' Peg sat forward on her chair and winked at me, as if to inform me that anyone who filled their tins every Tuesday had to be all right.

'Ginger gems,' Peg observed.

'Oh yes. I wouldn't be without my gem iron.'

Peg beamed. Even if Mrs Munn's ginger gems weren't as plump or cream-laden as hers, Mrs Munn had passed the test. Peg would personally vouch for anyone who filled their tins every Tuesday and had a gem iron.

'I think you're going to be very happy here, Tony,' she proclaimed.

Chapter Twenty-Five

'You're certainly conscientious, I'll give you that. I can't keep up with the number of times you been to one or other of the city's libraries in the last couple of weeks.' Mrs Munn rubbed at her dining room table with a polish-laden duster. 'But, I suppose that's what you have to do when you read English literature at university.' She turned to me with a look that might have been one of admiration. On the other hand, it could have been one of suspicion. It was difficult to tell. Her eyes seemed to be as thin as the rest of her. Either way, she made me feel uneasy.

Yes, 'I do have to read a lot of books,' I said. The smell of lavender polish was almost heady. It caught in my throat and I gave a lame cough to clear it.

'You're obviously a young man who doesn't like to leave any stone unturned. I've never heard of anyone trying out a different church every Sunday. Very devout.' I shifted from foot to foot.

'I … I … just like to check out their theology.' I was the biggest, most pompous hypocrite in Yipsley Street, in Christchurch, in the world. It wasn't my zealousness that drove me to visit them all, but in case, by the merest chance I found Fred and Lori in one of them. They could well be kneeling on a hassock, unaware I was there to bring my search for them to an end.

Mrs Munn gave her table another massage. 'I can assure you there's nothing wrong with my church's theology.

It's as sound, as sound as … ' She searched for the right words. 'As sound as the docks at Gibraltar.'

'Of course … I never meant …' I began backing out of the room. Mrs Munn could be fearsome when she was upset. 'I think I'll go into the city,' I said, grabbing my coat from the hallstand and fleeing out the door, past the fretwork butterfly and down the path.

Today, I would try another row of shops. I'd just about given up on the libraries. Anyway, the librarians were becoming wary of me combing the aisles of books without appearing to be looking at any. And, of course, I could only do the churches on Sundays.

Where else could I look for Fred and Lori? I couldn't live in Christchurch without scouring every inch of the place for them. If they were still in New Zealand, and I had to believe they were, Christchurch was just the sort of place they'd live.

It didn't feel like a city, at least not like London. Here you could wait all morning for someone to walk past the window. I knew it wasn't a glitch in my memory or some sort of mental conjuring trick when I remembered people passing our flat in Blountmere Street all through the day and well into the night.

Here, the buses were never full, nor were the shops, nor was the swimming pool nor the library. And although I had never been to an English beach, I couldn't imagine so few people on them, especially on days when the sky pulsated blue and the sun patterned the sea.

A bell jangled as I opened the door of a shoe shop. A young girl in shoes that were so pointed and high I wondered she could walk in them at all, asked, 'Can I help you?' in a bored sing-song voice.

'Have a man with sandy colour hair, and probably wearing navy blue and a woman with frizzy hair and a long scarf been in here?'

The girl scrutinized my sturdy brown shoes from Old Man Witchery's last shipment only ten years ago. 'I've got some winkle pickers that would suit you.'

'Um … no thanks. I just wondered if you'd seen these people. They're my … family. We've lost touch over the years, and I'm trying to find them.'

The girl gave my feet another disparaging glance. 'How old would they be?' I wasn't sure if she meant my shoes or Fred and Lori. I'd never thought of Fred and Lori having an age. 'Middle age. Well, perhaps a bit older than that.'

'Sorry, can't recall anyone who fits that description.'

I shrugged. 'Thanks.' It seemed all but impossible. I made my way to the next shop. There was nothing much else to do except study and attend lectures and tutorials.

I was enjoying university and doing well, but with my letter to Paula having been returned and with no address for Angela, finding Fred and Lori seemed my best opportunity. At least they lived in the same country as me, and this place didn't have a lot of people living in it. I had to find out what had happened to Mum and Angela – what had happened to the whole of Blountmere Street, for that matter. I knew I would never be able to move on until I did. The Millards might consider me family, but neither Jack nor Peg had ever called me son, like Fred had. I'd forgive him everything for that.

In my first lecture at university, I'd sat next to Pete. Now at lectures, we usually saved each other a place. Like me, he was in the first year of a Bachelor's degree majoring in English literature. To begin with, we mainly met on the university campus. When we did, we stopped to have a chat, usually about inconsequential things such as our lodgings or rugby. Sometimes we became more serious and talked about an essay we were writing or our latest assignment, but I never told him anything about being a child migrant or about my quest to find Fred and Lori. He told me his father owned a factory in the North Island somewhere. As soon as he'd completed his degree, he was off, he said; as far away as he could get from the factory and before he could be dragged into the business.

I completed another eight shops without success, and made my way to the university. Tomorrow, I'd be able to fit in at least another half a dozen more enquiries before my lecture.

Pete caught up with me a few minutes before we arrived at the university.

'Is that all you do, mooch about the city?' he asked.

'That and study,' I laughed.

'You'll never make friends that way.'

'Perhaps not.' Over the years, I'd become accustomed to my own company.

'Look, there's a few of us who meet in the pub most afternoons for an hour or so. Why don't you join us? It'll do you good. You can't stay cooped up studying all the time.' He sounded like Peg and I smiled. 'I'll think about it.'

'Do more than that. Come with me later this afternoon. You'll enjoy it.'

'Well, I don't … '

'We'll go straight after the lecture. No excuses, right?'

The group of undergraduates who met in the pub most evenings weren't much different to the Gang - four blokes and a girl (there was a difference there, of course) sitting around talking big talk that mostly led nowhere. A jug of best Canterbury bitter replaced the ubiquitous Tizer, and the chill fog of the bombsite had been exchanged for a warm smoky fug.

Mike, our self-appointed leader, wiped the beer froth from his mouth with the sleeve of his sweater. It was the same colour and in about as ragged a state as the one Dennis used to wear. It was the only thing about Dennis and Mike that was alike. 'As far as I can see, we don't have any alternative. We have to do something to draw attention to the evils of nuclear weapons.'

Had Mike always been this serious about life, or had the enormity of it descended on him when he entered the hallowed environs of the university, I wondered?

'So you think five measly people in a place thousands of miles from anywhere will sway world governments?' Linda asked as she flicked her hair back over her shoulders.

'At least we'd be doing something, not sitting on our backsides like the rest of humanity waiting for the planet to be blown to pieces.'

'You've got a point. We could stand in The Square.' Pete began.

'Demonstrate, Pete, demonstrate,' Mike interjected.

'Demonstrate in The Square?'

'What d'you think, Tony?' Geoff asked.

I took another sip of my beer. 'Why not? As Mike says, at least we'll be doing something.'

'You're right, Tony, I suppose it is the best way to go,' Linda's knee brushed mine.

'We'll carry banners, shout slogans; you know the sort of thing,' Mike brought the conversation back under his direction.

'Very effective, I don't think! Five undergraduates shouting slogans that nobody can hear.'

Pete told me Linda and Mike used to date, but their relationship had cooled. He thought Linda had been on the verge of leaving the group until I turned up. "Changed her mind when she saw you, mate," Pete had winked.

'I can get hold of a loud hailer and a couple of orange boxes.' Mike appeared not to notice Linda's sarcasm. 'And if five university undergraduates can't come up with some pithy slogans, who can? As I see it, we've only got a couple of years left at varsity. Let's take the opportunity while we can.'

'If you're willing, I am,' Linda moved closer to me.

'Right, that's it. Let's meet, same time, same place tomorrow to discuss the details. Anyone got a lecture or a tutorial?' Mike eyed each member of the group except Linda.

'Right, tomorrow it is. Drink up, there's a few minutes to go before six, so we've got time for one more before throwing-out time.'

'If you're walking home, I'll come with you. I'm going in the same direction.' Linda linked her arm through

329

mine, ignoring Geoff's wink to Pete and Mike sullenly staring into his beer.

Mr Munn called from his shed, beckoning to me in a gesture of secrecy when I arrived back after having walked with Linda to the flat she shared with three other students.

'Come and look at my latest.' Mr Munn ushered me into his shed. He was practically the same shape as his wife. However, his most striking feature was his head: pink, shiny and devoid of a single hair.

Inside on shelves neatly placed and labeled was row upon row of cigarette lighters.

'I've just got a new one. Look at this little beauty,' he chuckled. It was made in the shape of a guitar. Mr Munn pretended to play it. He looked like a pipe cleaner figure that was about to become untwisted.

'You must have had a win at housie,' I said.

Mr Munn covered his mouth with his hand to suppress a spluttered laugh. He was like a mischievous child. The only time Mr Munn added a lighter to his collection was when he won at housie. They were both hobbies of which Mrs Munn disapproved, and she watched tight-lipped as her husband cycled off each evening to a housie night in a different part of the city. "Housie and cigarette lighters!" She grumbled. "Tools of Satan! Why couldn't it be Scrabble and match boxes?" Mrs Munn usually followed her displeasure by patting my hand. "Such a comfort, such a comfort," she murmured, patting a few more times.

'I suppose you haven't ever seen an elderly playing housie? He's got sandy colour hair, and she's got frizzy hair and wears a long scarf.' I asked Mr Munn. As usual, when I enquired about them, I clenched my hands and bit my lips together.

Mr Munn rubbed his hand over the shininess of his pate and closed his eyes in concentration. 'Not that I can remember. Wait a minute, though, there was once a couple who came. He had sandy hair and hers was frizzy.'

I bit deeper into my lip.

'No, no, they were hippies. Your couple were older, you said? No, afraid not and there's not many who escape my attention at housie.'

Inside, I sagged with disappointment.

'Family are they?'

'Just a couple of acquaintances, that's all.' I was a liar as well as a hypocrite. They were my family, my precious family!

Mr Munn fingered his latest cigarette lighter. 'Sure you don't want to share a pipe with me?' he asked.

'Not tonight, perhaps tomorrow.' I couldn't stomach a pipe tonight.

'I have to say I'm disappointed a God-fearing young man like you should get involved in this ridiculous ban the bomb stuff. Making a spectacle of yourself in front of all those people.' Mrs Munn's eyes were thinner than ever.

'There were only about a dozen there.'

Mrs Munn ignored me. 'Associating with a lot of young hot-heads and getting carried off by the police.' She covered her eyes with her hands to obliterate the image.

We hadn't actually been carried off. When the police approached, we simply collected our placards, orange boxes and megaphone and sloped off. Next time, we wouldn't be so compliant. We would hold our ground and wait to be carried away. This had merely been a dress rehearsal, Mike said.

The next time, rain kept all but two spectators away, and the police didn't bother to turn up.

'It needs a march, like the Aldermarston one. That'll put the wind up Prime Minister Holyoake. Who's in for it?' Mike asked during one of our pub meetings.

'Just the five of us?' Linda was scornful.

'There'll be a lot of students who'll be interested if we let them know.'

'When, where, how?' Linda asked in a monotone.

'We'll stick something in the university rag, and we won't limit our protest to the city centre. We'll make our presence felt and march round the suburbs where the people are. Christchurch might not be a huge metropolis, but its voice will stretch beyond the Pacific,' Mike declared.

Linda snorted, 'Spare us the oratory, Churchill! Anyway, if you're not all too high and mighty for such things, who's in for the pictures tomorrow?'

'Great,' Geoff replied, but Linda stared at him and mouthed the word, 'No'.

'Sorry, I've just remembered I can't make it,' he complied.

'And you, Pete?'

'Um … got a date … with an old friend. Sorry.'

'What about me?' Mike asked.

'You'll be too busy organizing the march.' Linda pressed into me. 'Looks like it's you and me, then.'

Linda was already outside The Savoy Picture House when I arrived. She was wearing a yellow skirt that finished well up her thighs and long white boots.

'Sorry I'm late. I had to help my landlady move some furniture. I hope you haven't been waiting long.'

'Just got here.' Linda flicked her hair back over her shoulders, in the way she had, using both hands in one synchronized movement. It revealed her breasts pointing from a tight black sweater.

Since I'd arrived in Christchurch, I'd resisted going to the pictures. I wanted to preserve my memories of the Gang and Saturday Picture Club. I wasn't altogether certain how I came to be here now. Linda had a way of arranging things so that it seemed as if it had been all my idea. And I couldn't divulge my fear that my memories would be overlaid by new images. I was more than sure she wouldn't understand.

Inside, The Savoy wasn't much different from The Majestic, with its ceiling mouldings and dusty carpet. Like The Majestic, we passed beyond a black curtain, guided by an usherette's light and into the darkened picture house, which had always been for me both exciting and frightening.

The Gang always sat near the front so that they could throw whatever missiles they had to hand with a reasonable chance of hitting the manager. He usually spoke before the films, ineffectively threatening eviction for bad behaviour. Sometimes our ammunition was aimed at kids who sang or recited. On occasions, we even flung things at the screen itself if the film wasn't to our liking. Now, Linda and I sat at the back. Sitting any further forward, she said, gave her a migraine.

I had no need to fear my recollections of Saturday Picture Club would be marred. It was difficult to concentrate on the film at all with Linda so close. Her head gradually sank on to my shoulder. Her legs were tucked beneath her, so that even in the dark, I could sense her skirt had risen an inch or two. Her perfumed skin touching mine was an utter distraction. She was in my arms before I was aware how she got there. I'd never taken so little notice of a film. It wasn't the least like Saturday Picture Club.

'Ban the bomb and save the world!' 'Nuclear armament is an abomination!'

People tending their gardens straightened and stopped to watch the group of about fifty striding along the streets, carrying our banners aloft. Others stood at their front doors. Children followed, aping us, chanting.

The air was heavy with the scent of spring. Kowhai and magnolia vied with each other. Tulips still in bud would soon open to sudden maturity, then in one last and desperate effort, they would spread their petals in a glorious death. I lifted my voice and sang, "*We shall not be moved*". How could we let all this be destroyed? Lifting my banner higher, I smiled at Linda. It was a noble thing we were doing, marching for the future of the planet and what better place to find Fred and Lori, if they were here.

Linda grinned back and shouted, 'Groovy, eh!'

Back in Cathedral Square, Mike made an impassioned speech calling for an end to the Cold War and for nuclear disarmament, while a contingency of three policemen listened with their arms folded. Afterwards they too, like the rest of the marchers, melted away.

'Pity it fizzled out at the end,' Geoff observed later in the pub.

'At least we *did* something.' I defended the march, even though I hadn't found Fred and Lori and I fought to keep the disappointment from my voice.

'It might not have been Aldermarston or Hyde Park.' Mike, still flushed from his oratory, set jugs of beer in front of us. 'But we've made our voices heard.'

'So what next?'

'We'll wait for our message to reach the Russians and for them to absorb it. Then we'll march again.'

'I'm sure they'll be quaking in their boots!' Linda's earlier euphoria had flattened like the top of her beer. 'Get serious, Mike! How d'you think they're going to hear about a piddly little march on the other side of the world. And, if by some miracle they do, they won't care two figs about it.'

'Don't under-estimate the power of the people wherever they are.' Mike retorted.

'Sounds a lot of pompous rhetoric to me. Anyway, who's for an afternoon on the beach?' Linda asked, glaring at each of the others in turn.

'Sorry, we don't seem to be able to make it,' Pete spoke for Geoff and Mike, as well as himself.

'Oh well, Tony, that leaves you and me.' Linda flicked her hair back. 'Sorry you blokes can't come.'

The spring sunshine was warm on our faces as Linda let sand run through her fingers. She was so different to Gaylene and Merrin, and, come to that, to Paula and the girls I had known in Blountmere Street. Linda was intelligent and forthright, unafraid of what others thought. Yet she possessed a vulnerability I found alluring. She brushed her hands free of sand and traced a pattern on my face with her finger, laughing.

'What's funny?'

'I was thinking that although you've been protesting all morning you don't seem to be doing too much of it now.'

'None at all.' The smell of kowhai and magnolia lingered about her as I took her in my arms.

That evening after his housie session, Mr Munn and I perched on wooden boxes in his shed and rammed tobacco into our pipes. He rose to select a cigarette lighter and chose a cat. He flicked its tail alight and bent it towards my pipe. I sucked and puffed. I hadn't had much success in mastering the art of smoking a pipe, but I knew Mr Munn looked forward to our times together in his shed when he returned from housie. As for me, it was a break from my studies and somewhere to relax and mull over the day after I'd been out with Linda.

'Not been protesting about the bomb lately?' Mr Munn made smacking noises against the mouthpiece of his pipe.

'We're letting things settle a bit,' I said, quoting Mike. 'Anyway, with Christmas coming, there won't be much going on. Best wait until the start of the new term.'

'I thought you might have lost interest in it now you've got this young woman goggle-eyed about you. A man can't concentrate on more than one thing at a time, especially when a woman starts to put the pressure on.' Mr Munn took his pipe from his mouth and spluttered a laugh. 'And there's not too many women who don't. They're subtle about it. A bloke's hooked before he knows it. Take me and Mrs Munn. She was a beguiling woman if ever I saw one. A bloke couldn't resist her. Got her own way at every turn.'

I gave up my attempts at sucking and held the bowl of the pipe in my palm, tapping it as I'd seen Mr Munn do. I tried to imagine stick-creature Mrs Munn as an irresistible young woman and failed.

'Linda wants me to go home with her for Christmas.'

'And don't you want to?'

'It's not that. It's just that the Millards and Joe will be really disappointed if I don't go back. And I know Jack can do with some help on the farm at this time of year.'

'And your young lady's using all her feminine wiles on you, is that it?'

'You could say that.' If cajoling, wheedling and pouting were classified as feminine wiles.

'What do you think I should do? I've tried writing to Peg and Joe explaining I won't be coming this year, but I give up after the first few sentences. They've been so good to me. I wouldn't be here without them, nor Miss Jervlin, or even Uncle Rewi and Auntie Aroha. And old Murray looks forward to seeing me, especially now Fergus has gone.'

'Can't your girl come with you?'

'She doesn't want to.' I hadn't been very insistent. Taking a girl "home" meant you were serious about the relationship, and I wasn't sure I was. Look at what had happened to Joe once Ann Epsley's parents got hold of him.

'It'll only be for a few weeks. You'll both be back at varsity next year. Be a test for the pair of you, like Mrs Munn and me. She went to her brother's for a month or two when we were courting, but I couldn't get the ravishing creature out of my mind. Married her four months afterwards. It was nearly as exciting as a win at housie.'

Linda pouted and actually looked as if she was going to cry when I told her of my final decision to spend Christmas with Peg and Jack.

'Can't we at least meet up after Christmas? I'll be in Christchurch, then. We can get together sometime in the holidays, surely.' She took hold of one of my curls and wound it round her finger. I hated her doing it. It reminded me of the things Downston used to say about my hair and brought his cruel features too easily into my mind.

'I've promised Peg I'll take her down south to her son after Christmas. I might even stay on and help him with his business. It all depends when his business partner gets back.'

'Sod his business partner. What about me?'

I hated Linda swearing almost as much as I hated her curling my hair around her finger. 'We'll just have to wait and see what happens,' I said. 'We'll find a way to spend some of the holidays together.' My irritation of a few seconds earlier evaporated when Linda looked down at her feet and her shoulders slumped.

'How about I stop in Christchurch on my way to taking Peg to her son down south? Peg can have a rest and a

cup of tea with Mrs Munn, while we meet for half an hour.
That's the best I can do for the next few weeks.'

    'If that's the best you can do, then I'll have to settle
for it, won't I?' She replied with a touch of petulance.

Chapter Twenty-Six

Christmas at the Millards was the same as it always was. Peg had invited practically the whole township for tea, and although she produced plate after platter piled with home baking, she fretted there wouldn't be enough. This year, neither Neville nor Roger and their families had been able to come.

'Thank heaven at least you're here, Tony.' Peg squeezed my arm. I responded with a weak smile. I'd come close to giving in to Linda and going to her parents in the North Island.

Miss Jervlin disengaged herself from a conversation with Noeline Stott and made her way towards me. 'Now forget about being modest and tell me what marks you've been getting at university?' She looked directly at me.

'I got a fairly good average.'

'And what does that mean?'

'Well … '

'Spit it out. What was your average mark?'

'Actually, I averaged an A.'

'Well done! You've obviously studied hard.'

Until I met Linda and the others, I spent most of my time studying. I'd enjoyed being shut up in my bedroom buried in books, abandoning myself to words, letting them crowd my mind.

Searching for Fred and Lori, protesting about nuclear weapons, and my involvement with Linda had left me struggling to concentrate on my university work, and I'd stared at one page after another and scarcely noticed a word. I had barely finished essays on time, and swotting for exams had become a matter of incredible willpower. My reasonably good marks were a matter of luck. Miss Jervlin's admiration caused me to avert my eyes to the ground.

'And you're still keen to train as a teacher?'

'With a degree in English literature, what else can I do?'

'You could write. Your letters are wonderful.'

'One day, perhaps.' It wasn't as if I hadn't thought about it. I would write my story, but not now. If I wrote it now, it would seem final as if all the events had been packaged and dispatched. I wasn't ready to relinquish them yet.

'One day perhaps you'll do what?' Joe joined us.

'Write a book,' Miss Jervlin volunteered.

'I halways said you was a brain box. Personally, I'm too taken hup with the business.' Joe hoisted the baby he was carrying further over his shoulder and resumed patting her back.

'I'm not writing a book, at least not yet.'

'Not even one of those science fiction things?'

'And definitely not a science fiction one. I wouldn't know where to begin.'

'I s'ppose it's like 'aving a baby. You start off, then learn has you go along. Anyhow I reckon babies haren't much different from hanimals; feed 'em at one hend and it comes out the hother.'

'Well you certainly seem to have learnt quickly. You make a wonderful father, Joseph.' Miss Jervlin fondled one of the baby's feet.

'Her toes aren't as long as matchsticks. Aren't you frightened of hurting her?' I asked.

'These babies are 'ardy things, much more 'ardy than some plants.' Joe thrust the baby towards me. ''ere, go on, 'ave a 'old.'

Gingerly, I took the baby and held her against my shoulder as I'd seen Joe do.

'That's hit, you've got hit.' Joe straightened his yellow and blue striped shirt. One of Old Man Witchery's, I guessed. The baby stirred then settled against me.

'Joanne - her name is very apt,' Miss Jervlin continued.

'Yeah. I s'ppose hit is very … what d'yer say … hapt. I wanted to call her 'ariett hafter my dear, departed gran but Ann said 'arriett didn't 'ave the right ring when I said hit.'

Joanne squeaked and sighed.

'Is she all right?'

'Course she's hall right. Got a touch of wind, or 'aving a dream, that's hall. Dreaming her daddy's a millionaire. It won't be long. Got some very himportant deals in the pipeline.'

How could Joe be a father? Joe, who not so long ago had declared girls and everything about them soppy. Joe who, apart from a bit of extra weight, looked no different from when he had been fifteen. If I'd seen more of him over the last years, it might not have seemed so bizarre. I would have got used to the changes gradually. As it was, I couldn't equate this bloke who knew how to cradle a baby over his shoulder, and detect when it had wind, with someone who had trembled at the mere sound of the word, "baby".

I couldn't ever imagine myself with a child. I couldn't see myself married, and especially not to Linda. Our relationship, like our protests, didn't belong anywhere outside Christchurch and the university environs. Linda and I were made solely for moonlight on the beach and starlight in the hills. We were for now, not the future.

Peg seemed to take up even more room in the Morrie than ever, making it difficult for me to change gear without my hand brushing her thigh. Jack had told me she hadn't been so well of late, a bit of breathlessness and the odd dizzy spell. Nothing much, he had hurried to assure me. He had, however, confided that Doc Marthwaite had urged her to lose a bit of weight. "But you know my good lady," Jack had said. "Told Old Doc a good helping of wholesome food never hurt anyone, and that this nonsense of wanting to be thin was ridiculous." Jack had smiled, although I thought I detected some concern in his voice.

'It's good of you to take me all the way to Roger's place this time,' Peg said. 'He's really been busy, especially with his partner, Ron, taking his parents on holiday at what's a hectic time of the year for them. Not that I've seen much of Ron's parents. His father helps out from time to time, but I've only seen his mother from a distance when she's been sitting in the car. 'Roger and Ron, knew what they were doing when they went into agricultural machinery all those years ago.' The pride in Peg's voice was obvious.

'I thought you'd like to pop into the Munns' place for a freshen up and a cup of tea before we travel further south,' I suggested to Peg as we approached Christchurch.

343

'Personally, I'd rather go straight there, but I suppose there's sense in taking a bit of a break.'

I smiled at her, relieved. 'And while you're having a bit of a gossip with Mrs Munn, there's someone I've just got to pop and see,' I said, trying to sound casual. Peg wasn't fooled. 'You've got a girl in Christchurch! I should have known.' She paused. 'Pity it isn't Merrin Bensdyke.'

No sooner had Peg disappeared inside with Mrs Munn than Linda was standing by the Munn's garden gate as if she'd flown there. She pulled me to her and kissed me. I looked around to see if anyone was spying on us through their curtains.

'Jump in the car,' I said, opening the door and practically pushing her in, anxious to get away from prying eyes.

We drove to a nearby park. Almost before I had time to turn off the engine she was in my arms. It was several minutes before we spoke.

'I've got this wonderful idea,' she murmured.

'Have you?' I murmured back.

'You could put Peg and her luggage on the bus down south. There's a spare seat, I've already checked with the bus company.'

'And what would happen to Peg at the other end of the journey.'

'We could ring her son and tell him something urgent had happened here and could he collect her from the bus station.'

'I couldn't do that.'

'Why not?'

'Because I promised to take her.'

'You've taken her a good part of the way.'

'But her son might need me to help him.'

'Don't I need you? Just think we could spend our days on the beach and our nights …'

If I stayed in Christchurch, I could get Linda to help me look for Fred and Lori. The search would be quicker if we did it between us. If Fred and Lori were living in Christchurch, driving Peg down south would only take me farther away from them.

'I suppose I … '

'Of course you could. This way, you'll be able to please everyone. Peg will get to her son and you and I can have time together.'

I started the engine. It wasn't as if Peg wouldn't understand, now she knew I had a girlfriend in Christchurch.

Peg was coming out of Mrs Munn's door as we pulled up. I jumped out of the Morrie, and ran up the path with Linda following.

'This is Linda,' I introduced her first to Peg, then to Mrs Munn.

'Nice to meet you.' Mrs Munn extended her hand but to my surprise, Peg merely inclined her head. Still feeling peeved about Merrin Bensdyke, I wouldn't be surprised.

'Look, I was wondering if you'd mind …' I began addressing Peg. Suddenly I stopped. How could I let Peg down for a few extra days with Linda. I could see Linda when I came back. My search for Fred and Lori would have to wait. Somewhere inside, I felt a sudden certainty that I was about to make the right choice. It caused the heaviness I hadn't realised had been there to dissipate.

'I wonder if you wouldn't mind if we gave Linda a lift back to her lodgings, before I take you to Roger's.'

'You mean, you're not ...' Linda stammered.

'I'm sorry, but I'll see you when I get back.' But Linda was halfway along the path.

'You won't see me then, or ever, you creep,' she shouted over her shoulder.

I smiled in embarrassment and Peg said, 'She doesn't seem too happy, that young lady of yours. Personally, and, of course, it's nothing to do with me, I think you could do far better.'

The lightness in me persisted as we continued heading south, even though I'd just lost a girlfriend and missed several days in my search for Fred and Lori.

Everywhere lay indolent in the midday heat. The grizzled landscape craved moisture, and the road ahead dissolved into a shimmering mirage.

Peg produced a large handkerchief and dabbed at her face. 'What I wouldn't do for a nice bath. This time of year's a bit too hot for travelling. When I get this far, I usually start counting down the townships, not that there are many. Just the odd one or two. At any rate, it helps the last leg of the journey to pass quicker.'

'I don't know the names of that many places, especially not the smaller ones.'

'You've done well to know the ones you do, shut away on that awful farm for so long. But, then, you were always a clever young bloke.'

'Not always. When I lived in London, I had difficulty reading. The girl downstairs gave me lessons. We had them at her place and we kept it a secret in case everyone laughed at me.'

'Is that who you wrote to when your letter was returned?'

'She and her family must have moved.'

'I've never liked to ask; didn't want to pry into your past. I know you like to keep it to yourself, but isn't there anyone else you can contact? Surely, the authorities should be able to tell you where your sister is and … ' she hesitated. ' … where your Mum's buried.'

I thought of all those in authority I'd come into contact with. Not one of them had helped me. If they weren't downright bullies, they were weak and ineffective, like the Man from the Agency who had come to Downston's to check on us.

I wasn't sure how the conversation had come to this, and I ignored what Peg had just said. Instead I replied, 'Everyone I knew has moved. Even our godparents went to live overseas.' I didn't know why I hadn't come straight out with it and said, "Their names are Fred and Lori. They emigrated to New Zealand, and now I'm trying with all the strength I have to find them." But I hadn't said their names out loud for a long time. I was relieved Peg hadn't asked.

Not all of what I'd said was true, anyway. I didn't really know if everyone I knew had moved. The Gang might still be around. Perhaps they worked at Hendersons, the leather factory. It was where a lot of kids from Blountmere Street worked after they'd left school. But what if they didn't remember me? I could hear Herbie's mother saying, "Isn't that the boy who used to come round here, the one whose

347

mother died? Had a sister somewhere. The authorities took them away. Put in an orphanage, weren't they?"

'I'm sorry, Tony, I didn't mean to upset you,' Peg directed the conversation elsewhere. 'I think they'll have to prise me from this car when we get there. I'm so hot, I'm stuck to the seat. Thank heavens it's not far now.'

In spite of Peg's assurance, the road was sinuous and seemed interminable. I was glad we'd filled the car with petrol just outside Christchurch and that I carried spare water and fuel in tins in the boot. Petrol pumps, like cities, were a long way apart in New Zealand. Here there was space to take the deepest of breaths and stretch without touching someone; where even the sky had room to touch the earth.

'There's the sign. It's only a mile or two up the road from here.' Peg's voice carried a note of relief.

'Our Roger's business is up here, just off the main road. He, Jenny and the kids have a house at the back.'

'What about Roger's partner?'

'He lives a bit further up the road. He needed a bigger house, what with his family and his parents living with them, as well. They're from London, I believe - his parents, that is. Perhaps you'll be able to have a chat with them.'

I'd seek them out as soon as I could. Even if they were really old, perhaps we could talk about red double-decker buses and bombsites, *Dick Barton, Special Agent* and Saturday Morning Picture Club. I would look forward to that.

The premises of R & R Agricultural Machinery and Repairs, together with Roger Millard's house, were set back from the road. They looked as if they'd been dropped there amid the endless paddocks by mistake.

At the sound of the Morrie pulling onto the forecourt, Roger emerged from the side of the building, wiping his hands on a piece of rag. It was certainly different from Joe's velvet-waistcoated welcome bestowed on visitors to Epsley & Fisher's. As if reading my thoughts, Peg said, 'Roger always did like getting his hands oily.' She waved as enthusiastically as the heat and the restricted space would allow. Nevertheless, the flesh under her upper arm flapped like a wing.

'Happy New Year,' she called.

'Jenny's got the jug boiling,' Roger helped extract his mother from the Morrie.

'That's what I've been wanting to hear. It's never too hot for a cup of tea. There's a tin of baking in the car, chocolate and cherry slices. They'll go down a treat, that's if they haven't melted.' Peg hung on to Roger's arm. 'And what about those lovely grandchildren of mine? What're they up to?'

'Gone eeling, but it won't be long before they come to check you've arrived. They've been talking about you coming to visit since Christmas.'

'It was good of you to bring Mum down,' Roger addressed me. 'December and January are our busiest months. Thank the Lord, Ron's back today. We're expecting to see him and the family any time now. I hope there wasn't too much traffic.

I suppressed a smile. 'Not much.' When was there ever a lot of traffic on New Zealand roads! I doubted we'd passed half a dozen vehicles since we had left Christchurch. 'You've got quite a big place here,' I continued.

'I'll get Mum settled then I'll show you around.'

Jenny's cup of tea might have cooled Peg, but it had done the opposite for me, and I was grateful for the lower temperature of the showroom.

'We're one of the leaders in agricultural implements and irrigation systems. No horse-drawn ploughs now,' Roger laughed.

'Have you been in this business long?'

'About fifteen years. I met up with Ron soon after he'd arrived from England, and we set up the business. We've never looked back. Even got Ron's Dad out from England to give us a hand with the paperwork side of things.'

We ambled from the showroom into the workshop and then out into the heat of the forecourt.

'It sounds like Ron now,' Roger smiled. 'I'd know the rattle of that old bus anywhere. They've made good time. I was frightened they might break down in the middle of nowhere. It wouldn't have been too good in this heat for Ron's parents and the visitor from England they've got staying with them. The kids, of course, would have seen it as an adventure.

The bus shuddered to a halt and three children tumbled out, while a tall bespectacled man in khaki shorts and a brown check shirt jumped from the driver's seat. He walked round to the other side and opened the door for his wife, before helping his parents out of the vehicle.

'Real polite is Ron. Takes after … '

But I didn't hear the rest; only the roaring of a waterfall in my ears, and the banging of my heart against my rib cage. I passed my hand across my eyes to clear the image and steady myself. When I removed it, they were still there: she with her frizzy hair and a chiffon scarf that trailed the ground; he in his blue shirt. His shoulders were not as square as they had once been, but he had retained his naval bearing. I stumbled towards them, shouting their names over and over and over. Suddenly, I realised there was someone with them: a young woman about the same age as me and wearing a pleated skirt. It couldn't be … but it was.

I tripped, steadied myself and plunged forward.

They'd come – a little late, but they'd come, and they'd brought *her* with them.